The Western Way

A Novel

The Western Way

The Western Way - Written by R.F. Stewart

PUBLISHER'S NOTE
This is a work of Fiction. Names, Characters, Places, and Incidents either are the product of the author's imagination or are used fictitiously, and any resemblance to actual persons, living or dead, business establishments, events, or locales is entirely coincidental.

The publisher does not have any control over and does not assume any responsibility for author or third-party Web sites or their content.

Copyright © 2013
Second Edition – First Printing February 2014
Library of Congress Number pending

ISBN # 978-1-934615-90-4
1-934615-90-0

Published by Main Street Publishing, Inc., Jackson, TN.
Copy Editing by Shari B Hill Yetto and Melissa Drummonds
Cover Design by Shari B Hill Yetto
Edited by Pat Little
Printed and bound by NetPub, Poughkeepsie, NY.

For more information write Main Street Publishing, Inc.,
206 East Main St., Suite 207, P.O. Box 696, Jackson, TN 38302
Phone 1-731-427-7379 or toll free 1-866-457-7379.
E-mail: editor@mainstreetpublishing.com for managing editor and
            lanewble@mainstreetpublishing.com for customer service.
Visit us at www.mainstreetpublishing.com and www.mspbooks.com.

The Western Way

A Novel

R. F. Stewart

ACKNOWLEDGEMENTS

This book is dedicated to my friend and confidant, B.R., whose stories of the state hospital in the 1950's became the foundation for this novel.

I would like to express my gratitude to family and friends who encouraged me to write, provided artwork, and offered technical support.

The Western Way

KATE

PROLOGUE
1989

I found the patient cemetery on a brisk October morning. The discovery was completely accidental: I would never have been walking in the back corner of the psychiatric hospital if I had not started my day by slamming six charts on the nurse's desk and storming off the adolescent unit. By the time the echo finished reverberating around the concrete room, I realized that I should leave before I compounded my unprofessional behavior by shouting.

I was officially AWOL. I had abandoned my post without permission. Strangely, no one seemed to notice as the steel door banged shut behind me. The roar of a unit in turmoil faded as I jogged from the building, passing beneath the rusting water tower and beside the brick chimney that belched black smoke like a crematorium. I hardly noticed the depressing surroundings: I was too incensed over punitive nurses, children trapped in locked units and my own helplessness to make a difference. The system was so Byzantine and rigid that there was no way for me, a young psychologist just out of school, to bring about change.

When I was a quarter mile from the last building, I ducked into a tunnel of trees. My footsteps were immediately hushed by a carpet of pine needles. I slowed to a stop, letting my heartbeat return to its rhythm as the aroma of cedar trees reached me. I craned my neck to see around the bend, but the path, shrouded in trees and vines, curved to the left obscuring the end. Fears of being on an abandoned road would have outweighed my curiosity, but as I was debating my next step, a doe broke from the underbrush and bounded down the trail with her spotted fawn close behind. It seemed like a signal of safety. I took a deep breath and moved forward, imagining that I would find some beautiful, medieval cloister beyond the next thicket.

When I reached the clearing though, I saw with a sinking dread that I had stumbled upon an ancient and neglected cemetery. Under towering sentry oaks, chipped and crooked headstones were scattered like broken teeth in the long grass. I was 26 years old, and the only cemetery I had ever entered was the one where my mother was buried: a pristine lawn dotted with markers that looked like stepping stones.

Who was buried in this place, I wondered, as I knelt to read the pitted and stained granite. My fingers moved over letters and numbers while I sounded out the words. But most of the tombstones were simply unknowable, carved with symbols and pictures as mysterious as hieroglyphics. Next to a rusting barbed wire fence, I found a jumble of white bricks engraved with letters and numbers. They were half-buried in the ground, as if an old house had been demolished by a storm. I would later learn that these bricks were markers for indigent mental patients, the ones who had lived anonymous lives in the back wards of the hospital and had been buried unceremoniously in a common grave. Each numbered brick was an abbreviation for a human life, lost in the hospital before it vanished from all memory.

One double headstone of polished granite stood defiantly against the anonymity of numbered bricks and illegible inscriptions. With its three simple lines, it hinted of tragedy.

Billy Wayne Gordon and Lana G.
Age 21 - Age 24
Died May 15, 1957

I crouched before the stone, parting the grass that grew around the base. Two doves, their beaks touching, hovered above a ribbon of tiny letters: "Death could not part us."

Rocking back on my heels, I stared at their names: Lana and Billy Wayne. They must have been lovers who died in a common accident. How unjust for young sweethearts to find each other while they were patients at a mental hospital! And with their whole lives ahead of them, to die in their twenties, not much younger than I was. They slept together now in a damp grave instead of a bridal bower. The knot in my throat swelled with grief for them and pity for my own losses.

Wiping my eyes, I stood and threaded my way through the headstones, following the sound of gurgling water and coming to stop at a bluff over a narrow river. Below me, the mist rose like a gathering of nimble ghosts, turning in slow circles. *Surely these were the souls of the patients who had finally escaped from the hospital*, I thought, fiercely rubbing away my tears. And surely the two spirits near the shoreline, dancing above the current, were Billy Wayne's and Lana's. I watched from the bank until the sun dried my face, and then I turned back toward the hospital with a sigh of resignation.

The Adminstration Building stood at the end of the same aisle of trees that had led me to the graves. It was framed by leafy branches but the bricks were still the color of dried blood. It dominated the landscape like a gloomy fortress in the middle of a park. Generations of families who brought their broken relatives to this place for care or confinement, must have looked with terror at the towers and turrets. And Billy Wayne and Lana, standing on the sidewalk, must have shivered as its shadow fell across their upturned faces.

Despite official discouragement, I came to the cemetery again and again during my first year at Western. I felt close to Billy Wayne and Lana when I stood in that quiet clearing. And each time I touched their headstone, I silently promised them that I would learn their story and honor their love.

To begin with, I approached my co-workers, asking about the people who were buried on the grounds. They told me that patients had been buried in that plot of land for a hundred years, and they assured me that the dead had not been forgotten: the grounds crew still mowed around the graves during summer months.

No one, however, could answer my questions about Billy Wayne and Lana. The medical records department solemnly told me there were no patient records dating back to the 1950's, as if pens had not been invented until much later. I talked to employees who could remember the hospital decades ago, but I gathered stories that memorialized other people, not my young couple.

I did finally come to know Billy Wayne and Lana, but it was through no effort of my own. The Fates were simply disposed to make the introduction.

KATE

The Beginning

I came to Western Mississippi Psychiatric Hospital, located in Madrid, Mississippi, directly from college. I was still idealistic and naïve, and I clutched a newly minted diploma. The day I turned my overloaded VW into the front gates and saw the Gothic spires of the main building, I was frightened and stunned. I had expected a modern, concrete and glass hospital, not some nineteenth century asylum. With my heart beating wildly, my mind raced from one course of action to the next: I could make a u-turn in the parking lot and drive away without informing anyone. I could meet the head of the department to explain that a family emergency now prevented me from taking the job. I could travel to the nearest town and call to say I had not finished my dissertation after all and, therefore, would have to complete another semester in Mayfield. And if I didn't take the job, what would I do? I resolutely answered my own question: I could drive back to Mayfield and try another reconciliation with my ex-husband; or I could arrive at my father's home and hope my step-mother did not answer the door; or I could go to the nearest city and start looking for a job, any job, while I lived out of my car. None of my options seemed reasonable. With a sense of dread that may have been as strong as any patient's who was committed to this hospital, I set the parking brake and pushed open the door.

The Adminstration Building, or "The Castle" as the staff referred to it, was built in 1886. Its blue prints must have been drawn by a team of sullen German architects; I imagined them as sturdy and pragmatic men who designed the massive brick walls for eternal confinement. Slotted windows in the four towers might have given the patients a thin rectangle of light, but they could just as easily have been used to defend the grounds with a volley of flaming arrows.

At the front door, there was a deep indentation in the stone threshold, a testimony to the thousands of angry and resisting feet that had eroded the marble. I let my foot slide into the hole and I stood for a moment, wondering whose legacy I was following.

The lobby, eerily deserted, was dark and stately with intricately carved, Black Forest paneling, a high tin ceiling and uneven plaster walls. I started up the immense, creaking staircase following the arrows to Personnel, climbing in complete aloneness as I wondered if the entire hospital had been decimated by a plague.

Just as I was about to give up the quest for a human being, I found the personnel clerk, Rosie, in an office filled with file folders, school pictures of her six children and stacks of loose paper. She flashed a brilliant smile as I sighed in relief and settled into the wooden chair. "Kathleen McConnaughy?. . . I've been waiting for you! Psychology, isn't it?… Does Dr. Thompson know you're here? I'll tell him," she volunteered, cradling the phone on her shoulder as she rifled through a legal-size folder. "Dr. Thompson? She's here—Kathleen. Okay. . I'll tell her." She hung up the phone, briefly looking up at me. "I've just got a few things for you to sign and then you'll meet with Dr. Thompson. We sure want you to get on next week's payroll! Let's see…Have any dependents? No? Just check here. Sign here. Is this your correct Social Security number?" She returned to my file as she continued, "We've got a copy of your transcript from your undergraduate school. But did you mail one from Mayfield State?"

"I asked the college to send one," I responded. Before I could hear her next question, I saw myself standing at the grey Formica counter, marking "Change of Name" on a form that was meant to undo my marital status.

The registrar had looked on with unabashed curiosity before commenting, "Nobody stays married for very long in this town."

Our marriage had come to a close without children to be shared or property to be divided. Marrying a musician had guaranteed that there would be no valuables to incite a squabble. Looking back on our brief union, I could see that Russ had been a rejection of my father's button-down, well-organized lifestyle. Russ was spontaneous, energetic, fun-loving and artistic—all the things my father was not.

My father had his talents, too: he was gifted at interpreting actuarial tables in his insurance office, but he had been blindsided by my mother's cancer and her final, desperate bid for control of a life gone awry. Discovering her hours after the overdose, he had quickly and wordlessly set out to obliterate all reminders of their life together. Unable to discard his thirteen-year-old daughter, he simply avoided any prolonged contact with me, spending long hours away from home as I finished high school.

To make matters worse, the physical resemblance to my mother was startling and more than once in the first year after her death, he had suppressed a gasp as he came upon me unexpectedly in some pose of hers. The morning he entered the kitchen to find me sitting at her place at the table, idling stirring a cup of coffee, he wheeled away from the too familiar scene and abruptly left for work, slamming the door behind him. When I began college, I was still grieving for my mother and still furious at my father for emotionally abandoning me. Within a year, I had met Russ.

It was silent in the room. Embarrassed at my inattention, I raised my eyes to Rosie. She sensed that I had been mentally absent and reassured me that she would reissue a request for my transcript.

Papers in hand, I left the Adminstration Building and started across the green, shaded campus for the Claiborne Building—the most modern structure of the complex.

KATE

Chapter 1
My Circulum Vitae

Russ and I were introduced in a literature class but we became a couple at the "coffee house nights" sponsored by a local pub. He had a clear, beautiful voice and his strong fingers ran effortlessly across the strings of his guitar. During our first months together, I was at the club almost every night to hear Russ perform. The downlights turned his tousled hair into a blue halo and softened his face into an innocent version of the late Jim Morrison. I would perch on a wobbly stool and drink in his music, leaving my glass of beer to grow warm.

But the real magic began after the bar had closed, when the musicians gathered at one of the tables and talked into the early hours of the morning. Some nights I was so drowsy that I fell asleep on Russ's shoulder, weaving their words into my very dreams. The conversations always started with the music and the story behind the lyrics. Then it would drift into talk about prospects: who had been discovered from this same stage; who was looking for a new bass player; who had been approached about writing songs for a recording artist. Before dawn, there might also be talk of political resistance and conspiracy, but these theories aimlessly floated above the tables like cigarette smoke. I loved the atmosphere in the bar after the customers had left, when the musicians were deep in discussion, when Russ leaned forward into the debates with one arm thrown carelessly over my shoulder.

Most of Russ's friends were astounded that he was married to a woman on her way to being "a professional." But my friends in graduate school seemed to understand why I had married Russ. His passion for music and his unruly charm gave him an undeniable appeal.

Months after coming to Western, I looked back on our early

years together with a mixture of regret and nostalgia. We had lived in a neighborhood called "the student ghetto," where the unraked leaves crunched under our feet and music drifted through open windows. Our home was a garage apartment behind a seedy, two-story house that had been subdivided into six apartments. Our windows opened to branches and fluttering leaves, giving the impression that we lived in a tree house. The bathroom was so small that Russ would pull back the shower curtain and complain of the steam as he stepped into the water with me. With a mischievous grin, he would tease, "I might as well be in here with you—I can't see to shave." I was frequently late for class and arrived one day at my clinical internship wearing sandals that didn't match.

We were poor in the way that only students are poor. We struggled to pay the rent, and the only room in our apartment was furnished with folding lawn chairs, a mattress, and a wobbly table from Goodwill. But there were books and stereo equipment on make-shift shelves and Impressionist posters on the walls. Luxurious asparagus ferns were suspended from macramé hangers. We had a swarm of friends who visited unannounced, shared spaghetti and cheap wine with us, and liked the same music we did. No matter what I endured at school, I knew that soon after I got home, I would hear his bounding footsteps on the wooden stairs, would hear him call, "Hey, Babe!" as he came through the door, would feel his embrace from behind, his arms rocking me from side to side as he nuzzled my neck.

Lying on the ridged mattress in drowsy afterglow, we had talked endlessly of our future. Because once I finished school, we would move to somewhere like Nashville, where record producers would certainly discover Russ. I would get a job in a community mental health center, treating middle-class professionals who had some type of pesky neurosis. I would be able to buy steaks instead of the Ramen noodles that were the staple in our diet. We had struggled for years, but I was buoyed by the belief that our lives would soon improve.

But our future changed permanently the day I bought a drug

store pregnancy kit and locked the bathroom door to watch the strip change colors. I was so incredulous that I bought another and then one more, counting the quarters out of my tip money to pay for the third box, testing and retesting my urine; surely there must be a mistake. The angry accusations and threats that would swallow up the rest of our marriage began that night.

"How could you do this to me?!" Russ yelled, slamming his palms against the table and sending the salt shaker into a wild jig.

"To you?!" I raged back through tears. "As if you didn't have anything to do with this! How do you think I wound up pregnant?"

He stared with an icy steadiness I had never seen. "I don't know," he spat out. "I thought you were taking your pill every day."

"I was!" I shot back. "I did take it."

"Well, obviously you missed a pill," he said between clenched teeth. "Three pregnancy tests can't be wrong." He stood suddenly, almost overturning the table in his haste. "I'm going out," he said to the wall as he pulled open the door and picked up his guitar case.

Tears spilled down my cheeks and dotted my T-shirt. I paced and cried and cursed both Russ and my father for how they had failed me, until I fell asleep in a jumbled pile of sheets and old quilts. When I awoke the next morning, the sun was winking through the leaves and propelling the dust motes upward into silence. Russ returned at noon, wearing rumpled clothes and a resigned expression. He immediately went to the refrigerator and turned up the carton of orange drink as I peppered him with stinging questions.

Finally, he placed the carton on the cracked linoleum counter. "Well, if you *have* to know, I was at Doug's and had a couple of beers. I didn't think I should be driving."

"You could have called me."

"Yeah," he acknowledged, raising the drink to his lips again. He finished the juice with his back turned to me, settling the empty carton into the stained sink. "Listen, Kate," he started, his face turned to the window. "I'm not ready to talk about a baby right now. I need a few days to get my mind around it."

"We have to talk about it eventually," I persisted.

"Yeah, but just.. not.. right… *now!* Okay?" His shoulders slumped and then he took a deep breath, his hands gripping the side of the sink.

I went into the tiny bathroom to get ready for my shift at The Mystic. I remember crying in the shower, letting the hot water run over my neck and back, and knowing at some intuitive level that I would never see his hand on the curtain again.

I graduated a month after I had the miscarriage. We had argued interminably about an abortion, eventually letting our schedules separate us into roommates who hardly saw each other. When I miscarried, all the accusations, the guilt and the sadness hung in the little apartment like spider webs that no one had the energy to sweep down. Russ began to hedge on his promise to move away from Mayfield, spending more and more time at Doug's place with a new group of musicians that included a 22-year-old blonde vocalist.

When he suggested a separation, I was too hurt to allow him that victory. In a fit of pride, I picked up no-fault divorce papers and left them on the kitchen table. I found them signed with the same flourish Russ had always used for music contracts. As I laid the papers down, I felt sick with regret at how we were tearing apart our lives, heedless of the damage we were doing to each other and ourselves. Rising waves of nausea rushed to the back of my throat and left me heaving over the kitchen trash can.

My last day in Mayfield, Russ had helped me box up my textbooks, helped me put clothes and a photo album in the car and had tucked a $20 bill under the map on the front seat, a wildly extravagant sum for an unemployed musician. As I had started the engine, he had leaned through the open window, giving me a brotherly peck on the cheek. "Let me hear from you after you get settled down there," he instructed. Then, his voice husky with emotion, he had added, "And, Kate, take care of yourself." He patted the door of the car as if he were signaling a pony to trot away.

I took a ragged breath and said, "You, too." I must have cried the first 80 miles of the trip, knowing I had left behind an emotional security that I would not easily find again, grieving over the loss of his love. By the time I had crossed into Mississippi, my face ached, my skin was raw from the swipe of Kleenex and I was out of tears.

A slender, middle-aged man, wearing owlish glasses stood in front of the glass doors of the Claiborne Building. He introduced himself as Scott Thompson and invited me to his office, chatting as we walked. The Administration Building, he said with a wry smile, was referred to as "Frankenstein's Castle," especially if the superintendent was particularly loathsome. He laughed at his joke and kept up a steady patter of facts about the hospital as we walked.

After winding through a maze of hallways, he opened his office door and offered me a seat. His wooden desk was scarred and a collection of mismatched vinyl chairs lined the beige walls.

Dr. Thompson settled behind the desk and leaned back. "We're really glad you're here, Kate. It's a small department and we've had this vacancy for almost a year. Do you have any questions to start with?"

The uncomfortable chair squeaked a protest when I shifted my weight. I asked about job duties and unit assignments, and he answered by telling me I would be working on the adolescent evaluation unit.

"Teenagers?" I almost gasped, thinking how unpredictable and uncivilized they could be. I was questioning whether I would be up to the task.

"It's actually a forensic unit," he continued. "They've gotten into some kind of trouble so the juvenile judge sends them here for a 30-day evaluation. We test them, observe them, interview them and then write a report back to the court with recommendations."

"What kind of recommendations?"

"Oh, everything from 'go home with probation' to 'go to a juvenile prison.'"

I was taken aback with the idea of teenagers being sent to prison. My astonishment pushed Dr. Thompson to continue. "Some have murder and rape charges. But most have run-of-the-mill charges like burglary, possession of marijuana, assault, things like that."

Western seemed more like a prison than a mental hospital, in spite of the grove of trees and clipped lawn visible from the window. From Dr. Thompson's vantage point, the campus looked like a college. But when I asked about the patient use of the grounds, I was told that the children's unit was locked even though some of the adults had "privileges" to wander the campus during the day.

But violent juveniles! I imagined cells, bars, angry young faces and I felt my stomach turn with a stab of anxiety. Gambling on his empathy, I said, "Dr. Thompson, I'm not sure I'm ready for all this. I just graduated and I feel pretty overwhelmed about the idea of working with delinquents…" My voice trailed off.

"I understand," he immediately broke in. "The hospital can be pretty intimidating."

"Yes, that's a good word," I said miserably.

"Listen, Kate, you'll do fine. With your education you're miles ahead of the high school graduates who're technicians. They have NO background in the behavioral sciences, and they're the ones spending most of the day interacting with the patients. I know how you're feeling, but believe me, you'll see yourself as an expert after one week."

I kept returning to the other unspoken problem: I was completely alone, solitary, unconnected, friendless in a new place and a new job. I struggled to explain. "I think part of my hesitation comes from being single—divorced." I hurried to correct myself before I looked out the window, determined not to tear up.

"Well, you'll find that's not unusual here, either." He paused and then leaned his thin forearms on the desk, locking his gaze into mine. "This is not a place people come to as their first choice, Kate. There's a lot of staff that became employees late in life to get into the state retirement system. Some of the doctors are here as part of the Impaired Physicians Program or as a requirement for their citizenship. Some folks come here because they can't find a job anywhere else." He looked down at the desk calendar. "It'll be two years on the first of next month for me." He pushed his large, tortoiseshell glasses further up his nose. "I was in a private practice group that ended up in bankruptcy."

I didn't know whether to say, "I'm sorry" or to express some optimism for the ultimate good of his being at WMPH. With a solemn expression he reassured me, "I think you'll do fine here, Kate, and I'll help you any way I can. When we talked on the phone, I told you that your student loans would be forgiven by two years of state service. And you thought that would be a big help to you," he reminded me before he continued with, "Once you've worked a couple of weeks, Western won't seem so strange to you."

He was wrong, of course, but I wanted to believe him.

KATE

Chapter 2
Introduction To The Unit

After a few minutes of conversation, Dr. Thompson suggested we meet Don, the senior psychologist on the juvenile ward. When he unlocked the unit door, the first thing I noticed was the abundant light and the pervasive odor of disinfectant. In the empty Day Room, a bank of windows spilled sunshine onto the tiled floor and across the hard, vinyl chairs. To my right I saw a classroom and heard the drone of a video on the African Savannah. The boys seated close to the door looked at me with unabashed curiosity. Their faces were absolutely average: some black, some white; many with acne and greasy hair; some thin and others stocky. They wore jeans, T-shirts and sneakers and they all slouched at their desks. A few smiled at me, but it wasn't a menacing leer—just a greeting.

"Older boys' classroom," Dr. Thompson said, gesturing to the right. "Younger boys' classroom," gesturing to the left. He walked quickly down the concrete hall, which was lined with pictures that left me wondering if schizophrenics had coordinated the decorating. The cheap, framed prints had been bolted to the walls for safety. They depicted random themes: Martin Luther King and Lena Horne stood next to a luxurious scene of the Mediterranean, which hung next to a picture of a race horse, which shared a corner with a print of roses. "Bedrooms…Day Room…Nurses' station." Behind the safety glass, three women shuffled charts and talked on the phone in muffled silence. "I'll introduce you to them later. I want you to meet Don first." He took a few more steps and knocked on a door with a sign that seemed to admonish us to wisely use our time: "Don T. Tarry." Then under it, "Doctor of Philosophy and Licensed Clinical Psychologist," followed by, "Forensic Psychologist A.B.P.T;" "Certified by the Sex Offender Board" and "Marriage and Family Therapist." The rest of the door was decorated with colorful bumper stickers, cheerfully declaring, "Impeach Bush!" and "What would Jesus drive?" and "Saddam Hussein is NOT the enemy."

"It's open!" came the hearty shout. I expected to see a version of a 60's revolutionary but found instead an older man with a professorial dignity, standing by his desk. He was tall, had short grey hair and wore wire-rimmed bifocals.

He reached across his desk to extend his hand to me and announced, "I'm Don Tarry. Glad to have you aboard."

"Don's been with the juvenile program for ten years, and he's got everything pretty well organized," Dr. Thompson said by way of introduction. I had already surmised that Don was contentedly mired in obsessive-compulsive disorder: Two shelves lining his office were boldly labeled with cardboard signs declaring the psychological tests: "WAIS," "WISC," "RORSCHACH," "MAPI." Another wall held what seemed to be ancient, molding textbooks. On his desk, everything was laid out in a grid: the desk calendar, the telephone, the post-it notes, the stapler, the sharpened pencils.

"But it'll be good to have some help," Don responded. "Let's see…Emily left, what? Three months ago? Things have really piled up since then," he said, with a sweeping gesture toward a tray sprouting manila folders and loose paper. Before Dr. Thompson could deflect him, Don was well into explaining his system for completing the assignments. I tried to maintain my concentration but must have been daydreaming for the only part I heard was, "And after I dictate them, I take off these pink stickers and that shows I'm just waiting for the typist to get finished." He sat back in his chair with a look of satisfaction.

I caught a glance from Dr. Thompson, who checked his watch and told us he had to leave for a meeting with the assistant superintendent. "I'm going to leave Kate with you," he reported as he opened the door. "Just give her an overview; don't overwhelm her."

Don seemed surprised at this admonition, responding with, "Wouldn't think of it—being her first day and all!"

"And help her find an office," Dr. Thompson added as an afterthought.

I received an orientation that was excruciating in detail. Dr. Tarry's voice droned on, listing the tests that were used, the computer scoring system, the format for the court reports, the lists of judges and their addresses, the operation of the cassette recorder. He even took me down the hall to introduce me to the women at the nurses' station. Mildred Cox, RN set her thin lips in a tight line and looked me up and down disapprovingly, withering the hopeful smile I had fixed to my face.

"You do know you'll be working with adolescent boys," she hissed. "You need to watch how you dress." She scanned my loose top and stirrup pants. Reflexively, I tugged at the hem of my blouse, immediately chiding myself for responding to her scolding.

"Oh, Mildred! Don't worry about her!" Don intervened. "She's not a nurse." Silently, Mildred turned from us to resume work on one of the charts.

A mousy woman with her hair cut in a simple pageboy, glanced shyly at me and waved a hand. "I'm Linda….the clerk," she whispered as if she were apologizing.

"Patrice. I work in recreation," said a statuesque, black woman as she authoritatively snapped shut a three-ring binder.

"Nice to meet you," I said to the two of them and the back of Mildred's head.

"Where's her office going to be?" Patrice asked.

"She hasn't picked one out, yet. Come to think of it," Don replied, snapping his fingers, "That's what we need to do next." He flung open the door of the nurses' station and gestured for me with an expansive bow. "After you!"

As he strode down the hall, he cautioned me not to allow Mildred to control me. "She's the head nurse and she's in charge of the techs and the LPN's. But YOU are a psychologist! You are not under her supervision!" I listened without any surge of confidence.

Stopping before a locked door with grimy safety glass at the top, he continued. "Now, you could put a curtain over the window if you want this office." He pushed open the metal door, and I began coughing at the overwhelming odor of stale urine. The empty room had a slotted window at ceiling level, one light bulb protected by bars and a grimy floor that sloped to a center drain.

"Used to be the control room," he explained. "It could be fixed up, though. You could bring some plants from home and some pictures for the wall. It'd look fine once you got your things in here."

Once the coughing stopped, I stood in incredulous silence long enough to get his attention. "Or… we could move some of the chairs out of the room next door if you want that one." He opened the next door, revealing a spacious office with tall windows. One end of the room, however, was piled from floor to ceiling with broken chairs. Some with splintered wooden backs, some with metal legs twisted in odd angles, some with vinyl seats in shreds. "I don't know why they're storing these here," he mused.

"They look like they're broken," I said and he nodded in agreement. "Well, why don't they throw them out?"

"Oh! They could be fixed!" he exclaimed. "The carpentry shop could repair them if somebody needed some chairs…You might find one you'd like to have," he ventured. "For a side chair or something."

I pondered that suggestion briefly before saying, "I'd like to have this office. Can you and I move the chairs to the room next door?"

Don seemed scandalized by that suggestion. "Property Department does that!" he scolded. "I'll call them."

I'm sure he did call them, that very day, but it took three weeks before the two irritable men came to the unit with their flat dolly. They threw the chairs in a jumbled pile for a trip to the ancient Davis Building, which had become the mausoleum for everything from rolling ECT machines and broken furniture, to water-damaged records and patients' cast-off clothing. Nothing, it seemed, was ever discarded at Western. When I complained to Dr. Thompson

24

about the inertia of the staff, he smiled ironically and informed me, "That's the Western Way." I would hear that summation again and again. The staff excused the administration's inane decisions and poor planning with a shrug and the comment, "There's a right way, there's a wrong way and there's the Western Way."

The Western Way sent computer technicians to wire buildings that were about to be abandoned because the structure was "unsafe" and had to be "mothballed." A carpet of pecans crackled under the tires of our cars each fall because the Western Way prevented us from gathering them and "stealing State property." Meanwhile, Mr. Furley, the head of personnel, had the hospital grounds keepers cutting his yard with state tractors and state gasoline, once a week. The Western Way gave Patrice an Employee of the Year award for her exemplary work with the adolescents and then immediately transferred her to an adult unit where she languished for months until her supervisor could pull enough strings to have her reinstated.

In another version of the Western Way, a bonfire was fueled with antique, wicker furniture because the superintendent vowed that he would permanently stop state employees from stealing the beautiful rockers and settees. Employees used their lunch hours for trysts in empty buildings; for conducting their loan shark businesses; for selling Avon in the parking lots; for washing the superintendent's Cadillac.

Months after my first day of employment, when I agreed to dictate Dr. Givhup's admission reports for pay, I assumed that an employee could use a lunch hour as he or she wished. Imagine my astonishment when I was hauled in front of the assistant administrator and told I would have to cease these entrepreneurial activities or face disciplinary charges. The Western Way.

These ironies and contradictions were unknown to me, however, when I first started the job. My first day went by in a blur, and I had no contact with any of the teenagers because I spent an inordinate amount of time listening to Don describe my impending job duties. By the time I climbed the stairs to Dr. Thompson's office at 3:00, I had been given a beat-up desk, which was placed in the room with the broken chairs. I also had a key to the office and a key to the unit.

Dr. Thompson looked away from his computer screen to ask how my afternoon had been.

"Fine," I said, still wondering how I could complete a week at that hospital, let alone two years.

When he asked me where I would be living, I recounted a conversation I had with someone in personnel who had mentioned a dorm on the campus. I had thought I might stay there until I could find an apartment.

He rolled his eyes. "I guess they mean the student nurses' dorm," he surmised. "Well, it could provide basic shelter for you until you rent a place, but that's about all. Come on, I'll take you up there."

At its zenith, WMPH had provided training for legions of young student nurses. They came in shivering groups of 20 or 30 girls who stood in front of the Administration Building, waiting for their instructor. However, by 1989, students no longer lived on the campus for a two month's rotation because everyone commuted from home in a car.

I followed Dr. Thompson into a dusty, narrow stairway at the back of the Administration Building and then through a huge room with a stage at one end. Weak light filtered through sooty windows, and cobwebs hung in gossamer strands from the corners. "This used to be the auditorium. They had dances up here, back in the day," he commented as my steps scraped like sandpaper across the dirty plank floor. He pulled open another creaking metal door. "I don't think anyone's used this dorm for the last 4 or 5 years," he confided. "If you're tired, you could just 'crash' here, but you'll probably want to find something else by the end of the week."

It was a long, narrow ward with 20 beds pushed against the wall. The mattresses were rolled against the metal headboards. A steel chest of drawers stood next to each bed, and a group of vinyl chairs were clustered at the end of the room. No TV, no telephone, no area rugs, no posters on the wall, no colorful bedspreads, nothing,

nothing that would have made it seem like a dorm. When I surveyed that room, I felt such despair and loneliness that I collapsed into a chair, elbows on my knees, forehead in my hands. I ran my fingers through my bangs, checking my tears and tasting the salt as it ran down my throat. "I don't think I can stay here," I said quietly.

A mouse scuttled across the floor at the end of the room, propelling me to jump from my seat. Suddenly, I was staring directly into Dr. Thompson's glasses, into his odd expression of surprise and pity. "Why don't I check with my wife and see if you could stay in our guest room for a day or two?" he suggested. I was so grateful that I could hardly speak, just managing to choke out a thank you. And although Dr. Thompson and Carol were absolute strangers and although I never felt "at home" in their prim bungalow, I was strengthened by this one act of kindness into knowing I would be able to return to work the next day.

KATE

Chapter 3
A Room To Rent

A week later, I approached Carol in the kitchen as she fixed sandwiches for dinner. Precious, their fat poodle, sat at her feet, her watery eyes riveted to the counter. I asked if there were any news on the lady who might be willing to rent me a room.

"Oh, yes! I meant to tell you yesterday...I saw her at the library board and explained your situation. She's willing to consider it, but she'd like to meet you first. You know...on a social basis."

I met Carol's eyes with a quizzical look. "She's definitely got plenty of room, but she just wants to get to know you before she opens her home to you. Don't worry, Dear," she reassured, patting my arm, "I gave you a good reference." Smiling over the top of her glasses, she absently dropped a piece of ham for Precious. A snort was followed by a smacking noise, but when I looked down, Precious was still sitting at attention, watching Carol's hand.

"Miss Adele is quite independent," she continued authoritatively, "and she'll make up her mind right away. You wouldn't know she was 80! Why, she still gets up every morning and dresses in her nice things; puts on her jewelry, even if she's going to be at home all day. You've seen her house? It's the big, red brick house with white columns on Polk Street."

I was skeptical that the woman who lived in that antebellum mansion would be in need of a boarder.

"Well, it's the family home and Miss Adele is the last of the family. I'm sure they had plenty of money at some point, but the farm was sold off years ago so there's not much of a fortune left. Then there's the upkeep on a house like that! It's over 100 years old, so something's always in need of repair." She tapped down the last slice of bread while Precious kept time by vigorously nodding her head.

Once we were seated at the breakfast nook, I thanked Carol and Scott for their hospitality and ended by saying, "I don't think I could have made it this week if I'd had to live in that empty dorm room."

"That was an impossible situation," Dr. Thompson said matter-of-factly. "I don't know why Personnel ever suggested it."

Carol and Scott watched TV after dinner. I excused myself and settled in bed with a magazine. I was exhausted and soon fell into a fitful sleep, dreaming that Russ was pulling back a shower curtain that surrounded the little twin bed. He slowly turned back the covers and then lay next to me, nestling his familiar angles against mine. Russ suddenly disappeared and I was sleeping alone in the nurses' dorm. The mice were swarming over me, scratching my face and tangling themselves in my hair. I was inexplicably paralyzed, unable to move or even scream.

I woke up sobbing, my gown glued to my body with a sheen of perspiration, my mind second-guessing everything I had said and done from the first pregnancy test to the drive to Madrid. Maybe we shouldn't have rushed into a divorce. Maybe taking the job at Western was the wrong thing to do.

I finally fell back to sleep and awoke a few hours later to find that my eyes were matted and swollen. I splashed cold water over my face again and again, but when I said goodbye to Carol, I was sure she knew I had been crying.

KATE

Chapter 4
Treatment with a Team

The next day, Thursday, I attended my first Treatment Team meeting and had a phone installed at my desk. It felt good to have two connections with the outside world.

Treatment Team began at 9:00 a.m. or at any point thereafter when an RN, a doctor and a social worker were present. Psychologists were classified as "non-essential" members of the team so meetings could proceed without us. Treatment Team was held in a conference room on the unit where two long tables were pushed together and a line of chairs hugged the walls.

Dr. Givhup, seated at the head of the table, smiled shyly at me and idly rubbed the slick dome of his nut-brown head with one hand. "We are glad you are here," he said formally. "Please to haw a chair." He nodded toward an empty seat at the table. "Now, as you know," he continued, looking purposefully around the table, "we haw ten boys to see this morning and there are already three families here. So…" he splayed his hands out on the table, "Let us begin."

Mildred glared at me from across the table while I avoided her stare. What could I have done this morning to invoke her anger? I made a mental inventory of my clothing and comments, finding nothing but my own sense of sadness at having so deeply offended her.

Next to Mildred sat Karla, the German social worker. She had married her military husband while he was stationed in Frankfurt and when he retired, they had moved to West Mississippi. Karla wrote furiously on her forms without looking up when the doctor commented. The door opened and a thin, black teenager sauntered in and eased himself into the seat at the end of the table. He was so tall that his arms and legs seemed to spill over the edges of the little chair.

Mildred picked up her stacked papers and smacked them against the table to straighten the edge. "Tavaris, this is your treatment team," she began in a clipped Midwestern accent. "We meet every week on Thursday morning to go over your progress. We're going to introduce ourselves and then you can explain why you're here."

The boy looked around uncertainly as the introductions droned on. As the last name faded away, he sat quietly, waiting to be prompted. "Tell us why you're here," Mildred repeated.

"Buglary."

"We know the charge, Tavaris," Mildred said imperiously. "Tell us what happened that caused you to be arrested."

When Tavaris remained silent, Karla prompted, "Eet vill only halp you to tell ze troot."

Patrice, the recreational therapist, leaned toward him. "Tavaris, you remember how you told me about going in the store? Just tell them what you told me," she encouraged.

This seemed to jolt Tavaris into our world. He immediately began talking, but so rapidly that I could not write fast enough to take a readable note.

"We wuz at my cousin girlfriend house an' Marcus say, 'Les do some'n' so we got'n the car and rode aroun' an' wen ta Sonic an' got some drinks an' then we rode aroun' some mo'. Then Kevin say, 'Stop da car!' an' he got out and walked aroun' the Q-fashion to the back do' an when he come back, he had these clothes he was carryin' an he told me ta stay inna car and look out, case somebody was ta come up an' then they wen back in and got mo' stuff and then they come back t'the car an we lef' and somebody mussa saw us cause the *po*-lees started follerin us an' we wuz throwin' clothes out da winda goin' down da highway an' then Marcus tried t' outrun 'em and we wen down in a ditch an' they put us in a *po*-lees car an' took us t' juvie." He stopped, apparently out of breath.

Patrice coaxed, "Tell them if you've been arrested before."

"Shopliftin' an' fightin'," he announced.

Patrice, Mildred and the classroom teacher asked other

questions about his school behavior, his family, his use of alcohol and drugs while Dr. Givhup sat impassively at the head of the table like a mahogany Buddha, his eyes half-closed in meditation. As their questions subsided, Karla's pen continued to scrape angrily across her papers. Dr. Givhup started his Mental Status Exam:

"Umm. What ees your name?" Tavoris looked startled to be hearing from the short, brown man at the end of the table.

"Tavaris Jones."

"And what ees the date?" Dr. Givhup continued.

"Thursday."

"Yes, and the date?"

"September ... 15, I think."

"Umm, and what ees the year?"

"1989."

"Good! And where are you?"

Tavaris seemed amazed that Dr. Givhup didn't know where we were. "The hospital, of course!"

"That's right," Dr. Givhup said with a satisfied tone. But the questions were about to become abstract and Tavaris was already struggling to understand Dr. Givhup's Indian accent.

"Do you hear woices?" asked Dr. Givhup pleasantly.

"Huh?" said Tavaris.

"VOICES! VOICES! DO YOU HEAR VOICES!" Karla interrupted, suddenly slamming down her pen so that Tavaris and I both jumped.

"Huh?" said Tavaris with a rising note of panic.

"Voices!" said Mildred, "People talking!"

"I hear you all!" Tavaris answered. "I ain't got no trouble with my hearin'."

"No, Tavaris," Patrice interjected, gaining his attention. "Do you hear voices when no one's around?"

"Naw!" he responded, slowly wagging his head at the idiocy of the questions.

Dr. Givhup made some hash marks on the paper before him. "Do you see wisions?"

"Huh?"

"VISIONS! VISIONS!" Karla hissed.

"Huh?"

"Do you see things that aren't really there?" Patrice translated.

"Oh! Naw!"

"Do you need any medicine?" Dr. Givhup inquired.

"Naw!" Tavaris immediately answered, apparently understanding the word "medicine" quite well.

"Are you crazy? Are you mentally eel?" Dr. Givhup continued. Dumbstruck, Tavaris looked around the room as Dr. Givhup forged ahead, "Do you need any halp?"

"Oh!" Tavaris exclaimed, jolted by the question. "Naw! Naw!"

"You see," Dr. Givhup sagely commented, nodding to each member of the team, "He doesn't think he needs any halp." He made some more marks on the paper before he began again.

"What do you want to be when you grow beeg?"

Tavaris briefly looked down at his 6'3" frame before saying, "Huh?"

Karla tried to translate, "Vhat do you vant to be vin you grow **up**?"

Tavaris now knew to look toward Patrice, the closest black staff member at the table. He raised his eyebrows.

"What do you want to do when you finish school?" she prompted.

"Play basketball!" he enthusiastically answered.

Dr. Givhup rubbed the top of his shiny head. "Okay, he can sign," he commented and an attendance sheet was handed down the table to Tavaris.

Our next adolescent was Todd, a stocky, white boy with unruly hair, who plopped into the chair, crossed his arms over his chest and stared menacingly at Mildred. She ignored him. The questions began, but this time Patrice was in charge of the early comments, so things seemed to progress more smoothly. After initially declaring that he had nothing to say, Todd listened to Patrice's explanation of why he should cooperate with us and then he told his story: "I was in a fight in tha ole Walmart parkin' lot. I beat up mah best friend's boyfriend. He was gettin' loud and actin' like he was gonna hit her, so I whipped his ass…He went to the ER and I came here," he smugly informed us.

"Did she ask you to help her?" Patrice probed.

"Naw! But I wasn't gonna stand there and watch her get pushed around."

"Have you ever had to go to court before?" Mildred asked.

"Last year for fightin' at school," he said, laying his hands on the table to admire them. They were thick, square hands and next to the little finger was the hairline scar of a "boxer's fracture."

I felt compelled to break my newcomer's silence, and when I spoke, several people looked around as if they had forgotten I was at the table. "How'd you get that scar?" I asked, pointing to his hand.

"I broke my hand and they had to go in an' fix it."

"Were you fighting when you broke it?"

"Yeah," he admitted, then seemed surprised at his candor. "But don't tell my momma," he pleaded. "She thinks I broke it when I fell off my bike."

"How old were you when that happened?" I continued.

"'Bout 13.."

"Have you been fighting your whole life?" I asked, quietly.

He looked startled and then answered, "Pretty much."

Dr. Givhup began his questions. "Do you want to keel you-sef?" he asked politely.

"Huh?"

"Commit suicite!" interjected Karla without looking up from her writings.

Todd looked as uncomfortable and unsure as Tavaris had. I leaned toward him, emboldened by my earlier success. "Do you think about hurting yourself, or killing yourself?"

Todd looked me squarely in the eyes, locking his gaze into mine and letting several seconds pass before he responded, with a slow and distinct "No." I intuitively knew that he was taking me into his confidence long enough to tell me his denial was a lie.

Patrice began to tell him about the schedule for our evaluation. "You'll be here for about 30 days. This is the evaluation your judge wanted you to have…" Her voice, steady and confident summarized the weeks he would be spending with us. "Your levels will depend on your behavior, how you follow the rules… We want you to stay on good levels. You've made a good start. Just keep it up." Todd nodded his agreement and scrawled his name on the signature page that appeared before him.

When Todd left the room, Dr. Givhup looked at me appreciatively and his face crinkled into a smile. "Wery good work, Ms. McConnie!" he complimented. "An yur fust day, too!"

I caught a glimpse of Mildred's glare. "How did *YOU* know about a boxer's fracture?" she demanded.

"Oh, I had an old boyfriend who had one," I confided easily. "The scar looked the same."

"Wery nice! Good observer!" Dr. Givhup laughed.

When the meeting was over, Patrice praised my interview skills to Don, who met us in the hall. Giving me a pretend punch on the shoulder, he said, "Way to go!" and strolled to the nurses' station.

But despite the little bloom of familiarity, I ate lunch in my office, a meal of peanut butter crackers and a yellow apple from Carol's fruit bowl. I could hear Don, whistling as he locked his office door and could hear the conversations between staff members fading as they disappeared down the hall.

A feeling of profound solitude and then bitter loneliness washed over me. I threw away the rest of my apple and parted the blinds, gazing through the wire mesh screen to the bicycle rack outside my window. A few years earlier, an elderly donor had contributed ten bicycles to the hospital in a gesture of grand naiveté. The bikes now rusted in a metal rack next to the parking lot because juvenile delinquents on elopement status could not be offered a means of escape. I giggled, absurdly imagining Mildred slinging one careless leg over a bike and motioning for ten delinquents to follow her on a pleasure ride. This was definitely another example of "The

Western Way," I mused. In the distance, smoke boiled from the brick crematorium-chimney as if the memory of old patients were being changed into a dirty smear across the sky. I shivered, returned to my desk chair and pulled a sweater over my shoulders.

My mind wandered to the little tree house apartment, where Russ was probably still asleep. I imagined him, rolled up in a tattered quilt, his lips slightly parted, his long eyelashes brushing his cheek. I seemed to have rushed into a quagmire and now that I was trapped in this behemoth of an institution, I thought about Mayfield, about how I would be getting ready to leave for the afternoon shift at The Mystic. None of my reasons for coming to Western seemed to make sense to me anymore. I stayed locked in my office for the lunch hour, feeling more and more miserable.

The afternoon session in Treatment Team began at 1:00 and included several families. A set of snaggle-toothed, tattooed parents, clearly irritated by the difficulty of understanding Dr. Givhup and Karla, had demanded to know if there were any "American doctors" in the hospital. One mother, dressed in a halter top and short-shorts, arrived obviously inebriated. She wore a plastic hibiscus behind one ear and giggled each time Mildred mentioned a charge her son had incurred. "He's my bad boy," she scolded, tousling his hair and chuckling. Mildred called Security and had her escorted out of the building. I was worried about how she would be able to drive 50 miles to her home but Karla scolded, "Ve kant be vorried about zat. Eet ees for ze police."

Parents of a 15-year-old juvenile sex offender settled into the chairs at the table and declared themselves to be pillars of their church and community. They dismissed the 7-year-old victim's story by saying the girl couldn't be too injured since they had seen her on a seesaw a few days later. The father leaned in front of his tearful son and answered all the questions the Treatment Team asked, even when Mildred reminded him that we wanted to hear from Corey. The mother sat with her jaw clenched and her arms crossed over her chest, as if she could barely contain her outrage at the injustices being perpetrated on her son.

When Treatment Team was finished, I stopped at Don's opened door and found him standing in the middle of his office, checking items off a list.

"Treatment Team is finally over," I told him. "Got your grocery list?"

"This? Oh, no, it's a little 'memory jogger' for me. I want to be sure I turn everything off," he explained, laying his badge on the desk. Next on the list was evidently "Unplug the coffee pot," because he pulled the plug from the wall and marked the list. He picked up his travel mug and the odor of vinegar reached my nose. "This is my new 'memory jogger'," he enthused, swirling the contents of the mug so that the vapors filled the room. "Have you read the research on vinegar? It's very convincing!" He took a big slurp from the edge of the mug. "Well, it's almost 4:00 so I guess I'll go on," he said as he switched off the office light and made one last checkmark. "I have to stop by Medical Records before I go home."

He whistled "Waltzing Matilda" as he strode happily down the hall. I shuffled to my office and collapsed in the creaking chair, straining to hear any sounds of life from the unit. The boys were in the cafeteria and the silence could have indicated that the building had been abandoned.

Now that I had a phone on my desk, I had a WAATS line which would connect me with anyone I cared to call. I quickly looked at my watch and calculated where Russ would typically be at 4:00 p.m. Then I dialed the number for The Club. Marie, the manager, answered.

"Hey, Honey!" she crooned in her raspy voice. "How are you? We miss you here." Her motherly questions sent a pang of nostalgia through me. I quickly asked if Russ were at the club.

"Has been," she answered. "He must've stepped outside. Just a minute, let me see if he's in the parking lot." She put the phone down and several minutes passed before I heard Russ's voice, as warm and engaging as if he were coming in the apartment door.

"Kate? Hey, Babe! How you doin'?"

"Okay. I just wanted to let you know where I am," I responded automatically.

"Oh…Sure! Let me write down your number."

A stab of sadness, a longing for him started the tears welling up in my eyes. I didn't want him to hear the quiver in my voice so I hesitated, biting my bottom lip.

"Kate? You alright?"

"Not really," I whispered.

He paused, clearly perplexed over what his response should be to this recently estranged wife. "What's wrong?"

"I want to talk to you… in person," I blurted out. "Can you come down here? Maybe over the weekend or something?" Hearing my own pitiful request, I regretted the words I had chosen. *How it must sound!* I thought. Quickly I added, "I just need to talk to someone I can trust."

"Well, sure," he responded. "Next weekend, I'm only playing on Friday night, so I could come down on Saturday. Would that work?"

My irritation burned in my throat. I saw that everything still had to be done by the music calendar. Music, his very jealous mistress, demanded to be first priority always. I took a deep breath, checking my anger. Next Saturday was better than nothing, so I told him I'd be waiting for him.

"We've got a gig tomorrow night at the Blues Club," he continued, his voice brightening with optimism. "They've got room for 150 and I think we may fill the place up! A lot of folks have told me they're going to be there…So next weekend, then. I'll try to get to your place early on Saturday. "

I carefully placed the phone back in the cradle. I felt unreasonably hopeful that the visit might somehow evolve into a rescue.

Chapter 5
The Audition

My audition with Adele Cearley Forrest was on Friday morning and in the intervening days, I had learned all I could about "Miss Adele": Her family was considered landed gentry and before the Civil War, they were one of six families who owned the entire county. The Cearleys made their fortune in cotton and then built their columned house on a street off court square in 1859. When Adele and her five siblings were children, they lived with their parents, Sterling and Ada, in a rambling farmhouse five miles south of Madrid. Every Sunday the extended family gathered at the long mahogany table in Colonel James' Madrid home for dinner.

The grandparents died when Adele was in her late teens, prompting Sterling to move to town and to establish himself, like his father before him, as an absentee manager of the family holdings.

Adele had grown up neatly balanced between the two worlds: In the afternoons, she rode Tennessee Walkers with her brothers but in the evenings, she danced in silk chiffon, across parlors lit by chandeliers. She was as eager to prune the rose bushes as she was to arrange them into a bouquet. Adele was frankly intimidating to men her own age and when she married a man 16 years her elder, no one was surprised. After a brief honeymoon in New Orleans, they moved to Walter's farm in Braggadocio, and she glided into managing his household and business accounts as easily as she had organized charity bazaars and church committees. Adele's favorite advice to young women was, "Better to be an old man's darling than a young man's fool" and her own life stood as a testimonial to her philosophy.

Walter Forrest was frankly in awe of his vivacious and confident young bride. He referred to her as "My Baby" and good naturedly teased her about having to buy a new hat every spring. She shopped in Memphis, driving the 80 miles alone with no fear for her personal safety and no concern for her mother's dire predictions. She kept two favorite Walkers in the barn behind their house and rode down county roads and across the fields when the mood struck her. Walter eventually taught himself not to worry about her absences although early in the marriage, he told her he wished she would leave a note on the kitchen table if she were riding.

When the Great Depression tightened its hold, Walter and Adele lost their large pool of laborers in the migration of field hands to the North. Cotton, always a labor intensive crop, was no longer King. The Forrests diversified, buying mustangs from the West to train as saddle horses; increasing their herd of dairy cattle to sell milk to the wholesalers in Memphis; and tripling the size of the vegetable garden so that produce could be sold to city grocery stores. By these adjustments, the farm was managed with the help of only a few workers and at the depression's end, Adele and Walter still owned their original acreage. Sterling, however, had lost most of the family land, mortgaging it heavily to pay taxes, gambling debts and hospital bills for his invalid daughter, Belle.

Walter died in 1962 and Adele moved back to her parents' home. She resumed her life as the oldest daughter and the most outspoken child. Since 1970, she had been the sole tenant of the house, although Josephine and Albert, two former field workers, lived in a small cabin at the back of the lot.

The morning of the interview, I walked into Carol's kitchen, wearing a clean pair of jeans and a knit top. She turned from the sink and proclaimed that I would have to change, which sent me back to the bedroom for a skirt and a cotton blouse. I had learned not to question her judgment about the rules of this quaint little town.

During the short drive to Adele's, Carol gave rapid fire instructions, raising my level of anxiety with each warning of what to say and what to avoid. The car rolled through streets lined with arching oaks, and I had the startling impression that we were traveling through some sort of time-tunnel toward 1860. Cars grew fewer; an occasional resident sat on a columned front porch reading the newspaper; two children knelt on a buckled sidewalk and drilled into the dirt with sticks.

Carol stopped in front of the columned brick home. She imposingly assessed my appearance, smiling her approval as we stepped from the walkway to the wide plank porch. When she took the brass door knocker in hand, I glanced at windows that were tall enough to waltz through, a cushioned porch swing, and flowers that trailed from window boxes.

A tiny, black woman opened the door. Her grey hair was parted in the middle and spindly braids curled over each ear; deep lines crinkled from her eyes, running down her cheeks. She shifted her cloudy gaze from Carol to me. "Good morning Josephine," Carol said.

"Good moanin', Miss Ca-el," she drawled in a quavering voice. "Come on in. Miss A-dele 'spectin y'all." In a slow, rolling gait, she led us through a foyer dominated by a serpentine staircase to a parlor where Adele was enthroned on a Victorian sofa. A silver coffee service gleamed on a tea table to her left. Although I had resolved not to stare, my eyes swept over the worn oriental carpets, antique furniture and threadbare velvet drapes before I made eye contact with Adele. She was a tall woman with hair that had been dyed the color of burgandy. She was dressed in a peacock blue dress and wore a strand of pearls. A large diamond ring glinted on her right hand. She stood to greet us, taking Carol warmly by the hands and smiling down on her beatifically.

"Would you like some coffee,?" she asked in a melodious voice.

But when Josephine asked if there was anything else we needed, Miss Adele answered sharply, as if the offer were an intrusion. "I'll call for you if I need you, Josephine." Then, as she poured the first cup of steaming coffee, she began to talk without looking at us, her lilting accent returning.

"So, Kate, I understand you're new to our little town."

"Yes, ma'am," I answered. "I started work on Monday at the

hospital."

"And you're living with Carol and Scott right now," she continued.

"Yes, ma'am. Just temporarily. I'm afraid I didn't make good arrangements for housing before I took the job. The personnel department told me I could live in the students' dorm until I got my first paycheck. But the dorm didn't seem like a safe place to stay."

"I should say not!" exclaimed Miss Adele. "There hasn't been a group of students in that annex for five to ten years," she continued authoritatively.

"It looked like a pretty spooky place," I confessed. "So Dr. Thompson took pity on me and asked Carol if I could stay in their guest bedroom for a while."

Miss Adele smiled at Carol. She was already familiar with this part of the story. "Cream? Sugar?"

What followed was a series of questions about my family of origin and a passing interest in the fact that I had been married. She dismissed my divorce with a wave of her hand and the comment, "These men can be difficult, you know." In the middle of our exchange, she decisively settled her coffee cup in the saucer and called with rising impatience, "Josephine! Where are you? Bring us those cinnamon rolls on the kitchen counter!" I was taken aback and then embarrassed by her imperious tone, but Josephine silently appeared at the door, composed and unhurried. She set the platter on the coffee table before disappearing to the kitchen.

"So, Kate, what do you think of our great big hospital and our little town?" Adele asked, her voice returning to its previous cadence as she questioned me about my experiences.

"Well…" I hesitated. "Everyone has been really welcoming to me…." Imagining Mildred, I felt I should be crossing my fingers to tell that fib. "And it's a beautiful campus." Adele seemed to be waiting for more impressions. "Oh, and I think the county courthouse is really pretty!"

I had hit pay dirt. She wanted to give me the history of Madrid and had been waiting for an opening. "Our courthouse was built right after the War between the States," she advised me. "This town was occupied by the Northern Army for months. Why, General Sherman struck my staircase with his sword one day during a fit of temper, and you can still see the gash. He was standing right there in the foyer when he was told that Grant would be delayed." She pointed one long finger toward the entryway. "General Sherman threatened the people of Madrid every day, but our town was just too pretty to burn, so he never gave the order to set it afire." She paused before summarizing as if she had known him, "Even though he saved the town, General Sherman was an absolute scoundrel!"

I looked at Carol, who smiled encouragingly from where she was nestled in an array of silk pillows. Miss Adele put her cup on the table and leaned back on the sofa, finally acknowledging the purpose of our visit by offering to rent me a room. The room that had belonged to her sister, Belle, was the logical choice she said, since it was on the first floor and had an outside entrance. We settled on a rent that included breakfast and maid service at a rate that seemed absurdly low. Part of me felt that I should save Josephine from doing my chores but I thought better then suggesting it to Adele.

"Well, the only other thing we haven't talked about is gentlemen callers. Do you expect to have gentlemen friends coming to visit you?"

It was an unanticipated question, asked in a deceptively casual way. I took a deep breath to gain time to think. "I don't have any gentlemen friends right now," I answered truthfully. "Once I'm settled in, I may meet someone I'd like to date," I said, feeling for the nuances to each word before I spoke.

"And would you be entertaining gentlemen friends here?" she persisted as she tapped her finger against the brocaded couch, leading me to momentarily think of myself in a hoop skirt, sitting on the divan as I flirted with a riverboat gambler.

"I think that would depend on how you feel about it," I said carefully. "I might like to have someone stop by after work, maybe… for a glass of tea or something…" My voice trailed off.

"Do you think you might want to entertain in your room?" she pressed.

The direction of her questions finally became clear. "No, ma'am, I won't have overnight company, even a girlfriend," I assured her, both of my palms raised in a gesture of surrender.

Adele seemed satisfied with my answer and called for Josephine, who tottered into the living room.

"Take Kate to Belle's room and let her see the bathroom, too," she instructed. From the wide hall, Josephine opened the door on a large bedroom, furnished with an ornate walnut bed, a massive chest-of-drawers, a statuesque armoire. "This here Miss Belle's room," she told me, pulling the drapes behind brass hooks to let in the weak light. I peered out the grimy window to see steps that lead to a brick patio. The room had the smell of antique stores and pawn shops: dusty, moldy and tightly shut against any spring breezes.

"When did Belle die?" I asked.

Josephine screwed up her face in thought. "Mm, 'les see. I think it was 1960." She began to busy herself with straightening the airless room, rearranging the pillows on the bed and smoothing the dusty bedspread. Hopefully the sheets had been changed since Belle's demise, I thought.

"Do the windows open?"

"Yes'm. They jus' slide up," she answered without making any effort to open them. Instead, Josephine stepped back to the hall door and ushered me into a bathroom that was furnished with a claw foot bathtub, a toilet and a square sink with a separate faucet for hot and cold. I decided Adele's house would be suitable for a few months, until I could save money for a deposit and find a modern apartment.

Once I was reseated in the parlor, I responded to Adele's questioning gaze: "It's a beautiful room and I think it'll work out fine for me."

"When do you want to move in?"

Anxiously I thought of Russ's planned visit, knowing I should not be in Adele's house when he came to town. "What about Monday week? I'd planned to be out-of-town next weekend," I lied.

"Well, that's up to you," she sniffed. "You could move in sooner and have everything in place before you take your trip." Carol gave me an almost imperceptible nod and I acquiesced to Adele's plan.

"Good!" she said, smiling broadly and patting her hands on both knees. "I think we'll get along just fine together!"

In the kitchen, sitting on a worn metal stool Josephine strained to focus her eyes on the Bible picture book she had owned since Miss Ada gave it to her at age eleven. The picture of Jesus carrying the lambs was her favorite. His tunic was a bright blue and his mantle was scarlet, colors that were vivid to her failing eyes. Her hearing was still excellent: from the next room she could eavesdrop on the conversation as Adele's guests prepared to leave. Idly she wondered how this new boarder would fit in with this household.

Cataracts had clouded her sight to the point that she could no longer tell the cornmeal from the flour sacks by simply looking. She used her sense of smell to determine which she needed for cooking. Josephine was 90 years old and had lived on Cearley property for her entire life.

She was born at home in a two-room shack hardly more comfortable than slave quarters. She remembered clearly the day that Adele had been born and she had been brought to the white-folks' house to help her mother Clara with the additional chores the new baby required. Josephine was pleasant and unexcitable, traits that soon earned her the responsibility of childcare. She remembered holding the baby Adele and feeling a terrible pity for this scrawny, unsettled infant who seemed to be causing her family such distress. Adele's mother cried and wrung her hands over the baby's poor appetite; her father hollered for somebody to do something with that child! The older brothers begged to be allowed to sleep in the hay loft, away from the sounds of crying. Adele had the colic. She didn't eat well; she fussed and fretted when she was awake; and her sleep was poor unless she was being rocked on someone's shoulder. Josephine believed that she had rocked that baby all the way to Memphis and back. Clara said Adele was going to need help for the rest of her life and made Josephine promise that she would stay with her charge for as long as she was needed. In the eighty years she had been working for Adele, Josephine had never seen an indication that Adele was ready to live on her own. Oh yes, Adele fussed and fumed and complained, but Josephine refused to be ruffled by these displays of bad temper. Those little temper fits passed as suddenly as they came and then life returned to its pleasant domestic rhythms.

The kitchen in Adele's house was Josephine's territory and she could find any utensil or ingredient without the benefit of good vision. Josephine did not even have a kitchen in the cottage she shared with her husband because all of their food was left-overs, brought across their threshold in plates that would be returned the next day. She knew every piece of clothing in Adele's armoire and how they were to be cleaned. She could anticipate the rhythms of the year: when it was time to get out the Christmas decorations; when the ferns should be rolled from the library to the front porch; when the Episcopal Ladies' Club would be coming to the house to prepare for their annual bazaar.

Adele and Carol exchanged pleasantries as we ambled to the door. Although she was in her eighties, Adele stood with ramrod straightness, as if she were about to review the troops. She stepped without hesitation, without apparent stiffness or pain. Everything about Adele seemed to be a contridiction. She was gracious, but ill-tempered with Josephine. She was charming with me , but also rather over-bearing. I thought about how she must have looked as a young woman, dancing with her beaux in these spacious parlors, impressing them all with her wit and grace. I was certain that she had indeed been a force to be reckoned with. I hoped I was up to the challenge of living with her.

LANA

Chapter 6
Monroe County 1952

Lana thought it must be the hottest day of the year. The cotton plants that surrounded their house seemed to be melting into the clay soil, and high above the fetid air, two buzzards circled, endlessly searching for some small animal fated to die of a heat stroke. The metal window fan roared constantly, giving her kitchen the sound of an airplane hanger, but despite its steady growl, the kitchen was torrid. The yellowed wallpaper was covered with a fine sheen of moisture, and Lana's white-blonde hair, an inheritance from some long-forgotten Nordic ancestor, fell in damp tendrils. Her face had long since lost the plump curves of infancy. Her nose was straight and narrow, without any curve that might suggest saucy flirtation; her eye brows ran in a resolute line, without a trace of an arch. Her lips were thin and were held grimly against her teeth. Only the perfectly round, crystalline blue eyes broke the linear continuity. As Lana held onto the edge of the kitchen sink, trying to make her stomach stop churning, she heard Jerry's truck pull into the gravel driveway. His footsteps hammered against the wooden stairs before he jerked open the screen door.

"If supper ain't ready," he said to Lana's back, "I'm gon' run down t'Jake's for 'at tractor part." Without waiting for an acknowledgement from his wife, he let the door slam and jogged back to his truck.

She had been nothing but sick since she missed her period two months ago. And now that it was July, the heat brought nausea and waves of dizziness. With the back of her flour-caked hand, she pushed a lock of hair away from her eyes, leaving a white smear above her brow. She turned on the faucet letting tepid water run from her fingertips in milky streams. There was no need to let the grease heat up, she reasoned she reasoned as she walked to the cookstove, because she was too weak to stand over the pan. As she placed the floured chicken into the refrigerator, the cool air rushed around her, and she stood in the door for a much longer time than necessary, letting the wisps of cold caress her face and arms. She closed the door with a sigh and shuffled to the bedroom, tumbling into the damp sheets.

When Jerry walked into his house at 6:00, he found the grease congealed in the pan, the kitchen empty, and his fully dressed wife asleep in the bed. She had been so listless lately that he wasn't surprised but he was furious. He jerked the pillow from her head and began yelling, "What you doin' in bed at this time a day? You ain't done nothin' in this house and there ain't no supper cooked. You think I been working all day long so as you could lay up in the bed?"

She groggily raised her head and fluttered her eyelids to focus. "You can't even stay wake long enough t'answer one goddamn question!" He straddled her on the bed and grabbed her by the shoulders, shaking her until her head jerked violently into her breast bone. "Bitch! I can't make a livin' and keep house, too! You too lazy and good-for-nuthin' to even get outta this bed!" After a few more shakes, he pushed her backwards, banging her head against the iron headboard. The blow sent a blinding pain forward and shot fingers of lightning across her eyes. When she began to cry, he dismounted and strode across the bedroom. Then thinking better of it, he returned to the bed, picking her up by the shoulders as if she were a cloth doll and throwing her to the floor. "And stay outta that goddamn bed!"

He marched through the kitchen and out the door, his footsteps shaking the plank floor with rage. She heard the angry tires of his truck throwing gravel against the house. At the back of her head, her fingers felt warm, sticky blood, and she was aware that something was trickling between her legs. She lifted her head and with another wave of nausea, realized that it was blood. Then a grey veil seemed to settle over her eyes and she lost consciousness.

≈⟩∾

Lana was 20 years old and had been married just over a year. Although she had liked some things about school, it had mainly seemed irrelevant to farm life. She had finished a year in high school and then stayed home to run her father's household for her absent mother, Lois Gray, who had run off with a Fuller Brush salesman. Lana began cooking for the family when she had to stand in a chair at the stove and maneuver the iron skillets with both hands. She began hanging out baskets of laundry when she had to balance on tiptoe and stretch her aching arms to reach the clothesline. Her father was no stranger to hard work, either. When there were crops to be planted and hoed and harvested, he worked in Mr. Lanier's fields, taking a share of whatever crop was made. In the winters, he worked in the woods belonging to Mr. Cearley, logging with a team of mules. Now in his middle forties, he was as grizzled and stooped as a man twice his age.

On a sunny, spring morning, Lana become reacquainted with Jerry Wright, when she brought a forgotten lunch pail to her father at the sawmill. Jerry had turned off the saws and had settled on a log to eat his dinner when he saw Lana walking toward them, wearing a green printed dress, her legs long and slender under the soft cotton, her straight, white-blonde hair pulled back in a ribbon at her neck. As she walked, she swung the lunch pail like a little girl would swing a rag doll. She meandered through the tall grass and muddy puddles, scanning the trees for the smudge of chartreuse signaling spring. The men, silently admiring her from their perch in the open shed, misread her preoccupation for cool disinterest.

Stepping into the darkness, she walked toward her father with the pail extended. He received the news that she had walked from home to deliver his lunch with imperious gruffness. Questioning her about the contents of the pail, he satisfied his curiosity with a quick glance under the napkin, then waved her away, telling her to "git on home."

As Lana hesitated, Jerry wondered if she were daydreaming

rather than listening to her father. Her blue eyes had a hazy quality.

"Go on then!" her father said, louder than before, prompting Jerry to slide off the log where he had been sitting.

"Hey, Mr. John," he called to get her father's attention. "I ain't seen Lana in a month a Sundays. Lemme walk `er down the road a piece."

Her father shrugged and turned his back on them as Jerry lightly took Lana by one elbow and circled her away from the machinery. They stepped from the shed and started down the dirt path.

She didn't seem to know what to do with her hands, since they were unaccountably free from carrying a burden. She twisted her fingers around a button at her waist as she stepped through the grass, looking up at Jerry with a questioning smile.

"So what you been doin' since school?" he began.

"Not a whole lot….Keepin' house for Daddy."

"Bet you stay busy, with all them lil' kids."

The grass swished against his pants as he walked, as if it were whispering about his good fortune. "You ever get out on a Sat'dy night?"

She hesitated for a minute before saying, "Umm, not really."

"Don't ever go to the movies or out for a coke or somethin'?"

"Um-m."

He pushed his cap farther back on his forehead in exasperation. "Well, you want to?"

Her hazy blue eyes scanned his face as she seemed to consider all of the possibilities. Then, after several minutes had passed, she answered, "I guess so."

His heart was beating wildly as he gambled on asking, "Could I pick you up this Sat'dy and carry you out for a coke?"

One corner of her mouth turned up in a faint, crooked smile, as if she found the idea of a date immensely amusing. His heart pounded more violently, sending its beat up his neck and into his ears. His co-workers simply could not see him shuffle back to the shed with her rejection stamped across his face, he thought, waiting an eternity for her to answer. Holding his gaze with her eyes, Lana nodded twice and then continued walking. He was standing in the road, with the details not yet decided, helplessly watching her wander away from him.

"Lana!" he hollered to her back. With a startled expression, she wheeled around to face him. "What time should I pick y' up?"

Again, the hesitation and confusion. "Maybe 6:00?" she questioned before she began her meandering journey again.

"You be ready, now! Y'hear?" he called after her retreating figure. Jerry swaggered back to the shed where six men were grinning at him and Lana's father was avoiding his gaze. He picked up his lunch pail, as if nothing had happened, and took a bite from the cold biscuit.

He was true to his word and appeared at the weathered shack at 6:00. He had bathed, put on a clean shirt, and washed the dust from the truck. Her father, his shirt soaked through with sweat, was sitting on the front porch, smoking a cigarette.

Jerry walked through several disapproving chickens that were scratching in the dirt yard, while the sounds of children playing behind the house carried on the evening breeze. "Mr. John," he said formally, nodding at the older man.

Jerry stopped at the bottom of the uneven, wooden steps and looked up at Lana's father, silently asking permission to climb the stairs to the porch. Instead of an invitation to join him, Mr. Gray demanded, "Where you takin' Lana tonight?"

"I reckon we'll jus' go t' town and git a coke at the drug store." Jerry put his shoe on the second step and leaned forward, propping his right elbow on his knee, still waiting to be asked to join the older man. "Been real nice today, ain't it?"

"Well, at least it ain't rained," he growled. "We oughtta be able to get the tractors in the field by early next week."

Jerry relaxed, familiar with the language of farming and weather.

"Mr. Lanier gon' plant that 100 acres down by Indian Creek this year?"

"He ain't made up his mind. But I `spect he will."

Jerry nodded his head as if he were the previous owner. "It's good, rich land, but it's sure prone to floodin' out."

Mr. Gray grunted his agreement then heaved himself out of the chair and leaned into the open front door. "Lana!" Silence. "Oh, Lana! You ready?" Silence, again. He sighed and walked into the house, leaving Jerry standing by the porch, listening as the older man's heavy steps thudded across the plank floor. After several minutes, Mr. Gray reappeared, looking chagrined. "I don't know where she got off to," he confessed. "Jus' come up'n have a seat. She's bound to be back in a minute or two." Jerry took the three steps to the sloping porch with one leap and found a wooden chair that had a sprung cane bottom. He sat down uncomfortably, but Mr. Gray didn't seem to notice; he was preoccupied with his can of Prince Albert. He opened a thin paper and tapped a little tobacco into the fold, then rolled the paper into a cylinder, licking the seam and pressing it together with stained fingers.

When he offered it to Jerry, the young man shook his head. Mr. Gray shrugged and scraped a match across the rough wood of the porch, cupping his hands around the match and the cigarette. The movements were seamless, having been repeated so often that he could look out at the horizon while rolling and lighting his cigarette. The oppressive silence sent Jerry to pumping his leg up and down and tapping his fingers against the wooden arms of the chair. Mr. Gray continued to draw and exhale, squinting at the horizon, comfortable in his wooden chair. He smoked, worked a toothpick around his teeth and cleaned under his fingernails with a pocketknife.

At 6:30 Lana appeared in the front yard, holding a round dishpan filled with buttercups so yellow that she seemed be balancing a harvest moon on one hip. Her cotton dress fluttered in the early evening breeze. The crooked smile she gave her father seemed to be more of a question than a greeting.

"Where you been, girl?" her father growled.

She was apparently impervious to his tone of voice. "Down at the ole Hurley place."

"I tol'ju I didn't want you down there," he upbraided her. "Too close to where the niggers stay. You don't need t'be walking down there a-tall."

"Ain't nobody down there bothered me," she mumbled, her eyes downcast. Then she looked up, holding the dishpan for his inspection and saying brightly, "But ain't they pretty, Daddy?" Jerry, sitting in the shadows, thought for an instant that he was watching the artless girl he knew in second grade. When he stood up and she caught his movement from the corner of her eye, she joggled the pan, causing a few of the flowers to fall in the yard. A greedy hen raced over to see if food had been dropped and clucked her disapproval at the inedible flowers.

"I ain't studyin' those flowers, Lana," John scolded before continuing. "Jerry's been waitin' on you half the night."

Flustered with her own forgetfulness and ill-at-ease with Jerry's sudden appearance, she stammered an apology.

"It's okay," he reassured them both, stepping off the porch. "You still wanna go t' town, Lana?"

She set the dishpan down on the edge of the porch, relieved for the opportunity to escape her father's wrath and hurriedly said, "If you do….Jus' gimme a minute."

When she reappeared, her hair had been combed into a silver-blonde ponytail, tied back with a ribbon. She was wearing the printed green dress and she had exchanged her mud-caked "field shoes" for a pair of clean canvas ones. Stepping onto the porch, she spied the dishpan of flowers and exclaimed, "They'll die if I don't get 'em in some water," as she rushed into the house one last time.

Jerry opened the door on her side of the truck and helped her step in. She was impressed with his manners and made a mental note to wait for him to open her door after they had parked. The road to town was lined with miles of fields, lying fallow after the spring rains. Jerry chattered as he drove, commenting on the land

and who had owned it previously, while Lana listened absently, gazing at a crescent moon that reminded her of one of her mother's silver earrings.

The drugstore was busy with last minute shoppers buying necessities before the mandatory Sunday closing. Jerry nodded to a booth in the soda fountain and they sat down, facing each other. He ordered coke floats for both of them and as they waited for the drinks to arrive, he asked Lana about herself. She gradually grew more comfortable and reminisced with him about high school. Her laugh was high and silvery as he told her he was the seventh grade student who had ignited a stink bomb in the teacher's lounge. Clasping her hands together, she exclaimed, "Was that really you?! I always wondered who did that! We got to leave school early that day!"

As the high school boy came over to their table to wipe it down with a damp rag, Jerry realized that the drugstore was about to close. He put a quarter on the table for a tip and stood up. "I guess we'd best be goin'," he informed Lana.

On the way to the truck, he considered reaching for her hand but decided against it. The date had gone well so far, and he didn't want to push things too fast.

After that first date, Jerry was at the Grays' house almost every Saturday night with plans for a movie, for a ride through the county, or for a trip to a sandlot baseball game. Lana's happiness was countered by her father's resentment of the time she spent away from home. Mr. Gray complained bitterly, thought of more chores to be done before she could depart and finally threw an empty whiskey bottle, forbidding her to leave the house at all. All the next week, she nursed a bruise across her cheek and was too embarrassed to appear at the door when Jerry came to call.

He was desperate to find out why she had wordlessly rejected him, so he decided to wait at the edge of her garden one Saturday morning. When he stepped out of the shade, she dropped the hoe she was carrying and let out a high-pitched, little girl scream. He rushed to her and put his hand over her mouth. "Sh-h-h!" he insisted, looking around to see if anyone was coming to investigate. "Hush, now! It's only me," he laughed. When he took his hand away, he saw the yellow smudge under her left eye.

"What happened t'you, there?" She answered by hanging her head. "Your daddy do that?" he demanded. She made one small nod. "'Cause of me?" She was miserably rooted to the furrowed dirt. "I ought-a teach him t'keep his hands off-a you!" She was frightened by the menace in Jerry's voice and the hard, angry line that was his mouth.

"No! Don't you hurt him!" she insisted.

Jerry considered this for a moment before suggesting that they sit down in the shade and talk. As they leaned against the trunk of a felled oak, he told her that they should just go on and get married, start their own family. Lana seemed mildly surprised at the suggestion, but she didn't argue against it. When he pushed her for an answer, she considered his homespun proposal for only a few seconds before she smiled slightly and whispered, "Okay."

The next Tuesday morning, she dressed to go to the garden, arousing no suspicion from her father as she left the house, hoe in hand. She had placed the freshly pressed green dress and the canvas shoes in a brown paper bag on the thick log, and she knew that Jerry would be waiting in his truck, just down the path from the garden. While she stood under the poplar, her pale skin dappled in its shadows, she slithered into her dress and left her hand-me-down trousers and long-sleeved work shirt in a pile on the ground. Dangling the canvas slippers from her fingers, like the promise of a better life, she walked to the truck and left her muddy field shoes on the road.

As soon as she was seated, Jerry pushed the truck into gear and raced to Tupelo. There was no waiting period for a license and the Justice of the Peace kept an open-door policy. The ceremony finished, they returned to Jerry's home to set up housekeeping.

Mr. Cearley owned Jerry's house and the land that surrounded it. The shotgun shacks were one room wide and 3-4 rooms long. They were said to derive their name from the fact that doorways were aligned, so that a gunshot from the porch would have neatly sent its bullet through all of the doors to exit at the rear. Unlike her father's ramshackle cabin, Lana's new home had modern conveniences that she had never known, primary among them, indoor plumbing.

Although Lana would live just five miles from her father, he did not come to their house to protest his daughter's marriage. She had left a note on the kitchen table that Tuesday morning before she walked to his garden for the last time. It was neatly printed in block letters: "Daddy, I am gon to mary Jerry." She figured that Fred would find it when he came in from school and would read it to her father that night.

LANA

Chapter 7
Mrs. Jerry Wright

Lots-a people 'round home thought I was slow 'cause I was shy and didn't talk much. I never had a friend that could-a told 'em any diffrent. The girls at my school wore nice clothes and lived in town. They never saw me even though I sat behind 'em in class and followed 'em down the hall. I might as well-a been invisible for all they noticed me. Now the boys, that was a different story. I knew they watched me when I walked and a couple-a times I heard 'em whistle when I passed. But they never talked to me or asked me out…prob'ly 'cause they didn't want to tangle with Daddy. I don't know why Jerry thought he could ask for a date and get away with it, but he did.

That first day I saw him at the sawmill, I was surprised at how bold he was with Daddy. He wasn't much taller than me, but he was a broad-chested, powerful man, and he had those eyes that can look a girl up and down in an instant. Bedroom eyes, I called 'em.

I liked going to town with Jerry, but I suppose I married him mostly to get away from my life at home. I'd been cookin' and cleanin' and takin' care of babies ever since I could remember, with nothin' ever changin' for the better. When I was 20 years old, I already felt like an old, broken-down married lady. I thought that marryin' Jerry would bring me a better life.

All my growin' up, we lived in somebody else's house; it was miserable cold in the winter with the wind whistlin' through cracks in the boards and the woodstove heatin' just a circle-a chairs. I woke up lots-a mornins and found the pail-a water in the kitchen froze inna solid block-a ice. And there wasn't no money for extras: I never had a store-bought dress, and the boys never had nothin' but hand-me-down shoes that were too big or too small and left blisters on their poor lil feet. Daddy worked like a dog but he never got ahead. There was too much he owed for.

After Mama ran off with that Fuller Brush man, Daddy never could get over it. Leavin' us was the wrong thing for Mama to do, but she did a lot of wonderful things, too, and I couldn't stop lovin' her, just 'cause Daddy was mad at her. I remember how she liked to try out new hair styles; how she'd sit by the meer with a picture of a movie star taped to the wall, hummin' a tune as she combed her black hair, pinnin' it up so she looked just like Rita Hayworth! She told me one time that she named me "Lana" after one of the prettiest movie stars that ever was: Lana Turner.

Another thing Mama liked to do was dance. She'd turn up the radio on a Sat'ady night and dance in the kitchen. At first, Daddy'd dance with her, but he'd get tired quick. So, she'd laugh and pick up Les, who was still in diapers, and swing him round an' round. With his little legs stickin' straight out, he looked like he was sittin' in the air 'bove the floor. Mama'd dance so long that Daddy'd finally unplug the radio and tell her if she took another step, he'd whip her! Sometimes Daddy'd go on to bed and leave her to stay up; and sometimes Mama'd get into his whiskey and drink it 'til she fell asleep in the chair.

After Mama left home, Daddy never did have a thing to smile about or nobody t'dance with. I felt so bad for him! I'm prob'ly too forgivin', but I couldn't even stay mad at him for throwin' that whiskey bottle at me. I know he was just afraid he'd lose me to Jerry, like he lost Mama to the Fuller Brush man. And the funny thing is— that's just what happened.

The first couple-a months with Jerry were good ones. By the way he talked about the future, I could see he was smart and high-reachin'. We had a nice house with lights and runnin' water, and I thanked my lucky stars every mornin' when I turned on the faucet in that kitchen and the water gushed out. And to be able to use the toilet inside the house! It was so wonderful not t' have t'use the slop jar at night; not t' have t' use the privy in the summer, when the blow flies flew 'round your head and the smell of the outhouse'd make you think you were goin' t'gag 'fore you could open the door for fresh air.

Being work-brickle as he was, Jerry kept his job at the sawmill and did sharecroppin' too. He came home tired every night, but he did come home. I'd have supper ready and we'd eat together. Then, if the weather was nice, we'd go out t'the front porch and sit in the swing. Sometimes we talked 'bout what we'd have some day. Sometimes we just sat in the dark, listenin' to the crickets, while he smoked his store-bought cigarettes. The cigarettes lighted up his face when he drew on 'em, makin' me think of Daddy. Then I'd wonder what Daddy and the boys was doin' and wonder when I'd ever be able to see 'em again.

I learned pretty quick not t' talk about my family. Jerry couldn't stand for me t' have feelins for nothing but him. Why, he'd get mad if I said I missed Les and Fred, and he'd always say I had too much to do at home to be traipsin' down the road for a visit. Jerry was so jealous that he killed an old tom cat who'd taken up with me! It was that day I started hatin' him.

Ole Tom Gray came to my door the week after I moved in. He made me think of an old man who used to sit on a bench at the courthouse with his shirt tight 'cross the shoulders and so skinny in the butt that his britches just hung on him. Tom Gray was the same way—big and brawny through the neck and shoulders from fightin', but bony in the hips. One of his ears was torn and he was all stove up from his last ruckus. He was too weak to hunt his own food so I started givin' him leftovers out the back door. After a few months, Tom Gray let me run my hand down his back. It made me feel good t'see him gainin' back his strength. Some afternoons I'd sit on the top step, listenin' to Tom Gray purrin' while he napped in the sunshine. I liked to think that someday I'd be just as content and peaceful as he was.

But Jerry started fussin 'bout Tom Gray: didn't want no cat trippin' him up; didn't want food from his table bein' thrown out the back door for no cat; didn't want no alley cat hangin' round, tryin' to get inside every time the door opened. The more I begged, the more he saw Tom Gray meant somethin' t'me. He was more determined than ever to get rid of him. He tried to run Tom off by throwin' gravel at him, kickin' at him. But none of that worked, so Jerry shot him and left his poor, crumpled body for me to find when I came in from the garden. I stood there with my eyes closed for a long time, hopin' that when I opened 'em up, Tom'd be stretchin' and yawnin' from a long nap. But, instead, Tom Gray was layin' there still as could be, the wind rufflin' his fur and I knew he was dead. I picked him up, payin' no never-mind to the sticky blood that ran 'tween my fingers. I held his bony body to my chest and put his soft head 'gainst my cheek, like I always wanted t'do. I stood there a long time, tellin' Tom goodbye and feelin' sorry for his sad, hard life and when I looked up, I saw Jerry standin' at the windah, watchin' me cry, with the most satisfied look on his hateful face.

One summer mornin', right after Jerry left for the fields, I tol' myself I was tired of being sad and lonely. I pulled on some work clothes and I walked all the way to Daddy's house. Five miles it was!

When Les saw me steppin' up on the porch, his eyes got as big as saucers. He didn't know whether t'run to me and hug me or run back'ards into the house and get Fred.. So he just stood at the front door, like his feet was nailed to the planks. I held my arms wide open and said, "Come on, Les, I walked a long way for a hug!" And with that, his face broke in a big grin, and he ran to me and hugged me so tight I could barely breathe. He figured I was comin' back home for good. Fred even asked me where my clothes was. I had to tell 'em it was jus' a visit, and that made Les cry and made me feel like a heel for gettin' their hopes raised up for nothin'.

We sat on the porch together a long time, me with my arms 'round their shoulders. Every once in a while, I'd lean over and press my cheek against their soft hair. I closed my eyes and tried to think about every lil' thing so I could remember it all later on: how their bony shoulders felt under the worn-out cotton shirts; how their skin had a fresh air, little boy smell to it; and how the sunshine made me feel content as a cat by the woodstove. When I stood up t'leave, I promised I'd come back to see 'em again. And I asked 'em what they'd like for Christmas 'cause I knew that thinkin' 'bout Christmas would sure cheer 'em up. Their eyes lit up when they talked about the toys they'd like to have. I started for home, but I turned once to wave goodbye to 'em from the bend in the road. They was standin' right where I left them on the porch, their faces long and sad.

I got back home right 'fore Jerry came in, and there was nothin' fixed for supper, of course, 'cause I'd been gone all day. Jerry was right peeved about that and kept askin' me what the hell I'd been doin' all day. But I tol' him I'd gotten so busy with the garden that I'd lost track of time. Since he left the garden all to me and never even set foot out there, he didn't have nothin' else to say. I fixed him some cold cornbread in a glass of buttermilk, and that stopped his fussin' long enough for him to gobble it down and go on to bed.

But everyday after that, I thought-a my brothers, and I closed my eyes and remembered my visit. I thought 'bout how happy they were to see me, and how my heart seemed to swell toward their little chests when I hugged 'em. They were jus lil' boys now, but they were on the way to bein' grown men soon, and I was missin' out on all their growin' up 'cause I was married to somebody who was even jealous of a cat.

Some mornins when Jerry left, I'd go back to bed and just cry 'til I fell back t'sleep. Most days I'd get up by the early afternoon and cook supper, but the garden got less and less lookin' after and finally the Johnson grass just 'bout took it over. I was tired all the time and ever lil' thing seemed to take up more energy than I had any hope of gettin'. There was no need t'sweep up the mud from Jerry's boots 'cause he'd just be trackin' in more at nightfall. There was no need t'wipe the crumbs off the table after breakfast 'cause we'd be makin' more crumbs at supper. Clothes didn't really have to be washed cause they'd be dirty soon as he wore `em again. Finally, it was too much trouble to cook, too. Jerry didn't seem to notice most of the things I stopped doin'. But the dirty clothes and the end of hot meals came right to his attention. He was either fit to be tied or trying to help me, but nothin' he said or did mattered t'me. He ordered me t'take a tonic like the one his sister used t'take. Some days he hollered at me. But I jus' didn't care no more. And when he'd come t'bed, I closed my eyes and went somewhere else with my mind—like my Daddy's front porch. After a while, Jerry gave up on tryin' t'get me to do better and jus' stayed riled up, his temper so big that it came in the door `fore he did, and it squeezed me inna corner when he got t'the bedroom.

That day Jerry came home from work and found me layin' in the bed in my clothes was the first time he hurt me. He shook me so hard I thought my eyes were gonna slosh right outta my head. And God help me, when I saw I was bleedin' and losin' his baby, I was glad! I was glad she wouldn't have t'live in that house with Jerry Wright! I only wished I could go with her t'wherever it was that baby souls went when they left this earth.

LANA

Chapter 8
Carried Away

After I lost the baby, I spent a lotta time sittin' in the rocker on the porch, watchin' the leaves hang like rags in the heat. Jerry was real sorry for what he done and he tried t'make it up t'me. He said he didn't know I was expectin' and he said he wanted us t'start a family jus' as soon as I felt better. One night he brought me home a little white box from the drug store with some ruby-red earrings in it. I thought they was real pretty, as sparkly as some-a the jew-ry Mama used t'have. When I put `em on, Jerry grinned from ear to ear. He was really proud-a hisself.

Next day I put on those earrings and wore `em while I did my housework. I'd catch sight-a myself in the meer in the bedroom or the glass in the kitchen door and I'd say t' myself, 'Lana, you do look beautiful—jus' like your Mama did.' After I swept the kitchen and started dinner, I decided t'sit down for a while and thumb through the Sears catalogue, where I saw lots-a pretty ladies wearin' big earrings, wide-skirted dresses and long coats. I ran my finger `cross the pictures, over the fur collars and down the shoulders. I wanted a warm coat like one-a those so bad I could taste it!

Jerry was jus' carried away when he came home and found me wearin' those earrings. He was happy I'd been cookin', too, that's for sure. So while he sat at the table, eatin', I did all the talkin'. I told him `bout the coats in the Sears catalogue, but he just grunted and said there was lots-a tools in that catalogue that looked good to him. While I washed the dishes, he went out on the porch, waitin' for me to come sit with him. I thought I was workin' fast, but by the time I got t'the door, Jerry's head was leaned back and he was snorin' away. So I tiptoed back to the kitchen, cacklin' bout my good fortune, feelin' just as free as a bird!

But when I got to the kitchen, everything was so ugly and dark!

The linoleum by the sink was worn plum through and the curtains were dingy. I decided t'change things that very night! I took the bright yella pillowcases that Jerry's sister gave us when we married, (too pretty to sleep on, I always thought), ripped out the side seams, and basted a place for the curtain rod. If I only had my mama's ole sewin' machine. Why, I could've been finished with those curtains in five minutes! What a diffrence the curtains made when I hung 'em up! Even though it was dark outside, the kitchen looked like it was filled with sunshine.

After that I went to the bedroom and stripped the sheets off the bed so as I could wash 'em the next day. And I cleaned the meer with some vinegar water. And finally, 'bout two o'clock in the mornin', I went to bed. Jerry came in some time later, madder'n a wet hen 'cause I hadn't called him to bed. He was riled 'bout the sheets being off the bed, too. But I guess he was too sleepy to fuss for long, 'cause he fell in next to me, both of us in our clothes, layin' on the mattress buttons which made little O's on our arms.

Next mornin', I woke up 'fore Jerry. It didn't take much sleep for me to feel full of pep and I was scramblin' eggs when he came to the kitchen. The coffee'd been made and I was wearing my cherries dress and my red earrings. The new curtains made the kitchen look like buttercups were growin' at the windahs. Jerry whistled as he stood in the doorway. "What a sight you are for sore eyes!" He strutted over t'the stove and put his arms round my waist. "You look nice this mornin'," he said, kissin' me on the back of the neck.

I laughed at how clumsy he was when he flirted. "It's probably these earrings that some nice man bought me!" I teased, glancin' at him outta the corner of my eyes.

'Fore he ever opened his mouth, I knew I saw jealousy. "You better be talking 'bout your husband," he warned me without smilin'.

"Of course!" I said. Then I did somethin' I never done before: I didn't wait for him t'come t' me. I put my arms 'round his neck, and pulled him close, kissin' him hard on the mouth. When I turned him loose, he looked so surprised that I started laughin' and that sure made him mad.

He stepped back from me, holdin' my wrists in his big, calloused hands and lookin' me hard in the face, like he was tryin' to read me. After a minute, he let me go and told me t'wrap him up some biscuits t'eat on the way. He marched straight out t'the truck, but when he got there, he looked back at the house for a long time `fore he opened the door.

∾∾

Once Jerry was gone, I had the food put away inna flash. I was too full of get-up-and-go t'sit down so I paced through the bedroom and flipped through pages of the Sears catalogue. The day was just too pretty to waste! Since it was only 2 miles from my door to Main Street, I put on my sun hat and started walkin t'town. A couple-a times a truck passed me and honked. I smiled and waved back at `em.

The lady behind the counter at Sears was surprised t'see me. I was pretty dressed up for a Thursday mornin'. Anyway, I told her who I was married to and how Jerry was doin' so well, workin' for Mr. Cearley. And once the crop came in, I said, it was no tellin' how much money the gin was gonna be payin' Jerry. While I thumbed through the pages of the catalogue with her, we laughed `bout how men never kept up with the new fashions. She had good taste, that store lady did: she liked the brown coats with the Persian lamb collars, too. I tole her t'order me one, and she got out her pad and pencil and started writin down all kinds-a numbers. I picked out a few winter dresses and some new, high-heel shoes, too.

Once I finished at Sears, I went to the store where Jerry had a line-a credit for our groceries. Mr. Eddie seemed surprised t'see me cause Jerry was always the one goin' t'the store.

"How you doin' today?" I asked him, real dainty. He nodded t'me. "I'm goin' t'get some things for supper. It's Jerry's birthday, you know." He said he didn't know that. "Yes, Sir! And I'm goin t'surprise him with a real nice supper." I pointed toward the meat counter. "I'd like one of those roasts." He asked me if it was goin' on Jerry's bill and I told him 'yes.' So he scurried over t'the counter, pulled out a big ole beef roast and held it up for me to see 'fore he wrapped it up in butcher paper and wrote down some figures in his book.

"What else?" he said. I pointed out some cans-a ham and some cans-a black cherries and a loaf of white bread while I was there, too.

Once I picked out what I needed, I said hello to the men sittin' at the back of the store, playin' checkers on top of a crate. I told 'em all 'bout Jerry's party and how happy Jerry was goin' to be. And one of em said, "I'd be happy, too, if you was waitin' for me when I got home!" And they all laughed so I laughed too. When I started out the door, I could feel their eyes on me so I let my hips sway a little as I went.

The sack wasn't even heavy 'til I got about halfway home. Then the sun was up pretty good and the blacktop was sticky and the canned goods was gettin' real heavy. So, when I got t' Highway 200, I jus' took the cans outta the sack and left 'em by the side-a the road 'til I could come back later on and get 'em. The roast'd started leakin' blood, and the bottom of the sack was gettin' soggy and a few drops fell on the front of my dress. I hated that my pretty red-cherries dress had a blood stain on it! I'd have to put it in to soak as soon as I got home.

After I turned on the Braggadocio Road, I came to the Avon Lady's house. I was so hot and sticky that I thought it'd be nice t'sit on her shady front porch and maybe order some lipstick. She came t'the door, wipin' her hands on her apron, and then brought out a little magazine that had all kinds of pretty lipstick, face creams, and perfumes. It was hard t' make up my mind! I finally told her to order me what she thought was best, but t'be sure t'get the Passion Red lipstick and the Cherries Jubilee rouge for me. She gave me a glass of sweet tea while we was lookin at the magazine, and that helped me rest up for the last mile home.

The roast was spongy by the time I got t'my kitchen door. I wasn't sure it was still good, but I went on and put it in the oven. Then I took my dress off and left it in the sink to soak out the blood stains. The windah fan was goin', and the house was full-a shadows, and I walked 'round barefooted, in my underwear. I was cool for the first time that day. I sashayed 'round the kitchen, followin' the breeze. My panties and bra were so damp they stuck to my skin, and it seemed like a shame to have anything standin' between me and that breeze, so I took 'em off. Why, it felt wonderful! I was standin in front of the windah and the fan was blowin' my hair away from my face and the wind was ticklin' me all over. Then I heard the door open and Jerry's voice hollarin, "What the hell is going on here?"

"I got hot." I told him over one shoulder.

"Hell, Lana, put somethin on! You caint be standin in front of the windah, nekked as a jay bird!" He stalked to the bedroom and came back with one of my house dresses. "Here! Get this on!" I wouldn't take the dress from him, so he started punching it toward me, shoutin, "Take it, Lana! You take it and put it on."

When I ran in the bedroom, he came right after me. "Either get dressed or go t'bed!" he hollared.

I backed into the corner. "I don't wanna go to bed. It ain't even dark yet."

"Lana, I ain't foolin' with you. You get dressed now!"

Jerry was gettin' bigger and taller as he ran at me. I reached for the top-a the dresser where he kept his fillet knife and pulled it outta the cover. Then I told him he better not come any closer t'me. I looked at him as mean as I could, squintin' one eye. "You better leave me the hell alone!" I yelled, feelin' real satisfied with how those words tasted. I moved the knife back and forth in the air. Why, Jerry looked as scared as a rabbit at the end of a shotgun. Without takin his eyes off the knife, he backed toward the door and laid my dress on the chair.

"I'm goin' out for a while," he said, like he'd just made up his mind t'go get a Co-cola. His bigshot ways tickled me so much that once he was gone, I put away the knife and sat down cross-legged on the floor, laughin' til the tears ran from my eyes.

"Did you see his face?" I asked myself, between giggles. "He was sure scared! Big ole Jerry Wright, scared of lil ole me!" I laughed so hard that I got the hiccups! I wobbled back and forth on the floor, rockin' and laughin'. Once I was all outta giggles, I got up and went back t' the windah fan. Jerry couldn't stop me! I was goin t' stand in front of that fan til the sun came up!

I don't know how long it was 'fore I started gettin' a little sleepy. It was pitch black outside when I got in the bed. I didn't put on a gown and I didn't pull up a cover 'cause it was still too hot. I woke up to see Jerry standin' over me in the bed. I don't know how long he'd been there, lookin' at me nekked, but I'm sure he was enjoyin' himself. I roused up and rolled over on my back, stretchin' my arms out to him. "C'mere, you big ole thing," I cooed. Jerry just stood there, still as could be. I parted my legs. "Don't you want a little lovin'?" He was so quiet I could hear him breathin' hard, like he'd been runnin'.

"Go back to sleep, Lana," he said, pulling the cover over me.

That made me as mad as a hornet. I threw the sheet off and bolted straight up from the bed. "Don't you tell me nothin' about sleep! I know when I need to sleep!"

"Okay. Okay," he said, agreeable like. "Just rest, then. You don't have t'go t'sleep. Jus' lay there and rest." He went to the dresser and picked up the fillet knife, puttin' it in the cover and slippin' it in his pocket. He turned the fan on the table so it blew straight toward me.

Jerry tiptoed outta the room and soon I could hear the creak of the porch swing. I really didn't have any reason to fight him so I went back t'sleep with the breeze like a lullaby on my skin.

Jerry might-a slept in the porch swing for all I know. When I woke up, the sun was streamin' through the edge of the bedroom curtains. I put on a house dress and walked to the kitchen, where the yellow curtains were happy as a row of buttercups. He was in the kitchen, sittin' at the table with a cup-a coffee in front of him. He looked at me like he was waitin' for something to happen. I could feel the mischief bubblin' up in my chest and I decided to keep him guessin'. I went t'the stove and pulled out the iron skillet.

"Want some breakfast?" I asked, just as sweet as could be.

"No," he said, holdin' on to the cup of coffee with both hands like it might run away from him.

"You goin' t' work without breakfast?"

"Today's Sundee."

I looked back at him, surprised. "Sundee?"

He nodded. "That's right."

"I thought yesterday was Thursdee."

"When you went to bed, it was Thursdee."

I wondered if he was tryin' to fool me. I turned over in my mind how I could know what day it was, and I puzzled over walkin' down t'the church to see if there was services goin' on.

I yawned and stretched. "I didn't know I slept so long."

He kept watchin' my hands every time they moved, like he thought I had something in my pocket! I leaned my back against the counter and slowly put my right hand in the pocket-a my dress. His eyes followed my hand as it went deeper and deeper. I grabbed the hanky that was in the bottom and pulled it out real fast. Why, Jerry jumped clean out of the chair, knockin' it over backwards! It was so *funny* to see Jerry that nervous! I laughed and held up the square-a cotton. "It's just a hanky!" I said, waving it back and forth.

"Damn it, Lana, you jus' actin' crazy!"

I turned back to the stove. "I want some breakfast," I announced, "whether you're goin t' eat or not."

I turned off the skillet and settled in at the table. I was jus' starved! My first bite-a eggs quivered on the end of my fork, the steam risin' like a welcome. It was delicious! I didn't know I was such a good cook! The fried eggs had an edge that looked like brown lace. The sausage cozied up to a pool of grits, and the toasted light bread was swimmin' in a puddle of sorghum. I ate every bite, while Jerry sat 'cross from me, still holdin' that cup of coffee like it was his only friend, watchin' my fork go from the plate to my mouth and back again.

Finally he asked me if I was feelin' better since I had somethin' to eat, and I said I'd never felt better. He seemed happy with that. He leaned back into his chair and let his shoulders relax against the slats. "You be all right here t'day?"

I stopped chewin' and thought about that. "If it's Sundee, where you goin'?"

"I told Edna I'd stop by her house today."

Edna was Jerry's sister and she lived with her husband Raymond in Clemmons. She was old enough to be Jerry's mama, and she was the one who took him under her wing when their mother passed.

I told him I'd go with him to Edna's but Jerry was surely unhappy with that. He shifted in his chair and looked at the coffee cup. "I ain't stayin' for dinner or nothin'. I jus' told her I'd drop by on m' way to check on the crop."

When he left, I decided to go out to the garden. It seemed like it'd been a long time since I'd been there and when I saw how sorry it looked, I felt bad for lettin' it go. The rows-a peas and beans that were so full of promise early in the summer had been taken over by Johnson grass. Weeds were chokin' out the tomato vines, too, but there were a few tomatoes as big as a child's fist. I picked 'em all—red and green, and carried 'em in my skirt. The squash had run a race with the cucumbers and the vines were all tangled together. I picked a few squash—the ones that weren't the size of a gourd.

I'd always loved my garden. At my daddy's house it was 'bout the only place I could go t'be alone and at Jerry's house, it was a sure place to get away from him. I liked the way the dirt smelled after the rain, and I liked the tender green of the new leaves. I sat down on the kitchen step where Tom Grey used to nap. I dusted off the reddest tomato and took a bite, tastin' sunshine, the juice runnin' down the corners of my mouth and the seeds dottin' the front of my house dress. I didn't care. It was just an old rag of a dress, anyway.

☙❧

The house was unnaturally quiet when I got back inside. I put the vegetables up, washed the breakfast dishes and spent the day putterin' around. But everything went slow. I'd sweep a while and then sit down and thumb through the Sears catalogue. The brown coat I ordered would be comin' soon, and I saw that it was priced at $30, which was way too much for our means. I'd have to walk back t'town and cancel the order next week.

Around 4:00 I heard the rattle of Jerry's pickup and peeked out the windah to see him raisin' a cloud of dust on the gravel road. I put the Sears catalogue away and took the vegetables to the sink to wash `em. He was happy when he came in the door, pattin' me on the shoulder and tellin' me the cotton was makin' a good crop. He thought the field on the other side of Madrid would bring in several hundred dollars. We'd be havin' a nice Christmas, he told me. He took a bottle out of a brown paper bag and said, like he was just rememberin' it, "Oh! Edna sent you somethin', a tonic."

I turned from the sink and looked at the dark brown bottle with a cork stopper. "What's it for?"

"She says it's good for whatever ails you…but it's specially good for settlin' your nerves."

"I don't think I need that."

"Well," he hesitated, "you've been a little high strung lately. I figure it might have to do with female trouble….Anyway, Edna swears by it. Says she used it when she was nervous." He set it down on the table.

I was still lookin' at the dirty-brown bottle and thinkin' how awful it would taste. "Well, if I feel like I'm gettin' nervous, I'll take it," I said.

All through that fall, I didn't think I needed the tonic and Jerry didn't talk `bout it again. It sat up in the medicine cabinet next to the Mercurochrome, which didn't get used, either. The order from Sears came to the house `fore I remembered t' go t' town and cancel it. I wouldn't even let myself open the package and look at that beautiful coat. I flagged down the mailman the next day and asked him to send the whole thing back to Sears.

The Avon Lady stopped by one Tuesday with a pretty pink sack in her hand. She knocked and knocked at the door while I hid in the bedroom, waitin' for her to go away. She came back the next day and surprised me while I was comin' in from the garden. When she followed me inside, she was starin' at everything, sniffin' round my house like she picked up a trail of something gone rotten. She wouldn't sit down at the kitchen table, and I figured it was `cause she thought she might get somethin' on her dress. She tried to shame me when I said I didn't have the money to pay for the whole sack, right then. "Why the very idea, Mrs. Wright!" she said. "I ordered these cosmetics for you on good faith! I've already paid the company for this order!"

I went back to the bedroom and raked Jerry's change off the dresser, countin' every penny, hopin' it would be enough, but it wasn't. In the end, I had t' reach in the Prince Albert can and take some of Jerry's foldin' money he'd been savin for a new shotgun. I prayed I'd be able to put it back `fore he knew it was gone.

The bill for Jerry's birthday party was called t' his attention the next time he was in Mr. Eddie's store. I don't know what Jerry said to `em, but he came home and told me there had to be a mistake `cause he knew he hadn't bought no roast beef and ham on credit. I told him the truth and explained I tried t' make a birthday party for him. He asked me where all those cans of ham were and that's when I remembered that I took `em outta the sack and left em by the crossroads. I couldn't think of a lie t' tell him, so I told him the truth and I think he was madder about those cans than he was about the roast. He stomped `round the kitchen, askin' me if I thought he was made of money, and how could I be so stupid t' leave food by the side of the road. I was sick and tired of hearing him long `fore he quit yellin'. I just sat at the kitchen table with my head down, feeling dumb and miserable, while he marched back and forth and slammed his fist down on the table, makin' the salt and pepper shakers dance the jitterbug. He kept on askin' me questions nobody could answer and then, once he said everything four or five times, he put on his jacket and left and I finally had some peace.

LANA

Chapter 9
Married Christmas

The fall went by fast. Jerry was gone a lot, gettin' in the crop so I had plenty-a time t'make Christmas gifts. I knitted mittens for my brothers and put up a jar of chow-chow for my daddy t' have with his greens. I knitted Jerry some wool socks and a scarf t' go 'round his neck. When Christmas mornin' came, I got up my courage and asked Jerry if he would take me t' Daddy's. He thought about it a few minutes while I stood there with my hands limp at my side, feelin' too scared t' get my hopes up. Finally he said, "Why not? It's Christmas. We'll go see Edna, too."

I picked out my two prettiest jars in the pantry for Edna's present—a jar of green beans and a jar of tomatoes. When I held 'em next t' each other, the colors looked just like Christmas.

The sky was low and buckshot gray and it hovered over the fields of left-over cotton. It'd rained so much that wads of cotton hung from the brown stalks like wet quilt batting. By the side of the road, the cotton that'd fallen from wagons was mounded up like dirty snow.

The first thing I saw when we rounded the curve was how little and how tired Daddy's house looked. The tire swing hangin' from the oak tree wasn't even rockin' in the wind. The only thing I saw movin' was thin smoke, risin' up from the chimney. When I stepped on the porch, the boards seemed t' be more warped and splintered than ever before.

Fred came t' the door, wearin' a shirt that wasn't big enough for him. His little pale face broke into a grin when he saw it was me. He shouted, "It's Lana! She said she would come at Christmas!" As soon as I pulled open the screen door, he almost knocked me down with his hug. Was he always this thin? Les came in, jumpin' and hollarin' and tryin' to hug me by pushin' Fred outta the way. We stepped in the dark room, smellin' the smoke and the grease from last night's supper. Daddy was in the corner by the wood stove, his back t' us. He didn't get up and he didn't say nothing `til I stood right in front of him.

I smiled at him, holdin' out his present, my hand shakin' a little bit `cause I was scared he was still mad at me for gettin' married. "Merry Christmas, Daddy," I said. He just blinked at me, so I tried again, "We came t' wish you a Merry Christmas….I brought you some of your favorite chow-chow. . ."

He looked down at my hand and took the jar from me, twisting it to see all the sides. Finally he looked up at my face, jus' like he was wakin' up from a dream and said, "Much obliged."

"Y'all sit down," Daddy said, and he limped toward the table, draggin' his chair behind him.

As soon as we sat down, Jerry told him, "We can't stay long. We just came by to bring the presents."

The boys was hopping `round us and all talkin' at once. "Y'all hush!" Daddy yelled. "Sound just like a bunch of magpies." They got quiet right away, but they crowded `round my elbows, pointin' at the little brown paper packages spread on the table.

"Here you go, Fred," I said, handin' him his present. "And this one's for you, Les." They tore open their packages, tryin' on mittens and cacklin' over `em. When they hugged me, the scratchy wool rubbed against my neck. Jerry asked how Daddy's crop'd been this year and they talked about the sawmill. When Jerry stood up, I patted Daddy's arm and told him, "We got to go, now, Daddy."

My chair scraped over the planks of the kitchen floor. The boys were back to crowdin' `round me, talkin' at once. "Don't go, Lana!" Fred begged. "You just got here!" He grabbed me by my hands and tried to lead me back to the table.

"We got to go, boys," Jerry told `em, real firm.

`Fore we got to the door, Daddy called to me. "Lana? You ever think you'd use your mama's sewing machine?"

"All the time!"

"You wanna take it with you?"

I couldn't hardly believe he was givin' the machine t'me. It was the best Christmas present I could imagine. I thanked him five or six times while him and Jerry loaded it in the back of the truck. Jerry said his goodbyes to my daddy outside, and I promised the boys I'd see 'em again, real soon. Les begged me not to go, but I finally pulled his arms off my neck and told him I had to. They wanted to be brave, but they looked like they was about to cry. I hated to leave so bad! My goodbyes and my 'see you soons' were like thorns stuck in my throat.

When I got t' the truck, I could see 'em at the windah, watchin' me go. They looked jus' like lil tow-headed ghosts, with thin faces and hollow eyes. I waved t' em and smiled real happy, but once Jerry pulled outta the front yard, I put my head down on my knees and cried my eyes out.

"Stop your bawlin!" he yelled. "Hell, I won't let you go back again if you're gonna act like this!" I took the hanky he held out t' me and swiped it cross my face. "That's better," he said, lookin' me over. "We'll go on and see Edna, and then we'll go home and fix us a nice Christmas supper."

Edna and Raymond, they had a lil more than the sharecroppers livin' round Madrid 'cause Raymond worked at the cotton mill. Edna had store-bought presents for Jerry and me. A new, warm coat for Jerry and a few yards of different-colored material for me. She said she knew I sewed and maybe I could do something with it. Jerry tried on the coat and pulled the collar up 'round his ears. He pranced round the kitchen and declared it the warmest coat he'd ever had. I thanked 'em for the material, but I couldn't help but wish they'd bought that beautiful coat with the Persian lamb collar for me.

We just finished dinner when Jerry and Raymond said they was goin' down to the creek and see if the water'd been risin'. They left in Raymond's truck and they was gone so long that I'd 'bout decided I'd be spendin' the night at Edna's. I wasn't all that used to Edna and her ways. We spent a good bit of time with Edna showin' me all her knick knacks and tellin' me where she bought 'em.

`Round eight, I heard the brakes on the truck and then I heard a lot of loud talkin and laughin'. Raymond and Jerry staggered in the house, their faces red as a beet.

"Why, Raymond Lee Spencer! What business do you have coming home like this? And on Christmas Day!" Edna stood up to him and argued with him just like she was a man. He was takin' steps backward and she was leanin' forward, and they did that funny dance from the parlor to the kitchen and back. He kept tryin' to explain and calm her down. He said, "Aw, Edna! One little drink ain't gonna hurt nothin'." But Edna wasn't buyin' that and she wouldn't leave him alone. Jerry laughed at `em and then put on his new coat, grabbin' me by the hand.

"Thanks for the dinner and the presents!" he called at the door. "And thanks, Raymond, for the Christmas cheer!"

"Jerry Wright! You ain't too big for me t' turn you over my knee!" Edna threatened, but there was pleasure in her eyes when she looked at Jerry. Not like the mad look I saw when she hollered at poor Raymond.

Jerry laughed. "We'd best be headed home, now! We'll leave y'all to it!" The glass windah rattled as he shut the back door and trotted t' the truck. "Boy, is it cold out here!" he said, rubbin' his hands together `fore he touched the steerin' wheel.

"Want to go home and get warm, Baby?" He glanced over at me with those bedroom eyes of his and rubbed his free hand gainst my stomach. I never said nothin'. He drove and I looked out the windah at the low clouds, dreadin' what he had in mind.

By the time we got home, the sky was spittin' little, hard pellets of snow. The fire'd gone out in the woodstove and the house was awful cold. We went straight on t' bed, but the whiskey made Jerry fall asleep `fore I could even put on my gown. He laid on his back, snorin' and I curled up in a little ball, facin' the windah, wide awake, listenin' to the wind screechin' through a gap `round the front door.; thinking `bout my brothers, how there was nobody to cook and mend for `em, how sad they looked. I thought about how tired and old my daddy looked. And I thought about how Jerry didn't seem to care a thing about me. And with Jerry sound asleep next to me, I cried all the tears that I couldn't cry before, when the little ghosts stood at the windah, watchin' me drive away.

LANA

Chapter 10
The Hair of the Dog

The next mornin' I heard Jerry in the bathroom 'fore I got out of bed. He was retchin' and moanin' bout the drinkin' he done last night. He come back through the bedroom, sayin' he had a headache that was makin' him go blind. Then he staggered to the kitchen, rummagin' 'round through the cupboard, knockin' over glasses and cups and slammin' the doors as he went. I put on my shoes and walked to the kitchen, my gown swishin' 'round my knees.

"What in the world are you lookin' for?"

"Don't we have any whiskey in this house? Somethin' for the hair o'the dog?" When I asked what that was, Jerry pushed me hard and yelled, "Lana, get out of my way!" I stumbled against the sink 'fore I caught myself. "If you can't help me, dammit, jus' get outta my way!"

I wasn't sure what kind-a help he wanted, but I thought I could save him some trouble if I jus' told him we didn't have no whiskey in the house. That seemed to make him even madder. "I told you we needed to keep a bottle of whiskey in case somebody came down with a cough," he screamed, lookin' at me with eyes that were so bloodshot that I wondered how he could even see through 'em.

"Well, we don't have no whiskey."

"Don't you get smart with me!" The slap came 'fore I could even see it. He hit me so hard I thought my head was gonna spin 'round on my neck. Blood was runnin' in my mouth an my eyes started t'burn. I put my hand up to the smartin' place 'fore the tears started t'brim over. Jerry stopped for a minute like he wasn't sure what to do next but 'fore he could think of any more meanness, I ran outta that kitchen. I grabbed up his brand new coat from the chair, where he dropped it last night, and I put it on while I was running down the porch steps. He took a few steps t'come after me, but he was so sick from the whiskey that he couldn't move fast enough t'catch me. He was yellin' at me t'get back in the house, like I'd turn round and come back t'be slapped again! I could still hear him cussin' when I got t'the bend in the road.

It was a minute 'fore the cold bit into my bare legs, and I realized I was out in the road in my gown, wearin' a coat that didn't even cover my bottom. I didn't care how cold I got; I was not goin back home 'til Jerry had plenty a-time to calm down. I ran to the old Conner place 'cause it was only a quarter mile from our house, and nobody'd lived there for a long time. It was down in a little holler. The kudzu'd grown over the whole place so that it looked like somebody's pulled a quilt up over the roof. The doors were crooked on their hinges, and the windahs had mostly been broken out, but I knew it'd be warmer in there than bein' out in the open. There was some trash on the floor from the last folks that moved out, but no varmints. I found a corner that was full of sunshine, sat down with my back to the wall and covered my legs with newspaper. I don't know how long I stayed there; I didn't have a watch and it's hard to tell time by the sun in the winter.

When I couldn't stand the cold any more and my toes was so numb that I thought they might break off, I started back for home. I wasn't ten steps down the road when I heard a car comin' around the curve. 'Fore I could get off the road, the car slowed down and I could see a woman was drivin'. She was wearin' a coat with a Persian lamb collar and a dainty felt hat with a slantin' feather. Her dark red hair peeped out from around the brim. She rolled down the windah jus a little bit.

"Are you out walking in this weather?" she asked, her brown eyes dancin' like she was teasin' me. I didn't know how to answer that, so I just stood there. "Child, what in the world are you doing out here in your nightgown?" I felt so ashamed for being caught like that and I couldn't think of a thing t'tell her. She said for me t'get in her car and she'd take me on home. When I didn't jump right in, she started scoldin' me, "Get in the car, girl! It's too cold to stand out in the road just because the cat's got your tongue!"

The seats of that big, fine car was cold, but the air inside was warm as summertime. We passed Jerry's house and I didn't say nothin' t'her 'bout stoppin' t'let me out, but I did look up there good t'see if he was anyplace in sight. His truck was still parked in the yard but there wasn't a light on in any windah.

"I'm Adele Cearley… Forrest," she told me, glancing in my direction. That's the first time I knew who she was. My daddy logged in their woods and Jerry was sharecroppin' for 'em, but I never met any of 'em. Everybody knew they was richer than rich. My daddy always said those Cearleys had enough money t'burn a wet mule. But why anybody'd want t'do that, I never did know.

Next time Miss Adele looked over at me, I remembered the caked blood on my lip, and I put my fingers t'the corner of my mouth, trying t'hide it. "You're John Gray's girl, aren't you?" I nodded. "Well, what on earth are you doing out on a day like today, dressed like that?"

"I..I got excited and left the house 'fore I knew how cold it was," I said.

"You walked a long way from John's house," she said, lettin' me know she was wise to my story.

"No, ma'am. I didn't start out from my daddy's house. I live with Jerry Wright…I'm married to Jerry Wright," I corrected myself.

She was wearin' leather gloves, and her hands seemed like they were hoverin' over the steerin' wheel when she turned it. She tipped one finger toward my lip, sayin', "Did Jerry do that to you?"

I suppose she knew the truth without me havin' to answer, 'cause she pulled the car off the road and turned toward me, full face. "What's your name?"

"Lana."

"I asked you a question, Lana! Did Jerry do that to you?" I nodded. "Well, Mrs. Lana Wright, I've been around plenty of men just like your husband—big, tough men who like to knock their little wives around. And I can tell you that I have *no* respect for a man like that! Furthermore, my father will not stand for a bully to work for him. He despises that sort of low-life behavior and my husband does, too. Walter took a horsewhip to one sharecropper and made another one move off the farm for just that sort of thing." She was frownin' and shakin' her head so hard that the feather in her hat trembled like it was afraid of what was about to happen. I was scared too.

"Please, ma'am, don't tell your daddy," I whispered. "It never happened 'fore this."

She looked hard at me and slowly shook her head, suckin' in her lips with a lil disgusted smack. "Do you expect me to believe that? I'm sure he's done this to you before, and I'm even more convinced that he'll do it again. In fact, I'm sure he'll keep knocking you around as long as he thinks he can get away with it."

I looked away from her and out the windah where the stiff pines stood in frosty green thickets. "I don't want you t'tell your daddy about this," I said softly. "If we lose our home, I don't know where we'll go t'live."

She slapped the steering wheel with one hand, makin' me jump. "Lana! I'm just trying to get you to see that you don't have to put up with this. You can stop it!"

My stomach turned over from dread or hunger, I wasn't sure which. I felt like she was pushin' and pushin' me, like some big kid on the schoolyard who was determined to take my lunch pail. "I don't see how, Ma'am."

"By telling him you're not going to stand for it any more! And meaning it when you say it! You tell that husband of yours that if he hits you again, you'll come to me! I'll give you a job in my house."

"I jus' kept looking out the windah 'cause I didn't really know what t'say to Miss Adele. She was so determined for me to be strong, and she was so bossy! I musta sat there quiet for five minutes 'fore the car started movin' again and the trees began to fly by my windah. She was driving fast now and we were goin' further and further away from my house. I started wonderin' if I was gonna be workin' for her that very day.

She pulled the car inna gravel driveway and pointed to a painted house, with a porch curved all `round the front and a black roof that was tall as a witch's hat. "This is where Walter and I live," she said. "It's not more than three miles from your house to mine. Now, Lana, if you have any more problems, I expect you to come let us know and we *will* help you."

I couldn't figure why she was tryin' so hard to help me. It's not like we could be friends or nothin'. It's not like I could ever do somethin' for her in return. We sat in the car for a long while and then I finally jus' told her "much obliged" and that musta satisfied her `cause she went on and backed out.

Before she started drivin' again, she asked me did I want to go home to Jerry, or did I want her t'drop me off someplace else, like at Daddy's. That would-a sure been nice, but I couldn't go back to Daddy's house t'live. I was a married woman, now. And I married Jerry of my own free will. Daddy would-a said I'd made my bed and now I'd have t'lie in it. There was no use even thinking `bout Daddy's house.

I told her I needed t'go on home, and she pulled her car up next t'Jerry's truck and let me out. Then, with me openin' the door to that bitter cold, she told me again, "I mean it, Lana... You come to us if you need help."

I stared into the car one last time, tryin' to be brave and wantin' to remember every little thing: how Miss Adele sat up straight and tall in the seat; how she spoke her mind; how she was sure I could be strong and make Jerry stop hittin' on me. Then I closed the door.

Jerry was watchin' it all. I didn't see him `til I was almost to the door, `cause he was standin in the dark house, with all the lights off. I jumped when he jerked open the door. His eyes were clearer than they were in the mornin', but he hadn't shaved or combed his hair, so he still looked pretty wild.

"Where in hell have you been? And why you sashayin' down the road in your nightgown?"

I walked right past him. "I was tryin' to get away from you,

Jerry Wright."

He stopped for a minute, like he didn't spect me t' have an answer for him. Then he said with a real smart voice, "Well, you sure put on a show for everybody. Out there in the road in nothin' but your nightgown. But I guess that's the best thing to wear if you're gonna be whorin' around."

"I was out there in my nightgown 'cause I was in a hurry to get away from you!"

He seemed t'be considerin' this for a minute 'fore he said, "What'd Adele Cearley have t'do with that?"

"She saw me walkin' home and gave me a ride."

"Hhm!" he snorted. "D'ju cry on her shoulder? Tell her how hard you have it, livin' here with mean, ole Jerry Wright?"

"I didn't tell her nothin'," I said and I started walkin' away from him. I took off his Christmas coat and laid it over the back of a kitchen chair. Then I went straight to the bedroom and started gettin' dressed. I put on every stitch-a wool clothes I owned, just like I was fixin' t'be outside all day. Then I pulled a kitchen chair close t'the door and I dragged over a basket of sweet potatoes. With my sharpest paring knife, I started peelin' those potatoes, lettin' the skin fall in a bowl in my lap. Jerry stood at the door for the longest time, watchin' that little knife shine in the light.

Then without a word, he got his coat from the back-a the chair and left. When I heard his truck start up, I felt like my heart was dancin' in my chest! I won! Me, Lana, I beat Jerry Wright! He was takin his temper someplace else t'make somebody else miserable! I turned on the radio and danced to the music while the lil' paring knife took a rest.

I saw Miss Adele one more time that year. It was after Christmas, but 'fore I joined the church. I was out in the front of the house on a warm day, on my knees in the dirt, plantin' some bulbs I dug up from the ole Hurley place. When I heard something on the gravel road, I looked up, half expectin' to see somebody comin' to tell me I had to give back those stolen bulbs. But it was Miss Adele, ridin' a high-steppin', shiny black horse that pranced right up to me! For a minute, I thought she might not stop him in time, so I jumped up and took a step or two backwards to get outta his way. She kinda chuckled then and told me she didn't mean to scare me, just came by to see how I was doin'. While we was passin' the time, the horse got impatient. He wallowed the bit 'round in his mouth and stirred the gravel with his front foot.

Miss Adele didn't pay him no nevermind. She wanted to know what I was plantin' and if I ever had a flower garden before.

"This is my first try," I told her, and then feelin' guilty, like I should tell the truth 'bout it all, I said "I used to walk over to the Hurley place and pick buttercups every spring. I reckon I wanted some-a my own, so I brought these home."

She never blinked an eye 'bout me stealin'. She said, "Well, if you'd like to have flowers around your house, I'll remember that and send Albert over when I divide the irises. They'd probably do well right there." She pointed to a spot by the kitchen windah.

I thanked her and then she said, "You seem to be doing better today than the last time I saw you. I assume that Jerry Wright has kept his hands to himself." It wasn't really a question, but I nodded anyway. "Good," she said real quick 'fore she spun that horse around in a tight circle, throwin' gravel in all directions. She trotted off without even sayin' goodbye.

I stood there a long time, watchin' her go, that horse, prancin' down the road with his head up and his tail streamin' out like a flag and Miss Adele sittin' high in the saddle, her dark-red hair, blowin' out behind her, and me wishin' I could jus' get up behind her and ride off too.

LANA

Chapter 11
The Preacher Man

It must-a been `round March when Brother Paul, the preacher from the church down the road, came t'see us. It was a Sunday afternoon like all the rest. Jerry was taking a nap and I was washin' up the dinner dishes when I caught a glimpse of somethin' movin' across the yard, and I peeked through the buttercup curtains to see Brother Paul, walkin' to the door. His shoes were shined to a fare-thee-well, and his oily black hair was combed back from his face. Brother Paul was tall and thin and dressed in a black suit that flapped around his hips when he walked. He looked for all the world like a big crow, stalkin' up to the porch.

"Afternoon, Mrs. Wright!" he said, flashin' me a big grin soon as I opened the door. "How are you today? Can I come in?"

I let him into the front room. "I guess you've come to see Jerry," I said.

"Why, yes! But you, too."

I left Brother Paul and went to the bedroom to wake up Jerry.

"What's *he* doing here?" he grumbled, ill with me, like I was the one who invited him.

"I don't rightly know. But I don't think he's gonna leave' til you talk t'him."

Jerry sighed real big and got out of the bed, pulling his arms through the sleeves on his shirt and mumblin' to hisself. But once he got to Brother Paul, you would've thought Jerry'd been waitin' all week for the preacher to come by! I could hear his voice from the kitchen. "Brother Paul! How you doin'? Has Lana asked you if you wanted somethin' to eat or drink?....No?...Lana! Get Brother Paul a glass of tea." While I fixed the tea, Brother Paul and Jerry got in a big discussion and they was both laughin' and carryin' on. Jerry's voice reminded me of back at Christmas, when he'd been drinkin' down at Edna's; he was loud and jokin' round. I brought the tea and sat on the arm of Jerry's chair.

"Thank you, Lana," said Brother Paul, his eyes resting against mine for just a minute 'fore he looked away. "I've just been meaning to come by and invite y'all to come for worship service some Sunday. We start at 11:00 and we have singing and then preaching. On the fourth Sunday, we'll have dinner on the grounds after preaching is over. Sure do wish y'all would come join us!"

"Lana and me been talkin' 'bout going to church," Jerry told him.

"Well, I know that you're busy, Jerry. Sunday is the only full day you have off, but it *is* the Lord's Day, and we sure would like to have you in church."

"You'll be seeing us soon," Jerry promised.

Brother Paul took long sips from his glass of tea. He and Jerry talked 'bout some of the people Jerry knew who went to the church, and then Brother Paul set down the empty tea glass and pushed on his knees to stand up. "I'd like to have a word of prayer, if that's all right." He bowed his head and began to pray 'fore Jerry even told him it'd be okay. In his prayer, he called us "a fine young couple" and he prayed that the Lord would lead us to church soon.

While we was wavin' goodbye and watchin' his shiny Ford pull out of the yard, I told Jerry, "Brother Paul seems like a nice man. We ought to go hear him some Sunday."

"I'm too tired to go to church on Sundays, Lana, but you can go if you want to. You can walk down there without any problem." Jerry undressed and went back t'bed but I thought about the invite for a while. I'd been to a revival back when Mama was at home, and I liked the music and the way Mama swayed and clapped her hands when she sang.

It was a fine, warm Sunday when I went t'hear Brother Paul.

The singing had already started, so I came in the back door of the church and found a seat on the last bench. I had on my dress with the cherries and I was wearin' the red earrings Jerry'd gave me. The older lady sittin' next to me didn't have on a speck of jewelry or lipstick, either. She stared hard at my ruby-red earrings and pursed her lips together when I smiled at her. When she looked away from me, I pulled off my earrings and put 'em in my pocket.

Brother Paul stood up in front and welcomed everybody and the folks in the pews set up a breeze with fans from the Pearson Funeral Home. He said who'd been sick and who'd just had a new baby. Then he opened the Bible and read a passage about Saint Paul.

The near as I could tell, St. Paul had been a real mean man, a bad sinner 'fore he was baptized, and Brother Paul said every one of us needed to learn a lesson from that. When he said, "Your sins…washed away," and pointed toward the back row, I just knew he was pointin' at me.

"Amen," said the little lady next to me. I heard others say "amen" under their breath, too.

At first, Brother Paul gripped the stand that held the Bible with both of his hands, like he might be afraid it would get away from him. He leaned forward and talked in a soft, friendly voice, but then he left the stand and started pacin' back and forth, back and forth in the front of the church. Sometimes he stood still and shouted "Hallelujah!" while he raised the Bible high in the air. He talked more and more 'bout baptism and how important it was. I remember him sayin' that it could make us as white as new snow.

That's about where I stopped listenin' and started day dreamin'. I thought 'bout the time I lost the baby and how glad I was to lose her. I thought about all the mean things I'd done and the greedy feelins that had me orderin' clothes and perfume. The longer I sat there, the worse I felt. Finally, I wanted to be baptized, too, and get rid of all my sins.

When Brother Paul got to the end of the preachin', he stopped pacin' and looked out at us with a broad smile. He opened his arms wide, like he was going to hug us all together. "So who among you needs to be healed of your sins? Who is ready to start over again, just like a newborn babe?"

That's when I stood right up. Brother Paul looked surprised t'see me standin' there at the back of the church with my hand high in the air. I called out, "I am!"

"Why, Lana! How wonderful that you're ready to turn your life over to the Lord! Come up here and let's have a word of prayer." Brother Paul took both of my hands in his and I was surprised at how soft his hands were-not hard and calloused like Jerry's. He leaned his forehead toward mine so we was almost touchin'. "Let us pray, Lana," he whispered. I closed my eyes and waited. I could hear his soft voice, but I couldn't make out most of the words.

Finally, he moved back from me, put one hand on my shoulder and said to the folks on the benches. "Our sister, Lana, is ready to become one of the elect. We will baptize you today, Lana, in the pond behind the church….Miss Glady, would you take Lana and get her in a baptism gown?" A tiny, old lady took me to a room where there was white robes hangin' on pegs all along the wall. She told me to take off just my dress and then she slipped the robe over my head. I left my earrings and my dress with the cherries on the floor. All the men and women marched out to the pond, with me and Brother Paul leadin' the way.

We waded into the still pool of water. The sun was shining fiercely for a spring day, and I already felt the sweat poolin' under my arms. But the water was chilly and when we marched deeper in the pond, I shivered. Brother Paul must've felt me shake 'cause he said, "You don't swim, do you?" I shook my head. "There's nothing to be afraid of, Lana." We were waist-deep in the water, and he put his right arm under the small of my back and put his left hand over my nose and mouth. Then he leaned me backwards into the water and said, "Lana, I baptize you in the name of the Father, and the Son and the Holy Ghost." The chilly water sloshed over me and rinsed away all the evil and sin that'd been clingin' t'me since time began.

When he pulled me back up, the sin dripped from my hair and from the end of my nose, carryin' all the filth that was inside of me back to the pond. Brother Paul was smilin', almost laughin' now. He gave me a dry handkerchief for my face and then turned to the little group of men and women standin' on the bank. "Brothers and Sisters, welcome our new Sister—Lana Wright!" They was all smilin' at me as we waded outta the pond, Brother Paul with his arm' round my waist to steady me while I stepped along the muddy bottom.

When we got back to the church house, Brother Paul told me there'd be a towel in the room where my clothes was so I could get dressed. But I looked at my dress with cherries on it, layin' in a heap on the floor and I thought about how I'd worn that dress for all my sinnin'. I wanted more than anything to have something pure and white to wear home. Somethin' that'd look like an angel's gown. I leaned my head out the door and called t'Brother Paul.

"Could I wear one of them dry gowns home today? I'll bring it back on Winsdee."

Brother Paul seemed surprised, but he said I could. So I took off all my wet underclothes and put on a clean white gown, just like the one that was drippin' pond water all over the floor. I rolled the cherry dress, the underwear and the earrings in a ball, held my shoes in the other hand, and walked barefoot to the back of the church. I never felt so free! The gown swished 'round my ankles and rubbed against my nipples when I walked. I ran my fingers through my wet hair, pushin' it back from my cheeks and laughin' at their faces when they saw me. They all looked surprised, even though Brother Paul said I could wear the gown home.

"I feel so clean, so good!" I told Brother Paul as I came to a stop and smiled up at him. He was so handsome, with his shiny hair and his pretty brown eyes, and his big, white teeth. I was full of happiness and it was all 'cause of him. He saved me! I took a step closer to him, so our faces was real close together and I stared into his brown eyes 'til I could see the little flecks of gold there. "Thank you, Brother Paul," I whispered. "Thank you for saving me."

I wanted to kiss him and let him know how much I loved him and loved Jesus. But he stepped back and said real quick, "I didn't save you, Lana. Jesus did. Praise be to Jesus!"

"Yes, praise to Jesus," I whispered. The other men was standin' behind Brother Paul, real quiet and still, like they was waitin' for something. I decided it was time for me to go home. "I got to get home, now," I told 'em. "But I'll be back on Winsdee night." When I started down the plank steps, I knew they was all watchin' me walk away from 'em. I let myself sway so the gown kissed my hips, first the left and then the right, with every step.

It was gettin' to be the hot part of the day and I could feel the sweat, tricklin' down from under my arms and runnin' down my sides. But the loose gown swished as I walked and made a lil breeze against my skin. When I came in the kitchen, I laid my bundle of clothes down on a chair. Jerry was sittin' at the table, cleanin' his rifle, and there was pieces all in front of him. He seemed to be surprised to see me.

"Lana, what in hell have you got on?"

I turned in a little circle with my arms straight out, so the sleeves hung down graceful and long. "It's the baptizin' gown," I explained. "Ain't it pretty?"

"What are you doin' coming home in that? Where're your clothes?"

I picked up the bundle. The cherry dress looked like it'd been stained with lipstick and wine and fast livin'. "Right here," I said, droppin' them in the garbage can. One of the earrings rolled out of the dress and landed on the floor with a plop.

"You're not throwin' away your good clothes!" he yelled. "And these are the earrings I jus' bought you!" He scooped the earring off the floor and held it to my face.

"They're sinful," I told him, takin' another glide around the kitchen.

"Ain't nothing sinful about this dress!" He pulled it out of the garbage and the coffee grinds from breakfast tumbled on the floor. "Damn it, Lana! I told you that you could go down there and hear Brother Paul. I didn't tell you to go crazy over church!" He threw the dress on the floor and the other earring rolled out of it. "Now stop all this foolishness and get this mess cleaned up." I kept on dancin' from the table to the cabinet and back again. I could just imagine the piano playin' that pretty hymn they sang at church. It would be nice to dance at church. Maybe I should mention that to Brother Paul.

Jerry stood still and watched me for a few minutes and when I danced in his direction, he reached out quick as a rattlesnake and grabbed me by the wrists. He pulled me up to his face and I could see little flecks of spit in the corners of his mouth. "You get that gown off *Right Now* and put your clothes back on!" he said real slow and real hard, like he was spittin' out the words.

"You're hurtin' my arms!"

"I'm gonna hurt a lot more than just your arms if you don't take off that silly gown and get your clothes on. Do you hear me?"

I blinked hard, tryin' to think what to do. I couldn't believe Jerry was blind to how I was changed. The gown was pure against my skin and I was clean inside and out. I belonged to Jesus and I knew that He would love me, no matter what I was wearing. "Okay," I told Jerry. "Let go of me." He dropped my wrists, and I unbuttoned the placket at the front of the gown and let it slide over my shoulders. It fell in a white heap round my ankles. I was standin' there nekked before Jerry and Jesus. But Jerry acted like he'd never seen me nekked. He reached down t'pull the gown back up, but I was faster 'an him. I jumped back and raised my hands up high. "I praise and worship you, Jesus!" I called out.

"Good God!" Jerry hollered. "Have you been in church with nothin' on under your clothes?" I leaned my head back and laughed at his foolishness and then I began to pray, thankin' Jesus for my deliverance.

Jerry acted like he was just frantic to get me back in some clothes! He ran to the bedroom and grabbed an old housedress. "Lana, cover yourself up!" he begged, puttin' the dress ` round my back. Then he tried pushin' me in the bedroom. He told me if I wanted t'pray, I'd better go where it was cool and dark. I thought that made sense, so I let him lead me t'the bedroom and I prayed by dancin' and singin' with my hands upward to heaven. After a while I felt like I'd told Jesus everything he should hear. I went to the kitchen and got the gown from the floor and put it back on so I could cook supper for the saints.

Jerry stood in the doorway, watchin' me. He never said another word about the gown. I danced in it, and cooked in it, swept in it, and wore it to the garden. By Winsdee, it was grimy 'round the hem, but Jesus could tell that it was still being worn by a pure woman.

I didn't need much sleep that week. I felt better 'an I ever had before. I could dance longer, talk faster, laugh louder, and pray harder than anybody else. In the kitchen, the buttercup curtains sent out a vibration tellin' me to "Remember the Spring; Remember to Spring! Spring and Fling and Sing on the Wing!" And the plank floors sang about Jesus when I slid my feet along the cracks. Outside, the wind said that Heaven's voice was closer than anybody knew, but I could hear every word. God'd sent his Son to Braggadocio to purchase a new bride and I was ready t'go with him.

Jerry wasn't home on Winsdee night. I walked to the church in my baptism gown and got there while the singin' was goin' on. I could hear the pretty piano music comin' from the open windahs of the church and I could hear the angels hummin' in the trees. Jesus told me not to go inside the church just yet. He said t' walk t'the pond, where He could see me. The wet grass was cool and soft under my bare feet. I stood on the bank of the pond and listened to Jesus' voice, sweet and soft, tellin' me how He had six hundred and thirty-four Heaven Dollars to buy me. I told Him I loved him very much, more than I loved anybody or anything else. He said to show him how much I loved Him and trusted Him, to get in the water and walk to Him. I couldn't swim, but Jesus said He could swim for both of us. The water rose 'round my knees and I started singin' to Him. I could feel the gown billowin' up and floatin' round my arms as the spirit of the water hummed to my feet. I took another step and the water was up to my shoulders, pattin' me and singin' a lullaby. I raised my hands to Him and called out, "I love you, Jesus."

That's when I heard a woman scream, "She's drownin'! It's Lana! She's in the pond!" A herd of feet came poundin' down the wooden steps as my Brothers and Sisters ran outta the church. I smiled at 'em and sang louder. Brother Paul jumped in the water and thrashed his arms about. He called, "Lana, I'm comin'! Don't panic!" I smiled at him. He was Jesus, and he was going to swim for both of us! What a sweet, loving look He had on His face.

"I love you, Jesus!" I whispered as He pulled me toward the shore by one arm.

When we got to the shallows, two Brothers waded into the water to help. The cool, wet baptizin' gown lay tight against my skin. I leaned toward Jesus. "I love you, Jesus," I said again, real soft, and I kissed Him on the mouth. I could feel electricity running between us, makin' me shiver. I circled my arms round Jesus' neck and held him tight t'me, kissin' him again and again. I don't know why those other people pulled us apart. They should've seen that Jesus loved me and that we was goin' to be married soon as He paid the six hundred thirty-four dollars. But they didn't understand nothin' and they shouted at us and pried us apart. I reached out my hands and cried for Him t'come back t'me, but Jesus just turned away from me and climbed up the bank. Two Brothers held me by the arms and they dragged me from the shallows and set me down hard on the grass, and I cried and cried til they took me home.

Chapter 12
Jerry

After I married Lana Gray, I had more trouble `an you could shake a stick at. I knowed Lana back when we was both kids in grade school, but who paid attention t' girls back then? We was all poor farm kids, most of us livin' on somebody else's land, our daddies raisin' us t' work in the fields. By the time I was 9, I could hitch a team of mules good as any grown man. So bein' a farmer was way more interestin' t' me than any girl in pigtails.

Every one of us farm kids missed school in the fall, when it was time t'pick cotton. That was one miserable job! We pulled long tow sacks behind us `til they was full. Workin' in the hot sun, movin' down the long rows, the sweat drippin' off the end of my nose. There was a bucket of water at the end of the row but nothin' t' drink `til you picked all the cotton that stood between you an' that bucket. The cotton bolls was so hard and thorny that your hands'd be bloody if you picked without gloves. But it was faster t'pick with your bare hands, so most of us got used t' doin' it that way. I had enough of that kind of life way `fore I married Lana Gray. I wanted my own farm, my own field hands, my own place t' live and if hard work was the price I had t' pay, it was alright by me.

When I saw Lana that day at the sawmill, I thought she looked like an angel. I never remembered her bein' that pretty when we was in school. She had blond hair and a figure like a movie star— tall and long-legged and she looked up to me like she saw what I'd be some day. I started takin' her out on Sat'days. Why, I don't think she'd ever been on a date `fore I come along! Her daddy wasn't mean, but he needed her t' stay home with him and the little boys and so he did everythin' he could to discourage any courtin'.

Lana's family never had a pot t' whiz in. When I married Lana, I pulled her out of a life of misery an' took her t' live in a house that had everythin' she'd done without: electric lights, runnin' water, indoor bathroom. You'd think she would-a been grateful, but it seemed like nothin' made that girl happy for very long.

I will say our first few months together was pretty good. Lana kept the house clean and she sure knowed her way 'round the kitchen. She liked t' sit with me on the porch swing after supper and make plans for what we'd do, once I'd made a few good crops.

I guess everythin' changed after she lost the baby, but hell, she wasn't that far along! I couldn't even tell she was expectin'! She just started layin' 'round all day long. Wouldn't cook or clean. Stayed in the bed from the time I left 'til I come home. Can't you see how I felt? Comin' home tired an' hot from workin' all day, and Lana laid up in the bed like the Queen o' Sheba. It was plain that she was takin' advantage of my good nature! I did talk rough t' her that one day an' I shook her a lil' bit to make her listen t' me. But it was after I left the house that she fell outta the bed an' lost the baby. That didn't have nothin' t'do with me.

Anyway, after a few months of her moonin' round the house, sad-eyed, refusin' t' even look at me when I talked t' her, she finally started getin' some better. I bought her a pair of earrings at the drug store one day an' boy was she proud of 'em! Strutted into town wearin' 'em on my birthday.

At Christmas, we stopped by my sister Edna's place. Her husband Raymond gave Edna money t' buy presents for everybody and then he bought hisself a bottle of Jack Daniels. I tell you, good whiskey is jus' like a tonic! My mama always kept a bottle in the top of the kitchen cabinet, in case somebody had a cough. I tole Lana and tole her again that she needed t'get a bottle t'keep in case of sickness, but she never paid me no mind. So that mornin' I needed somethin'; there wasn't a thing in the house. And instead of tryin' t' help me, Lana run off down the road in her nightgown and stayed gone until supper.

The last straw for me was when Lana got started in church. I tole her she could go t' church, but I had no ideal she'd get it in her head t' be baptized and then take on, like she did. After a few days, she was wearin' that baptizer gown all day and all night, singin' and prayin' and dancin' round the house. She was just plumb crazy with religion! I couldn't do a thing t'settle her down. The people at church tole me that she got in the pond on Winsdee night and damn near drowned. Then, when Brother Paul got in the water t' save her, she threw her arms `round him and kissed him on the mouth. The men from the church came t' see me about Lana, an' said I had t' do somethin' `bout her. One of `em tole me I should check on puttin' her at Western State. I really didn't want t' hear any of that, but I knowed I couldn't keep her at home. I could lock her in the bedroom, but I couldn't keep her from stayin' up all night, singin' and hollerin'. When it would get real quiet in there, she was up t' no good. So I couldn't sleep and I couldn't work and finally there was nothin' else t' do but take her t' Western State.

The day I put Lana in the truck and carried her there I didn't know what I had in store. Jus' seein' that place from the road gave me the heebie-jeebies! Those big high towers lookin' like some kind of jail. And Lana sittin' on the seat next t' me, laughin'. She had no ideal where I was takin' her. Even when I got her outta the truck an' in the front door, she didn't act like she knew what was goin' on.

The doctor was sittin' behind a big desk with lots of papers piled on top of it. He tole me t' have a seat while he finished up with his writin'. So I sat in the chair with my cap in my hands, waitin' and waitin' like I was `bout to get some charity. When the doctor did look up, he wanted t' know how long Lana'd been actin' like that. He tole me she'd be safe there with `em at the hospital and they'd try some treatment for her. He said I could come t'visit her whenever I wanted to. From what he said, I believed that Lana'd get well so I could bring her home for good.

Once all the spring plantin' was done, I did go t'see Lana a couple-a times. The nurse'd lead her outside by the hand, like she was a little girl. Most of the time, she just stared off in space, actin' like she couldn't hear nothin' I was sayin'. After a couple months of that, I decided I'd just as well forget about Lana. She wasn't really alive any more, in my way of thinkin'.

KATE

Chapter 13
Todd's Story

I went back to the hospital when I finished my interview with Miss Adele. The adult male patients, out of the building on grounds privileges, were roaming unsupervised from picnic table to parking lot. One man, grinning broadly at me, broke into the song "Wild Thing," then put both hands over his chest as he sang, "you make my heart sing." I waved casually and quickened my step. Before I got to the entrance, however, a small, wiry man ran up to me, inserting himself between me and the door. "Got a quarter? Some coffee? Wanna have sex? For a quarter? With some coffee?" I tried to move around him, but he was like a professional dance partner: when I moved to the left, he moved with me.

This continued for several minutes until he put one hand on my forearm. I drew back angrily. "Get your hands off me!" I yelled. He stepped back, muttering to himself, then hurried to where another patient sat on a bench with a cup of coffee.

"Gimme some coffee!" he demanded. The other patient hunched over the steaming cup to protect it from theft.

My dance partner thus distracted, I quickly ducked into the foyer and walked to the juvenile unit. No one seemed to have missed me. I wandered down the hall to my office without anyone looking up or asking where I had been, further confirming my feeling that I was "non-essential" in every way.

I found a message from Scott, telling me there would be a psychology meeting in the afternoon. After I scanned it, I opened the file for Todd and began to review the test materials: He had an above average IQ, his academic skills were woefully deficient and his personality test indicated that his aggression was a cover-up for feelings of inadequacy. Nothing surprising about any of that, I thought. I read further in the chart, coming upon an assessment by someone named Jack Gordon. The handwriting was neat but angular. Mr. Gordon had written about Todd's history of fighting and how he had been suspended from school and banned from the community center for physical altercations. He noted that Todd was worried about his younger sister, and since he was locked up for thirty days, he was acutely concerned about who would look out for her.

I found Todd in the cafeteria, sitting at a large table by himself, his back to the corner. He was hunched over the tray of food and was eating hurriedly, as if the plate might be taken away at any minute. Between bites, he looked around the room, apparently scanning it for any threats.

I greeted him as I approached. "Hi, Todd. When you get finished with your lunch, I'd like to talk to you for a few minutes."

He shrugged nonchalently and responded, "Okay by me."

He arrived at my office door after he had dumped the paper plate and plastic utensils from his tray. I began to explain the evaluation procedure that would eventually be sent to the court.

Todd sat impassively as I talked, seemingly disinterested in the process. I redoubled my efforts to engage him. "First of all, your judge wants me to go over some things with you and be sure you understand what goes on in court. Have you ever been to court?" I asked.

"Lots of times."

"For what?"

"Fightin'."

"So you understand how things work in a court?"

"Sure."

"Then tell me, Todd, what does the judge do?"

"He decides if he's going to send you home on probation, or lock you up."

"Is there anything in between those two?"

He looked thoughtful and paused before he admitted that he did not know.

"Well, the juvenile judge can do a lot of things. He could put you on probation, but he could also put you on house arrest, give you community service, make you take drug screens, or send you to counseling."

"Yeah, that's right," he agreed.

"Then there are places that aren't lock-ups. Places like drug rehab, group homes…"

"Most of 'em are lock-ups," he informed me with an authoritative tone.

"Well, maybe some of them have locked doors, but..."

He interrupted. "So whadaya think the judge is gonna do with me?"

"I don't know. So far you've been doing fine on the unit. You haven't gotten in any fights. You're helping yourself the best way you can by cooperating with the staff."

This seemed to satisfy him and he settled back in the chair.

"There's some things I need to ask you, Todd, so I can fill in the blanks on my forms. Is this a good time?"

He seemed pleased to be asked for his permission. "Yeah…I'll miss the afternoon part of class," he told me, grinning.

"I don't think your teacher will hold it against you. He knows you're talking to me. Let's see, we'll start with the charges: Aggravated Assault. Tell me what happened that you ended up fighting with this guy."

"Well, we were all in the parking lot out by Walmart and Jimmy kep' sayin' he was gonna have ta teach my friend Jennifer a lesson. She's not mah girlfriend, but she's mah best friend and I've known her since second grade. I could tell he was gonna hit her, so I just got in between 'em and told Jimmy to leave her alone. Then he pushed me and told me to get out the way and I pushed him back. Next thing, we was punchin' each other. He fell down and I kicked him in the ribs pretty hard. He didn't get up, so I put Jennifer in my truck and we left. Somebody else called the ambulance. Then that night, the police came by mah house and said I had to go down to juvie with them."

"Did he ever actually touch Jennifer?"

"Naw, but he was 'bout to."

"What did the court do when you got the other assault charges?"

"Probation. Intensive Probation. Boot camp."

"How'd you do on probation?"

"I never violated. All my drug screens were clean."

"That's good. Did you ever go to a mental health center for counseling?"

"Naw. I ain't crazy or nothin'."

"I know that. I just wondered if you'd ever talked to a counselor or been to anger management classes."

"My mama wanted me to take a class like that, but I got these charges before I could start."

I asked about his family and he described a working, single mother who provided for him and his 12-year-old sister with 12-hour shifts at the factory. Moving on to leisure activities, he described weekends when they rented DVD's or games, and I believed him when he said he had a good relationship with his mother and his sister.

"Tell me about your father. Where is he?" I ventured.

Todd's face immediately darkened. "He's in Stantonville."

"That's close to where you live, isn't it? Do you see much of him?"

He glared at me before answering in the negative.

"Why not?"

His face seemed to contort, collapsing into creases of anguish. "He don't care nothin' 'bout me," he said in a raspy growl.

I was taken aback at the brutal honesty of his statement, but I forged ahead, asking why he believed his father was uncaring.

"'Cause he don't ever try t'see me or talk t'me on the phone. An' if I go t'his house, he jus' talks on and on about my sister and how she's doing." His voice rose to a shout, "He don't care nothin' 'bout me!"

I hesitated, wondering what I could say that would be helpful. "Maybe your father just doesn't know how to show his love. Does he have some serious problems? Like alcoholism or mental illness?" I ventured.

"Yeah. He's got `em both. But that ain't no excuse!" he insisted.

"You're right. It's not an excuse."

He tucked his face into his sleeve and began to sob. I didn't ever think I'd see the boxer cry, and I was caught off guard, stunned and silent, sitting across the battered desk from him as his tears darkened the sleeve of his shirt. Eventually I remembered the box of Kleenex and I slid them toward him.

"I don't need it," he answered fiercely, his words coming muffled through his shirtsleeve.

"Okay." I sat back in the chair and waited, wondering what I should say. Nothing I had learned in school seemed to fit Todd's situation. He regained his composure slowly, eventually reaching for the tissue and rubbing it violently against his eyes before he continued, "I just don't get it. He's got time for everybody else."

I used this comment as an opening, encouraging Todd to talk about his father and their very rocky relationship. He was close to his mother and sister, but he was furious at his father for his rejection. After several minutes, I asked him if he felt he had ever been abused.

"By my dad?"

"By anyone," I said definitively.

"Well, yeah, by my dad. He used to whip me with a belt that had a rodeo buckle. He'd get mad and hit my back, head, whatever he could reach. My mom stopped that…she moved out and got a divorce."

"What about sexual abuse? Did anyone ever touch you in a way they shouldn't have? Or ask you to touch them?"

"Not that. But my mom had a real bad boyfriend for a while, when I was ten. I hated him. He tried to make me suck his thing one time. I told him 'No way!' so he left me alone after that…" Todd took a deep breath. "But he didn't leave my little sister alone. I came in on him one day and he was making her do that."

He heaved a sigh and began to tear the soggy Kleenex into pieces. "I didn't do anything!" he said, furiously condemning the

10-year-old boy who had seen his sister molested. "I let it happen."

"You were just ten years old! What could you have done?"

He looked up angrily, the tears standing in the corners of his eyes, "I could-a done something! I could-a fought him! I could-a taken a baseball bat and hit him or SOMETHING!" He was shouting, the veins standing out across his temples and down his neck. Then he began to sob again and softly said, "I let it happen."

As he cried, I sat quietly, wishing I knew the right words. Were there magic words that would make this hurt ebb away? I rejected three or four ideas before I finally said, "Todd, it wasn't your fault. I know it feels that way, but it wasn't your fault. You were only ten, and a ten-year-old can't fix a problem like that."

He sniffed and reached for another tissue. "I never told anyone before," he said.

"So your mother doesn't know what happened?"

"Naw." He looked up at me quickly. "And I don't want you t'tell her, either."

"I don't intend to tell her. But someone has to tell Children's Services. They'll want to keep this man from ever doing that kind of thing again."

He looked at me doubtfully. "I ain't gonna talk to `em," he asserted.

"They'll want you to tell them what you know. It could put the man in jail."

He wagged his head from side to side in a slow, determined motion.

"It's your chance to do something, Todd. It's not too late."

He seemed to consider that point and then slowly said, "I'll think about it."

"Good. Let's talk about it later on. Maybe Monday, okay?"

He agreed to revisit the subject. We finished with a few more questions and he went back to the classroom. I sat back in my chair, my mind reeling with all the emotions and information he had shared. Such a scared, guilty kid! He was still fighting the "bad guys" to protect the helpless girls in his life. And no amount of fighting could ever make up for the day he watched, paralyzed with fear, while his sister was molested. I wondered if he could ever work through such terrible trauma. I made a few more notes and then closed up the office and started for the psychology staff meeting.

KATE

Chapter 14
Illness Strikes

The psychology meeting held in Dr. Thompson's office gave me the first opportunity to meet my "colleagues." They were seated around a large conference table in a windowless room: Dr. Garcia originally from Cuba, elegantly slim and dressed in tailored slacks, dress shirt and tie. He had a languid Spanish accent and a courtly air. Dr. Garcia stood when I entered the room and for a minute, I thought he might kiss my hand, instead of shaking it. Susan, an overweight white woman whose thin hair hung in long wisps, barely glanced in my direction. Georgia, a middle-aged woman with a tall, imposing presence, had been an army nurse before she changed careers to become a psychologist. She nodded curtly when Dr. Thompson introduced us. Jim, a retired Air Force psychologist, propped his heels on the table, paring his fingernails with a pocket knife. Kenneth, the only black psychologist at the hospital, leaned back in his chair, his hands laced behind his head, and stared up at the ceiling. At the head of the table, as if he were preparing to order dinner for a group of unhappy teenagers, sat Dr. Thompson with papers in hand, waiting for the meeting to come to order. He pushed his large glasses farther up his nose and said in a soft voice that hardly commanded attention, "Well, I guess it's about time to start." Glancing at the industrial-sized clock on the wall, he commented, "I guess Don will be here in a minute."

As if on cue, the door flew open, banging against the tiled wall, and Don rushed into the small room as if he were being pushed by a blast of air. "I'm sorry I'm late," he panted from a corner of the table. "I've had diarrhea all day and it seemed like it just wasn't going to get any better! The cramps have been killing me. I've been drinking Sprite and eating crackers all morning. But I was still having this terrible diarrhea, you know the kind that is just *All Water?*

And you never know if you're going to make it to the bathroom in time!" I glanced at Dr. Thompson, who seemed to be nauseated, too. "But," Don continued triumphantly, "I went home at lunch and took some Imodium and I haven't had any bowel movements since then!"

With his chin raised in disdain, Dr. Garcia looked down his chiseled Spanish nose to where Don had taken a seat. "We are so hauppy for you, Don," he remarked, his Castilian R's rolling across the table.

Apparently Don didn't hear the sarcasm, for he continued with, "Well, I'm glad to be better, too." He shifted in his seat, catching the attention of Jim, who casually looked up from his manicure.

"It's all that vinegar you've been drinking," Jim observed coolly. "It's pickled your system."

Don was undaunted. "Well, we all have our own opinion. But the research is absolutely amazing. A little apple cider vinegar can do wonders for arthritis!"

"What ever!" Jim said, dismissing him.

"Don, I was just letting every one know what changes would be coming on the adult units," Dr. Thompson interrupted in an attempt to gain control of the discussion. Doctors would be moved; group times would be changed. None of it seemed to be related to me until he commented that Susan would be off for a week in November, and I would probably have to cover her groups. I didn't feel comfortable working with chronic patients, but protesting didn't seem to have any effect, so I decided to accept it.

When the meeting was adjourned, I stopped in the hall to talk to Dr. Garcia, who told me he had come out of retirement to work a few days each week at the hospital. "As long as it's meaningful," he explained, "I will continue to come." Georgia approached us as the others strolled away from the office. She shook my hand with brusque, military precision.

"We're glad to have you working with us. If there's anything I can do to help you, let me know."

At that point, a stocky, middle-aged man approached, carrying a can of paint in his beefy fist. When I turned to face him, he unabashedly assessed me from head to toe before asking, "You Miss McConnie? You need t' unlock your door. I'm ready t' paint your office."

I was surprised that the hospital would think a coat of paint would improve the state of my office, but I asked what color he intended to use. He looked at me through hooded eyes and put a toothpick in one corner of his mouth. "Everything's white unless you want t' work out somethin' on the side." A frank, sexual interest permeated his gaze, leading me to assume that I would have to be willing to have sex with this man to have the office painted mauve. Georgia crossed her arms over her chest and rolled her eyes heavenward.

"White will be fine," I said quickly. "When are you planning to start?"

"Now."

Dr. Thompson stepped from his office door. "Kate, I called yesterday and asked them to put a fresh coat of paint on your office."

"It seems kind of late in the day to get started."

"Yes, it's too late for today, Ted. She'll be leaving in the next 30 minutes or so, and she'll need to lock the office door as she goes."

I glanced at Ted who seemed furious that his plans were being thwarted. Had he intended to do more than paint? Was he planning to install a camera under my desk or something? His jaw clenched as he glared at me. "Well, I don't know if I'll have time t' get to it on Monday. It might have t' wait 'til later in the week."

"That'll be fine," Dr. Thompson said, ignoring the anger in his voice and watching Ted march away.

"Why does he want to start painting the office on a Friday afternoon?" I mused.

"Who knows," Dr. Thompson laughed, "That's the Western Way."

"Pl-ease!" Georgia said in exasperation. "Ted's scoping out the new girl on the block. He thought you might be next in line," she informed me.

"Now, Georgia," Dr. Thompson interrupted. "We don't know that."

"I do!" she insisted. "Ask Joan, the clerk on Unit C. Last year Ted…"

"Don't let him bother you," Dr. Thompson pointedly interrupted her. "Just keep a close eye on him," he advised me.

When I got back to the adolescent unit, I paused at the nurses' station. With Mildred gone for the day, it might be a pleasant stop. Patrice, who was putting assessments into the charts, looked up as I came in. "Make it through the psychology meeting? Did you wonder if any of `em were patients?" she chortled.

Before I could think of an answer, a man who appeared to be in his middle thirties sauntered into the nurses' station. He moved with the natural grace of an athlete, skirting his way around the tangle of desks, chart racks and copy machines. He seemed to be preoccupied with something and did not see me standing in the corner, which gave me a few minutes to observe him. This was no musician. He had the build of a baseball player with broad shoulders and sinewy arms. His features were too craggy to be handsome; the bridge of his nose was slightly crooked, probably from being broken; and his face was a little too square. His wiry hair was cut short, with a few sandy-blonde tufts standing rakishly above his forehead. He had a confident air about him and when he caught sight of me, his eyes crinkled in a smile.

"Jack," Patrice called, breaking my reverie. "I was sure sorry to hear about Mr. Clyde… I always thought a lot of him."

"Thanks, Patrice," Jack responded. I saw the same sadness flicker in his eyes that I had seen in my own reflection after my mother died. Another orphan, I surmised. I glanced away from him, hoping to give him some privacy.

"Mr. Clyde worked in the hospital his whole life, didn't he?" Patrice pressed.

"Yeah, 45 years." He flipped through some pages in the chart, avoiding her sympathetic gaze. I wished that she would find another way to express her good intentions.

There was an uncomfortable silence as papers rattled against the metal binder. "Oh, I didn't introduce y'all," Patrice hastened to say. "Jack, this is Kate. She's the new psychologist on the unit. This is Jack Gordon; he's our recreational supervisor." Putting her hands on her hips in a sassy pose, she winked at me conspiratorially. "Jack's in charge of me and Darrel."

"Yeah, right," Jack responded before offering me the obligatory. "Nice to meet you."

So this was Jack Gordon, I mused: the man who had seen Todd as something more than just an unruly kid. With a dawning realization of my identity, Jack snapped his fingers, grinning broadly. "You're the lady that got the best of Tommy Beal this morning, aren't you?"

"At the front door? I think he got the best of me, instead of the other way around," I muttered in embarrassment.

"I don't know about that!" he chucked. "Patrice, you should have seen her telling Tommy how it was going to be! After she told him off, the old boy started after George Hill," Jack summarized with admiration.

"Tommy tests everybody when they're brand new," Patrice pointed out.

I nodded, still wishing that the loss of my composure had not been witnessed.

"I don't think you'll ever have trouble with Tommy again," Jack confided. "But if you do, just holler for security. He's afraid of anyone in uniform." He turned his attention back to the record, rifling through the pages and complaining that Darrell's assessment should have already been finished.

"I need to see it before Cody's family comes for treatment team. I hear they're real mad about him being here." Jack interrupted his comments about difficult families to look up at me and quietly observe, "I imagine it'll take a while for you to get used to all this." I feigned an optimism about the job until he continued: "Who's your supervisor? Don? I don't know if you'll ever get used to Don!" As he re-shelved the heavy notebook, he said, "Well, the weekend's almost here! Let's call it a day."

I had forgotten that the empty weekend lay before me. Unlike Jack, who probably had plans and people to be with, I had two days at the Thompsons' house, wondering what Russ was doing in Mayfield.

Once I was back at their home, I changed to a worn sweatsuit and had something to eat, consoling myself with thoughts of Russ's coming visit. I spent Saturday and Sunday lounging in the den and taking long walks down streets of arching trees. Scott and Carol, who planned to visit with elderly relatives, repeatedly encouraged me to come along for the drive, but I declined and watched with relief as they backed out of the driveway, taking Precious with them.

KATE

Chapter 15
Flashlights and Duct Tape

Monday morning, Don ejected himself from an Olds 98 that seemed to have been roasted on a spit and then camouflaged with green and brown paint. As I stared at the car, Don informed me that he had bought the vehicle for his teenaged son. Since it was built like a tank, he reasoned that it would be safe for a teenager just learning to drive. Evidently, his son had felt so comfortable in the car that he had used it to go "mudding" with friends and had haplessly mired it in a farmer's field, where the exhaust system ignited the stubble. The boys extinguished the flames with their coats, but not before the paint job was ruined and the tail lights were melted. In Don's estimation, the car was still driveable, regardless of his son's sworn testimony that he would never be seen in it again. To demonstrate that it is not possible to die from embarrassment, Don had declared that he would use the car for his commute to work.

He patted the side of the door fondly. "It still runs just fine," he announced. "But I did have to tinker with some things." He strutted to the back where the ruined tail lights had hardened into plastic lava, trailing down the rear fender. He had taken two large flashlights and had colored their lens with a red magic marker before he secured them to the trunk with duct tape. Don switched on the flashlight closest to me. "If I leave work after dark, I can just switch these on, and anyone would assume they were taillights," he explained. Even though the faint, pink glow from the lens looked like a child's toy, I refrained from commenting. Don switched off his flashlight, and we started for the building.

He pleasantly asked if I had enjoyed my weekend and suggested that the next time I had a free Sunday, I could visit the Unitarian church in Jackson with him and his wife. "I appreciate that; I'll let you know," I said, wondering if we would have to arrive with the flashlights on.

This non-committal agreement seemed to please Don, and he whistled as he walked the rest of the way to the door. Jack and a few men from the recreational department were leaning against their trucks like high school boys, laughing and talking. I caught his eye and waved.

"Got a minute?" Jack asked, catching up with me as I passed the rack of deteriorating bicycles. "What was Don telling you about that car?" As I told the highlights of the story, Jack said, "I can't believe that's his car! I saw it parked at Walmart on Saturday, and I figured it belonged to some poor devil who was one step away from being homeless. I thought about leaving a ten dollar bill on the seat so he could get something to eat." Jack was shaking his head as he talked. "I can't believe he's driving that thing! It's not like he can't afford something better. He's just too cheap to spend the money."

"He's definitely one of the most eccentric people I've ever met."

"Or ever will meet," Jack remarked as he opened the door on the unit. "Well, have a good day, Kate" he called as we parted.

The week seemed to glide past me, faster than the first one. There were boys to be tested and interviewed, treatment teams to attend, and parents to be reassured. By Friday, I realized that I had hardly left the unit each day until it was time to go home.

Tuesday after work, Dr. Thompson helped me load the little VW with all of my possessions, and we drove to Miss Adele's house, where she and Carol caught up on the gossip while Dr. Thompson and I carried the four dog-eared boxes to the back bedroom.

He set the last box on the wide plank floor and looked at the crown molding in admiration. "These ceilings seem to go up forever.

Can you imagine what it would cost to build something like this today?"

I shook my head. "It's a beautiful home, but it seems like a sad place. So empty now that it's just Miss Adele living here."

"That's true," he hesitantly agreed. "But Adele's very active and she keeps a full schedule of events here: Bridge Club, Book Club, Daughters of the Confederacy, Episcopal Women's Club. " His eyes twinkled as he added, "You may be wanting to miss work to get in on some of the fun."

"You don't have anything to worry about," I reassured him. "I never learned to play bridge and I haven't been to church since I was in Junor High." I almost added, *since my mother died.* The church and I had not had a reconciliation and I wasn't interested in organized religion.

Carol hugged me before she stepped off the porch, making me promise I would visit often and keep them updated on everything. In reference to Russ's planned visit, she whispered that she would see me Saturday. As Miss Adele pushed the tall, wooden door closed, it shuddered and creaked against its rusty hinges.

"I know tomorrow is a work day for you, so you may be starting to bed in a little while. But if you want something to eat, there's peanut butter in the pantry and milk in the refrigerator."

When I said I had already eaten supper, she confided, "Well, my program comes on every Tuesday night, so I'm going to the den to watch it. You're welcome to join me," she commented.

Believing it was an invitation not to be refused, I followed her into the "den," which looked like a library with its tall, glass-fronted bookcases. An oak reading table stood in the middle of the room, flanked by two leather wing-backs. Miss Adele settled in front of a miniature TV that sat on a small end table, but I was too fascinated with the books to sit down. All of the classics, from the Iliad to Pride and Prejudice, were contained in the shelves. There were dusty anthologies of poetry and modern bestsellers: *Ship of Fools, All the President's Men, The Confessions of Nat Turner*, as well as ancient medical books with cracked spines.

"You probably have more books here than the library!" I exclaimed, feeling a small stirring of embarrassment as I confessed that I had never read most of the classics. She graciously demurred, pointing out that the collection had been started by her great-grandfather.

As Adele turned toward the prime time soap opera, I began to flip through the pages of *Jane Eyre*. This was a book I *had* read back in junior high, when I felt like an orphan, too. I had never met my Mr. Rochester, but I would be living in a stately manor like his. I thumbed through the copy, finding a picture of the insane wife imprisoned in an attic room. Repeatedly she escaped, and each time she attempted murder by arson, I recalled. This book might bring nightmares, I decided, as I hurriedly pushed it back onto the shelf.

I faced the TV but floated into a daydream that revolved around Russ's visit on Saturday. It was going to be a perfect fall day: Russ and I would take a picnic lunch to Chickasaw State Park, a mere 30 minutes away. We would talk about putting our lives back together, try to find a way to make all of this hurt go away, commit ourselves to the future and let love overcome all the obstacles.

At the next commercial, I excused myself, feigning sleepiness. I pushed my shoulder against the bedroom door to close it and fell on the quilted bedspread. I imagined myself as Belle, lying in this bed, my eyes following the crack that stretched across the plaster ceiling, my hands resting listlessly across my chest. It was all too believable. I bolted upright from the bed and began searching for my pajamas.

The evening activities would be repeated without variation for the next several months: I would leave work hungry, lonely and confused to find a hot meal waiting for me in a formal dining room. I would share an evening of TV or reading with Miss Adele, before I retreated to my bedroom to prepare for the next work day. And as the heavy door closed on the hall, the moan of the hinges would remind me of all the sadness, isolation and regret that had rushed into Belle's bedroom before I could shut the door.

KATE

Chapter 16
The Boxer's Rebellion

After a fitful night in the towering walnut bed, I awoke to the heavenly smell of bacon frying. I quickly bathed and dressed, then followed the aroma of bacon and coffee, surprised at my hunger. Josephine was standing over a sizzling, black iron skillet and an elderly black man was sitting at the kitchen table, nursing a cup of coffee. He looked up pleasantly as I entered. I greeted him and pulled out the chair next to his.

Josephine turned from the stove. "This Miss Kate," she explained laconically.

He introduced himself as Albert, but before the conversation could progress further, Miss Adele walked by and saw me sitting with the Black Help. "My goodness, Kate," she exclaimed, fluttering into the kitchen "We have breakfast in the dining room!"

I shrugged an apology to the help as I left the table. In the dining room, a carafe of coffee stood majestically at one end of the polished mahogany table and two placemats were set with china. The palatial setting was so cold and formal that I wished I could eat at the cozy, linoleum table with Albert and Josephine.

As Adele poured steaming coffee into the delicate cups, I asked who was in the kitchen with Josephine.

"That's her husband, Albert. He's my yard man and general handyman."

It was hard to imagine Albert, who appeared to be frail and elderly, pushing a lawnmower. "How old are they?"

"I don't really know: they don't have birth certificates. But I imagine they're in their eighties."

"And to think, they can still work!" I exclaimed.

"Pshaw!" she scoffed. "I haven't gotten a day's work out of either one of them in the sixty years they've been here."

I was stunned at the idea that the couple had been with one family for sixty years. And it was so unattractive of Miss Adele to criticize their long service. "Why did you keep them on, if they wouldn't work when they were young?"

"Oh, you don't understand about that generation," she admonished me, waving her hand as if she were shooing a pesky fly. "Albert and Josephine were living out on my father's land, sharecropping. But once there were cotton-pickers and combines, we didn't need help to bring in the crop. Most of the sharecroppers got jobs in the city. But a few stayed on, and they were given something to do to earn their keep. Josephine and Albert always wanted to stay with us, so my father gave them the gardener's cottage at the back of the property. I'd say they get by pretty well. They draw their social security and they get food stamps."

It was hard to believe that this type of arrangement still existed. My mother had told me about families in her little town that had black dependents, but that had been 50 years earlier.

Josephine tottered into the dining room with a tray of eggs and bacon. I quickly ate every morsel, while Miss Adele smiled and commented that I had started my day off right. I finally checked my watch, wiped my mouth with the cloth napkin and ran to my bedroom for my purse and keys.

Chaos reigned on the boys' unit at 8:03 a.m. Mildred ran from the nurses' station with a syringe in one hand. "Move!" she barked as she passed me. From the end of the hall, there were sounds of techs yelling and furniture crashing into the wall. Mildred never hesitated: She ran straight into the melee and immediately came out of the Day Room, holding a struggling boy by the ear. A tech was behind her, forcing the boy's arm into his shoulder blades. They disappeared into the "Quiet Room," where the yelling continued.

"I said lay down on this bed and take the shot or you'll be tied down first!" Mildred ordered. I could hear the boy's voice arguing, but couldn't make out his words. In another moment, I saw Todd ejected from the Day Room by a muscular tech. He stumbled into the wall and then righted himself.

"I told you I didn't hit him!" Todd screamed. "I was just sitting there and he came over and started punching me! It was self-defense when I kicked him!"

"I don't care what it was," bellowed the tech. "You're on Level IV for fighting. Go to the Quiet Room or I'll have to take you"

"Man! I don't see why I should get punished!" Todd yelled as he started to the other Quiet Room. About halfway down the hall, he saw me standing at the nurses' station and his face brightened. "Miss Kate! Miss Kate! Can I talk to you?"

"You ain't talkin to nobody, Boy," interrupted the tech. "Get to the Quiet Room NOW!"

"I'll come to talk to you later on," I told him quickly. "Just settle down, now, and do what the staff is telling you."

Todd disappeared in the room, and the tech pulled a chair to the doorway to keep him in sight. I plodded to the nurses' station and sighed as I signed my name to the attendance sheet.

"Looks like it's going to be another one of those days," said a voice from the door. I turned as Jack came in.

"What happened down there?"

"The kids say it was a gang fight," he confided. "They say Todd was cracking his knuckles and Kevin thought he was 'dissing' him. So Kevin got up from his chair and started punching Todd. After that, no one's sure. Chairs got thrown; boys either ran toward the fight or away from it. It was a real mess."

"Do you think Todd's in a gang?"

"Kevin's in one. I don't know about Todd—he says not."

I asked what the current situation was and Jack responded: "Kevin and Todd are in separate Quiet Rooms. Everybody else is in a seat in the Day Room. No one was seriously hurt—there was no blood," he summarized.

Mildred came back into the nurses' station and forced the empty syringe into the sharps container mounted on the wall. "That should take care of him for a while," she said with a satisfied tone. "He'll think twice before he starts another fight on *My Unit*." She glowered at me. "And you, young lady, have got to learn to either help or get out of the way."

"I didn't know I was on the unit long enough to be in the way," I said defensively.

She sniffed. "Standing in front of the nurses' station is being in the way." Mildred turned her attention to contacting Dr. Givhup. When he answered her page, she gave him an abbreviated version of the fight, her voice dripping with honey. "Yes, sir. Well, there's no reason for you to rush right over. It's all been taken care of for now. That's right." She hung up the phone and started on her paperwork.

After working on test data for half an hour in my office, I poked my head out the door to check on Todd and to ask if I could talk to him individually.

The tech shrugged. "It's all right with me." He looked back into the Quiet Room, calling Todd to report to my door.

Todd sauntered past the tech with a cocky expression and plopped down in the vinyl chair before I could take my seat.

"So what happened this morning? You've been doing so well—all Levels I and II."

"I know it! And now Kevin's ruined everything for me. Are you going to tell the judge I got in a fight?" he asked.

I said the judge didn't need all the details, but I still needed to know what happened.

"Kevin's been on my case ever since I got here. He's always braggin' 'bout how tough he is and all the people he's whipped. I been tryin' t'ignore him, like you told me to. . ." He swallowed hard. "Well, I ignored him for a whole week, but today he was talkin' about Miss Annabeth, you know her?" I nodded. She was a cute, young nurse with boundless energy and a ready smile. "We got back from breakfast this morning and Kevin starts talkin' about her, what a great ass she's got. What he'd like to do. You know, Miss Kate, the kinda stuff he was sayin!" he summarized in embarrassment.

"That's what started the fight?" I asked incredulously.

"I couldn't let him talk about her that way!" Todd exploded. "There wasn't nobody else to help her!"

The tech pushed open the door in response to the shout. "You okay?" he asked. When I nodded, he disappeared again.

"Todd, Miss Annabeth doesn't need any help. She's a grown woman and she can stand up for herself."

"It ain't right for Kevin to talk about her that way."

"It's not right, but it's not hurting Miss Annabeth. It's just words."

He put his head into his hands and said miserably, "You just don't understand."

After I asked him to help me see his point of view, Todd looked up with an earnest expression. "Kevin could hurt her if he got the chance. Somebody had to teach him that he shouldn't try it."

"So you're going to teach him a lesson? And protect her?" He nodded his agreement. "How're you going to protect us all, Todd?" I replied in exasperation. "There's a lot of young women in the world. And a lot of jerks, too. It's a job that's too big, even for a boxer like you."

He was silent, hunched over in his chair for several minutes. "What are you goin' to tell the judge?"

"I'm going to tell him that you're a good kid who's made some bad choices."

This didn't satisfy Todd in the least. "What kind of recommendations are you gonna make?"

I explained that the entire Treatment Team would be deciding the recommendations—not just me, and I encouraged him to return to his cooperative behavior. After receiving my permission to go back to the classroom, he stood at the door, gazing longingly out the window, unaware that Jack had stepped through the threshold.

"Talking to Miss Kate?" he casually asked, effortlessly turning

Todd's attention from the outside world. "I hope you're listening to her—she's got some good advice." Jack put his arm over Todd's shoulder. "You've had a tough time this morning, haven't you, Bud? Everybody's entitled to a bad day now and then. But you need to get your levels back up and stay clear of Kevin."

Todd bent his head, mulling over the advice. "You know he wants to see you blow up so it'll ruin your chances of going home," Jack pressed. "The only way to win is to let Kevin sink his own ship."

Todd chewed on the corner of his lip before answering, "I'll be back on Level II by tomorrow."

"Way to go," he said, patting Todd on the back. Jack gave me a "thumbs up" over Todd's shoulder as he steered him toward the door. When I caught a glimpse of Todd's quick smile, it was the first time I'd felt any optimism about his future.

KATE

Chapter 17
Like a Refugee

Miss Adele, ensconced in a brocade chair in the parlor, raised a hand in goodbye without lifting her eyes from the Saturday paper and when I arrived at the Thompsons, they were distracted by a last minute change of plans. The morning gave me the unsettled feeling that I was partially invisible. In spite of their hurried exit, Shirley stopped at the door to tell me again I was welcome to entertain Russ at their house, if I decided not to have a picnic. "Either way, help yourself to the snacks," she said waving toward the kitchen cabinets.

At noon, I was still waiting for the sound of Russ's car. It was another dead Saturday. I flipped through all of the TV channels six or seven times, thumbed through the stack of magazines, tore into a package of pretzels as I waited for him. I could imagine all the reasons he was late and reluctantly concluded that the visit probably meant more to me than it did to him.

Russ pulled his rattling Datsun into the Thompson's driveway at 1:30 p.m., and before I opened the door, I took a moment to compose myself. I didn't want to seem either overly eager or petulant. I affected a slow saunter toward his car and I smiled as I walked. The all-too familiar attraction was still there, giving me a catch in my throat. How could it be that he still looked so good to me? The thick, curly hair, the hazel eyes that crinkled into a smile, the lean frame. "Hey, Babe!" he called, advancing toward me with arms outstretched. "You look great! Must be something about this place that's agreeing with you." My feet dangled above the ground as he lifted me in a tight hug. "I've been thinking about you all week!" he whispered in my ear before he settled me back on the sidewalk, continuing brightly, "This where you've been living?"

"At the first, but now I'm renting a room in this big Civil War mansion!" I laughed. When I gave him the details, he wanted to know why we wouldn't be staying in my room.

"Long story," I said by way of diversion. " I'll explain it to you in the car. Here—take the cooler. It's got stuff for a picnic."

"Great! I'm starved," Russ said, rummaging through the ice in search of a soft drink.

We drove past Adele's home on our way out of town, and Russ, awed by the grandeur of the place, referred to it as *Gone with the Wind*. I forgot to be miffed about his late arrival as I fell into easy conversation with him. I told him story after story of the hospital, Miss Adele and the Thompsons. He laughed at the flashlight tale, before catching himself in the middle of a giggle and accusing me of making up the story.

When it was his turn to describe the weeks in Mayfield without me, he hummed the new songs he and Doug were writing and hinted that a scout from Nashville was interested in the band. We were so engrossed in our conversation that we missed the turn to the park.

By the time we found a concrete table, we had passed deserted campgrounds, stacks of boats stored for the winter, and a swimming pool drained of its water. We were alone in a small state park known only to the locals.

Russ held up a bottle of red wine as we unloaded the car. "Look what Marie gave us! She said she sends you her love." I took the bottle, sensing that it was far more expensive than Marie's usual "House Wine," knowing that she must have ordered it especially for our date. We ate sandwiches and drank the good red wine from Styrofoam cups, poking sticks in our little fire while we talked.

"I brought my guitar," Russ said, pulling the case from his car. He sat on the bench with his back against the table, strumming it idly for a while, making ripples of chords and tightening the strings again and again. Eventually he announced, "I've been working on a new song…well, a new song for me. It's actually one of Tom Petty's."

In an unhurried, sensuous rhythm, he began singing "Refugee." He had changed Petty's hard-driving song into something slow and bluesy so that the languid words alternately soothed and stung: "Somewhere, somehow, somebody must have put you down…. maybe you were tied up, taken away and held for ransom… You don't have to live like a refugee."

By the time the last chord floated into the trees, I felt a new stab of regret for having left Russ behind. Tears were crowding the corner of my eyes and when he looked up from the guitar to see them, a knowing expression flashed across his face. Despite all our differences, he understood me, and wasn't that what marriage was all about?

He carefully put the guitar into the case. "You know, Kate, I'm with Petty: You don't have to live this way. I don't even know why you're down here—it's like you're trying to prove something."

I put my head down on my knees and rubbed away the salt in my eyes, my words muffled by the sleeve of my jacket. "I didn't want to leave, Russ, but … I had to take care of myself, find a job. You acted like you didn't want us to be together."

"I never said I didn't want to be with you, Kate," he insisted. "You've got it all wrong. You just got completely focused on your career and the job took first place, over everything, over being with me."

I thought about this for a while, vaguely aware that the silence between us was filled with the sound of wind in the trees but little more. I knew he was wrong but I wanted to be careful as I explained myself. "The real problem was… that the baby… never meant anything to you, Russ." I whispered, almost afraid to bring the truth back to the forefront.

He was quickly exasperated. "What baby? The pregnancy was over before we even talked about it!"

"We never talked because you didn't want to discuss it. You never wanted the baby, and you were happy when I lost him." There! I had said it. I had put the awful truth into words that stung my own lips.

He took a deep breath and let it out in a long sigh, trying to be patient. "I never said I didn't want us to have a baby…eventually.

But this just wasn't a good time to be starting a family."

I nodded silently, thinking, *I didn't plan the timing.*

Russ continued, pressing his point, "I don't really see what the problem is! You got upset and wouldn't talk to me about it. The next thing I know, you've left divorce papers for me to sign." He paused and then said through his teeth, almost as if he were cursing under his breath, "*You* walked out on *me* and I was never even unfaithful to you."

I nodded, suddenly believing he was telling the truth, certain that Michelle was only a vocalist for the band, a hired singer. For a moment, the whole idea of leaving him seemed crazy. I could just give up the fight, stop living like a refugee, get in the car and go back to Mayfield. I felt like I was careening toward another disaster. Before I answered, I pulled the tattered pieces of my emotions back, seized the unruly part of myself that wanted to fall into his arms and answered the small voice that urged me to talk about our baby, to explain so that he would finally understand.

I started slowly, saying. "Russ, when I found out I was pregnant, I was as surprised as you were. You didn't believe me, but the pregnancy was an accident." I stopped, longing to hear him say, 'I believe you now' but since he remained silent, I forged ahead, "After I got over the shock, I began to think about the baby as a real person—a boy. And somehow I knew he'd have my dark hair and your hazel eyes. I could actually *see* him when I closed my eyes at night. And I could see you rolling a ball to him at the park or carrying him on your shoulders. Then one morning I woke up cramping and bleeding and in a few hours, that little boy was gone....." I swallowed hard, fighting the tears that threatened to spill down my cheeks, begging him in my mind to understand. "Some days I felt like I should be searching for him in the preschool down the street instead of going to work. I..I just got sadder and sadder."

"I knew it was bothering you, Kate, but I didn't know what to do about it."

"There was nothing for you to *do*. I just wanted for you to be sad with me."

The edge was back in his voice. "I'm just not like that. I can't be sad about something that never really happened. It was real to you….but it was just an abstraction to me"

"Not 'it.' *He*," I insisted, feeling the anger rise in my throat.

Russ hesitated before saying, "O.K. *He*, then." After a few more pokes to the fire, Russ pressed for a resolution to his mission. "We don't have to talk about this again, Kate. I can forgive you for running away if you're ready to come home and pick up the pieces."

I watched the angry flames as they gnawed into a thin branch, feeling indignant that I was the one who needed forgiving. "I don't see how I can come back," I told him tersely. "I've got huge loans to pay off and no way to do it in Mayfield."

"Shit!" He threw his Styrofoam cup into the fire, where it hissed and then imploded. "It's not even about the baby, is it, Kate? It always comes down to the money. You know we made it for three years on your part-time jobs and my gigs. Then all of a sudden, you want more. And you've got no faith in me and my music! No faith that I'll make it all up to you later on!"

"I believe you want to…" I said, keeping my eyes on the fire.

"That ought to be good enough!" he hissed, standing abruptly. He marched the guitar to the car before he wedged the empty cooler into the trunk. "It's getting cold," he announced. "I'm ready to go."

Wordlessly I rose from the log where I'd been sitting, brushing the splinters from my pants, wishing I could walk back to Madrid, dreading the forced intimacy of the car. As he silently drove me back to the Thompsons, I stared at the evening star, low on the horizon. It was burning spectacularly, the light that was reaching my eyes already thousands of years old. The star might have been extinguished decades ago, and I could be the last one know about it, I thought, just like the love that I had lost.

LANA

Chapter 18
Lana's Hospital

Lana danced through the arched portico of the Administration Building, with an aide at her side, veering away from the foyer, where Jerry stood with his cap in his hand. Chatting gaily with the nurse, she insisted that she was on her way to Hollywood to star in a big picture with Clark Gable, or else to marry Jesus. Both men were waiting for her to make up her mind! Helen smiled, hoping this new patient would be easily led all the way to the locked unit, reminding herself again that manic patients were unpredictable. She had been slapped and punched by women who looked no stronger than this one. Nodding in response to Lana's harangue, Helen stopped at a metal door, fumbled in her pocket, and took out a large ring of keys. Lana abruptly ended her monologue and stared at the brass lock.

"Where you takin' me?" she demanded.

"Some important people want to meet you," Helen answered breezily, propping the opened door against her hip. "Come on in, Mrs. Wright. They're waiting for you."

Lana drew herself up to her full height and tossed the pathetically dirty scarf over one shoulder. She glided into the ward where thousands of patients had walked, some begging for release and others begging for sanctuary. Helen's hand no longer rested on Lana's arm; they were walking in a secure area.

The ceilings were twenty feet high and crowned with a layer of patterned tin. Doors with transoms ajar opened from each side of the hall into rooms that housed 6-8 women and were furnished with metal beds, chests of drawers and nightstands. Chairs were largely confined to the Day Room, where they were arranged in a monotonous line against the walls. At the end of the ward, the head nurse had a small office that served as a break room for the aides, as a pharmacy, and as an admitting office.

Helen unlocked the office and ushered Lana into one of the heavy, metal chairs while she slid behind the desk and reached for a form.

"What is your name?" Helen asked, pleasantly.

"Lana Turner," she answered imperiously, seemingly unaware of the soiled scarf hanging limply from her neck.

"Do you have another last name, Miss Turner? One that's not your stage name?"

"Gray. Well, Wright since I married Mr. Right." She giggled at her little play on words and then stood up in front of the desk, her feet gliding to the tune she hummed.

"Can you tell me your birth date, Lana?"

"Well, of course. But it's not polite to ask a lady's age, is it?" She wagged her finger to and fro, scolding Helen for her faux pas.

"Can you tell me where you are now?" asked Helen, unruffled by Lana's charade.

"I thought *you* would know," Lana teased.

As Helen pressed for an answer, Lana became oppositional, saying that she would not be the one to tell Helen such a secret. Sighing, Helen laid her pen on the desk and called for an aide named Rita. The young woman with short, blonde hair appeared almost immediately. "I don't think Mrs. Wright is ready to talk to us yet. Why don't you just take her down to Room 5 and get her settled in? She's going to need a bath and some clean clothes," Helen added as she wrinkled her nose in disgust.

Rita's voice was as sweet as a song, Lana thought, and she liked her from the first. As they traversed the wide, tiled hall, she confided her plans to go to Hollywood or to go to Heaven, and she gave Rita at least thirty similarities between the two destinations, ticking them off on her fingers as she talked. In the large bedroom, four of the beds were empty and three contained patients who were lying on the covers, napping in their day clothes.

"This will be your bed," Rita told her, patting the mattress. "And we'll put your clothes in this chest, when they get here."

Lana looked around the room and blinked at the strange, grey shapes, reclining on the beds. It seemed an unlikely place to be meeting important people. She leaned toward Rita with her index finger over her lips. "Sh-h. They're all asleep," she cautioned.

Rita nodded. "Let's get you a nice bath," she whispered, leading the way to the bathroom where three stalls and a large tub lined one wall. Leaning over the tub, Rita let the water cascade over her hand and felt for warmth. Lana's bare feet pattered against the tiled bathroom floor as she danced with an imaginary partner.

"We'll take these clothes off and lay them here in the chair," Rita coaxed. "What a pretty scarf. Can I see it, please?" Lana stopped in mid-twirl with her arms outstretched and stared intensely at Rita. Still cajoling, Rita touched the knitted scarf with the tips of her fingers. "That's some fine needlework, there. Did you make it yourself?" she asked, slowly unwinding the scarf from Lana's neck. "Look at the colors! I like the way you used dark red and gold together." Once the scarf was in Rita's hands, she slipped it quickly into a pocket of her smock, preventing any tug-of-war over the ownership.

"Now, let me help you with this dress," she continued, unbuttoning the front placket, while Lana stood stiffly with her arms at right angles to her body. "Put your hands over your head and we'll just slip you out of this! Skin the cat!" she called cheerfully, as she pulled the filthy dress above Lana's head and tossed it to the chair.

Rita had worked at the hospital for two years, but she was not prepared to see the signs of abuse that now confronted her: Lana's trunk was covered with dark, purple blotches and raw burns. Rita sucked her breath in through her teeth, realizing that someone had tried to deal with this young woman the way men broke horses—with rope restraints and beatings.

"You poor thing," she whispered under her breath as she gingerly unhooked the brassiere. Lana, docilely followed all directions, and since they were in the bathroom alone, Rita felt profoundly grateful for the cooperation. "We've got a nice tub full of warm water here,

Lana. Just step on in and sit down. Be careful and don't slip," she cautioned, still holding Lana's arm. "Doesn't that feel good?" Rita cooed, scooping up metal cupfuls of water to pour over Lana's back. Although Lana babbled on nonsensically, Rita could see her shoulders relaxing as the warm water streamed down her bruised back. "Let's get your hair washed, too," she asserted, hoping her luck would hold out. Without asking permission, she poured water over Lana's head and created a luxurious lather with handfuls of thin, state-issued shampoo.

When the bath was finished, Rita waited patiently while Lana dried herself and stepped into the hospital-issued cotton dress. Listening absently to the disjointed monologue, Rita wondered whether she might have met Lana on the street, or if they could have been students at the same school. Despite her bruises and burns, Rita could see that Lana had been a pretty woman. Her chiseled features and white-blonde hair made her stand out from the ordinary and with a little primping, Rita thought she would be beautiful.

Lana spent the rest of the afternoon dancing up and down the wide halls and excitedly telling disinterested patients that she would be leaving soon for Heavenwood. In the Day Room, Evie and Daisy leaned around her to keep their eyes trained on the afternoon soap operas. Some of the patients shouted at Lana when she inclined her face toward theirs. The catatonic patients sat in weird positions with their hands in ballet poses over their bobbed heads. Their rigor mortise led Lana to the conclusion that they were already dead and she avoided them.

As she made revolutions around the edge of the Day Room, she was surreptitiously observed by the aides, who chain-smoked while they gossiped and watched TV. Rita told her coworkers that Lana Gray Wright had done well in the bath. She doubted that the evening shift would have to deal with violence. Cindy, a voluptuous redhead who giggled and fluttered through the life of the hospital, overheard the comments and called her "Lanagray" for the rest of her life. At 3:00 Dr. Lundsford appeared at Helen's door and announced that he was ready to see the new patient.

He touched Helen's shoulder in a proprietary way, then threw himself into the swivel chair behind the desk. He watched her move around the office, mildly stirred by the sway of her hips against the starched, white uniform. Although she was from a working-class family, Helen was an attractive young woman; and he enjoyed the evenings he spent with her. She had a charming laugh, an upturned nose, and inquisitive eyes. Best of all, she had never made any demands for a lasting commitment.

Dr. Lundsford was a tall man with long, graceful fingers and the manner of aristocracy. He had come to Western to complete his residency and had decided to stay for a few years longer to enlarge his savings. He lived rent-free in one of the ranch-style houses built on the edge of the hospital campus. Other than an occasional trip to Franklin to visit his elderly mother, he had no expenses to speak of. A female patient came to clean his house twice a week. He paid her with whatever pocket change he happened to have. He was welcomed in the staff cafeteria whenever he wanted a quick meal, and he was also the recipient of the dietary department's gifts: milk from the dairy; hams from the smokehouse; brown eggs from the henhouse; fresh vegetables in season from the garden. His cook, Hazel, was the wife of one of the maintenance workers. Her dishes reminded him of the meals prepared by his parents' black maid— nothing fancy, but always savory.

The youngest of four children born to his prominent parents, he wore sailor suits as a toddler and starched oxford-cloth shirts as a teenager, his mother's fastidiousness creating a vanity about his appearance that would continue into his dotage. Being raised in a household with three much older sisters gave him a spectator's view of the strategies of feminine wiles. He watched as his sisters fluttered around pieces of jewelry and gold-edged invitations. They doted on him when they were at home and he grew up in many ways like a favored pet: showered with affection for a few minutes at a time and then expected to entertain himself for hours on end.

Dr. Lundsford picked up a pen from the desk and fiddled with the clip, then threw it down when he heard three sets of footsteps. Lana barged into the office, slinging her elbows back and forth to break the grasp of the aides who tried to restrain her.

"Let me go! You're hurting me!" she yelled.

Dr. Lundsford stood next to the desk. "It's okay. You may release her." The aides looked at each other quizzically and then dropped their hands. "Now, Lana," he began in his cultured and polite voice. "No one's touching you. Would you like to have a seat?" She blinked at him, momentarily confused about his identity. She became certain that she had seen his picture in a movie magazine.

"Are you from Hollywood?"

He hesitated before answering, "Why, yes. As a matter of fact, I am."

She leaned toward him and began to tell him what would happen when she reached the promised land. Her words were strung together nonsensically, the theme of Hollywood frequently derailing into talk about Brother Paul, Jesus, wife-buying and horseback riding. He sighed impatiently. Since she was hopelessly confused and disoriented, there was no reason to continue the interview. He would talk to her later. "She can go back to the Day Room now," he told the aides.

He turned to call for his favorite nurse and immediately felt a blow to the back of his head. The tape dispenser clattered to the floor as he whirled around to face his attacker. Lana's arms were again pinned by the aides, and she was furious.

"And if you're so important, why ain't you smokin' a cigar?" She pronounced it as "cee-gar," which the doctor had heard from other rural patients. "I am ready t' go to Hollywood *Right Now!*" she screamed, straining against the aides. "I got a black horse waitin' for me, outside this windah!" She jerked her head toward the glass that overlooked the campus. "And Jesus is waitin' to see me dance for the six hundred thirty-four dollars he brought from Heaven."

As he instinctively rubbed the back of his head, he felt sticky blood oozing into his closely clipped hair. "Get her out of here!"

he ordered. The aides struggled to move her to the door, but despite her small frame, Lana had planted her feet and was proving to be formidable.

Helen appeared, instantly assessing the situation and instructing another aide to help remove Lana to the control room. As they struggled to take her from the office, Lana continued to hurl epithets at Dr. Lundsford, using four-letter words and gibberish that sounded like another language.

"Are you hurt?" Helen asked as she retrieved the tape dispenser from the floor.

"No, I'm not hurt," he growled. "I'm just bleeding all over my shirt collar; that's all!"

"Where'd she hit you?"

"Here," he answered, putting his fingers to the spot.

Helen pulled his head toward her and examined it, suggesting an application of hydrogen peroxide. He collapsed in the swivel chair, watching her open a cabinet to extract cotton balls and a brown bottle of peroxide.

"We knew she was manic, but we haven't had any trouble like that with her." Helen said apologetically, "I didn't think she'd try to hurt you."

He was irritated and his pride had been wounded more than his scalp. "Well, you should have thought about potential weapons in this office," he lectured. "Manic patients are almost always irritable." She dabbed his scalp with the peroxide as he continued to scold. "I want her in that control room until we can give her a big dose of Thorazine and put her to sleep," he said. "She's in no shape to roam the unit. She'll end up hurting someone else."

Helen finished the ministrations and put the cap back on the peroxide bottle. She twisted it with quick, bird-like motions. "I'll see to it myself," she said brusquely. He realized then that Helen was chafing under his directions, and he was in no mood to smooth it over. So he walked to the metal door without waiting for an escort, unaware that as he retreated, Helen was sticking out her tongue at him.

LANA

Chapter 19
Mr. Hollywood

Lana spent the rest of the afternoon naked, pacing around the padded control room. The hospital required that clothing be removed before seclusion, in order to prevent the patient from harming himself. Lana screeched her anger and pounded on the metal door even though no rescue was forthcoming. She paced in endless circles, her bare feet pattering against the tile floor. When she had to use the toilet, she begged at the door for someone to take her to the bathroom, but since there was no response, she squatted over the drain in the sloping floor and urinated. By 6:00 p.m. when the nurse appeared with sleeping medicine in hand, Lana was cold; her voice was hoarse and her steps had begun to slow.

Three faces looked at her through the mesh in the door and the tallest aide spoke curtly. "Mrs. Wright. It is time for your medicine." The scrape of the key in the lock led Lana to believe she was about to be released, and her heart raced with the anticipation of freedom. The lead aide advanced toward Lana while two others followed, holding an olive-green blanket between them. Instinctively, Lana backed away until she felt the cold wall against her spine. The lead aide locked her gaze into Lana's while she extended two small pills in her palm. "Put these in your mouth, and I'll give you some juice to drink with it," she promised. Lana looked from one face to another, desperately wondering why Jesus had been delayed but when her eyes darted to the door, the lead aide called, "Now!" The other two rushed Lana, pinning her to the wall with the scratchy blanket. They pushed their shoulders into hers and pulled the blanket taut.

Lana began to scream, "Help! Help me! I can't breathe!" The terrible army blanket was like sandpaper against her skin, torturing every pore of her body.

Putting her face close to Lana's, the lead aide covered Lana's nose with one beefy hand and pinched her nostrils together. As she began to struggle for breath, Lana opened her mouth and felt two, fat fingers on her tongue, driving the pills to her throat. When the aide pulled her fingers away, she pushed up Lana's chin, snapping her teeth together. "Swallow that," she demanded, holding her hand over Lana's mouth and immobilizing her head against the wall. The other two aides grunted with the effort of keeping her still.

Lana's eyes rolled from side to side in terror. These women were trying to kill her! The blanket was so tight across her chest that she could not raise her rib cage to gasp for precious air. When she looked toward the door for Jesus, she saw four women of varying ages and heights standing in the hall, watching the drama. All of them had their hair cut in short bobs, with heavy bangs across the front, and they all had heavy eyebrows that met ominously in the middle. The smallest woman was agitated by the scene and pulled on the sleeve of her plump companion, hollering, "They're a-gonna give her monkey juice! They're a-gonna give her monkey juice!" When the stocky woman tired of the tugging, she first slapped the little woman, then said, "Top it, GaGa!" Holding her stinging cheek, GaGa jogged down the hall, still sing-songing, "They're a-gonna give her monkey juice!"

The bitter taste of the dissolving pills began to slide down Lana's throat. Her mouth was full of sour saliva that she could not spit out so she was finally forced to swallow. The aide noticed her Adam's apple involuntarily jerk up and down. "That's a good girl," she said matter-of-factly. "You'll feel better soon." She took her hand away and offered Lana a cup of juice. Still pinned to the wall like a butterfly in a specimen jar, Lana refused the juice, shaking her head violently. "Don't want it. Don't want it," she panted.

The lead aide shrugged her shoulders. "Suit yourself. I thought you'd like something to drink," she summarized as a stocky patient shuffled into the control room and grunted for attention. "Jui-sh-sh," she said, holding her palm out.

"Evie wants your juice. Don't you want to drink it?" Lana

continued to shake her head. "All right. Here, Evie," she said, handing the cup to the woman who turned it up like a shot of whiskey. "Now, go on back to the Day Room," she instructed her, taking the empty paper cup.

Within minutes, Lana could hardly hold her head up. The blanket was choking her, she thought, as her mind reeled drunkenly from one possibility of death to the next. She was too tired to beg for mercy and when she tried to turn to a better position, the blanket held her fast. Her eyes felt gritty until she closed them. Finally, she gave in to her exhaustion and began to doze as she stood against the wall. Still supported by the blanket, the aides allowed her to fall slowly forward so that she finished her descent at the concrete floor. Pulling the blanket tightly around her left side, they rolled her over and over, then secured the blanket with bands of cloth. In later years, mental health workers would refer to this restraint as "the green burrito," but for now, it was just a way of controlling an unruly patient. Retreating from the control room, the lead aide turned off the wire-enclosed light bulb and pulled the door shut.

For weeks, Lana felt as if she had been imprisoned in some carnival spook house. She was terrified of the leering faces, which floated out of the shadows and then faded from view. Rooms were changed on an hourly basis into new mazes and barricades. Meals were served at nonsensical times, the gorilla-like aides bringing trays when she was asleep and later removing the plates filled with long, white worms writhing in some kind of bloody, red sauce.

Mr. Hollywood, as Lana referred to Dr. Lundsford, always appeared with Betty Grable, who dressed in a nurse's uniform. Lana begged him to take her away from this frightening place and offered to give him half of her dowry when Jesus came, but the doctor refused her every plea. More days followed when Lana walked in a shuffling gait, sat in chairs with her back to the TV, was bathed by aides, urinated where ever she happened to be, and picked at the cold food that was brought to the unit. Her cyclical agitation was treated with doses of Epson's salts, which brought such violent diarrhea that Lana, too weak to move, would lie on the floor of the control room, only rising long enough to defecate into the drain hole.

Normally, the staff would not have allowed Jerry to visit while she was in such a compromised state, but he insisted and then accused them of trying to hold his wife hostage. So Helen approached Dr. Lundsford and told him that Jerry had been on the campus several times, interrogating the aides as they left the building at the close of their shift.

"So, why shouldn't he visit?" Dr. Lundsford asked as he flipped through a stack of papers in his lap. He leaned back in his leather chair, his highly polished shoes on the desk top. Helen put the clipboard in her lap and looked up at him.

"I don't think she's ready to see him," she said carefully. "She is making some slow progress: there are some days she requires less medication. But before she came in, her husband had evidently beaten her."

With a disinterested expression, Dr. Lundsford gazed out the window to Western's lush foliage, remembering the picnics he had enjoyed on the lawn of his parents' summer home. Those were wonderful, carefree days, he thought, smiling at the memories. He pulled himself back to the present and the nurse who waited on the other side of his desk. "I don't see how we can protect her from her marriage, no matter how bad it may be. He has his rights, too, you know." He looked at Helen's studious expression and smiled at her idealism. "Just send an aide to sit in on the visit. He won't do anything while someone's watching."

Helen had faith in her own common sense and her knowledge of the different classes of people. She chafed at his misguided logic. Dr. Lundsford, it seemed, was too aloof from the struggles of the common person to understand the women on the ward. Helen knew that the Wrights, for instance, were farm people. Country people lived in isolated homesteads, where they proceeded with a form of self-sufficiency that unfortunately included wife-beating and incest.

She, on the other hand, had grown up in Stantonville as a child of factory workers, and had enjoyed some advantages, primary among them, a mother who saved to give her a "nursing course." Helen knew her place in Stantonville society, where she was still just Lulabeth's daughter, and at Western, where she was in the enviable position of being younger than and better educated than the platoons of aides she supervised. Having authority on the unit was something she roundly enjoyed. At times she wished her contact with Dr. Lundsford was confined to dates instead of these debates about patients and their treatments.

Helen spoke assertively, "I don't think this is a good time to start visits, regardless of who's watching. Mrs. Wright's not ready."

Her lack of deference irritated him. "Helen, I've made my decision: Her husband can visit. He's the one who committed her so he will be allowed to see her." Dr. Lundsford dismissed further discussion by pulling a memo from the stack and holding it in front of his face.

The Western Way Helen thought, ironically: Get the patient on the road to recovery and then do something to make her sick again. She clamped her teeth together and hissed, "Where do you want him to visit then?"

"It doesn't matter to me," he said, taking his feet from the desk. He let her sit silently, clipboard in her lap for a few seconds, and then moved the memo to one side to catch her eye. "I need to check in with the other unit," he informed her. He gathered his fountain pen, carefully clipping it to his shirt pocket before he turned at the door. "By the way, Helen, I've been thinking about this weekend," he began, pausing when he saw that she was pointedly ignoring him. Not a good sign, he noted. Well, he wouldn't beg, especially not a dumb nurse in a backwater psychiatric hospital. He recovered his bearings and continued, "Normally, we'd plan to have dinner or something, but I have several things to take care of on Saturday. I'll call you later." She stood stiffly without acknowledging him and passed through the doorway without speaking.

Two days later, when Jerry phoned the hospital, Helen was summoned to take the call.

"This is Jerry Wright," a gruff voice said loudly.

"This is Helen Summers. I'm the nurse on your wife's ward."

There was a moment of hesitation before Jerry launched into his diatribe. "I want t' see my wife and ain't nobody at that hospital got the right t' keep me from her. I been tryin' t'see her for weeks now and I'm tired-a bein' put off."

"Okay."

"And another thing is, nobody's tellin' me nothin' 'bout how she's doin'. I think y'all may be holdin' her prisoner or somethin'. *I'm* the one put her in that hospital," he insisted, "and I want t' see her."

"Okay, Mr. Wright. That can be arranged."

"And another thing, when I come by, there's crazy people outside, everywhere. But she ain't never outside. Hell, she coulda been killed by now! Y'all probably killed her and hid the body. I tell you, I ain't goin' to be satisfied 'til I can see her!" His voice was raised in an angry crescendo.

"I said you can see her," Helen responded, never varying her tone of voice. Her acquiescence confused Jerry, who paused in his harangue, giving Helen the opportunity to continue. "We can arrange for a visit any day. Just let me know what would be best for you."

"Sata'dy."

"That will be fine. Check in at the admissions office and they'll bring her out to see you."

He continued to hesitate, so Helen took the initiative again. "Is there anything else I can help you with today, Mr. Wright?"

He found his voice and told her no, as he hung up the pay phone.

When Helen returned to the ward, Lana was sitting in a chair at the window of her bedroom. She turned toward Helen with blank eyes as the nurse took a seat on the bed. " I just got a call from your husband." Lana's expression melted into profound sadness, her gaze shifting downward and frown lines settling between her eyes. "He wants to come for a visit."

Her face crumpled into anguish. "No!" she screamed. The response was so immediate that it unnerved Helen, who stood up and prepared to call for help if Lana left the chair. Lana clenched her fists and screwed her eyes shut, the torrent of words tumbling like stones from a cliff. "No! No! I don't wanna see him! No! I ain't gonna see him! No!"

"Sh-h-h, Lana!" Helen commanded as she stood by the chair. She jerked her hand in a horizontal motion, as if she were slicing the air. "Sh-h. You don't have to see him today. Just settle down." But Helen's words had no effect until she dampened Lana's fear with a threat: "You need to settle down. *Now!* If you can't do it on your own, you'll go to the control room. Is that where you want to go, Lana?"

Lana's voice dropped to a whisper as she shook her head, repeating "No, No, No, No." Helen backed out of the room, refusing to turn her back on the woman in the chair. Sitting in the dusk alone, Lana's words grew slower and softer.

When Rita came to call her for dinner, she found Lana in the same chair; her knees pulled up to her chin; legs encircled by thin arms; her eyes unfocused toward the wall. Rita crouched by her side and touched her lightly on the shoulder, the unyielding position making her wonder if Lana was catatonic. "Are you ready for supper?" There was no response, not even a blink of the eye. Rita asked again and again and was finally rewarded with a slow turn of the head and a flicker of recognition in the blue eyes. "Come on, Sweetie. I know you must be hungry," she coaxed, patting Lana on the arm. After more cajoling, Lana slowly stood and shuffled with Rita to the Day Room, where trays had been delivered for the patients who were too unpredictable to leave the unit.

LANA

Chapter 20
Jerry's Visit

Jerry appeared at the admission office wearing a clean chambray shirt and blue jeans. Standing in the foyer, shifting his weight from side to side, he waited for the elderly telephone operator to acknowledge him. She finally nodded her blue hair in his direction, said she knew who he was there to see, and returned to her task of plugging and unplugging cables from the board. A half an hour later, Lana appeared, escorted by a young woman who identified herself as an aide.

"Hey, Lana," he called. The thin woman seemed to be a shadow of the girl he had admired in the weedy road. She raised her face to his voice but looked past him with a blank stare.

Rita's suggestion that they visit outside brought palpable relief to Jerry. He strode ahead of the women, inattentive to Lana's slow, unsteady steps, to the fact that she was led by the aide as if she were blind. Jerry threw himself onto a park bench and watched while Lana lowered herself onto the other end.

Jerry's persistent attempts to engage his wife and Lana's mute unresponsiveness frightened Rita. After only a few minutes, his fists were clenched and he was leaning over Lana as he talked. Rita's heart raced with anxiety. When he began shouting at his silent wife, Rita couldn't watch any longer.

"Mr. Wright! Mr. Wright! We'll set another day for a visit." He blinked his eyes as if he had forgotten she was present. Without waiting for his response, Rita gathered Lana to her side and walked her back to the building, leaving Jerry rooted to the ground.

In September, Rita began to see gradual changes in Lana. The medicine insured that she slept all night; the routine of the unit provided a sameness; the food, grown on the campus and cooked in the traditional Southern way, supplied consistent nourishment. But, most importantly, Lana's manic energy finally ebbed away, leaving the personality, the interests and the memories she had owned before her admission.

Rita was still struck by the fact that Lana never asked about returning to Mr. Wright. Most of the other married women constantly talked about going home. Lana did repeatedly ask Rita why she had been admitted, when she had arrived, what had Jerry done with her belongings, and when she might see her brothers. When the questions turned to Jerry, Rita told her about his insistence on visiting and his angry impatience. They were folding sheets and towels one day when Lana asked again about her husband.

"He came to see you, but he got really angry when you couldn't talk to him."

"But why didn't I talk to him?"

"You weren't well, yet."

"Am I well now?" she asked guilelessly, the words catching in her throat as she imagined her mysterious sickness.

Rita smoothed the wrinkles from a sheet and looked at Lana's pained expression. "I think you're getting better," she said slowly. "And the nurse and the doctor think you're improving, too." She spontaneously reached to pat Lana's arm.

"Do you think my daddy could bring my little brothers to see me?"

"Why sure, Sweetie. They could visit with you by the duck pond. I bet the boys would like that, wouldn't they?"

Lana nodded, then questioned, "How will they know to come visit me?"

Rita hesitated. "Maybe you could ask your husband to bring them."

She slowly shook her head. "He won't do it. He don't like `em."

What kind of man could hate little children, Rita asked herself as she drew a blank on how to proceed. After a few minutes, Lana broke the silence. "Rita, do you think they'll ever make me go home?"

Rita held the edge of a towel in midair. "Don't you want to go home some day?"

Looking down, Lana said under her breath, "No, not to Jerry's house."

"Well, then, we'll just have to see what the doctor can work out," she pronounced with a forced cheerfulness.

They continued to fold and stack the linens that would be used by the entire ward. The aroma of sunshine on clean cotton gave Lana a stab of homesickness and she buried her face in one of the sheets, drinking in memories of hanging wash on her daddy's clothesline. *Who would have ever thought,* she said to herself, *that I would miss doing the laundry.*

Rita, watching Lana from the corner of her eyes, began again, "Sometimes it's best to just think about what you can do to feel better today, Lana. For right now, you're in a safe place." Lana took the sheet away from her face and smiled.

LANA

Chapter 21
The Magic Bus

When her behavior became more predictable, Lana began to eat in the hospital cafeteria with the other patients. She liked to sit next to Lucy, who was known as "The Bird Lady." The thin, elderly woman had been a resident at the hospital for so long that no one could remember when or why she had been admitted. She was mute but could sometimes be heard whistling in the tiled bathrooms. The aides thought she must enjoy hearing the echoes of her birdcalls. Lucy had "grounds privileges," which allowed her to leave the unit at any time, wander the campus without supervision, and return to her ward as she pleased. Although she was encouraged to eat everything on her tray and although the other patients were discouraged from sharing food, Lucy routinely filled her pockets with leftover bread. She communicated by pointing to the biscuits while begging with her eyes. Some of the women vindictively stuffed their bread in their own mouths, making their cheeks into chipmunk pouches. Many of them, however, surreptitiously placed the bread from their trays into Lucy's waiting palm. Lana, who quickly became one of the "givers," also learned to follow Lucy to the Black Gum tree where the songbirds waited. Lana watched in silent wonder as wrens and sparrows fluttered around Lucy, as if she were an emaciated St. Francis.

On Thursday afternoons, the Recreation Deptartment provided rides in the white bus, sporting a State of Mississippi seal on each door. Lucy never wanted to leave the campus, but Lana had noticed how eagerly the other women waited by the door. After she had been at Western for several months, she shyly asked Rita if she could go. Rita cocked her head to one side and surveyed Lana from that artist's angle before saying that she thought it would be fine.

Two weeks passed and then, as the women returned to the ward one Thursday after breakfast, an aide told Lana to get in line at the locked metal door. She took her place with the group of excited patients and waited to hear why they had been herded to the parking lot.

Lana climbed the steps of the bus, astounded at its height and length. The seats were so elevated that she was looking down on the heads of the patients still waiting to board. She scanned the campus from this new perspective, seeing groves of trees, a rose garden and a lake where ducks serenely floated. Her attention was arrested by a short, bald-headed man who had taken up a position by the right, front tire. He bowed grandly to each passenger, his round face flushed with pride. "Ladies First!" he recited, smiling broadly and offering his hand to the women who were boarding. As the restless male patients milled around the bus, he glowered at them and silently dared them to approach the door. When the bus was full, Lana expected him to take the driver's seat but was surprised to hear a male aide say, "That's enough now, Buster! Go sit down." His gallantry deflated, the little man shuffled to the back of the bus and collapsed in a seat.

With the last patient seated, the driver gripped the chrome pole and swung himself into the bus, plopping down behind the wheel. He looked at the faces in the large, rear-view mirror. "Everybody ready?" he called. As he caught Lana's attention in the mirror, she could see how young he was—barely out of school, she thought, watching his brown eyes crinkle in a smile. "Hey, Missy," he called to her. "This your first time on the Magic Bus?" She nodded. "Well, we'll have to do the grand tour today, just for you." Billy Wayne pushed the stick shift down into first gear and the bus lurched forward.

Seated just behind him, Lana was struck by how much the driver seemed to enjoy his job. He bounced in the seat as he worked the pedals with both feet and shifted the gears. The bus shuddered as it struggled up hills and whined as it gathered speed toward the valleys. The driver smiled constantly and kept up a good-natured patter with patients and fellow employees.

As they left the hospital grounds, Billy Wayne patted his shirt pocket and extracted a pack of gum. He put a stick in his mouth and then looked at Lana in the rear view-mirror, offering her a piece. She declined with a shake of her head, but Evie, who was sitting next to her, eagerly reached for the package and quickly stuffed all four pieces in her mouth. Billy Wayne laughed good-naturedly at her greed. "Don't choke on that, now!" he cautioned her.

During the next hour, they passed farmhouses and fields, while Billy Wayne tried to engage Lana with observations on the scenes passing her window. "Now that's Pearson's Pond," he said nodding his head toward the right. "It's got some of the best bream in the county. Rodney knows all about it." Billy Wayne confided in a stage whisper, "He fishes over there any day he can sneak away from work! That is, if he ain't out fishing for a new girlfriend!" One of the aides laughed and said that Billy Wayne had been to the same fishing hole. "Shoot! The Pine Ridge Club's too rough for me!" Billy Wayne hooted, wagging his head from side to side. The bus slowed to a crawl at a fork in the road.

The country store that sat in the road's fork was known as "The Y." The generous front porch was decorated with tin signs, advertising RC cola, Prince Albert snuff, and King Biscuit flour. The signs left trails of rust on the weathered, grey walls. When the bus screeched to a halt, the little, bald man immediately jumped from his seat and ran to his post at the front of the bus. "Ladies first!" he called out triumphantly. The women on the bus stood and shuffled to the door, where he carefully took their hands to guide them down the last step. When an errant man appeared in the aisle, Buster bellowed, "Ladies first!" in an increasingly menacing tone. Lana sat quietly, unsure why everyone was leaving the bus since they clearly had not returned to the hospital. When all the other women had stepped down, Billy Wayne turned in his seat and said, "Missy, that means you, too, don't you think?" She stood uncertainly. "Come on, it's time to get off and stretch your legs," he encouraged.

She started down the steps where the little man still stood, wiping the sweat from his red face with a dingy handkerchief. He quickly put the square of cotton in his shirt pocket and gallantly extended his hand to her. "Ladies first!" he said, beaming. Lana stepped to one side, barely avoiding the rush of male patients who thundered from the bus. As she blinked in the glare of sunlight, Billy Wayne jumped down the stairs to the gravel parking lot.

"Want a cold drink? It's okay. I got money for everyone," he reassured her as she followed him up the steps to the cool, dark store. At the counter, patients asked for cigarettes, candy and lighter fluid as Billy Wayne elbowed his way to the front. He told the merchant how many cold drinks he would be buying and left the patients to pick out "the extras" with their own spending money. The thin storekeeper, bending over the cash drawer looked to Lana like a question mark. And the cool, dark interior reminded her of Mr. Eddie's store. She remembered his interrogation about who would be paying for the pot roast and the unwelcome memory made her shiver so that she turned on one heel and retreated back to the front porch. When Billy Wayne reappeared, he had two RC's from the cooler. A mist wafted from the opened tops and ice slivers ran down the sides. He handed one bottle to Lana and then took a seat in the rocker next to hers.

When he took a long swallow from his bottle, Lana did the same, gratefully letting the cold liquid slip down her throat. She cut her eyes in his direction, shyly thanking him for the drink.

"Oh, you're more 'an welcome, Missy."

Groups of patients began to reappear on the porch, some talking and laughing, others silent. They wandered among the trees that framed the little store or sat on the edge of the porch, letting their feet dangle in the dusty air.

Billy Wayne ignored them as he continued. "So this is your first bus ride. Well, what'd you think?" He looked hopefully toward the somber woman, who was taking tentative sips from the cola bottle.

"It's nice," she answered laconically, temporarily crushing his hopes for conversation.

"Want t' go back by a different way?"

She considered this option, wondering if the bus might round an anonymous curve and suddenly be in sight of her father's house. If that happened, would she see her brothers in the yard? Would she be able to call out to them against the wind that rushed through the windows? Would this man stop the bus and let her get off? It all seemed too much to hope for. She shrugged her narrow shoulders. "It don't matter t' me how we go back…I just like being off the ward."

"I feel the same way myself" he confessed. "It's good to get away from the hospital sometimes."

They sat in silence for several minutes, Lana lost in thought about summer and what must be happening at home. The garden, her brothers playing in the dirt front yard, either Jerry or her daddy coming home wearing a shirt that was dark with sweat. She felt momentarily confused about the identity of the tired man entering the house, but Billy Wayne was talking again, so she released her memories and turned her face to his.

"I haven't even asked you what your name is," he said apologetically. "Mine's Billy Wayne," he announced, extending his calloused palm. "Billy Wayne Gordon."

She took the tips of his fingers carefully, as if she could break the big hand by squeezing it. "I'm Lana," she said, as she pulled her hand away and took another sip of the RC.

"Pleased t' meet you, Lana. So this the first time you've ever been to the Y? Or d' you live around these parts?"

"First time."

"It's a nice store," he mused. "I've known Mr. Dan all my life. When I was little, I'd come up here to buy bait; and then I'd go fishing down there on Caney Creek," he said, pointing to a line of trees and bamboo that edged the cotton field. "The creek's just on the other side of that cane break. There's some good fishing spots down there. A couple of deep pools where the fish like t' rest in summertime. You ever seen Caney Creek?" She shook her head.

"That's a shame. It's real pretty back there." He took another swallow of his drink. "Mr. Dan, he's always been good to me. I think he'd put in an extra cricket or two for me when I was a kid." He winked at her, then scanned the line of trees. "I sure have caught some good crappie down there," he said, more to himself than to Lana. "You like to fish?"

She turned his simple question over in her mind and then responded, "I don't know. I never been fishin'."

"You're kidding!" he said, incredulous at her deprivation. "Never been fishing?"

She shook her head.

"Why, it's one of the best things you can do in the summer! Catch a mess of fish; then have you a fish fry; invite all your kinfolks and friends. I've had a million of 'em at my house!"

The corner of Lana's mouth turned upward in a thin smile, and Billy Wayne realized it was the first time he had seen even the hint of amusement on her face. He corrected himself, "Well, maybe not a million, but plenty of them. Enough to feed half the county. You think I'm joking, but my daddy used to have forty, fifty people in the front yard, waiting on the fish to get done." He hesitated. "You ever cooked fish?"

Her eyes crinkled into a smile as she said 'yes.' "Well at least you know about that!" he remarked, shaking his head again at the thought of someone who had never held a fishing pole.

The last aide emerged from the store, sliding a pack of cigarettes into his front pocket. "I guess everybody's got what they wanted," the aide surmised. "We'll be ready to go whenever you are, Billy Wayne." Continuing down the stairs, the aide joined a group of smokers standing under the wide branches of an oak tree.

"Miss Lana," Billy Wayne began, gaining her attention. "Sometime when we have a fishing trip down on the river, I'll be sure you get to go, too. Would you like that?"

She smiled an enigmatic, crooked grin, before adding hesitantly, "I'm not sure I'd be any good at it, but I'd like to go."

Billy Wayne slapped his palms against his thighs. "Well, we'll be sure you get to go on the next one. The Recreation Department plans a fishing trip every month or so in the spring and summer. See that heavy-set lady sitting under the tree? She's one of the best fishermen at the hospital. Likes to use Catalpa worms. I'll see if I can line you up to sit next to her. You'd learn a lot just by watching her."

Too soon, Lana thought, they were called to board the bus and start back to the hospital. She had forgotten how much she enjoyed sitting outdoors, and she felt a creeping despair as she shuffled with the other patients toward the bus.

LANA

Chapter 22
The Ceramics Shop

Some of the patients had spending money for the canteen where they bought "the extras": gum, cigarettes, candy, soft drinks. Eventually Lana gained the courage to approach Daisy, a thin, elderly patient who had been unfriendly but not unkind. When Lana asked how patients received their money, Daisy looked at her hard and long, her mouth moving from side to side in a chewing motion. Finally she laid aside the piece of gingham she was gathering and said, "Ceramics Shop."

Her terse answer confused Lana. "You mean they give you money there?"

Daisy picked up the fabric and resumed her basting stitch. "You sell your things," she said with a note of finality that told Lana the discussion was over.

Later that day when she sought out Rita, the young aide laughed at Lana's questions. "Daisy works in the ceramics shop and she makes the clothes for those porcelain dolls. When one of her dolls sells, she gets part of the money."

Lana was eager to be included in a program that involved crafts, and she pestered Rita about the privilege until Rita gained permission from the hierarchy of supervisors and nurses. *It's nice to see Lana become interested in something*, Rita thought. She had spent entire months either in a manic tear or so medicated and weak that she could barely speak.

The ceramics shop in the new Claiborne Building was a place of wonder for Lana. Greenware in all shapes and sizes lined the walls, and long tables with assorted brushes and paints stood in the middle of the room. Fellow patients were already at their seats with projects in hand, carefully painting eyelashes on doll heads or tiny flowers on vases. Lana walked behind them, exclaiming at the beauty of their work and complimenting the women on their artistic flourishes, while two disinterested aides stood in the corner, deep in conversation. The aides answered what few questions the patients asked without ever losing eye contact with each other. Lana believed they were telling secrets because they whispered to each other. She hesitantly approached them, asking what she should do.

"Just get anything you want from the shelf by the window," the taller aide told her, pointing briefly in the direction of the sunshine. Lana slowly walked to the shelves of greenware, marveling at the selection of bric-a-brack. As she reached for a candy dish, a loud voice protested, "Don't touch that! It's mine!"

"Sorry," she said over one shoulder. She gazed at the greenware on the top shelf; surely it had not been claimed.

Again she reached with a tentative hand and heard another voice command, "I'm a gonna work on that one next!"

This little scenario was repeated four times before Lana hopelessly turned from the shelf and found an empty chair at the table. Unwilling to risk any further ill will, she folded her hands in her lap and watched the women as they painted.

Another fifteen minutes passed with Lana simply observing, before a large woman at the end of the table stood up and glared at her. "What're you looking at, Bitch!" she yelled.

"Why, n-nothing!" Lana stammered, her heart racing uncontrollably. She leaped to her feet, instinctively knowing she should run away.

"Don't give me that! I seen you watching everything I was doin' so you could steal it later!" The big woman slammed the doll head on the table, shattering the porcelain face as well as a nearby cream pitcher. "There! Ain't nobody getting it now!" she proclaimed with a self-satisfied smile.

Flora let out a wail, "Oh-h-h! My pitcher!" She picked up the larger pieces and examined the jagged edges before looking toward the aides, who were reluctantly breaking off their conversation. "Miss Effie! Mavis broke my pitcher!" She held up the shattered pieces as fat tears rolled down her cheeks.

The aides moved toward the table, but Mavis stood defiantly glaring at the paint brushes raised in midair and the fearful faces. She pointed at Lana. "She's botherin' me!" she bellowed, pointing at Lana who stood with her palms frozen in a gesture of surrender.

This skinny little, blonde woman is too meek to pose much of a threat to Mavis, the taller aide thought as she took Mavis by the left elbow. "Come on back to the ward, Mavis," she said.

Mavis turned slowly to look at the aide and said with a malevolent grin. "I ain't goin' no where. It's my turn to be in the shop."

The other aide took Mavis' right elbow. "You can come back another time," she placated.

Mavis slung her elbows free and dived forward on the table, flailing her arms as she landed. Lana and the other patients jumped away from the flying greenware as the melee began. The aides struggled to subdue her, but Mavis' size and strength were formidable. "Get help!" the smaller aide panted, and Daisy ran to the door and jerked it open, Lana close behind her. Lana didn't know where they were running to or for whom they were searching, but she believed any place would be safer than the ceramics shop. As they rounded the corner, Daisy bounced off a startled Billy Wayne, who had been talking to another worker in the hall.

"Fight! Fight!" she hollered.

He looked at Lana, who was wringing the hem of her blouse. "Where's it at?" he asked.

"Fight! Fight!" Daisy bellowed.

"Lana! Where's the fight?"

She was so frightened that her thoughts were mired, and she couldn't remember the word "ceramics." So she grabbed Billy Wayne by the hand and began running toward the work room. As they drew closer, he could hear the sounds of shouting and of glass breaking. He broke Lana's grasp and pushed open the door to see Mavis backed in a corner with her hands on the open shelving. As reinforcements entered the workroom, she heaved her shoulder against the shelves and sent the bookcase toppling to the floor. The crash of breaking glass was deafening.

"Jackie, get everyone back to the ward," Billy Wayne instructed the smaller aide, who herded the women from the room with outstretched arms. Lana, like the others, trotted away from the workroom but continually glanced over her shoulder to catch a glimpse of the scuffle.

Billy Wayne and two aides stood blocking the door. There was nothing left to break. When Mavis drew a deep breath and proclaimed that she wasn't going anywhere, Billy Wayne spoke quietly, "You know you can't stay in here, Mavis. There's not even any place to sit down."

"I ain't tryin' to sit down," she proclaimed, still a little breathless from the strenuous clearing of shelf and table.

"Come on, Girl," Billy Wayne said, stepping toward her. "Let's go." She let him step within striking distance, the other two behind him, before she grabbed a gallon of paint and swung the can toward him. He ducked, then rushed her, tackling her at the hip. As they fell backwards, the other aides ran to grab her arms. They were scuffling in shards of glass, and some of the pieces were piercing their clothes, leaving a growing smear of blood on the floor. Other aides heard the cursing and shouting and ran to help.

Someone found a nurse, who appeared at the door with a syringe of brown liquid. By the time Mavis was subdued, three male aides were considered late for their shifts, Billy Wayne's hands and knees were stabbed with slivers of glass, and Mavis had gashes in her trunk, legs and face.

The medication caused almost immediate lethargy. They dragged Mavis to a control room on the nearest unit, and she was already snoring when Billy Wayne hobbled to the door.

"Where d'you think you're going?" the nurse demanded.

"Home."

"Not `til we get this whale undressed," she insisted.

"That ain't my job," he protested, taking another step. "Well, I'm in charge of this unit and I say it *is* your job. Now help me roll her to one side."

Seeing no other option, Billy Wayne crouched on one side of the sleeping woman and put his hands under her massive shoulders and hips as the nurse pulled Mavis by the arm. She flopped on her back and the nurse began unbuttoning the blouse, muttering about her plight in life. She deftly pulled the clothing from the mountain of flesh.

Billy Wayne would say later that Mavis wasn't the first naked woman he had ever seen, but she was the one he tried his best to forget. With her clothing removed, Mavis looked like a shapeless piece of dough that had been carelessly dropped on a slab of concrete. The folds of skin on her abdomen hid most of her pubic hair, and her ponderous breasts were slung to each side, the nipples pointing toward the floor. Varicose veins, the size of fat, purple worms, lay across her thighs.

Billy Wayne stood painfully, the pieces of glass working their way back and forth into his knees. He staggered from the room before the nurse could insist on any other chores. The sound of Mavis' snoring grew dimmer as he reached the door to the hall.

He crossed the rolling campus, limping down the gravel road to his brother's house as he reasoned that he would surely find someone at home who could treat his injuries. Clyde was in charge of the dietary department and his wife, Betty, was a housewife who didn't drive. He opened the screen door and stepped in without knocking.

"Yoohoo!" came the answer from the kitchen. When she turned from the sink, her plain face paled with fear. "Billy Wayne! What in the world has happened to you?" She wiped her hands on her apron and hurried toward him, her eyes darting from one bloody smear to the next. He collapsed in the kitchen chair before answering.

"Got in a scrap with a patient," he explained. "She tore up the ceramics shop and then we had to wrestle with her in all that glass."

Betty was already dabbing at the blood on his face with the corner of her apron. "Sakes alive!" she whispered.

The screen door slammed and a heavy footstep sounded across the plank floor to the kitchen. "Good Lord, Billy Wayne! I hope the other man looks worse `an you do!" Clyde exclaimed.

"Woman," Billy Wayne corrected him.

"Woman?! Hell, brother, what you doin' fightin' a woman?"

Billy Wayne let his head fall back to look up at Clyde, who was standing behind his chair. "She's a patient. She tore up the whole ceramics shop and the aides couldn't handle her, so they called for help."

"Well, you're goin' hafta figure out a better way to help than this! You're a mess."

"I know that," Billy Wayne responded tersely. "Everybody that was wrestling with her looks just like this."

"Uhm," Clyde muttered, unimpressed. As he walked out of the kitchen, he called back over his shoulder, "Betty can probably get you doctored-up, and you can stay for supper if you're a mind to."

Having Billy Wayne share a meal with them was something Betty always welcomed. In most ways, her life with Clyde had been lonely and isolated. Her own family lived an hour away, and visits with them were rare. She didn't allow herself feelings of self-pity, however, and reminded herself that at least she had a home of her own. She didn't have to share living quarters with her elderly parents and maiden aunts.

On the ward, women were milling through the halls and dayrooms, too agitated to sit and watch TV. Helen gathered them in the dayroom while she stood in the doorway with her clipboard resting against one hip.

"Listen, everybody!" she commanded. "I know that Mavis caused a problem today at the ceramics shop," she said loudly, gaining the attention of most of the women, if only momentarily. "She is in the control room on Unit K and she will be there until she can behave. I don't want to have to put anyone else in the control room," she ended ominously. "You need to sit down and be quiet now."

Patients were milling in slower circles and some were finding seats. Lana had been pacing around the beds in her room, before joining the others in the dayroom. She wasn't sure that she would ever ask to go to the ceramics shop again. The safest place in the hospital seemed to be in her own bed.

Billy Wayne fell asleep in the rocking chair after dinner, and his sister-in-law insisted to Clyde that he be allowed to stay for the night. "He's exhausted," she argued. "What's the point in makin' him drive home?"

"He needs to grow up," growled Clyde. "When I was his age, I was already workin' with Uncle Jim in the loggin' woods. Mama spoiled Billy Wayne 'cause he was the baby."

"That's not his fault," she persisted as she jerked back the chenille bedspread. "Billy Wayne's a good-hearted boy, and I don't hear nothin' about him at the hospital but compliments.

"He wouldn't even *be* at the hospital if I hadn't talked to Art."

"Well, everybody needs a little help when they're first startin' out. You'd still be loggin' and I'd still be choppin' cotton if somebody hadn't helped us," she pointed out.

Clyde glared at her across the expanse of white sheets, momentarily considering a night on the couch, before realizing that Billy Wayne was bound to spend the night there. Clyde set his jaw as if he were about to lie down in a bear's den. He climbed into the bed, rolled to face the wall and fell asleep.

Since the next day was a Saturday, Betty again opposed Clyde by insisting that Billy Wayne be allowed to sleep late, another vice that her husband frowned upon. Even though Clyde stormed around the kitchen and let the screen door bang behind him, Billy Wayne did no more than adjust his shoulders against the scratchy brown sofa. When he awoke, it was 10:30 and his brother was at the hospital, supervising the Saturday kitchen workers. His sister-in-law greeted him as she swung open the kitchen door, a laundry basket on one hip. As Billy Wayne looked up from his cup of coffee, she was struck with how much this younger brother looked like her husband. They shared the same broad faces, the same sandy-brown hair. But Billy Wayne's smile was dazzling, while Clyde's mouth was usually downturned in an expression of disapproval. Fleetingly she wondered if Clyde had ever been as good-natured as the young man who sat at her table.

Offering him breakfast, she expertly pulled a black skillet from the oven and put a dollop of bacon fat in the bottom. Billy Wayne was more grateful for the company than the good food, although he considered himself fortunate on both accounts. He often felt isolated, almost forgotten, in the little clapboard house where his parents had once lived. Subsequently, his meals were mostly snacks, eaten while he stood over the sink or relaxed on the front porch.

The Gordon family home, built on Indian Creek, was less than a quarter of a mile from the hospital grounds. After their mother died, Clyde had urged Billy Wayne to stay on at the homeplace, pointing out that no one was ready to see the property sold to strangers. And since Billy Wayne had no other prospects, staying in the old family home seemed to be the best resolution for everyone.

But sometimes Billy Wayne ruefully wondered if he had made the right decision. When he returned home later that morning, he pondered the fact that he knew the home as intimately as he knew his own body. He was born in an iron bed in the back bedroom, the last child, the "change-of-life baby," the supposed cure for his mother's female problems. Letting himself in the front door, his eyes slowly adjusted to the gloom and he could see his family everywhere: his mother at the cookstove with her back to the door; his father in the chair by the hearth, a poker in his hand to jab at the logs; his brother Mac, whittling in a chair by the fireplace; Ben, sitting at the table, cleaning his shotgun with an oily rag. The ghosts of his family were more alive to him than his brother Clyde.

He eased himself into the chair that had been his father's and dozed for a while; then he awoke and filled the bathroom sink with water. Gingerly sudsing and rinsing his face, he studied his injuries. His left eye was puffed and purple and he had shallow cuts and scratches on both cheeks. His injuries, he concluded, were more embarrassing than serious.

Spending a Saturday at home, with no plans and no projects, brought Billy Wayne to the point of claustrophobia. Eventually he pulled a kitchen chair to the front porch and busied himself by cleaning his guns, sharpening his knives, and making idle plans for squirrel hunting. By Monday morning, he had lived with boredom for what seemed like weeks, and he had conquered the shame over his injuries. He took a fair amount of good-natured ribbing from the other men in the recreation department, but most of them were sympathetic because Mavis was legendary for her malevolence as well as her strength.

LANA

Chapter 23
Rose Gardens and Dances

With grounds privileges, Lana was free to wander the campus, and she slowly realized that the vast gardens she had seen from the window were tended by patients. She longed to work with them, believing that if she could just sink to her knees and let her fingers knead the soil, she would somehow regain the rhythms of her earlier life.

Platoons of patients were assigned to keep the vegetable garden free from weeds, and a few worked in the stately rose garden, nestled against the entrance gate. Occasionally someone complained about having to "chop weeds," but most patients were working in the gardens because they wanted to, because they had always had a vegetable garden at home and because they felt useful when they had a part in growing food. Lana approached Rita to ask how patients received these assignments, but with a disapproving frown, Rita told her not to get started with a garden assignment or she would be working there "from sunup to sundown." Rita added matter-of-factly, "Your complexion isn't suited for working out there."

Rather than seeking permission, Lana decided she would simply stroll to the rose garden on the next sunny day and offer to help. She had mixed results: Most of the patients saw the rose garden as a privileged place, and they were not interested in sharing their territory with an interloper. She sat on a bench near one grizzled little man, whose concave cheeks told her that he had lost his teeth years ago. She watched him working lime into the soil around the roots and then closed her eyes to savor the warmth of the sun and the fragrance of the roses. When she opened her eyes, the little man was still on his knees, but he was squinting hard at her face.

"'Bout t' go t' sleep, ain't you?"

"Just wonderin' about this garden," she confessed. He abruptly returned to his task at the roses' roots, threading his fingers tenderly into the soil. "I'd like t' learn how t' take care of roses," she said wistfully.

"Humph."

"You been tendin' `em for very long?"

"Been here thirty-two years."

She almost gasped. Surely he couldn't have been in the hospital for so long! As she began her mental arithmetic, she thought about him coming to Western as a young man. Perhaps as a vigorous young man, who sauntered up the streets in town and smiled broadly at his girlfriend. So he came to Western in the 1920's. How did people come to the hospital then? By wagon? By train? With family members leading them, bound and gagged? Her mind flitted from one scenario to the next as she watched him work.

"I know what you're a-thinkin'," he said, watching her from the corner of his eyes. "That it's a lo-ong time. And it is. A whole lifetime."

She nodded, afraid to ask the questions that circled through her mind.

"I used to see about leaving," he continued, turning his attention once more to the soil. "But after a while, I didn't want to have to start all over again out there." He punctuated his disdain for the wider world by jerking his head toward the highway. "Even if you go home, there's always somebody watchin' you, followin' you, tryin' to trip you up."

He picked up a sharp trowel and began to stab the dirt. "One of my neighbors was like that," he said abruptly. "Always sneaking `round my house. I could hear him at night, walkin' around in the rafters. Sometimes he'd peep in the back windows, tryin' to catch a look at my wife. I'd have to run out on the porch and fire a warnin' shot in the air. But after two or three times, I got tired of warnin' him and decided I'd just shoot him the next time he set foot on my property." He made a few more jabs into the soil and then concluded, "I didn't have to wait long."

The conversation was over and Lana knew it. She silently stood and tiptoed away from the paranoid murderer, who lovingly tended the fragrant tea roses.

The weeks inched by and the village that was known as "Western" moved in a kind of parallel universe, next to Madrid, but not quite of Madrid. As fall turned to winter, the rose bushes were pruned to ugly stubs, and Lana no longer saw the gaunt man working in the beds. Mavis was allowed to return to the ceramics shop on Tuesdays, when there were fewer patients in the room. She was also allowed to put her works-in-progress into a locked cabinet to prevent other patients from tampering with them. The poker game, which had been played in the dairy barn for the last twenty years, continued after Rudy's death, and his seat was eventually filled by a newcomer to the hospital, who had only been a patient for nine years. Rudy had enjoyed a full life at Western State but had wronged a fellow patient, who later doused his bed with lighter fluid and incinerated him while he slept. The doctor always thought it was a gambling grudge that had been dramatized to the extreme, but there were no family members to complain, no investigation to launch and no one to accuse of murder. Rudy was buried in the patient cemetery beneath a brick numbered 1029.

Daisy began to make smocked pillows and baby clothes out of pink and blue gingham. The new items sold well in the patient store, providing her with money for cigarettes and candy bars. Occasionally she broke off a piece of her Baby Ruth and gave it to Lana, while they strolled back from the canteen. Buster was still the self-appointed guardian of etiquette on the bus. But if someone else managed to say "Ladies First," Buster flew into a rage, balling up his fists and shaking them in front of his chest, while his face and bald scalp turned beet-red. "Ew-w-w! I wanted to say that!" he screamed between clenched teeth. The laughter of the aides only fueled his anger and brought him to the point of aggression. He pushed one unsuspecting worker face down in a mud puddle and earned a two-week stay in the control room. The flock of birds that waited for Lucy had grown ever larger, and some of the nurses had begun to grouse about the droppings on their cars. There was talk of revoking Lucy's ground privledges.

In the eastern tower, "Squirrel man" lived in isolation due to three previous attempts to harm his fellow patients. He was a brilliant man who had once graduated from the University of Mississippi, magna cum laude, with a degree in literature. His real name was Mullins, but he was known as Squirrel man because he fed the squirrels crumbs from his cornbread. After Squirrel man tried to suffocate his roommate for snoring, he was placed in isolation until Dr. Lundsford could declare him safe to return to the unit. He had been living in the tower, now, for three years. The isolation did not seem to dampen his passions. He spent most days composing epistles to his relatives and to the Memphis *Commercial Appeal*, delineating the injustice of his commitment. The staff allowed him to write with crayons on scrap paper. Squirrel man may have been able to read his tomes, but if they had been mailed, it was unlikely anyone else could have deciphered them.

The smiling, wiry man known as "Lo-lo," (because that was the only sound he made when speaking) continued to act out his obsession about lint, methodically collecting it and storing it in his shirt pockets. With a steady pincer-grasp, he picked lint off any patient or staff member who was unfortunate enough to be within arm's length. One Saturday while the Candy Stripers were helping with a Halloween carnival, Lo-lo noticed a piece of lint on one of the young volunteers who leaned into a booth. Stealthily he approached her and carefully but firmly pinched the lint from her buttocks, sending the terrified teenager over the counter in a screaming somersault. "Lo-lo-lo-lo!" he responded. happily holding up the offending piece of lint for everyone to admire.

No one punished Lo-lo for his breach of etiquette, but the Candy Striper spent the rest of the carnival imprisoned in the nursing supervisor's office. "That's the Western Way," explained Rita when Lana questioned her about the incident.

Dr. Lundsford and Helen had forgotten their squabble and were spending most Friday and Saturday nights at his home. Knowing that the telephone operators kept track of the whereabouts of all professional staff, Dr. Lundsford insisted that Helen go to her own apartment after their lovemaking sessions. Helen resented the banishment, but she acquiesced to his demands because she believed that Dr. Lundsford might eventually be inspired to propose. She knew that prayers were sometimes heard, and she occasionally sent up a small one for an engagement ring.

During the chaplain's prayer time on the men's unit, one patient prayed that God would make Dr. Lundsford start the dances again. Another man said he hoped that God would let him kiss that "pretty blonde" he had seen standing by Daisy in the canteen. Still another said he hoped God would let Cindy come back to the paint shop, where he worked, because she was "just full of lovin'."

In the basement of the Administration Building, B.F. ran a bait shop, where he sold worms he had collected from the banks of the Neshobee River. His schedule allowed him to collect worms and crickets on pretty days and sell them when he didn't want to leave the shelter of the hospital. Occasionally Luther went with B.F. to the riverbank, but Luther was more interested in building a lean-to than digging worms. By stealing lumber from the carpentry shop, Luther eventually built a hut, where he could rest from the demanding hospital routine and entertain lady friends he met at the dances.

In the big auditorium of the Administration Building, dances had been held for decades. Originally it may have been a fiddle and a man to "call" the square dances, but by the time Lana came to the hospital, music was provided by a local country band. The dances had been temporarily suspended after "Big John" decided to borrow a guitar and take his place on stage. When the musician protested, Big John broke the guitar over the owner's head and sent him sprawling on the floor. The resulting fracas led Dr. Lundsford to suspend the dances until the agitated patients could be sorted out from the aggressive ones. There was also the problem of finding a new band, for word had spread among the local musicians that Western's dances were a risk to instruments.

When the dances were reinstated that fall, Lana watched the preparations with ambivalence. She was eager to attend yet fearful of being in another group that might include Mavis. Some of the women made appointments to have their hair coiffed at the hospital's beauty salon and returned to the unit with ribbons and ringlets that bounced as they walked. Surprisingly, Lucy wanted to go to the dance, although Lana couldn't imagine her relating to anything but a bird. Cindy had spent several hours putting on makeup, but she was unconcerned about the boundaries of her lips, so her bright red lipstick stretched from one ear lobe to the other. Daisy had used her money to buy a new pair of rhinestone earrings that sparkled as she laced her tennis shoes in the slanting afternoon light.

Rita had used her own money to buy a new skirt and blouse for her favorite patient, and she happily nodded her approval as Lana got dressed. They were not fancy, Rita thought, but the periwinkle flowers on the blouse brought out the blue in Lana's eyes. When she turned to thank her, Rita took a satin ribbon from her pocket and wordlessly pulled Lana's hair into a high ponytail. "Pretty as a picture!" she proclaimed, assessing her handiwork.

Except for the patients who had been aggressive during the previous week, everyone climbed the stairs to the third floor auditorium. The aides chattered about the people who would be there, wondering if a worker from maintenance, dietary or recreation would be ready to dance.

The band was beginning the first song as Lana stepped through the door, and she was spellbound by the gleam of the guitars. The musicians swung them in time to the music. The auditorium was packed with patients and staff, many of them already on the dance floor. Every style of dance imaginable was on display. Some of the patients were dancing the jitterbug with wild kicks and flailing arms.

Others were standing in one place, hopping from one foot to the other as if the soles of their shoes were on fire. Still others were shuffling cheek to cheek, oblivious to the rapid beat. A small man with a receding hairline had been captured by Mavis, who locked him into a tight embrace and lumbered onto the dance floor, oblivious to the fact that his shoes were dragging against the planks. The music seemed to be vibrating from every wall and buzzing through the wooden floor into Lana's shoes. She tapped her foot and grinned at Rita.

"I like that music!" she mouthed before Rita was pulled to the dance floor by an elderly patient in clean overalls. She laughed, waved to Lana and good naturedly became his partner. As Lana scanned the room to identify other dancers, a tall young man approached and held out his thumb as if he were trying to hitchhike. "I don't know how to…" He ignored her protest, grabbing her by one hand and jerking her behind him. Once Lana was among the gyrating and hopping patients, she forgot her shyness and began to sway to the rhythm. The young man, who towered over her, gently held her left hand and danced to a different beat.

Very shortly, other patients began to break in. Sometimes she was surprised to look toward her partner and find someone new. The music was loud and there was no reason for conversation, but one man with a grimace and a left arm frozen across his chest leaned toward her and said in a stage whisper, "You pretty!" as the music slowed to an end. When Luther became her partner, he was unwilling to be interrupted. He simply ignored the men who tried to cut in and stubbornly refused to release Lana's hands. Eventually this caused the expected amount of resentment and frustration, and several men offered to "step outside and settle this." Billy Wayne was propped against a corner when he belatedly noticed the squabble. He sprang away from the wall and inserted himself between Luther and the angry interlopers.

"Luther!" he shouted above the music. Luther opened his eyes and gave Billy Wayne a blank stare. "Luther! It's time to find another partner!" he ordered.

"I like this one," Luther whined.

"I know, Fella, but look at all those other women who are waiting for you to dance with `em," Billy Wayne said, gesturing to the clumps of female patients milling at the edge of the dance floor. "Go on, now," he insisted, taking Lana's trembling hand from Luther's big paw. "Go on and ask one of them to dance." Pulling Lana into a slow dance step, Billy Wayne moved away from Luther. Two other men stood close behind Lana, hoping to cut in, but Billy Wayne grinned at them and chided, "It's my turn now, Boys. Let me have a dance or two." He swung Lana away from them, causing her to stumble and step on his foot.

"Oh! I'm so sorry! I didn't mean to do that. I'm really sorry! I-I never been to a dance before."

"It's okay," he assured her. "Everybody starts out as a beginner."

He took her right hand and placed it on his shoulder, carefully touching her waist with his left. Then he lightly held her left hand and smiled down at her confused expression. "It's not hard," he assured her. "Just rock back and forth to the music." They continued through three songs, Billy Wayne discouraging interruptions by quickly shaking his head at any approaching patients.

After the slow music died and a song with a rowdy beat began, Billy Wayne led Lana to the long tables at one end of the room and ordered two glasses of Koolaid. She noticed that Lucy was loitering at the refreshment table, surreptitiously hiding cookies in her pockets. *So this is why Lucy came to the dance,* Lana thought, *to collect food for the birds.*

"Want to go outside for some fresh air?" he asked hopefully before leading her through the crowds to the staircase.

They stepped from the stale, sweaty auditorium into the bracing air of an autumn night. Passing the shrubbery that flanked the corners of the Administration Building, they heard a raucous giggle and then Cindy's voice teasing, "I think Mr. Winkey likes to be kissed!" A man's voice responded, more laughter ensued and then Cindy burst from the shrubbery in a game of hide and seek with her suitor. She clutched her open blouse with one hand and held her swirling skirt with the other. Without acknowledging Billy Wayne and Lana, she disappeared into the foyer of a basement door, waiting to be found.

Billy Wayne decided not to intervene in Cindy's romantic misadventures—the nurse on her unit had evidently decided she should be allowed some freedom. He veered away from the building, even though Lana was making an obvious effort to see where Cindy was hiding.

With no trees to block their view of the sky, the stars seemed to be within touching distance. Lana tried to think back to when she had last seen the night sky. Was it from the porch of her daddy's house? With Les sitting by her in the darkness? It seemed like another lifetime. "It's beautiful, isn't it?" she whispered, her face tilted upward. "There's the Indian Chief," she told him, pointing to Orion. "I learned that from my daddy. He said that's a knife hanging at his waist."

Billy Wayne followed her pointed finger, then looked down to study her profile. With a pang of sadness for her derailed life, he wondered what she could have done to end up at Western State. Every time he had been around her, she had seemed as sane as anyone else. He was still puzzling over her plight when she turned toward him and smiled. He was taken aback by her loveliness and swallowed hard to keep his bearings. Lana's platinum hair glowed with light from the heavens, and her eyes were unwaveringly focused on him. Her stunning good looks, he thought, had been victorious over the sadness she had worn like a shroud that first day he talked to her on the porch of The Y.

Reminding himself that she was a patient, he began telling her about the Neshobee River, which was just beyond the line of trees, and he ended by asking her if she would like to see it some day. When she agreed, he resolved that the first time Lana looked upon the wild beauty of that river, he would be standing next to her. Strolling back toward the Administration Building, they heard the strains of "Good Night, Ladies."

"Looks like they're just wrapping it up," he commented. "You want to go to the auditorium or back to the ward?"

"I guess back to the ward. Everybody else will be down there, soon, won't they?"

Billy Wayne walked Lana to her ward, as if he were walking her to her parents' front door. He felt a small, involuntary shudder at the thought that she was about to be locked in. Lana seemed resigned to her imprisonment, he thought, as he watched her knocking timidly on the metal door. When he heard the scrape of the aide's key, he turned on one heel and walked away without saying goodbye.

LANA

Chapter 24
The Mid-South Fair

The Mid-South Fair came to Memphis every fall with a swirl of thrilling rides, games of chance, talent shows, outdoor country music concerts, livestock shows and the haze of bar-b-que smoke. Western State traditionally took the trustworthy patients to the fair on a Wednesday night, when church services thinned the crowds. The year before, Billy Wayne had had his first experience with threading an ungainly State of Mississippi bus through the unfamiliar Memphis streets and then shepherding ten patients to the end of the fairgrounds and back. It was one of his more challenging workdays because Buster was insistent on ushering the women into every ride and tent with his gallant "Ladies First" while Luther was obsessed with attending every peep show he could find. The next workday, Billy Wayne told his supervisor that his experience at the fair was "about like herding cats."

This September, he was less frustrated about the assignment, however, because extra workers had been appointed and Billy Wayne had seen Lana's name on the patient list. He was also relieved to see that Mavis would not be in attendance.

He frequently glanced in his rear-view mirror as he drove in a caravan with three other buses, west on Highway 64. Lana's hair was pulled away from her face into a barrette at the crown of her head. She wore jeans and a blue plaid shirt, tied at her slender waist. Pieces of the conversation between the women patients drifted to him.

"I never been to the fair before!" Lana gushed, scanning the horizon for the first view of the adventure.

"It's a good-un," Daisy commented.

"Are there pretty things to buy?"

"There's lots of ways to spend your money down there," Cindy informed her, applying another coat of Tangee to her lips. "How much you got?"

Lana reached into her pocket and pulled out the zippered coin purse Rita had loaned her. She shook limp bills and tarnished coins into her palm, "four dollars and some quarters," she said.

"That'll do you about fifteen minutes, Lanagray," Cindy authoritatively told her.

While the money was still in her hand, Rose leaned across their seat and peered at Lana's savings. "There's ways to make money at a fair, too, you know," she hinted, cutting her eyes from Lana to Cindy.

"Girl, you are sure right!" Cindy chimed in. "And it's easy 'work,' too!" They laughed conspiratorially before Cindy settled into the seat by Rose, whispering as the bus bounced into potholes.

Lana looked at Daisy with a confused expression. "Can you get a job at the fair?"

Rolling her eyes, Daisy said, "No, not a job."

"Well, how do they make money?"

Daisy set her mouth in a disapproving line and leaned in to whisper hoarsely, "Sex." Having spoken, she threw her back against the seat, crossed her arms and stared straight ahead, leaving Lana to ponder exactly how this would be happening at a fair. She gave up her meditation when Billy Wayne called to her.

"What you want to do when we get to the fair?" he asked.

"I want to see it all!"

"Well, we can walk from one end of it t' the other, and you can see what's there. Then maybe you'd like t' get on one of the rides or see one of the talent shows."

"It all sounds good to me!" she told him, radiantly smiling at his reflection in the mirror.

The buses parked in a separate lot, a block from the main gates. Billy Wayne told the patients they would all need to be back by 9:00 and as they stepped down, he gave them their admission tickets and $5.00 of hospital money. "Don't spend it all in one place," he teased Luther, who would most likely stay at an "adult show" until his funds had vanished.

As the patients streamed toward the gate, Billy Wayne caught up with Lana and described the available entertainment. They strolled through the midway first. He laughed at Lana's astonishment as her first bite of cotton candy melted on her tongue. At the games of chance, he chose the booth with marching tin ducks and air-guns bolted to the counter. The carnie looked glum when Billie Wayne picked off three ducks and chose a pink teddy bear to give to Lana. She accepted it like a little girl, hugging it to her cheek.

At the home demonstration shed, Lana dallied at each exhibit as if she were at a jewelry store. Each blue-ribbon jar of preserves, each basket of perfect apples, each bouquet of flowers was more beautiful than the next. Billy Wayne leaned up against a post, a stick of gum in his mouth, and watched her meander through the tables. Her beautiful hair cascaded forward when she leaned over the tables, and her round eyes searched for him at every new corner. He saw the liquid grace in her movements and imagined her as a girl with advantages: someone who had grown up in one of the stately homes in Madrid or maybe someone whose father had worked at a bank. Someone who had come to high school wearing pretty clothes or maybe someone who had cheered for the team as he ran across the football field. He deduced that family cast the dice more than heredity, and he wished that Lana had had a fighting chance to be a person in her own right. After an hour, Billy Wayne pushed away from the post and joined her, touching her lightly on the elbow.

"Lana, don't you think we better move on? There's a lot more of the fair to see, and we're about to run outta time."

She apologized but glanced regretfully at the tables she had not visited. Returning to the milling crowds outside, Lana was distracted from her grief at leaving the flowers, and she happily pointed out rides that spun and raced by with alarming speed. In the end, Billy Wayne asked her if she were afraid of being "up high" and when she said she didn't know, he guided her to the line for the Ferris wheel. The ride left her alternately frightened and spellbound as their seat swung to the top of the arch. With nothing but a thin plank under her feet, she told him she was suspended "like a bug in a spider's web." At the first rotation, she gasped and buried her face against his shoulder. Soon her curiosity overtook her terror and she pushed away from him to peer at the spectacle below. The lights of Memphis, she told him, were like magic, like some kind of fairy-land.

Again and again she described the fair as "the best night of my life," leaving Billy Wayne to wonder just what kind of marriage she had had. When they returned to the parking lot, a knot of patients stood beside the bus, and the rest rapidly appeared a few minutes after 9:00, except for Squirrel man. They waited for him until 9:30. Then, with the rest of the patients frustrated and restless, Billy Wayne and one aide hiked back to the gates. Billy Wayne was furious with this delay and assumed that Squirrel man had eloped from the hospital, despite the nurses' assurances that he would "be no problem at the fair." Squirrel man was almost immediately sighted, however, when they re-entered the fair and glanced toward a bank of phone booths. They could see him in the first booth, talking excitedly and gesturing crudely with his free hand, his face red with the stifling heat of the glass enclosure.

Squirrel man had spent the entire evening in the phone booth. He had used his money to repeatedly call every one of his relatives and the night desk of the *Memphis News*. He berated them all for his commitment and informed them of the government plots that kept him in the hospital. Billy Wayne put his shoulder to the door and collapsed it, throwing Squirrel man against the corner. Grabbing the receiver from the startled patient, he put it to his own mouth, saying, "Sorry, wrong number," before he slammed it into the cradle. With Squirrel man still reeling from the blow, Billy Wayne jerked him out by the collar of his shirt.

"What the hell do you think you're doing?" he shouted at the sweaty patient. "You've made a whole bus load of people wait on you! And for what?! So you can stir up a bunch of shit!" Billy Wayne grabbed one arm and wheeled him to face the gate. The aide grabbed the other arm and they grimly marched him back to the bus. Squirrel man offered no resistance and no explanation for his behavior. He was deposited on the bus, found his seat in the back and promptly fell asleep.

The ride back to Madrid was eerily quiet. Patients rested their heads against the windows or fell asleep on the shoulder of another. Lana fell into a dreamless sleep with her head propped against her arm, while Billy Wayne, occasionally wiping his heavy eyelids with the back of his hand, calculated the miles that separated the joys of the fair from the ways of Western.

KATE

Chapter 25
Settling In

After Russ's ill-fated visit, I sank into a routine of sameness that belied the fact that I worked in a facility for criminals and the insane and lived in an antebellum mansion with the president of the Daughters of the Confederacy. On weekdays, I woke in time to rush through a bath, pull my hair into a loose ponytail and eat a quick breakfast at Adele's table. Once at work, I attended treatment team meetings, gave psychological tests to the teenagers and wrote exhaustive reports to the courts, wondering at times if they were ever read. I tried to stay focused on my assignments and ignore the feelings of loneliness that constantly threatened to unravel my composure.

The long, leisurely weekends presented a greater challenge: On Friday afternoons I typically drove the VW to its assigned space under the towering magnolia and left it parked until Monday morning. The library and the Dollar General Store were within walking distance from Adele's house, and they were my most frequent destinations. Otherwise, I slept 10 and 12 hours on weekends and lounged in Adele's "den," casually reading random pages from antique books and watching PBS shows on gardening. Sometimes I wondered about my father and why he had not responded to the note that gave him my new address. But I was at a loss for what I would say in conversation, so I did not telephone him.

As the sunny fall turned into a dreary winter, bruised and dimpled clouds hung on the spires on the Administration Building, threatening rain every morning. I knew I was becoming depressed, but I was too confused to fight it. I began to leave my office at lunch and hike along the asphalt ribbon. My walks first took me around the Claiborne Building. and later in widening circles to the ballfield, the abandoned buildings and to the cemetery. Often when I approached the crooked tombstones, does scattered with their spotted fawns bounding after them. The fawns had been born so late in the season that I felt sure they would not survive the winter, and I felt a rush of sadness as I watched them duck into the woods. Standing in front of Lana and Billy Wayne's marker, I could feel the futility that lay against their tombstone as well. I ran my fingers over their names, wondering who they were, what they dreamed of, how they died.

The first day I wandered onto the ballfield, I took a seat on the damp bleachers and scanned the scene before me. The grounds crew kept the field mowed and the board-and-batten concession stand painted white, as if a line of cleated players would soon be standing for the national anthem. I could imagine the crack of a patient's bat and the cheers from the staff sitting behind home plate, but I had been told that the last baseball game had been played in the sixties.

A towering sycamore at the southern edge of the campus provided a canopy for some of my lunch hours. The bark on its trunk scaled like chipped paint and lightning had seared a gaping hole in its breast, but the spreading branches were beautifully smooth and white. Although the lawn was littered with pincushion seed pods, only one of its offspring had been allowed to live, and that spindly daughter was poorly anchored, leaning precariously toward its parent. I strove diligently, though unsuccessfully, to understand the lesson that nature seemed to be presenting. I sat between the massive, criss-crossed roots and leaned my temple against the scaling trunk, hoping to draw out the story of a damaged but triumphant life. Dozing with my cheek cushioned against the bark, I dreamed that I had fallen asleep on a pile of jigsaw pieces that scattered in all directions as my hands clumsily drew them together. Each week the spindly daughter tree leaned farther and farther toward the giant sycamore, as if it were yearning to fall into a mother's arms.

Then, after a windy November night, I found it lying in the grass and the next day, I found only the tracks from the bulldozer that had dragged it away. I was irrationally distraught about this little botanical tragedy but willed myself not to talk about it for fear that my coworkers would think I was too eccentric even to work at Western.

A week later, avoiding the road to the sycamore, I was walking along the eastern edge of the grounds and found a mangled hawk lying in the road, its back broken so that the red-tipped tail feathers were fanned out like a losing hand of gin. One wing saluted the heavens, where earlier it had swooped in spectacular dives. Dizzy with grief, I swayed as I stood by the side of the road, until the indignant horn of the laundry truck broke my trance.

KATE

Chapter 26
Winter Solstice

The winter slid toward its solstice, forcing me to wake in the dark and drive home in the dusk. I could almost feel my body sinking toward hibernation. I thought constantly of crawling into a warm bed, pulling a comforter over my head and sleeping until spring. It seemed like every winter took me off guard so that each November I was surprised to find the damp gloominess returning and settling into my blood. I remembered feeling depressed at this time of year, even when I was married to Russ and busy with school.

I parked the VW and walked to my back entrance with the cold biting into my face and hands. The door was swollen against the jamb and I had to push against it with my shoulder. My dark room was hardly warmer than the outside, I grumbled, throwing my jacket over a chair, kicking off my shoes and then burrowing under the bedspread. I thought a half hour nap would revive me, but I awoke three hours later with Miss Adele, knocking on my door and asking if I were okay.

"I'm fine," I called to the closed door. "Just a little tired… I decided to lie down."

"We've finished with supper," she informed me. "Josephine has put away the food so if you want something, you'll have to get it from the refrigerator and warm it up."

I thanked her, but she continued to hesitate at the door, listening for sounds of life. I turned on my side and went back to sleep. The next morning, I woke up very early and was disgusted to find my pillow wet with drool and my work clothes tangled and wrinkled. Shivering, I undressed in the cold, wishing for some better source of heat than the radiator that was tapping a cadence from the corner. I wrapped myself in a robe and tiptoed to the bathroom for a hot bath, hoping the morning routine would lift my spirits.

When I opened the bathroom door, the smell of frying bacon made me realize that I hadn't eaten since yesterday's lunch. I paused at the door of the kitchen and watched Josephine. She stood first at the counter and then at the stove, humming a gospel song as she worked. Despite her age, her hands were steady. She moved efficiently in the kitchen that had been her workspace since childhood.

Miss Adele was just taking her seat as I appeared in the dining room and she seemed relieved to see me. As we ate breakfast, she told me about the annual Episcopal Church Christmas reception to be held at her house on the evening of the eighteenth. She cocked her head to one side and asked if I wanted to be part of the festivities. My first reflex was to say no. The thought of making polite chatter with a group of strangers seemed exhausting. Miss Adele smiled, "I think it would be good for you to meet some new people. And it's an opportunity to have a little glamour in your life, Kate. You can buy a new dress, have your hair done, get a manicure. Doesn't that sound good to you?"

"I don't know, Miss Adele. I've never been very good at chitchat."

"Humph!" she snorted. "You talk to strangers every day at work. I don't think you'd have a minute's trouble. But if you did, there's always the Christmas wassail to relax you!" she laughed, wagging a finger in my direction with surprising humor.

I paused and spread some of Josephine's pear preserves on my biscuit, asking if I might know any of the expected guests.

"Why, of course!" she answered. "The Thompsons will be here and several of the doctors from Western. You don't have to decide about it this morning, but you really should think it over. Anyway, what would you do while the party's going on in the parlor? Read in your room? That would certainly be a miserable way to start the holidays." I pondered her comments while I finished my biscuit, wiping my mouth with the cloth napkin that was ubiquitous to her table, and promising to let her know my decision soon.

She waved me away. "An RSVP is not required," she announced.

I thought about her invitation (or was it a command performance?) as I drove to work. She had summed up the situation: I had nothing better to do, and it would surely feel strange to be a prisoner in my room while the sounds of the party filtered under my door.

Still, I dreaded all the festivities of the coming holiday season. I had some dim memories of the holidays before my mother had been diagnosed with cancer and I could remember wonderful aromas: sugar cookies that I decorated with colored crystals, a tall cedar tree with homemade ornaments from Girl Scouts and school. I could hear my mother's high-pitched laughter if I remembered hard enough. When I closed my eyes, I could see her sweet face when she was young and healthy.

But in the last years before she died, Christmases were a sad and embarrassing affair. My father never had time to take me to the store, and I was left to try to craft a present from things I could find in the cabinets. One year I put four clothespins across the bottom of a wire coat hanger and demonstrated how she could hang her nylons to dry. Although she was pleased with my gift, I remember being angry at my father for his thoughtlessness. She spent the last Christmas of her life on the couch, propped up on pillows, watching TV holiday specials with me. Most of the music was sappy and sentimental, and I hated the fact that someone would wish for a "White Christmas" or "Two Front Teeth" when I longed for a mother who could get well.

My mother died a few days after New Year's when I was 13. Standing by my father at the side of a gaping hole, hearing the slow whine of the machine that lowered her coffin into the earth, I wept without shame and choked on my tears, while my father stoically and silently looked on. In fairness, he was probably relieved that my mother's suffering was at an end, but he was also helpless to explain why she would shorten her limited days with suicide.

My car rolled past the plywood reindeer that grazed on Western's front lawn. The guards in Security nodded to me as I walked through the front doors. The children's wards were decorated with artificial trees and ornaments that the patients had made. Church ladies had been to visit earlier in the week and had brought the children sacks of candy, pencils and puzzle books. At three weeks before the 25th, the unit was rapidly becoming vacant, since judges and DCS workers tried to get the children to a home, any home, for the holidays. The children who were left were losing hope of being placed off the unit for the week. Christmas on a children's psychiatric unit might be the saddest place imaginable, I thought, as I pushed the key into my office door. Sadder than losing your mother, but keeping the memories of her; sadder than losing contact with your father; sadder than losing a marriage on the heels of losing a baby.

KATE

Chapter 27
Wards of the State

When Georgia took a week's vacation, I was sent to the Acute Adult unit to provide leadership for the morning therapy groups. Before her departure, Georgia had introduced me to the nurses on the unit, given me a tour of the therapy rooms, and handed me a worn syllabus of her group topics. Despite her efforts, I knew I was unprepared to work on Unit K. These adult patients had been recently admitted, but they were not members of the neurotic, "worried well," who had been the focus of my graduate training. They were by and large the "frequent fliers," people who came in and out of the hospital in a revolving door pattern. They were psychotics who had decided to discontinue their medication, or substance abusers who needed detox, or people who lived in psychiatric boarding homes, or the wandering homeless who refused a shelter cot.

The small, austere room had a slotted window close to the ceiling and eight chairs arranged in a circle. Georgia's hand-lettered flip chart had been left in place, so I perused the first few sheets. The syllabus indicated we would be talking about "anger management" and the ways our hostilities could be channeled into healthy endeavors.

The aide led a group of shuffling adult patients into the room, and they immediately found their seats, hardly noticing that their group leader had changed. I smiled self-consciously at them, nodding and repeating "good morning." Most of them made no eye contact, and so I believed they were sublimely unaware of the scheduled group or the substitute leader. I started by giving a brief introduction and remarking that we would be talking about anger. None of them seemed to have any idea why their doctor had referred them to group.

"I ain't even supposed to be in this hospital!" insisted Alfred, as soon as I paused in my introduction. "The judge don't have no jurisdiction over me! I need you to talk to 'The Lion' at KQED and find out what I got to do to get out of here!" I tried to placate him into talking about the topic of anger, but Alfred would have none of it. "I'm tired of being in here. The staff be messin' with me at night while I'm asleep. Somebody put a snake down my throat, and I can feel it on days that it's rainin'." Since I was having no luck redirecting Alfred, I finally interrupted him by turning to the next patient and asking him about anger.

Jacob was a beefy white man with close-cropped, brown hair. His eyes shone with rage and his words tumbled out in a torrent. "Ma'am, I don't know why my doctor wanted me to come to this group. I ain't got no problem with anger, Ma'am. 'Cept when my wife gets me mad but that was when the TV said 'you can't go to Horn Lake no more' 'cause them McKnights been bothering me since the Civil War, and they been tellin' lies and booby trapping my boat so I was talking about an axe. You would too, Ma'am! Not a shop axe like you cut down a tree with…a voodoo axe to put a hex on 'em and anybody would do the same thing if you have enough you can't TAKE IT NO MORE!" He stood, spittle flying from his lips as he shouted.

"Jacob! Sit down!" I pleaded, frightened at his escalation. He glanced at me, mumbling an apology as he collapsed in his seat. I suddenly felt weak in the knees from the rush of adrenaline. I steadied myself against an empty chair, waiting for my heart to stop pounding.

"Miss Hattie," I said, turning my attention to a tiny black woman who rocked in her chair, mumbling to herself. She looked up at me, revealing two large warts on her nose and hair that was parted in the middle to bush out over each ear.

"Ma'am?" she cackled.

"What can you tell us about controlling anger?"

"Well-ll-ll," she drawled. "I don't rightly know. 'Cept sometimes you get mad at your husband and you could have trouble 'cause maybe one of you be Church of Chri-i-st and one of you be Baptist and you not really married if you not married in the Church of Christ." She resumed her rocking.

"Okay, so does that cause someone to be angry?" I pressed.

"You not supposed to be with that man. You not supposed to be married to him. The Bible Book say so. I don't rightly know if that's true or not. But it say so in the Bible Book; yes it do," she paused and looked intently at me. "It could be true or it could be not true," she said, casting a suspicious glance toward a dozing Jacob. "You don't know who be putting things in that Bible Book," she warned us.

Cindy, a middle-aged redhead, unlaced her delicate fingers from their resting place across her large abdomen and leaned forward. "Sometimes you're supposed to be together, even if you're not married!" she declared as Hattie began to rock in her seat and mumble to herself. "Sometimes they won't *let* you get married but you're supposed to be married! Lanagray was supposed to marry Billy Wayne, but she was married to the wrong one!"

An electrical charge ran up my spine. Could this patient know the same couple I had been searching for? It had to be the same people! Even though she said Lana's name as if it were one word, this woman surely had a personal knowledge of the two people buried in the Western cemetery! She must have talked to them, walked across the grounds with them, eaten with them in the dining hall. I licked my dry lips and tried to sound casual. "Cindy, who is Lana?"

"Lanagray! She's gone to be with Jesus!" she bellowed, giving her head a forceful shake that sent her double chins quivering. "She's living there right now and he's the wrong one. He didn't love her like Billy Wayne did."

"What happened to Lanagray and Billy Wayne?" I whispered, feeling a twinge of guilt for indulging my curiosity.

"Gone! Gone to live with Jesus like the Good Book says. I'll fly away Sweet Jesus! In the sweet By and By! By the time I get to heaven! Get my wings for what I buy and love everybody 'til I cry…"

I seemed so close to learning about Lana that I couldn't let it go, even though I knew Cindy had lost her focus and was rambling nonsensically, even though I knew my questions were now bordering on unethical, perhaps even harmful. I leaned forward in my chair, oblivious to the other patients, focused completely on the redhead who rambled nonsensically. "Cindy, what happened to Lanagray?"

She stopped in mid-sentence and looked at me as if for the first time. A haughty and seductive expression crept over her bloated face. "I was always prettier than her and I had more boyfriends, too! When I went to dances, everybody wanted to dance with me. We'd go down in the basement, and I kissed their Mr. Winkeys and they liked it! And Elton gave me a baby to take to Memphis but they took her away! For good!" Her voice had turned to a wail of anguish. "All gone! The baby's all gone!"

The aide laid her newspaper on the floor and stepped into the group room. "Now, Cindy, we're not going to talk about all that old mess with babies. You want to stay in group or you want to go back to the unit?"

Cindy buried her face in her hands and wept copious tears as the aide persisted, "Come on! Get up and we'll go back to the Day Room!" She pulled on Cindy's elbow to no avail.

"Stay in group!" Cindy shouted as she wiped her nose with the back of her hand. When the aide backed away, she cried silently, patting away the tears with the collar of her blouse.

Even a heartless person could not have interrogated her further. Feeling that I had done too much damage already, I turned my attention to Stephanie, a pretty brunette wearing a pink sweater and tight jeans. She raked her manicured fingers through her hair as she told me she didn't have a clue as to why the doctor would put her in this group. "I never get mad!" she insisted, although she did describe several passive-aggressive episodes that had been intended to take revenge on her husband.

Sheila, a slender young black woman, slouched in her chair with her arms folded across her chest. She answered all of my questions with either, "I don't know," "Nothing," or simply, "No."

Whatever secret she had would not be revealed in this group.

Amy responded to questions with an emotionless and succinct description of her last suicide attempt before she stared off into the space just above Georgia's flip chart.

Mr. Niven, an older white man with a too-long crew cut that stood up as if he had been recently frightened, insisted that when he was angry, he always talked things out with his wife of 50 years. He punched the air with a long forefinger as he made each point.

By the time an hour had passed, I was exhausted and the patients were bored into a new level of inattention. The aide put her arm around Cindy's quivering shoulders and walked her down the hall, the other patients following close behind.

Later that morning I read the charts, learning their stories in a way that they could not have articulated. Both Alfred and Jacob were paranoid schizophrenics, who had auditory hallucinations and were often noncompliant with their medications. Miss Hattie was an undifferentiated schizophrenic who had put Red Devil lye in her husband's stew because she believed the Bible said they were living in sin. Stephanie was addicted to Valium and had embezzled money from her husband's business to buy her pills. Sheila lived in a group home, where she isolated herself from the other women and was typically silent. Amy had a long history of opiate abuse, and when she lost her nursing license, she fell into an intractable depression. Mr. Niven, a retired Army colonel, was an alcoholic who had threatened to pistol whip his wife if she did not go to town to buy him more beer.

Cindy, my hoped-for informant, was diagnosed with a form of Bipolar Disorder that typically hovered in the manic range, inclining her toward promiscuity, reckless behavior, religiousity and rapid, disjointed speech. As soon as her sleep and appetite had been minimally stabilized, but long before I could talk to her in any meaningful way, Cindy was discharged back to the group home, where she lived between hospitalizations. Although she was never a functioning member of society, her medicines had allowed her to reside in a Tupelo home for mentally ill women, after having spent 20 consecutive years in Western. Her brief reference to Lana and Billy Wayne made them real for me in a way the tombstone never could. I renewed my search to find someone who could tell me about them.

KATE

Chapter 28
Believing in Santa

The Christmas potluck dinner for our patients and staff was scheduled for December 10th. Josephine had graciously contributed a tray of her famous fried apple pies so that I wouldn't have to arrive with a tub of grocery store coleslaw. By 11:00 the hustle of table decorating and food placement had taken over all other sounds on the units. Classwork had been suspended, and taped Christmas music filled the hall. With a collection of picture books in hand, I offered to read to the youngest students, prompting the teacher to gratefully disappear. Four elementary-age children were out of their seats, moving restlessly around the room, talking among themselves. The two boys were laughing and pulling books from a shelf each time they passed the bookcase.

"Hey, guys!" I called, projecting my voice so it hit the concrete walls and bounced back to me. They were stunned for an instant and stopped their revolutions to stare at me. "I've got a book I want to read to you about Santa." I didn't give them an option as I continued: "Come sit up here, close to me, so you can see the pictures." The girls came forward obediently and settled into the desks while the boys ignored me and resumed their horseplay. Julia leaned forward, the shiny pink barrettes on the end of each braid nodded in my direction.

"Well," I said, shrugging my shoulders. "It looks like the girls will get all of the treats when I'm finished." I opened the books dramatically and began to read, asking the girls to put their fingers on Rudolph's nose, or on Santa's hat, making the stories as interactive as possible. I thought the boys had simply grown curious about the story when they took a seat at their desks, but as I looked up from the pages, I saw Dr. Givhup at the door, smiling broadly.

He waved at me as he walked away. "Cally on!" he called like a

British general. When I finished my story about Santa's workshop, Jason folded his arms across his chest and announced with a disgruntled tone, "Santa is for babies. I don't believe in Santa!" It was a declaration of independence from the largest and most worldly boy on the unit. His short military haircut made him look even older than his eleven years. The other three children hesitantly looked at him and then me. They didn't want to be babies, but they weren't ready to give up St. Nick either.

Jack sauntered in and sat on the back row, folding his frame into the child-sized desk. "I believe in Santa!" he countered. They turned in curiosity; even Jason looked back. "I believe because there are presents under my tree every Christmas!" Jack leaned forward in the child's desk, an earnest expression giving credence to his every word. "Did you know that Santa stops coming when you don't believe in him?" The girls nodded with solemn eyes and Jason looked momentarily concerned.

"Do you have another book about Santa? Why don't you read that one?" Jack suggested. I opened the second book to a much quieter and more appreciative audience. When the last page was turned, Jack encouraged the children to go to the hall where the food had been placed on long tables. The spell was broken: they jumped from their desks and bounded from the room, the boys resuming the wrestling match as they started down the hall.

"Oh, wait!" I called after them. "I forgot to give you your treats!" I handed each of them a bag with a miniature box of chocolates, small games and playing cards. They didn't take the time to look inside, and I later found the bags unopened and abandoned on vinyl chairs and metal dressers.

When I expressed my gratitude to Jack, he smiled and responded: "I didn't do a thing! I just came in to see the kids and decided to stay and hear you read."

"They wanted to be on their best behavior for you. You made a difference by being here."

"We're all here to make a difference, Kate," he observed philosophically, a wan smile flickering across his face before he walked silently from the room.

I followed him with my eyes. He moved around the knots of patients and staff like a running back, side-stepping would-be tackles. Laughing, he stiff-armed Jason, who had scuffled into his path. When Jack disappeared through the unit doors, I took my place in line with the staff. We ate on our laps, supervising the children in the dining room. The teenaged boys ate purposefully, scooping up each pinto bean with long, sweeping strokes, their table silent except for the scrape of plastic utensils.

The boys who had been patients when I first came to work had been discharged weeks ago to face their charges in courthouses scattered throughout the region. I wondered briefly about Todd, whether the judge had let him go home to protect the honor of his sister, and whether Tavaris was still associating with a peer group that seemed intent on turning him into a criminal.

KATE

Chapter 29
Antebellum Open House

The night of Miss Adele's Christmas reception was bitterly cold and windy. As I left my car, I paused to marvel at the stars, which looked like shards of broken glass on dark velvet. Once inside, it was immediately clear that the ladies from the Episcopal Church had worked all day to decorate the Cearley House for Christmas. Branches of waxy magnolia leaves reclined across the mantel; wide gold ribbon spiraled down the staircase and ended in a swag on the newel post. The dining table, covered with a plaid cloth, groaned under the weight of chafing dishes and china platters. Albert had kindled a blaze in each fireplace, and the logs were crackling and hissing against the cold. I had never seen Adele's home look so lovely; the signs of age and wear had been erased.

Josephine, holding a silver tray of sliced fruitcake and miniature pecan pies, tottered into the dining room with Miss Adele close on her heels. "Josephine!" she called sharply, waving a handful of serving spoons. "You've forgotten the spoons and forks! How do you expect people to serve their plates? With their fingers?"

Josephine ignored the scolding as she put the tray on the table and started back to the kitchen. Placing the serving pieces by each dish, Adele muttered her disapproval as she worked, eventually glancing up to see me standing at the end of the dining table.

"Kate! You don't have all that much time to get ready!" she chided. "You need to get dressed."

Like Josephine, I wordlessly retreated. I had taken a Wednesday afternoon to drive to Jackson, where I purchased the dressy outfit, now hanging on the door of the armoire. The black silk bodice danced with dark sequins and dipped to a low V in the back. I sat on the bed for a few minutes, fingering the dress and trying to remember if I had ever owned anything so elegant. Christmases with Russ had been decidedly casual affairs and when I lived at home, I had never shopped for semi-formal clothes. While I dressed, music came from the front rooms; then the repeated ring of the doorbell; and finally the voices of the first guests. I quickly swept my long hair into a chignon, securing it with a rhinestone barrette and leaving a fringe of bangs to fall across my eyebrows. Then, I slowly turned in front of the ancient, smoky mirror, thinking of Jack Gordon, wishing he could see me in this new dress. Taking a deep breath, I stepped from my room and walked down the dark hall to the parlor.

The party was noisy with tinkling laughter, Christmas music and the deep bass of men's voices. People chatted over the dining table while they speared the delicacies. A few guests stood close to the parlor fireplace, holding their cocktails with one hand and warming the other hand in the glow of the flames. Miss Adele, who was giving another order to Josephine, broke off her instruction in mid-sentence to smile broadly at me. "Don't you look like a dream!" she pronounced. "That dress is just exquisite." She looked me up and down, lingering at the rhinestone barrette before she nodded her approval. "Get something to eat and then I'll introduce you to some of the guests."

Holding a plate of miniature sandwiches and fruit, I was escorted to the group by the fireplace. In order to introduce me, Adele boldly interrupted the razor-thin gentleman, who seemed to be holding court with a small group of admirers.

Dr. Lundsford nodded at me politely and smiled without the effort of showing any teeth. "A pleasure to meet you, Miss McConnaughy." He turned to the portly man on his left. "This is Mr. Nuckols." Then nodding to the stylish woman beside him, he added "and my wife, Rachel." As a flushed man in a frock coat bustled to the small group, the doctor continued, "And this gentleman is Father Riley." The priest murmured a hello with a quixotic smile.

"So how long have you been working at Western?" Dr. Lundsford asked, smoothly including me in the little circle of royalty, who monopolized the warmth of the fireplace. The more I tried to appear confident, the more ill-at-ease I felt. Mr. Nuckols, who may have sensed my discomfort, left the circle and returned with a cup of rosy punch. "Have some wassail," he encouraged, handing me the drink.

I gratefully sipped it, tasting the blend of rum and spices, as Dr. Lundsford pontificated. "A little wassail never hurt anyone and it can certainly warm the blood."

"And on a night like this, we all need warming up!" The priest giggled, taking another swallow.

I felt the glow of the alcohol making its way to my face. We talked about the cold weather, the midnight mass that would take place in the ancient Episcopal Church, and, of course, the hospital. I began to feel a sense of inclusion as Dr. Lundsford told me he had worked at Western as a young doctor. "It was a valuable experience for me," he confided. "I was only thirty and by the time I spent two years there, I knew more than any psychiatrist in Nashville. That's where I went to practice, you know."

Mrs. Lundsford leaned forward and told me in a conspiratorial whisper, "He's treated all of the country music stars!" She scanned the room to assure a pseudo-confidentiality before she continued, "He got Brooks Ferris over his drug addiction!"

Dr. Lundsford put his free hand in his suit pocket and looked casually toward the ornate mantel. "Well," he said with false humility, "Brooks was ready to give up the drugs or I couldn't have done a thing for him."

Warmer and certainly more relaxed after finishing the wassail, I excused myself and walked carefully to a chair in the corner, testing my gait against the effects of the liquor. Dr. Garcia emerged from the library, holding one of Adele's leather-bound books in his long, graceful hands.

"I don't have the courage to ask if I may borrow this beautiful book," he confessed as she protested to the contrary. "I only ask that I be allowed to read it here in your home."

"Spend the evening with a book? When there are all these lovely people to visit with? I think not!" Adele responded, laughing. "I insist you take it home with you. I know you'll return it."

He bowed slightly from the waist, assuring her that he would care for the book as if it were his own. When he strolled into the parlor with the antique book, I waved to him.

"Kate, I am delighted to see that you are here tonight! I did not realize you were a friend of Adele's," he confided, his soft Spanish accent suggesting luxury and privilege.

"Oh, I live here," I said, giggling at his astounded expression. "I'm renting a room from Miss Adele," I confided.

"You couldn't be in a more gracious home," he told me. "I have known her for at least ten years, ever since I came to work in Madrid. We serve on the Library Board together."

An overweight woman with frizzy grey hair approached us, prompting Dr. Garcia to introduce me to his wife, Victoria. She was decidedly American; they had married years ago, shortly after he had emigrated from Cuba.

As the Garcias left my side to circulate among the guests, Carol and Scott arrived, heralded by a sudden blast of Arctic air. Albert put his shoulder to the tall door, pushing it shut before he disappeared with their wraps.

"Everything looks beautiful!" Carol exclaimed to Adele as she scanned the dining table. "Why you've outdone yourself again this year!" Carol glanced at me and then looked back with a more direct stare. "Why, Kate!" she exclaimed. "You are absolutely stunning! Stand up and let me see that dress!" I obeyed, turning in a pirouette. Carol pulled at the sides of her reindeer blouse as if she were about to curtsey. "You have put us all to shame!" she laughed.

I basked in their approval, until Adele introduced an ill-at-ease young man who had been hugging the door to the library. In response to her comment that he was a friend's nephew and also a new hospital social worker, Calvin nodded miserably before escaping to the wall of books. At that point, I realized that Jack Gordon would most certainly not be attending this party: the guests either had ties to the Episcopal Church, the library board or the Daughters of the Confederacy. Others were present by virtue of being the grandchildren of Adele's childhood friends. By 11:00 the crowd was thinning out and guests stood at the door, waiting for Albert to retrieve their coats. When the last person had stepped onto the cold front porch, Miss Adele collapsed into the loveseat and pushed an auburn curl from her forehead.

"Josephine?" she called. The elderly maid appeared at the door as Adele continued, "I already put away the leftovers so we'll clean up the rest tomorrow. You and Albert go on home and get some rest. I know y'all must be as tired as I am," Adele commented, both fatigue and concern in her voice. It was the first time I had heard her address Josephine with anything other than directives.

Adele turned her gaze to where I sat on the fringed ottoman and asked my opinion of the evening.

"The party? I thought everything went very well. The food was wonderful; the wassail was delicious and all the guests seemed to have a good time."

"They did, didn't they?" she murmured, perusing the room and letting her eyes rest lovingly on the mantel. "It's so nice to see the old house dressed up for the holidays," she mused. "It's been many, many years since my sisters and I could decorate it...I wish you could have seen this house back in the twenties. We had parties and dances that lasted `til dawn!" She sighed and then fell silent, lost in her reverie. After a few minutes, she rocked forward in her chair and stood up. "It's time for bed!" she declared, leading the way from the parlor. She turned at the door to be sure I was dutifully following.

"I think I'll stay up a while longer," I told her. "I'd like to enjoy the fire."

She shrugged her indifference before climbing the stairs to her bedroom. I kicked off my shoes, nestling my back into the club chair. For a long time, I faced the fire, listening to it sizzle against the branches, watching it slowly lose its vigor. I let my mind quietly drift away from the parlor, starting with idle thoughts about Jack Gordon. I knew that this Christmas would be especially hard for him since his father had died a few months earlier, and I wondered what he was doing on this bleak December night—if he were alone or with company.

I thought about the last campfire I had watched and I wondered where Russ was, what kind of Christmas he would be having, where he would spend the holidays. In Marie's bar? In a hastily arranged family get-together?

Finally, I thought about my own parents and the holidays they had shared before my mother's cancer. I imagined them as they had appeared in old photos: a young married couple, excited at sharing their baby's first Christmas, holding me close to the tree so I could see the ornaments.

My thoughts seemed to be warmed by the red coals in the fireplace. I realized with a sense of wonder that in Adele's comfortable parlor, watching the fire make a familiar dance from long ago, the hurt seemed to melt from the edges of my awareness. And, in its place, I felt only a drowsy contentment.

KATE

Chapter 30
Western 1989—Christmas Eve

Christmas Eve was a workday, but as I drove into the parking lot, I realized that few of my co-workers would be present. The units were almost deserted of children and even the nurses' station was empty. I looked on the rack to see only two charts from the "Eleven and under" unit and only four charts from the older boys' unit.

The day would stretch out interminably, I thought: I had no deadlines looming and no reports to be finished. I also had no books to read, I grimly realized, since I had left my library book on the dining room table. I decided to go to the older boys' unit and see what activities had been planned for them. Although the TV roared, their Day Room was empty, and I did not know where the patients were until I found Annabeth on the phone in the break room.

"Oh, Honey, the two little ones are on their ward and the big boys are down in the gym with Jack. He thought they'd be happier if they worked off some energy."

I found the basketball court empty, but I could hear the sound of splashing and laughing, echoing from the indoor pool. Jack and the four older boys were engrossed in a game of water polo, their shouts and laughter ringing from the tiled walls to the choppy surface of the water. One of the boys immediately pointed me out to the others, prompting Jack to wave me toward the water. "You ought to come play with us! We would use a good point guard," he teased.

"Maybe some other time!" I called.

The boys put on a show as they worked to impress me with their swimming and jumping. Jack acted as both referee and teammate for the underdog. Their total focus on play and their resounding cheers completely distracted me from Christmas.

Gleefully I clapped each time someone made a point, but the exuberance came to an abrupt stop when a group of long-term male patients shuffled to the pool deck.

Jack quickly cleared the teenagers from the water, the boys complaining about having to give up the pool, and Jack relentlessly herding them up the stairs. He climbed the ladder at the end closest to me, grabbed a towel that had been draped across a plastic chair, and unselfconsciously rubbed his face and hair as he talked. I was uncomfortable standing in my prim sweater and slacks, talking to a man who was half-naked, but Jack appeared to be completely unaware of our unequal clothing status. Before I looked away, I stole a glance at the powerful shoulders and the sinewy arms of an athlete.

"Y'all go on to the locker room and get dressed. I'll be there in a minute," he shouted before smiling at me conspiratorially. "They'll be taking naps all afternoon!"

I told him I was surprised to find him working the day before Christmas when surely he had the annual leave to be off. His answer was characteristically self-effacing: "Well, Patrice and Darrell have little kids and they want to be home with them. Besides, the boys that are left on the unit during the holidays really need more attention than the nurses can give `em." He finished drying his arms and then slung the towel around his neck. As he started for the locker room, he turned back once, grinning at me. "Next time, Miss Katie, no excuses...you'll have to get in the pool with us."

On the younger children's hallway, I entered another deserted nurses' station. The TV in the dayroom rolled infinitely upward with no hand in sight to adjust it, for the one aide assigned to the unit was on the phone, absorbed in placing an order for her lunch. Julia and Jason, the only little ones left, were playing a board game with Dr. Givhup. They sat on the floor, rocking back and forth on their heels and giggling loudly. The doctor was obviously making the wrong moves and answering questions with spectacular mistakes, prompting the children to laugh and correct him. He winked at me almost imperceptibly and went back to playing the buffoon for the entertainment of the last two children on his unit.

When the game was finished, Dr. Givhup questioned the children about their Christmas wishes. Jason was skeptical, but Dr. Givhup urged him to say what he would like to have. Finally, Jason quickly replied, "A bike," as if saying it rapidly would cause less of a disappointment when Santa did not appear. Julia, on the other hand, needed no goading. Her dark face glowed with pleasure. "A Baby Wipe and Dipe!" she sang out, mimicking the commercials on TV.

Dr. Givhup clapped his hands together in glee. "We will see what Santa brings tonight!" he said in his sing-song voice, gracefully rising from his seat on the floor and floating to a standing position. Putting his palms together, he bowed slightly to the seated children.

The next day "Santa" had come and all of the requested toys were parked in the corner of the Day Room, courtesy of Dr. Givhup. The two children who had no home to go to for Christmas had Christmas delivered to them. I decided that day that the good Dr. Givhup, Hindu from birth, was the best Christian I had ever met.

LANA

Chapter 31
Christmas 1955

In the weeks following Thanksgiving, Billy Wayne and the rest of the recreation department worked feverishly to prepare for the hospital's Christmas. The noise of the TV, the movement of patients and the conversations of the aides were now superseded by radios blaring Christmas music. Recreation workers began to sort through the fruit, candy, socks, underwear and cigarettes that had been sent to the hospital in large boxes from Central Office in Jackson. Each patient received a variety of edibles, new clothing and toiletries that would be rare unless provided by family members. It seemed to Billy Wayne that he spent all day with red felt "stockings," stuffing them and then sorting them by ward and building. He wished he had the time to take the patients for a walk to the "Rec center" or on a bus ride to look at the Christmas lights. However, for the month of December, the stocking stuffer chore monopolized his time.

Since Lana ate with her unit during the first lunch shift, he typically broke away from his chores long enough to lounge in the cafeteria for a half hour. As he talked to his brother in the kitchen, Billy Wayne would repeatedly glance at the dining room, looking for the patients from Lana's ward. Bringing his cup of coffee to her table, he would sit across from her and tease with the patients seated nearby. The women loved his good-natured charm and were happy to make a space for him on their benches. Several of them would pat his arm and tell each other that Billy Wayne was their "boyfriend." He liked to see Lana's eyes following their hands as they fluttered over him, but he was also pleased that she didn't take part in the persistent flirtation.

With his back to the kitchen, Billy Wayne was unaware that "Big John" was watching the activities at the table with more than a passing interest. Mavis knew he was observing them. She winked at John and waved coyly.

"Big John" had entered the hospital 10 years earlier, at the age of 22, because the townspeople of Rose Hill believed he had killed a woman in their community. Mrs. Brantley was a stocky, middle-aged woman who had hired John to cut her lawn. He was a "slow learner" who never attended school and spent his days roaming the village without supervision. But when her partially clothed body was found on the floor of her bedroom, John was the only suspect. For one thing, he had recently been seen raking out her flower beds.

But the most compelling indictment was the fact that he had spent years tagging along behind a group of teenaged boys who had dropped out of school. Because John agreeably acted out their fantasies, the group made him a quasi-member. They incited him to steal lace underwear from Miss Latimer's clothesline, to plunder Coach Brantley's pornography in his tool shed, and to write the "F word" in the snow of Miss Angela's yard.

Since there was no evidence to convict John of the murder, and his retardation prevented a trial, he had been sent to Western State for the remainder of his life. After a short period of adjustment, John gained grounds privileges and was prized in the dairy barn for his rugged build and his willingness to work.

When Billy Wayne finished his coffee, he ambled to his office and found a new crate of donations to be sorted. Muttering under his breath, he raked his fingers through his hair in frustration but as he opened the boxes, he thought immediately of Lana and how pretty she would look in one of the lapis blue earring sets. The Shalimar perfume had been packed next to the jewelry and left its soft scent on the white cardboard box. Newly inspired, he grabbed an empty stocking and carefully filled it with the best presents in the crate, locking it in a desk drawer when he finished.

A week later, while he was taking a break from the Christmas preparations, he found a piece of notebook paper and carefully printed: "To Lana. One fishing lesson at the Ox-Bow lake. From

Billy Wayne" He folded the paper carefully and retrieving the felt stocking from its hiding place, pushed the note to the toe.

Christmas Day was unseasonably warm with a cloudy sky that foretold a change in the weather. Billy Wayne volunteered to work the holiday. He placed the boxes of Christmas presents in one of Western's flatbed trucks and began delivering them. At the doors of the units, crowds of bright-eyed patients rushed toward him and had to be physically restrained until he could march the boxes to the Day Rooms. He was amused to see the harmless melee that resulted under most of the Christmas trees. When the cardboard flaps were pulled back, eager patients thrust their hands into the boxes, grabbing as many stockings as they could reach. But as fistfights broke out on some of the units, Billy Wayne was unwittingly pulled into the aides' attempts to maintain order. Control rooms were full, vats of Epsom's Salts were depleted and nurses were short-tempered all over the hospital.

On Lana's unit, Helen considered herself a veteran of Christmas festivities, and she knew that before she could share Christmas dinner with Dr. Lundsford, she had to finish her shift. She was, therefore, intent on getting the presents distributed equitably and calmly. Under the garlands of artificial holly and mistletoe, Helen had seated all of the women in a circle of chairs. Clipboard resting against her hip, she dared anyone to get up without permission. After Mavis nonchalantly stood and stretched her muscular arms, Helen made an example of her by immediately locking her in the control room. By the time Billy Wayne arrived, the other women were sitting quietly, hands folded in their laps, listening to the muffled sounds of Mavis cursing and screaming.

His hopes at being able to spend some time with Lana were buoyed by the sense of order. The aides took several stockings in each hand and walked around the circle of chairs, handing one to each patient. Cindy reached into her stocking and seized the bottle of "Evening in Paris" cologne. Using the atomizer, she sent a saccharine mist lingering in the air. Giggling, she ducked under the haze before the aide seized the bottle and absconded with it.

Cindy began to argue about this injustice but was instructed by Helen to sit down or join Mavis for the rest of the day. She slumped into a chair, looking suddenly insignificant.

Most of the women immediately dumped the presents into their laps and happily began to sort through the items. Lana slowly retrieved her gifts from the stocking, pausing to hold each piece of fruit, each pair of socks, as if she were saying grace. She heard Helen announce that they could leave their chairs as long as they didn't squabble with each other. With Mavis' continual stream of profanity providing a warning, most patients stayed in the Day Room, peeling their oranges and trying on their new socks. Lana had gathered up her gifts and was starting for her bedroom when Billy Wayne interrupted her course.

"Why don't you put your things away and take a quick walk with me," he suggested. "It's pretty warm outside today."

She quickly agreed, returning with a Christmas-plaid headscarf tied around her hair. Rita unlocked the door for them, admonishing Lana not to be late for the afternoon Christmas party sponsored by the Presbyterian Ladies.

Billy Wayne and Lana walked down the long marble steps of the Administration Building and strolled to the baseball field. Taking a seat beside him, Lana took deep breaths of the damp air as if she could somehow save enough to protect herself from the coming weeks indoors. When she surveyed her surroundings, she realized with mild confusion that she had probably been to this ball field during the summer. She wished she could be sure. She trolled the recesses of her memory, trying to picture Billy Wayne as a coach who herded the young patients onto the field; or perhaps as a player, tapping the end of his bat against home plate. Neither fabricated memory seemed correct, however. She pulled her attention away from the baseball field and turned to look at Billy Wayne.

Unbuttoning his jacket, Billy Wayne reached inside for the red stocking, warm from being carried close to his chest. He had written an awkward "Lana" with glitter and realized as he retrieved it that there was now a smudge of gold on his flannel shirt. Lana noticed the glitter before she noticed the stocking. Reflexively she brushed her hand across his chest to rake away the gold sparkle, then stopped as she realized the level of intimacy it presumed. She blushed as she took her hand away.

"It made a mess, didn't it?" he laughed, glancing at the front of his shirt. Then he thrust the stocking to her folded hands. "Here, Lana. Merry Christmas." He was disappointed with his brusque and artless phrasing, but he could not pull the words back so he waited for her response. She blinked her eyes at him in surprise before she looked down to the heavy felt stocking lying in her hands.

"But I already got my Christmas in the Day Room," she protested.

"I know, but this is something extra….I wanted you to have it."

She reached into the stocking and slowly removed the jewelry box, opening it carefully and running the tips of her fingers over the smooth stones, her lips parted in wonder. She sprayed a light mist of perfume on her wrists. Finally, she lay the stocking in her lap and looked up at him with a clear, unwavering gaze. "Billy Wayne, I don't know why you've done all this, but I do appreciate it." She paused and then ended regretfully, "And to think: I don't have a thing to give you."

"I didn't expect to get something back!" he insisted before his face broke into a broad grin. "Oh, you've got one more thing in the bottom of that stocking!"

She looked puzzled but ran her slender hand to the toe of the stocking and pulled out the note. "One fishin' lesson on the Ox-Bow lake," she read aloud, glancing at him in confusion. "Are we goin' fishin' today?"

He laughed. "No. You'd best save that present `til spring, when the fishin'll be better."

She was embarrassed at her ignorance and fell silent until he suggested, "We *could* take a walk down there though and just look around." The hike would make her unavailable to any afternoon visit from Jerry, she thought. Lana quickly agreed to go.

As they started toward the edge of the campus, Billy Wayne told her, "The shortest way to the Ox-Bow is through the patient cemetery. If you're not superstitious about things like that."

"I always heard the dead were at peace," she said, trotting to keep up with his brisk steps.

They were traveling on a grassy path through an arch of bare trees. After a quarter of a mile, the field road opened to a large clearing with marble headstones. Billy Wayne stepped confidently around the areas where patients had been buried, while Lana slowed her steps and looked about anxiously.

"What's all these bricks doin' on the ground?" she asked.

"That's regular markers for the graves. The families buy the tall ones when they want something better than the bricks."

Although she had agreed to walk through the cemetery, Lana was overwhelmed by sorrow for the people buried there. Shunted off to Western by family who abandoned them twice. People like "Bird Lady" whose real name had been surrendered at the hospital gates and who in death would be reduced to a numbered brick. Her eyes filled with tears as she stopped to read a thin marker, pitted by the years and overgrown with grass. Billy Wayne realized Lana was no longer walking behind him. He turned to see her kneeling in front of a headstone, one long finger tracing the letters across the grainy surface. She said more to herself than him, "Ada Cearley. Born 1872. Died 1890. Rest in peace." Her fingers brushed downward to caress a carving of a reclining lamb. Billy Wayne took a step toward her as she raised her eyes to his. "She was only 18 when she died. What could've happened to her? Do you guess she was one of Miss Adele's relatives?"

"I don't know, but she probably was. I think all the Cearleys are related if you go back far enough."

"Poor little thing," Lana sighed, looking again at the marker. "She died before she could even have a life. I wonder why she had to come to this hospital." She glanced at him for an answer.

Billy Wayne crouched at the back of the marker and draped one arm over the top. "I never heard the story about her," he confessed. "You want me to ask some of the old-timers about her?"

She nodded. "I'd like to know if she was related.... to Miss Adele." She paused briefly, considering whether she should talk about her past but then plunged ahead, relying on her instinct that Billy Wayne could be trusted. "Miss Adele, she was 'bout the only one that was good to me when I was having a real hard time with my husband."

Billy Wayne scanned her face, looking for the hardship she had borne but finding nothing but a troubled frown. He waited wordlessly while she traced and re-traced the outline of the lamb, his silence compelling her to continue. "Miss Adele found me on the side of the road one mornin' after Christmas and gave me a ride. It was so cold that day! And I was out there in my nightgown." She smiled to herself, the crooked grin giving her an ironic expression. "Now if there ever was a time I looked crazy, it was that day! I s'ppose Western State would have taken me, no questions asked!"

When Billy Wayne asked why she was outside in her gown, she turned her head to the side and looked at the dead grass brushing against the headstone, "I was tryin' to get away from Jerry and I didn't have time to get dressed," she explained and then added hesitantly, "He was hittin' on me."

"What?!" Billy Wayne sputtered as he scrambled to his feet. "Hittin' you?! Why in the world was he doin' that?"

"He didn't have to have no reason why, Billy Wayne. That mornin' he was mad 'cause there wasn't no whisky in the house."

Billy Wayne ground his teeth and felt his face growing hot despite the cool breeze that filtered between the trees. "Did he hurt you bad, Lana?"

"No, not that morning."

He pounded one fist on the cold granite before he began to pace. Lana took a deep breath and continued without looking at him. "Well, that mornin' I decided to just get out of the house as fast as I could. I didn't really think 'bout how cold it was. When Miss Adele stopped for me, I was just about froze to death. I think she knew what Jerry'd done. She told me I didn't have to live like that. She said if I wanted to leave Jerry, she'd give me a job at her house." Lana stopped and directed her gaze to Billy Wayne's eyes. "I'll never forget how she talked to me. I thought she must be the smartest, strongest woman I ever knowed," she concluded.

He turned his back to her and blurted out, "If I'd a known you back then, I would've done something to help you."

Lana blushed. "I'm sure you would've, Billy Wayne. You've got a good heart."

When he turned back, she was standing. He scanned her face, looking at the strands of fine blonde hair that had worked loose from the scarf, blowing in wisps across her cheek. He looked into the eyes that were such a crystalline blue that he felt he could dive into them head first. Quickly he distracted himself from these unsettling thoughts by asking her to walk to the riverbank.

She took his hand as they stood on the bluff over the swirling brown waters. "Right up from here," Billy Wayne said, ignoring her warm fingers while he pointed to a bend in the Neshobee, "is where I was telling you about catchin' enough fish t'have everybody over for a fish fry."

As he talked, Lana's eyes never left the river. She was mesmerized by the flow of the brown water. He came to the end of his observations and stood next to her in silence, occasionally glancing at her profile to see that the statue-like expression was unchanged. Twenty minutes later, with the sun snagged in the black fingers of the trees, Billy Wayne said it was time to start walking back and Lana responded softly, "I hate to go back to that hospital. I wish I could stay right here forever." He had never heard her express bitterness about the hospital, although he had wondered if she were really so content in a locked building. She went on, "This river's so wild and so strong that nobody could ever hold it down, could ever lock it up."

"It is," he agreed quietly.

"Nobody could change it. Nobody could make it go a different way. It's been running free since God put it here." He lamely confirmed this as she continued, "If you put a boat in, right here, could you go all the way to the ocean?" She took his sleeve into a tight fist, her eyes flickering with excitement.

"Wouldn't you like to, Billy Wayne?" she persisted, tugging at the sleeve. "Don't you wish you could just get in the water here and go 'til you touched the ocean? Have you ever seen the ocean?" As he shook his head, she continued, "There was pictures of it in my school books. Wouldn't it be wonderful to see it in real life, Billy Wayne?"

They stood in silence for a few more minutes, Lana's eyes following leaves and branches that passed them in a swirl. Finally he broke the spell to insist that they start back. She walked beside him without complaint, but she paused several times to look behind her at the trees that bordered the water.

LANA

Chapter 32
A Mess of Fish

With the first days of spring, Lana longed to be outside, feeling the sun's rays needling through her clothes. The "grounds privileges" allowed her to come and go from the ward and when it wasn't raining, she quickly finished any chores and left to wander the paths and the rolling lawns. The aides on the afternoon shift insisted that she be on the unit by suppertime, and she was scrupulous in abiding by this curfew.

She had almost forgotten about Billy Wayne's offer to take her fishing when he appeared one warm March day, holding two cane poles, a small cooler and a carton of worms. Rita called her to the door of the ward, where Billy Wayne was waiting. Even in a faded work shirt and slacks too large for her slender frame, he thought Lana looked beautiful. He recognized an unwanted tug of attraction each time he glanced at her.

Lana, excited about the outing, chattered most of the way to the Ox-Bow lake, telling him funny stories about Mavis, Dora and Daisy. He knew them all: They went to the fair in Memphis, took rides through the countryside, and attended every festival that he organized for the campus.

While she scanned the bank, he set the cooler on the damp ground and crouched to thread a hook through a fat, red worm.

"Look over there, Billy Wayne," she called to him, pointing to the cattails that grew in profusion. She remembered seeing the funny exclamation marks in her school books, and now the cattails seemed to be an army of exclamations, in lock-step along the shore. "!!!!!We're marching to the lake!!! In our brown uniforms!!! Attention!!!" they seemed to call out to her. She giggled until Billy Wayne looked up from his tackle box.

"Yeah, they grow where it's wet," he said absently.

"They look like an army…"she started, then let her voice trail away, feeling utterly foolish at her inability to explain.

He glanced at the shoreline without responding, then handed the pole to Lana. Standing just behind her, he put his right hand on her forearm, guiding her to toss the cork into a tranquil spot just off the bank. "Just hold it still, now," he whispered against her ear, "and be real quiet. You'd be surprised what a fish can hear."

When the cork bobbed under the current for an instant, he yelled for her to pull hard and in an instant Lana's first glittering bream appeared on the bank. It flopped and twisted in the grass, compelling her to drop the fishing pole to admire it. He re-baited the hook and took up his position behind her. This time she pitched the cork into the water with a slow, underhanded motion. "That's good!" he encouraged, still whispering. Within an hour, she had landed 15 bream and crappie. Laughing at her good fortune, she grabbed Billy Wayne in a spontaneous hug. "I caught us a mess of fish, didn't I?"

He tilted his head to look down at her face, saw her eyes dancing with excitement and in that instant, before he could consider the questions of right and wrong, before he could reason out the consequences, she moved toward him, brushing his lips in a soft kiss. And a second later, she leaned heavily against him, tightened her grip around his neck and kissed him more urgently. Billy Wayne stepped back from her with an expression of alarm.

"Well!" she said, breathlessly, pushing a wisp of blonde hair away from her eyes.

His big hands dangled at his side, while his mind reeled from one scenario to the next. "I-I'm sorry, Lana," he stammered. "It just happened."

"Sorry?" she questioned, the crooked smile giving her a look of amusement. "Sorry?" she repeated. "Well, I'm not….I'm not a bit sorry about it." She looked directly in his eyes, suddenly brazen in her confidence.

He didn't know what to say, but he fervently hoped he had not offended her and he was completely bewildered by her comments. She took a step closer to him and lifted her chin. "I'm not sorry because I liked it." On tiptoe, she kissed him again. Billy Wayne had come to his senses in the intervening seconds. He grabbed her wrists and stepped back from her, saying that they needed to start back for the hospital. Picking up the cooler of fish, he marched down the path, listening for her footsteps to follow him.

They came to the edge of the hospital lawn. He turned to face her and said, "Lana, what happened back there…it shouldn't have happened. I'm sorry for my part."

"You keep saying you're sorry," she scolded him. "But I thought it was nice. I liked it!"

Flustered by her insistence, his face turned red and he shook his head. "You're a married woman. It ain't right."

She laid her hand against his arm and searched his eyes, suddenly very solemn. "It felt right to me," she told him simply and then ambled toward the Administration Building, leaving him to watch her meander between the trees as if she were enjoying a day of leisure. When he saw her enter the front door, he tossed the cooler in his truck and drove to Clyde's house, where he made a gift of the fish. Betty asked him to stay for supper, but he declined and drove home to brood over the events of the day.

March had reversed itself and was now cold and raw, after the auspicious, mild beginning. Lana spent long, boring days in her room, watching from the window as the wind and rain shredded a forest of tender leaves. Daydreaming about her brothers occupied much of her time. They would be inside the house on days like this, staying warm by the woodstove, while her father planned the work that would come with warmer weather.

Billy Wayne eventually returned to his post beside the cafeteria coffee urn, gradually succumbing to his habit of visiting with the women while they ate breakfast. His eyes followed Lana when she entered the dining hall and lingered on her while he talked to patients at her table. "Big John," watching from the kitchen, let his hands dangle at his sides and stared at Billy Wayne and Lana when Clyde was too busy to notice.

During an ordinary Thursday breakfast, Lana told Billy Wayne that she had been thinking about her family almost constantly. She complained about her isolation and wistfully said she sure wished they would come visit her. He smiled at her, asking if she'd like pencil and paper to write a letter. No, she responded. Her father couldn't read or write, and her brothers might not be able to help him if the words were big. Billy Wayne nodded sympathetically before he offered, "You want t'go down there and see `em?"

Had this possibility of a visit been present all along? Could it have been hers, just for the asking? And what about Billy Wayne— had she ever met anyone with such a kind face and with such concern in his eyes? The other women had taken their trays to the sink and were lining up by the door. The aides admonished her to hurry so Lana whispered, "Yes! Thank you!" before rushing to the door. There, she turned twice to wave at him before she disappeared with the procession of patients through the door.

As he walked back to his office, Billy Wayne called himself every derogatory name he could think of. "Stupid! Idiot! You dumb bastard!" He berated himself as he walked with his chin tucked into his collar. "What the hell d'you think you're doin'? You know you don't need to be alone with that girl! Look what happened when you took her fishing! She's goin' to get you in a mess of trouble." He marched along the sidewalk, glaring at the cracks in the concrete.

LANA

Chapter 33
Her Daddy's Place

The howling of the wind woke her before dawn. She had slept fitfully all night, her dreams and thoughts running together in a confusing stream of images from her childhood and the years with Jerry. Pulling on her clothes, she smiled to herself at the thought of appearing as if by magic at her father's door. She imagined her brothers' faces, their smiles, and their arms around her waist. She told the aides she was not hungry for breakfast and stayed behind on the unit to pace in the hall, waiting anxiously for Billy Wayne. When the door was unlocked for him, she arrived at his side just as he was signing the pass sheet. He handed it to the aide, who disinterestedly stuffed it into a pocket and declared, "I don't know why anyone would want to get out in this weather."

It was not raining, but the low clouds threatened a deluge at any moment. They ran to Billy Wayne's truck, Lana holding the knotted scarf at her throat to keep it in place. As Billy Wayne turned the key in the ignition, she pulled the scarf from her hair, tossed the gleaming ringlets and exclaimed, "That feels better!" In response to his look of amazement, she explained, "Rita put it up in curlers for me last night, 'cause I wanted to look nice for my visit."

"Well, you do," he said laconically and then doggedly turned his attention to the drive.

As the hospital receded into the distance, Lana became increasingly talkative and gay. Billy Wayne listened to her with smiles and furtive glances, asking occasionally where he should be looking for the turns.

"Oh! We're not near there, yet!" she assured him, returning to her story about the boys putting up a tire swing. A few minutes later, he swung the truck off the highway and onto a barely-graveled dirt road. It twisted through the trees, occasionally sinking into puddles and causing the truck's frame to creak in protest.

Lana knew something was amiss as they drove into the yard, but she told herself that her father's truck was gone because he was in town on an errand. When they stepped onto the rickety front porch, she told herself there were no faces at the window because the boys couldn't hear her steps over the moaning wind. Her fist, raised to the unpainted door, trembled momentarily before she knocked. Telling Billy Wayne that they were probably asleep, Lana pounded her hand against the wood; then with her head down in determination, she pushed open the door and called, "Fred! Les! It's Lana! Come on and get up!"

Billy Wayne stepped into the gloom of the empty house and felt his heart go heavy in his chest. A few worn pieces of furniture were left in the room, but it was obvious that no one had lived in the house for weeks, if not months. The place even smelled deserted to him. The wood burning stove smelled of wet ashes and rancid grease. The peculiar odor of mice announced their presence before the dry scurry of their feet. Lana, however, seemed unable to comprehend the emptiness. As Billy Wayne stood helplessly by the cold and sooty woodstove, she began to run from room to room, calling her brothers and father in a voice that grew more desperate with each name. She opened doors and shouted into dark spaces. At one point she raised a back window and called in piteous tones, "Les! You answer when I call you! You hear?" Her voice breaking, faintly she cried, "You hear me, Les?"

Billy Wayne shuffled into a back room and found her sitting on the edge of a torn, grey mattress, her head in her hands, the silver curls shielding her face. Her shoulders shook convulsively, and the tears ran through her fingers and streaked her forearms. He hated to see a woman cry; and no matter how many times he had been forced to watch it at the hospital, his throat had always spasmed into a tight knot, as if he were going to shed tears, too. Watching Lana cry now was almost unbearable. He sat on the bed next to her, patted her on the back and stroked her hair, feeling helpless and foolish.

She uncoiled her body and leaned into him, clenching the soft flannel shirt in both fists. Billy Wayne held her and let the torrent of sorrow flow over and around him, feeling as if he were immobilized in a raging current. She sobbed until her cry ebbed into whimpers, and then she collapsed on the torn mattress, pulling him down to lie beside her. She whispered his name, running her fingertips against the face where she saw only sympathy. Tracing the curve of his cheek, she swept her fingers to his mouth, then leaned over him and kissed him gently. The fragrance of shampoo drifted to him. As she pressed her lips against his, he could taste the salt from her tears. "Please, Billy Wayne, please say 'yes,'" she murmured, kissing him more insistently. She took one of his hands and put it under her blouse, shuddering as his palm touched her nipple.

Despite his resolution, Billy Wayne found that refusing Lana would have been as impossible as swimming against the current of the Neshobee. She took the lead, unbuttoning his clothes, and touching him tenderly but urgently. The blood pounded in his ears as he watched her slithering out of her blouse; and when she sat atop him and moved with her own rhythm, he felt exquisitely paralyzed. Her pale skin and blonde hair were luminescent against the shadows of the bleak room. The curtain of silver-blonde hair fell forward and cascaded back as she rocked against him, mesmerizing him with her fierce beauty and desperate sexuality.

In the abandoned shack, their lovemaking was almost silent. They whispered their endearments as if her brothers were listening at the door. All morning and into the afternoon, Lana tangled her long arms and legs around him and smothered him with her kisses. When he gave in to exhaustion, she insistently placed her palm against his face and turned him toward her whispered pleadings. Their bodies came together again and again, temporarily belying the emptiness that surrounded them, soaking the grey mattress with sweat and semen, until a leaden fatigue finally overtook both of them.

With Lana's head pillowed on his shoulder, Billy Wayne pulled his flannel shirt from the edge of the bed and spread it over her shoulders. They dozed with the wind raising a howl of protest at their bliss. It rattled the loose panes in the window and raked the skeleton hand of a leafless bush against the clapboard.

"Lana, you awake?" He felt her eyelashes flutter against his skin. "Lana, I just want you to know that I'm gonna look until I find your family." He waited for a response, but none came. "We can start by askin' the neighbors where they moved off to. And we can check with your relatives that live in the county, too."

Her words were slow and deliberate as she summarized her family's lack of kin, but he urged her to consider the neighbors as a source of information.

"I don't think it'll do no good," she responded listlessly. "I think Daddy just fell on hard times and had to move to another farm."

Billy Wayne talked further of the ways he could investigate, pressing for her permission to talk to people on his own, until she finally acquiesced with a murmured, "It's alright by me."

With his confidence restored he admitted, "I'm sorry about your family being gone, Lana, but I ain't sorry 'bout what happened today."

"Me, neither."

He could feel her rhythmic breathing returning and knew she had drifted back to sleep. The instinct of protection radiated warmly across his chest, causing him to tighten his embrace before he let himself relax enough to doze. When he awoke, the window framed a gloomy dusk. Seized with panic, he called for Lana to wake up. "It's almost night!" he gasped.

She bolted from the bed and began pulling on the clothes that lay in a heap on the floor. As he buttoned his shirt, he watched her glide underclothes across the very skin that he had just caressed, and he fought an urge to bring her back to bed, to let the hospital be damned. He dared not make such a suggestion.

He stood and pulled Lana to his chest in a tight hug. "I ain't gonna wait another week to see you," he vowed, his voice muffled by her hair.

"We'll do what we can," she told him stoically, then broke his caress to walk to the front door. As he followed her through the kitchen, he saw her shoulders sag under the weight of grief. She hesitated briefly, then raised her chin and walked with her eyes steadfastly on the front door, avoiding the scraps of memories that lay in the room's corners.

LANA

Chapter 34
Billy Wayne

For a long time I fooled myself into believin' that I could jus' be a friend to Lana Wright, could help her through her troubles. She had a husband that beat her and no family to care about her. I must of told myself a hundred times, "Be careful, Billy Wayne; keep your mind on your job; don't do anything you wouldn't do for any other patient." Every time I saw Lana, I reminded myself that I was an employee and she was a patient and a married woman. I did a pretty good job holdin' everything in check 'til that day we went to visit her family. I never seen anybody so heartbroken! I tried to comfort her, but it seemed like the only comfort she wanted was for me t' love her. I jus' couldn't turn her away and after that, I couldn't think of her as a patient again.

While I was in high school, I had my share of girls to date. Some of 'em spent time in the backseat with me. But I had to plan every date and even so, we were always in a hurry. There was fumblin' with clothes and worries about being caught. But Lana! She slithered out of her clothes and came to me with her mind made-up. She is a beautiful, headstrong woman.

As the time went by, I did a lot of thinkin' about our future. I wanted Lana to be my wife, but she was already married and divorces were hard to come by. For a while, I thought about talkin' to Jerry man-to-man and makin' him see that he needed to turn Lana loose. Other days I was so frustrated that I thought I'd jus' take Lana out of Western and run away with her. But I didn't want to spend the rest of my life lookin' over one shoulder, tellin' lies t' everybody we met. That's not who I am.

After that day at her daddy's, I didn't get to see Lana again 'til the Thursday bus ride. I remember her standin' in line, lookin' from window to window, tryin' to catch a glimpse of me, worried like she thought I might-a gone away for good. When I opened the door and waved, she looked thrilled, givin' me the biggest smile I'd ever seen from her. I had piled some jackets on the seat behind me to save it for Lana, and once she came on the bus, I pushed everything over t' make room for her to sit down. We couldn't talk at first, but I caught her eyes in the rear-view mirror and smiled at her every chance I got. Once the bus was moving and the patients all got to talking, we had a strange kind of privacy.

Lord, the bus was noisy that day! The main things the patients were talkin' about were Cindy's discharge and Benny dyin'. Benny was at a cookout on Wednesday and I saw it happen. He put three hot dogs in his mouth at the same time and tried to swallow `em. He started turning red and he grabbed his throat. Jimmy, one of the recreation workers, was standin' next to him when it happened. I was across the way, helpin' Inez put more food on the picnic tables. When I looked up, Jimmy was pounding Benny on the back and Benny was turning beet-red. Before I could get around the picnic tables, Benny's knees buckled and he fell on the ground. His lips were blue, like he'd been suckin' on a blueberry popsicle. I loosened his shirt to try to give him more air, but Benny wasn't breathin'. He may of been gone before I even got to him.

Well, on that bus ride, half of the men in the back of the bus were talkin' about Benny dyin'. Charlie said, "Thas the way it happen sometimes. Yo' spirit jus' get loose from yo' soul and yo' soul jus' gotta go on." When I looked in the rear view mirror, I could see Charlie sprawled all over the seat. He had his tongue pushed against his bottom lip, which made him look like he had a big wad of tobacco in there. He moved his tongue out of the way and went back to talking about the soul. "Yo' soul, it caint stay down here, when that happen. It jus' had'ta go on up," he said, looking straight at the ceiling of the bus. The way Charlie was talking, it was like Benny's soul was living in the bus.

Before I could reason that out, Elbert took off his shoes and socks and sniffed his toes. He wasn't any more interested in what Charlie was sayin' than a man in the moon. Elbert was one of

Benny's roommates, but he didn't seem to care that Benny was dead. I thought the noise was goin' to die down, but then Sid started to rock back and forth in his seat, cryin'. He hollered over and over, "I HATE that man……… di-i-ed! He my roo-oo-mate! He my roo-oo-mate! I HATE that man……….di-i-ed!" The aides had their hands full. First they tried to soothe Sid. "It's okay, Sid; don't cry now." But finally they lost their patience and said if everybody didn't quiet down, the bus would be goin' back to Western.

Three women sittin' behind Lana were talkin' about Cindy bein' gone. "She was gettin' bigger'n a cow!" Annie said, and she held her hands in front of her stomach to show that Cindy was expectin'.

"She might have twins!" Zelma giggled.

"Or a whole litter of young `uns!" Winnie said. They put their heads together and cackled just like hens in the chicken yard.

The next time I caught Lana's eye, I told her, "I'm gonna get you a pass on Saturday mornin'. We'll drive over to Braggadocio and see if anyone there knows about your family."

Lana always seemed to be grateful for any little kindness. She nodded her head and whispered, "I'll be ready."

As soon as we got to the Y, I handed out the spending money and all the patients left the bus. I told Lana to wait a minute and once the last patient was in the store, I sat down next to her and kissed her. "I've been wantin' to do that all week!" I said as she smiled that little crooked smile back at me. Truth be told, I'd rather just stayed on the bus with her, but I decided we'd best not raise any suspicions, so we followed the patients to the store. We sat on the plank floor of the porch, had a coke and talked to each other without ever taking our eyes off the bus. I told her to be ready to leave the hospital at 8:00 on Saturday, and I told her all the places I intended to check on.

She seemed real discouraged to me. "Do you really think we'll find `em?" she asked over and over.

"I don't know. But we'll never find 'em if we don't try," I pointed out to her.

We got out every Saturday for a couple of months and had no

luck at all findin' anybody that knew anything. I musta talked to 30 women who stood in the shadows of the door with their kids hanging onto their dresses, and not a one said they had ever heard of the Grays. Lana didn't want me to do it, but I finally decided to drive over to Adele and Walter Forrest's and see if they knew anything 'bout her people.

After I pulled my pickup into the driveway, I could see this tall woman, wearin' a big straw hat and baggy, old men's clothes, standin' in the flower garden. Even with the way she was dressed, I figured it had to be Adele. For one thing, she had four black boys standing around her, watchin' her hoe. They were propped up against the trees in the shade, takin' it all in, cool as can be. Adele was tellin' them how she wanted things done and really showin' 'em how to do it.

When I walked up to 'em, I could hear her sayin', "Just like this!" while she chopped at the grass around the rose bush. There was something else said about fertilizer and roots, but those boys didn't seem to be payin' much attention to her. One of 'em standin' with his back against the tree looked like he was nappin'. When I was a few paces away from her, I cleared my throat and she spun around with her hoe up in the air.

I told her who I was, and she just listened, didn't say anymore than, "Yes?"

"Well, ma'am, I wondered if I could have a word with you…if it's not too much trouble."

She pulled her straw hat off and swiped her sleeve across her forehead. "What about?"

I asked her if I could talk privately, and she answered with a quick nod before she turned back to the boys, "Now! I've shown you what to do: surely you can work for a few minutes on your own." She leaned the hoe against the tree and led me to the shady front porch. Miss Adele threw herself into one of the chairs and told me to have a seat. While she was fannin' herself with the straw hat, she asked, "What can I do for you, Mr. Gordon?"

"I'm here 'cause I thought you might be able to give me some information. Help me find somebody." She raised one eyebrow, so I went on. "I work out at Western State and I'm a friend of Lana Gray, Jack Gray's girl. She's been tryin' to find her family for the last few months. The house they used to live in is empty and …."

"How do you know Lana?" she asked me, real sharp.

"I work at the hospital and I got to know her there."

"You mean she's a patient out there?"

"Yes, ma'am."

She shook her head slowly and then said, more to herself than to me, "Western State!" She went back t' fanning. "I guess she just had a nervous breakdown. Is that what happened, Mr. Gordon?"

"I guess so, ma'am. But by the time I first met her, Lana'd been in the hospital a few months and she seemed just fine to me. She was always askin' me `bout her father and brothers comin' to see her and I felt sorry for her, so I told her I'd help her find `em."

Miss Adele sighed and then looked at me out of the corner of her eyes. "Well, I'm afraid I can't be of much help to you…and your *friend*." She said "friend" in a way that let me know she saw more than a passin' interest in Lana. After she paused, she said, "John was working for Mr. Lanier most of last year. But he just up and moved away sometime in the early spring. Didn't show up at the sawmill for a week or so, already behind on his rent. Mr. Lanier sent Prentice to check on him and he found the house empty, all their things gone. No one ever knew what happened, but Prentice thought the older boy got real sick and the family just fell on hard times. They may have moved in with some of their kinfolks."

I swallowed hard. "How could that happen and nobody know where they went?"

"It probably happens more than you and I imagine," she told me. "These families living with one foot in the poorhouse, they don't have anything to fall back on. And most of them are too proud to ask for any help."

I threw my head back against the clapboards and closed my eyes. How in the world would I tell Lana this? We'd spent months lookin' for people who had disappeared into thin air! This was the last place to check and it was a dead end, too.

I stood up and said my goodbyes to Miss Adele, thankin' her for her help. She looked at me hard and said, "I do have one piece of advice for you, Mr. Gordon: Help Lana all you can. She's a lovely young woman. But you be very careful. Her husband Jerry is so mean and violent that Walter's threatened to move him off our place."

KATE

Chapter 35
Juvenile Court

The subpoena had been unceremoniously shoved under the door, causing me to leave a treadmark on the page when I stepped into the office. Brushing off the grit, I read the words that commanded my presence in Monroe County Juvenile Court to testify on Tavaris. I let my hands drop, the paper brushing against my thigh. I had never been to court, but during childhood had seen every one of the Perry Mason episodes on TV and, therefore, believed the court room was a dignified place, where lawyers asked trick questions that compelled reluctant witnesses to confess their crimes.

I walked to Don's office and found him as busy as an alchemist. He was orchestrating a percolator, an electric tea kettle, a jug of vinegar, three travel mugs and a collection of herbs to concoct a tincture of health. When I showed him the subpoena, he tilted his head back to read the print through his bifocals. "Hmm…" he said thoughtfully. "A subpoena, huh? Well, you'll do fine, Kate. "

"But I've never been to court before," I whined.

"First time for everything," he chirped cheerfully, turning back to the laboratory on his desk.

Jack was more sympathetic but unable to give me advice. He had never made an appearance in juvenile court, he told me, but he'd been a character witness for one of his hunting buddies who had been sued for alienation of affection in a divorce. "It wasn't bad," he reassured me. "I just told what I knew about Ted and then I left. I don't think Judge Walker will let `em be hard on you, Kate." I miserably scanned the subpoena. "Would you feel better if I went with you?" he asked.

I was stunned by the generosity of his offer. "Could you do that?"

He assured me that it would be no problem to arrange his

schedule, and we planned to leave Western immediately after lunch the next day.

While Jack chauffered me to Court Square, I opened Tavaris' folder in my lap and re-read the report I had written in the fall. It all seemed so long ago that I was afraid I would be unable to even recognize Tavaris among the people in the room. At the courthouse, we climbed the creaky walnut staircase in tandem, like two high school students in the 1920's, walking to our biology class. The massive door to the courtroom was closed. The bailiff asked for the name of the case and then instructed me to enter. "You'll have to wait for her, Jack," he said apologetically, "since you haven't been subpoenaed."

Jack promised he would be right outside the courtroom, flashing me a grin as the door closed with a thud. I took a seat on a wooden pew in the empty courtroom. The curved hand rails, patterned tin ceiling, highly polished tables, and floor-to-ceiling windows reminded me of the courtroom in *To Kill a Mockingbird*. While I was lost in my daydream, attorneys and officials trickled in, their voices rising into a gradual crescendo of good-natured banter. It was easy to spot Tavaris: His shackles clanked ominously as he shuffled to the table where his young lawyer waited to meet him, apparently for the first time. The defense attorney motioned for Tavaris to sit down and then began an earnest conversation, leaning toward Tavaris and conferring in a low voice.

At the next table, the elderly prosecutor was lounging in his chair, engaged in jovial conversation with the bailiff about duck hunting. At a pause in the story, the bailiff answered his query with a nod in my direction. The prosecutor, who resembled Colonel Sanders, rose from his seat and advanced toward me, smoothing his blue seersucker suit across his ample belly.

He leaned over me and carefully took my fingertips into his beefy hand. His white goatee framed a dingy smile. "Sidney Cupples," he said in a low, tidewater accent. "Thank you for comin' in today, little lady. Judge Walker wanted to hear from you, directly." I raised my eyebrows. "I imagine he was interested in just *who* could be writing those nine page reports!" He winked at me before returning to his conversation with the bailiff. I was left to wonder if the judge was pleased with my work or only irritated with the volume.

Then it was the defense lawyer's turn to approach. He was dressed in a new grey suit, burgundy tie and starched-white shirt. Since he appeared to be my own age, I wondered briefly if he, too, could be making his first court appearance that day. Gingerly he sat next to me and quizzed me about how I would answer hypothetical questions. "You don't want to see him go to juvenile corrections, do you?" he chided when I told him Tavaris had little family support. Then he advanced his own theory: "None of this would have happened if the school system hadn't failed him. Tavaris never got the help he needed and he was just frustrated."

Before I could respond to this misguided logic, we were interrupted. "All rise!" boomed the bailiff as the young lawyer hurried back to his seat by Tavaris. "Oh yes, oh yes. The Juvenile Court of Monroe County is now in session, the Honorable Robert T. Walker presiding. All who have business before this court draw near and you shall be heard. Come to order and be seated," he intoned, the monologue echoing along the walls.

The portly judge, dressed in what appeared to be a black choir robe, read Tavaris' charges aloud: "Aggravated Burglary: Theft over $500, Vandalism." He asked the lawyers if they had worked out any agreement and then impatiently declared he would have to have a full hearing, as if he were punishing the attorneys for their indolence. "Call your first witness, General," he instructed the prosecutor.

The bailiff motioned me to the front and swore me in. I took my seat in the witness stand, nervously fingering the file folder. My mouth was parched, and I licked my lips without any sensation that they had been dampened. Pitchers of ice water stood on each lawyer's table, a constant reminder that my thirst could be slaked if I simply sauntered away from the witness seat.

"State your name for the record, please," the judge instructed me.

"Kathleen McConnaughy."

"And what are your credentials?"

"I am a clinical psychologist, working at Western Mississippi Psychiatric Hospital on the adolescent unit."

Judge Walker nodded his approval. "General, your witness."

Mr. Cupples stood at his table and hooked his thumbs into his belt. Rocking back on his heels, he began, "Miss McConnie..." He halted, cleared his throat and started again, "Miss Macaroni." The defense attorney bowed his head and stifled a chuckle while I sat frozen in the chair. What would be the proper thing to do? Correct Mr. Cupples or remain silent? My thoughts were interrupted by his voice. "Miss MacNaughty!" he blurted out. The judge smiled at this slip of the tongue, but Mr. Cupples plunged ahead, apparently unembarrassed. "Can we just call you..." He paused dramatically before coyly suggesting, "Miss Katie?"

"I...I guess so," I answered, even though it seemed terribly informal for a court proceeding. But then again, surely Mr. Cupples knew better than I.

"Now, Miss Katie, you say heh-a in your psychological RE-port that Tavaris has average intellectual abilities but surris behavior problems," he read aloud as his thick forefinger slid along the typed copy.

I nodded. "Yes, Sir."

"Well, Miss Katie, can you put that in layman's terms?"

I floundered. Was this a trick question? Something Perry Mason would use to gain a confession? Did I have any wrongdoing to confess? Casting around for a simple description, I stuttered and hesitated. "Umm...well, I...umm...Tavaris has normal intellectual skills, but there are some...umm.. significant problems with his behavior," I finished lamely.

"Miss Katie, would it be safe to say that this young man has plenty of smarts, but he has a loose marble somewhere?"

I could hear my pulse pounding in my ears. This had to be a trick question! How could I answer it without ruining my credibility? "I guess…I guess you could say that," I stammered.

Mr. Cupples continued, "And in your experience, do such young men need the extra help of a full-time program? A place where they can live while they get rehabilitation?"

He was asking about a residential program. I understood the question. "Many times they do need…"

He interrupted me. "And here in the RE-port, you say that Tavaris needs residential treatment. Now, Miss Katie, did you base your opinion on the testing you did?"

"Yes, Sir."

"You see, Your Honor, Miss Katie was hired by the State of Mississippi to work with these disturbed young men and to probe their minds!" he proclaimed, throwing out his right arm in my general direction. "She has thoroughly tested Tavaris, and it is her professional recommendation that Tavaris go to a facility for some help. I submit that we should follow her recommendations since she is, after all…" He paused again for dramatic effect "…the Mind-Prober!" He bowed stiffly toward the judge and then took his seat at the table. I couldn't believe he was finished with his questions! I had been unable to give my full opinion, but the expected legal ambush was apparently not going to happen.

"Mr. Tate, your witness," the judge told the defense lawyer.

Rising from his chair with great energy and conviction, Mr. Tate came to an abrupt stop in front of me, as if the toes of his polished shoes were resting against the witness box. "Dr. McConnaughy," he said flawlessly, emphasizing the title of *doctor*. "In your training, did you learn the importance of a child's family life on his well-being and development?"

"Yes, Sir," I responded, glancing again at the rivulets of condensation, which slid down the sides of the pitchers. Evidently Mr. Tate was about to assume the role of grilling the witness, I thought, glumly realizing that the dreaded ambush could still happen. I dabbed at my temples with the back of my hand, feeling the dampness at my hairline.

"Well, under what circumstance would a family be detrimental to a child?"

"In cases of abuse or extreme neglect."

"Ah!" he said, raising his index finger as if to test the direction of the wind. "In cases of abuse or extreme neglect," he repeated slowly, looking meaningfully at the prosecutor and judge. Then he turned his gaze back to me. "Did you know, Dr. McConnaughy, that the Joneses have never been accused of abuse or neglect? Did you even bother to check on that? Did you have even one conversation with the Department of Children's Services about this young man?" He gestured toward Tavaris, who sat impassively in a starched shirt and jeans, with nary a parent in sight.

"Objection!" bellowed the General. "Multiple questions! He needs to pick one question and let her answer."

"Sustained," the judge droned, shuffling a stack of papers.

"Let me rephrase the question," Mr. Tate acquiesced. "Did you have *any* conversations with the Department of Children's Services about Tavaris Jones?"

"No."

"Did you have any conversations with his parents?"

"They were not present for treatment team meetings," I countered.

"Thank you, Dr. McConnaughy," he responded between clenched teeth. "I suppose that means you didn't talk to them by phone either. Is that correct?"

"That's correct," I admitted.

"Now, let's look at Tavaris' school record…"

"Objection!" Mr. Cupples called out without bothering to stand. "These charges have nothing to do with school."

"But, Your Honor!" Mr. Tate interrupted. "If the court please, I believe I can show that his frustration at school directly contributed to his unruly behavior."

"Overruled," Judge Walker said without looking up, as if he were bored by the proceedings.

"Thank you, Your Honor," Mr. Tate said, bowing slightly toward the judge before he turned his attention back to me. "Dr.

McConnaughy, are you familiar with Tavaris' school record?"

"Yes, Sir. I am," I answered conclusively, feeling that we were returning to an area where I had more than a passing knowledge.

"Tell the court what you found when you examined his record."

I opened the file folder and focused on the Xeroxed report from Tavaris' school, feeling a small surge of self-confidence. "Tavaris has had eight disciplinary events since school began in August…"

"No, Doctor. We are interested in his grades and…"

"Objection!" called Mr. Cupples. "Mr. Tate wanted her to testify on his school records, and she should be able to testify about the entire record."

"Sustained," said Judge Walker. He glanced briefly at me. "Go on, Doctor."

I licked my lips again before continuing. "Tavaris has been called to the office eight times since school began," I summarized. When Mr. Tate did not challenge me, I plunged ahead. "He's been in trouble for cursing at teachers, disrupting classrooms, fighting in the hallway…"

"Dr. McConnaughy, are these the behaviors of a frustrated child?" Mr. Tate interrupted.

"They could be, but they could also be…" I started.

"Thank you, Doctor. Let's look at your answer more carefully: "They could be…" Mr. Tate repeated slowly. "Behaviors of a child who cannot do the class work; a child who has learning problems and is failing every class but P.E. Such a child *could be* expected to act out his frustration at school. Could he not?"

I marshaled my resources in another attempt to tell the whole story. "At times children…"

"Yes or no, Dr. McConnaughy!" he roared. "Just a 'yes' or 'no' will do." I must have flinched at his sudden shout, causing Mr. Cupples to give another objection. Once he had the judge's attention, however, he apparently had nothing to protest other than the fact that Mr. Tate had rattled the witness. In the ensuing silence, the judge called, "Overruled."

Mr. Tate looked meaningfully at me, waiting for my answer. "Yes," I replied tersely.

"Thank you, Doctor," he said smugly, looking down at his own copy of the school records. "Now, let us hear about Tavaris' academic progress," he suggested, waiting for me to turn the page on the stapled report. "You have testified that Tavaris has average intellectual abilities. Is that correct, Dr. McConnaughy?"

When I affirmed his statement, he immediately countered: "Are you aware that he was failing every class but P.E.?"

"Yes, Sir."

"Well, tell us how you would explain that. How could it be that a 16-year-old with an IQ of 102 would only be able to read on a third grade level?"

I winced at the public mention of an IQ, a number I had been taught was strictly confidential. A number that should never be revealed to the client. But Tavaris's frozen expression never varied and I decided he wasn't listening to the proceedings. I began my answer: "It could be due to a lack of motivation, to a lack of family support, to a learning disability…"

He interrupted my list. "A learning disability!" he called with artificial amazement in his voice, as if he would end the sentence with *imagine that!* "And, Doctor, just what does that mean *in laymen's terms?*" he sneered, parodying Mr. Cupples' earlier remarks.

"It means that he has the ability to do the work, but he is not able to learn academic material due to…"

"Laymen's terms!" he reminded me.

"It means he can't read even though he is smart enough to be able to," I finished hurriedly before he could interrupt again. I could hear the edgy irritation in my own voice and told myself to take a deep breath and regain some composure.

"Thank you, Dr. McConnaughy. And are there special programs that schools can offer for learning disabilities?"

"Yes."

"And was Tavaris enrolled in such a program?"

"No."

"And is it possible that if he had been getting the help he needed at school through a special program, then he wouldn't have had to associate with older boys who had a history of criminal behavior?"

I was suddenly too exhausted to try to educate the court about educational theory and conduct disorders. I felt myself surrendering as I said, "It's possible."

"So if the school system had not failed Tavaris, we might not be here today."

"Objection! We are not here to put the school system on trial!" Mr. Cupples insisted, apparently rousing himself enough to return his attention to the hearing.

"Sustained."

"No further questions, Your Honor," Mr. Tate smirked. "Your witness, Mr. Cupples."

"No further questions, Your Honor," said the prosecutor, as I gratefully let myself exhale.

"You may step down," the judge informed me.

I felt like I was staggering toward the door, weaving past the enticing pitchers of water in my quest to escape from the witness stand. What could this exchange have accomplished? I asked myself. Could anyone have gained any insight about Tavaris' problems from my testimony?

Passing through the tall doors, I was distracted, with an unexpected twinge of jealousy, by the sight of Jack, lounging against a pillar as he chatted with a young woman. She absently twisted a lock of her hair around her finger and stole sidelong glances at him. As soon as he saw me, Jack pushed away from the pillar, with a hasty goodbye to the coquette, joining me as I clattered down the staircase.

"How'd it go?" he asked pleasantly.

"Water!" I whispered hoarsely. "I need a drink of water."

He led me to the water fountain on the ground floor and watched with a bemused expression as I took long swallows from the arching stream.

"Must `a been some hearing!"

"You don't know the half of it," I said, returning my lips to the icy water.

"Well, you survived it. That's the main thing," he reminded me as we walked to his truck. My spirits were rising with every step away from the courtroom. It must have been the way criminals felt when they were escorted to the exit door of the jail. I recounted my testimony for him, and he laughed uproariously at my mimicry of Mr. Cupples. "Sounds just like Mr. Sidney!" he told me as I used my best tidewater accent to say, "Can we just call you…. 'Miss Katie'?"

"Well, Miss Katie, I think you deserve something more than a drink at the water fountain," he pronounced, abruptly turning the truck into the parking lot of the local diner. "C'mon, let me buy you a cup of coffee and a piece of pie."

I was surprised that we would be at a restaurant on the State's time, but he apparently was unconcerned about being truant. We took an hour's break at The Top Hat Café. Jack seemed to be spellbound by the account of my misadventure. He crossed his forearms on the plastic tabletop and leaned toward my words, a mischievous glimmer in his eyes. Both of us had been Perry Mason fans, so we laughed about the TV characters, imagining them confronting Mr. Cupples and the other characters in my Monroe County courtroom drama.

KATE

Chapter 36
Driving on the Autobahn

The largest snowstorm of the decade descended on Northwest Mississippi on January 29, 1990, and it arrived without much warning. I noticed that the sky was a steel grey and that it hung low over the bare trees when I left Adele's house that morning. Karla had agreed to take me to work because the VW was in the shop with a broken water pump, and the mechanic had told me he would have to order one. "Don't get much call for this sorta thang," he pronounced, looking disdainfully at the VW. "Ain't many furin cars here in Madrid."

Karla seemed surprised that I was living in such grand style. "It's just a 'room and board' situation," I assured her. "I don't own it."

As we arrived at the hospital, I thanked her again for the ride, proposing to pay her for getting me back and forth to work, but she waved away my offer by saying, "It is no trouble." By noon, the sky was beginning to spit hard pellets of sleet and the wind was whipping spitefully through the trees. I wandered the halls, eventually stopping at Karla's office door.

"Do you think we need to leave early today?" I ventured hopefully. "Linda said they've let out the schools and Patrice said the roads are…"

"No, no! It's not time to leaf now. It hasn't schnoed that much!"

I hesitated. "But when the roads get slick, it's a real problem to drive on it. Most Southerners are like me—they don't know how…."

"I am not a Suzenor!" she proclaimed. "I can drive in the schnoe! I have driven on the Autobahn!"

I tried to reason with her, but she cut me off with a wave of her hand. "I have vork to do, Kate. Don't vorry…ve vill leaf before it is hazardous."

I accomplished nothing for the rest of the afternoon. I wasted time gazing at the snow falling in a steady flurry over the permanently racked bicycles, the park benches and the chain link fences. With my stomach tied in a hard knot, I stood at the office window, watching the constant trickle of staff members leaving early. Don had called in sick, Dr. Thompson's phone rang endlessly, and I was uncomfortable asking a total stranger to risk life and limb to drive me home. By 3:00 the professional staff was gone, and the nurses were battening down the hatches as they prepared to be locked in the unit for the next 24 hours without replacements. The asphalt ribbon that wound through the campus had become invisible.

At 3:30 Karla appeared in my office, announcing that she had finished her work and would be leaving 'early.' Grabbing my coat, I rushed through the doors ahead of her. She started the engine and backed out of the parking space, her tires spinning briefly as she accelerated. We had just passed the second sweeping curve when the car slowly veered off the road and rolled silently to the bottom of a grassy ravine.

"Acht!" she exploded. "Zees American roads! Zey are not vell-markt!" She put the car in reverse and confidently stepped on the accelerator, causing the back tires to spin merrily against the snow.

"We can't back out of here," I insisted. "We'll just have to walk to the building."

"No, no! I vill call my husband, an he vill send a vrecker." She pulled a purse-sized bag from the backseat and connected it to the cigarette lighter, quickly calling her husband, and telling him about the mishap. She hung up the phone with a satisfied smile. "Somevon vill be here zoon."

With the windshield wipers turned off, the car slowly became blanketed with white stillness. I briefly opened the door to survey the hill before deciding it was too steep to climb. The storm was churning around us, softening the outlines of the closest building and obscuring the others. By 4:20, there was no help in sight and I was beginning to panic. Would we be spending the night in the car? Without enough gas to keep the heater going? I blew repeatedly on my fingers, which felt as if staples were being jabbed under the nails. Finally I pulled my hands out of the sleeves of my coat and burrowed them under the hem of my sweater.

A shadowy figure knocked at my door, startling me until I saw that it was Jack swiping the snow from the window. He yanked open the frozen door. "Y'all okay?'

"Thank God you stopped," I stammered. "I thought we were going to be spending the night out here!"

The snow blew off the door jamb and landed in my lap as fine powder. "You can barely see the car from the road," he explained. "Y'all are so far in the ditch that you're just about invisible."

I was inching across the seat, sliding toward the open door, telling him how grateful I was that he had seen us. He extended his hand and pulled me out of the car to stand next to him. The snow sifted over the tops of my shoes and instantly turned to ice water against my feet. I reached for his arm, hoping I could maintain some sort of balance.

"Come on, Karla. I'll help you out," he volunteered, extending his hand. But Karla sat rigidly at the wheel, her hands gripping at a perfect 10:00 /2:00 position.

"I vill vait for ze vrecker," she announced.

"What wrecker?!" Jack exclaimed.

"I kalt my husband on ze phone and he said he vould send a vrecker."

"Ain't no wrecker gonna come out to the hospital on a day like this!" Jack insisted in an exasperated tone. "There are cars off the road all up and down the highway. I don't even think a wrecker could even get here."

"I vill vait," she insisted, glaring at him.

"Look, Karla, I've got a wench on my truck and if it's so damned important to get the car out of the ditch today, I'll pull you out."

"No! No! Zis is a new car! It vould damage ze bumper!"

"It's not going to damage anything!" Jack shouted. I was

shivering beside him; a tingling numbness had spread across my feet; snow covered our hair and shoulders in a fine powder. He saw what must have been a miserable expression on my face and said, "You're going to catch pneumonia out here! Go on to the truck." I released my grip on his arm and tried to climb the hill, but the slope and the dress shoes made it impossible. I slipped and then fell forward on my hands and knees. Jack turned away from Karla, trudged to where I crouched in the snow, and pulled me up by the crook of my arm. He escorted me to the road where his truck idled patiently against the howling wind. "Didn't get hurt, did you?"

"No, I'm okay. Just wet and cold."

He opened the door to the passenger side and helped me step into the high cab. Pulling a tattered, plaid blanket from behind the seat, he said, "Maybe this'll help. Wrap up in it and I'll be back in just a minute." Karla shut the passenger door before he could get to the bottom of the hill. Again he yanked the passenger door open, first gesturing with wide sweeps of his arms, then slamming the door. His face was red and his mouth was stretched into a taut line when he neared the truck. He got in and savagely pushed the stick shift forward.

"I'm gonna save her arrogant German ass even if she's too stubborn to take help from any American," he declared. I sat dazed and silent under the blanket as he maneuvered the truck to an angle on the road. Furiously he pushed open his door and half-slid down the hill, the hook from the wench in his left hand. He quickly fastened the hook and tramped back up the hill to the front of his truck. As the wench made a slow whine, Karla flung open the passenger door.

"Stay in the damn car!" Jack shouted.

"Stop it! Halt!" Karla commanded, twisting her body to give orders from the seat. She slammed the door but continued her edicts from the opened window while Jack ignored it all. With Karla's car back on the road, he resolutely unhooked the wench.

Karla hurled herself from the car and stamped her foot on the pavement, crying and screaming at him in German. With an amused expression, he calmly said, "You can try to drive home now, or if you want, you can run the car back in the ditch and wait for the wrecker. Anyway, my work here is done." He settled into the driver's seat and pushed the gear shift into first, gently easing the truck down the road. Through the back window I saw Karla standing in the snow, waving her fist and hurling epithets toward us.

"Got a temper on her," he observed, glancing in his rear-view mirror.

She was getting smaller as we drove, and the snow was blurring the outline of her car. "Do you guess she'll be okay?" I asked anxiously.

He looked at me in exasperation. "There's nothing else I can do for her, Kate! Do you think she'd get in this truck and leave her car sitting in the road?'

"Probably not," I acceded.

"Where d'you want me to take you?" he asked as the Administration Building receded from view.

In response to my comment that I lived on Walnut Street, he stopped the truck and twisted in his seat to face me. "I'd be happy to take you there, but I don't think it's possible. They tell me that most of the streets in town have been blocked by abandoned cars."

I considered this scenario and was at a loss for a solution, finally asking him for advice.

He hesitated before suggesting, "You could stay in the old nursing dorm for the night. I'm sure there's heat in all of the buildings." I shuddered involuntarily and then violently shook my head at the memory of my only visit to that dorm. "Or in the on-call doctor's quarters in the Claiborne Building," he went on, lamely.

"Who else would be there?"

"Probably whatever doctor is pulling on-call for the night." I imagined sharing a fold-out couch with Dr. Givhup and immediately rejected that scenario. He continued, "Well, if doesn't bother you, you could stay at my house. I live at the back of the grounds."

"Why would it bother me?" I asked incredulously.

He was flustered. "I don't know. Maybe you'd be worried about what people would say."

"At this point, I'd have to quote Rhett Butler and say, 'Frankly, my Dear, I don't give a damn!'"

I thought he blushed at the idea of being called "dear." However, he didn't debate the issue, but cheerfully said, "Okay, then. Home it is!" as he turned the truck toward the woods at the edge of the campus. "At least I can promise you a warm house and something for supper," he continued.

"You don't know how wonderful that sounds," I murmured, looking down at my dripping shoes.

"I've probably got a pair of old sweats that would fit you, too," he volunteered, adding, "You'll be warmer once you get those wet clothes off."

The truck inched through the twilight toward a yellow light flickering in the gloom. Holding his arm, I slid down the walkway toward the white frame cottage. When he pushed open the wooden front door, warm air, the smell of coffee and the sight of overstuffed furniture greeted me. I kicked off my shoes and sank into the pillows of the couch while Jack disappeared in the kitchen, returning with a mug of coffee. At the first sip, I looked up to see him shedding the wet jacket he had been wearing and then putting on a coat. "I'll be right back," he said matter-of-factly.

"Wait! Where are you going?" I cried with a child's anxiety at being left behind.

"To the woodpile for some more logs." He stopped at the door and added over his shoulder, "And to check on Karla." Then the screen banged and he was gone.

It seemed strange to be alone in the quiet house. I had no idea where the phone was or if it would still work. If I needed help, there was no one close enough to hear my shouts. I felt like I was miles from the patient areas of the hospital and from the closest human being. The silence surrounding me could have been the solitude of frontier Wyoming. I redirected my thoughts, telling myself that I would be fine at the little house, no matter how long

Jack was gone.

Before I finished the mug of coffee, he entered the house with four logs in his arms and news about Karla. "She went on home," he chuckled. "Security saw her go out the front gate a few minutes ago. I don't know how she'll get all the way to Tupelo, but I guess she'll give it a good try."

He opened the door to a pot bellied stove in the corner and carefully added two of the logs, the roar of the fire briefly dominating the room. "I came home around 1:00 and started a fire. I knew we were in for some bad weather, and I didn't want to have to look for kindling in the dark." After he dusted the woodchips from his hands, he turned back to me.

"How you feeling now, Kate?"

"Better. Warmer."

"That's good. You want me to see if I can find some wool socks and some sweats to fit you?" He disappeared into the hall and returned with a gray sweat suit, neatly folded. "The bathroom's down the hall."

I put down the empty mug and stood to take the clothes. For an instant, I felt an impulse to stand on tiptoe, lean across the bundle of gray fabric, and give him a kiss. Instead, I smiled a thank you and went to the bathroom to change. Once the wet clothes were peeled away from my raw skin, I did feel warmer. And when I got back to the living room, Jack was stringing a make-shift clothesline over the woodstove. "Where's your wet clothes?"

In a gesture of endearing domesticity, he carefully laid the blouse and slacks over the cord. "I don't think they'll get too hot there," he confided. "But we probably need to check `em every now and then."

Sinking into the cushions of the couch again, I drew my knees up under me. "Want some supper?" he asked, offering me grilled venison from the night before. "The tenderloins'll probably warm up good."

He insisted that I relax in the living room instead of helping with the kitchen chores. From my warm perch, I heard the sounds of plates clinking and pans rattling. I gazed out the window at the swirling snow. Jack leaned through the door asking, "Want a beer while you're waiting for supper?" When I reached for it, I noticed the square shape of his hand and the appealing sprinkle of golden hair across the back.

We ate on our laps, occasionally setting aside the plates to peer from the window at the snow. By seven, the lights had blinked a few times and Jack, predicting that the electricity would soon fail, brought a kerosene lamp from the kitchen. With a few more flickers, the room was in shadow, the lamp giving off only a weak circle of light and the pot-bellied stove glowing red in the corner.

We started the evening talking about the snow and Karla. But eventually the conversation veered to work: the staff at the hospital and the boys on our unit. Around eight o'clock, I suddenly realized that Miss Adele would be concerned for my safety at such a late hour on a work night. I jumped up from the couch exclaiming, "I need to use the phone!"

Jack looked startled but motioned me toward the kitchen. "It's on the wall by the table. Take the lamp if you need to."

With the lamp in hand, I made my way to the kitchen, passing a table with a shapeless black purse lying on it. Momentarily I wondered about the woman who owned the handbag but then reminded myself that Jack was, by all accounts, single and entitled to date whomever he pleased. It was surprising, though, that a date had left behind her purse.

I dialed the phone number, looking around at the small, spare kitchen as I waited for an answer. Miss Adele picked up the phone on the third ring.

Before I could finish my first sentence, she demanded, "Where in the world are you, Kate?"

"I got stuck at the hospital because of the snow," I started. "And I…"

"I'll send Albert after you right away!" she proclaimed. "Which building should he go to?"

"No, Miss Adele. There's no need for that," I said, with visions of poor Albert driving aimlessly through the blizzard. "The roads are too bad for anyone to go anywhere. I'll be fine right here. There's several out-of-town staff members who are having to stay."

"Well, if you think it's best…" she said doubtfully.

I hung up the phone and returned to the living room, chagrined. "I feel like I just checked in with the housemother at the dorm." He grinned at me.

Setting the lamp back on an end table by the couch, I finished with, "By-the-way, I thought dinner was delicious."

"You're welcome to come eat anytime," he offered. "I've usually got something on the grill. I guess it comes from all those years when my dad was in charge of Dietary." He smiled at the memory. "He was the General of the Western kitchen."

"I didn't know that about your dad…Did you grow up here, living on the campus?"

"Yeah, right in this very house. Western was a great place for a kid back then. Not anything like it is now." He leaned back in his chair, lacing his fingers behind his head as he reminisced. "I rode my bike all over this campus, played pool in every dayroom, fished in the creek, and stopped by the dairy for milk whenever I was thirsty. The patients were like family back then. We knew them all and they knew us."

"No one ever bothered you?"

"No. I don't remember anybody even threatening to bother me. Back then it was mainly an old folks' home with a few wards for the young people. Ninth Male and Sixth Female: that's what we called the forensic units. And they did have some crazy people there. They could get violent in a second.

"Once I turned 18, I got a job as a tech on Ninth Male. It was tough: we fought every single day. I refused to be mean to the patients, but some of the staff held 'em down for a beating or knocked 'em to the floor and jumped on their chests. I saw one guy bleeding from his mouth, his eyes, his ears…"

"Did he die?" I asked breathlessly.

"No…We just took him down to the bathroom and hosed him

off. But it's a wonder he didn't die. I look back on that stuff, and I don't know how some of those staff members can sleep at night."

I sat silently, thinking of Western as it must have been. "Did you ever work in the Administration Building?"

"Yeah, when I first started out."

"What about those towers on the ends of the building?"

"They were control rooms. They'd put patients in there when they were fighting. They'd take their clothes off first—I guess so they couldn't hang themselves or choke themselves. The control room and Epsoms Salts: that's about all we had for dealing with violent patients. We didn't have the medicines we do now."

"Epsoms Salts?"

"Yeah. They'd make 'em drink it and it gave 'em terrible diarrhea. So before long, they'd just be too weak to fight. Working on the wards back then was kind of like frontier justice."

I opined that working on the boys' unit must be fairly easy after his first experiences.

"Well, most of the boys aren't mentally ill. They've just got behavior problems...and family problems."

I agreed with his assessment. We must have continued talking until it was almost midnight. At that point, Jack stood up, yawning and stretching. "I need to head on to bed," he announced. "I guess we'll have to go to work tomorrow because we won't have an excuse to stay home." He walked down the hall and came back with a pillow and blanket. "You can have the couch or the bed. Whichever you like."

"Oh! The couch would be fine," I stammered, unnerved by the choice, wondering if the offer of the bed would include sleeping with him.

Putting down the blanket and pillow on the end of the couch, he asked, "Do you want the lamp on?"

"No, it's okay to turn it off."

He turned the wick and the flame sputtered and dimmed. "Well, good night then," he said as he stepped through the living room and down the pitch-black hall. I noticed that Jack didn't have to feel his way—he knew it by heart. I fluffed the pillow and spread the blanket over my legs, mulling over the Jack I knew and the young Jack who had roamed the hospital grounds before he began shepherding patients. I thought about how kind he had been to me as a stranded co-worker. And I thought about how completely safe I felt on that couch in his living room. And then I fell into a dreamless sleep.

෧ৡৎ

KATE
1990   Breakfast at Jack's

I had only worked at Western a few months when major changes disrupted my little routine. The boys' unit was moved to a squat, brick building that sat at the outer edge of the campus. It had once housed the tubercular patients, I was told. Just as I learned to recognize Dr. Ghivup's humanitarianism, he was transferred to a long-term unit for the most chronic and truly unreachable patients. Don Terry, who had provided my orientation, was moved to the forensic unit for adults. This may have been due to the fact that he placed a picture of himself in the Madrid Daily Times with a heading that read, "Forensic Psychologist."

I dreaded the introduction of our new physician, unsure of how the unit would receive a Jewish psychiatrist who quoted psychoanalytic theory. Dr. Levy had been trained in as classical Freudian when he was a young man. He had been in private practice, had traveled throughout the South as a consultant and had taught in medical school. Now he was retirement age and in failing health. He took the job at Western expecting to finish his career in an undemanding position with health insurance. He was in his late sixties and four times divorced. Dr. Levy took an immediate liking to Jack and was fascinated with his self-sufficiency. He had never done more to obtain dinner than stop at the corner deli for a Reuben sandwich to go. Jack could bring home the game from a hunt, dress it, season it, cook it and serve it.

It was Dr. Levy who talked about his deceased parents and encouraged me to talk about my mother. It was Dr. Levy who told me that the very fiber of her being was quivering in my DNA, in my mannerisms, in my speech patterns. "She hasn't died," he insisted as I sat mesmerized by his liquid speech. "She's living on, as part of you, Kathleen."

He was also fond of quoting famous psychiatrists as if they had been college friends. One often quoted psychotherapist had said the happiest adults were the ones who were playful, joyous children and only serious grown ups when it was necessary. Dr. Levy encouraged us to enjoy each other, to laugh and tease as if we only came to work to learn by playing. When he opened a box of Cracker Jacks in treatment team and found no candied peanuts among the sweet popcorn, he imperiously called customer service. With the phone on speaker, he charmed and flattered the young woman until she promised to send us a complimentary crate of Cracker Jacks, guaranteed to contain peanuts. When he hung up the phone, the treatment team erupted in applause. An observer would have thought that we had collectively won the lottery instead of twelve boxes of popcorn.

Don's position was filled by Dr. Elizabeth Barr, a petite psychologist recently employed by the hospital. She was in her fifties and looked to be thirty five. She was instantly recognizable as the only staff person who wore Ralph Lauren suits and drove a Jaguar. Her straight, blonde hair swept against her shoulders as she walked and when she donned a pair of over-sized sunglasses, she looked strikingly similar to Gloria Steinam.

Having been raised in a rather patrician home in Memphis, Dr. Barr had on-going difficulty understanding the spoken language of the Madrid townspeople. She lived on the hospital grounds in one of the small houses that was originally built for the physicians and she shopped in Madrid stores for the necessities.

A few months earlier Dr. Barr had decided to buy a pair of prescription sunglasses from the local optometrist, only to be so stymied by the encounter that she retreated to her car, still squinting in the sunlight. Liz, as she wanted to be called, had strolled into the optical business and greeted the stalwart, middle-aged woman who stood behind the counter. She said that she would like to buy some aviator glasses. The clerk cocked her head to one side and appraised Liz from head to toe. "We have a few Ah-viators up against the wall," she declared, putting the emphasis pointedly on the first syllable. Liz followed her gaze toward a corner. She pulled a pair of sunglasses from the rack but before she could slide them up her nose, the clerk bustled to the corner and asserted, "Those is men's Ah-viators!" Liz gingerly placed the glasses back and tentatively reached for a smaller frame. "Those is men's Ah-viators, too!" the clerk warned. "All our Ah-viators is for men."

"I think this pair would fit me, though," Liz suggested.

"I cain't sell you men's Ah-viators!" the clerk warned. Her face had turned red with the effort of educating this stranger.

"But all aviator glasses look basically the same," Liz countered.

"These Ah-viators is for men!" the clerk insisted, grabbing the frames from Liz's hand and glaring at her until she excused herself and exited the store.

Her second problem with the language occurred when she went to a small garage to buy new tires. The owner/mechanic assured her that he could get tires for her car. As Liz waited for the mechanic to consult a catalogue for numbers and prices, the phone rang. "Yeah! Naw! Well, I'm not sure, I said! I don't know right now." His voice was rising in irritation until he grew too impatient to talk to the caller. "I cain't talk to you right now!" he exploded. "I got a lady in here who's brought her Jag-U-war for four new tires! Four of 'em! I don't know how long that will take me! I got to go!" He slammed the receiver down, scratched his scalp under his billed cap and went back to turning pages in the catalogue. Liz said the exchange left her wondering if most Madrid townspeople bought only a tire or two at a time.

Although she encountered a multitude of difficulties in the community, Liz was the first to recognize the bond that had grown between Jack, Dr. Levy, herself and me. One morning as we relaxed in Jack's office, she commented that the four of us should just get married in some type of commune-style ceremony. "We could live together in a house with four bedrooms," she suggested half-seriously. "If we all shared expenses and income, there would be plenty, and besides, we could enjoy each others company without the jealousies and power struggles that are always part of a traditional marriage," she explained. Jack good-naturedly offered to do all of the cooking. Liz said that since she had four new tires, she should be in charge of transportation. Dr. Levy simply listened with a bemused expression. Eventually he summarized his position by quoting some little-known Freudian comment about sex so that Jack chuckled and Liz and I ducked our heads and went back to eating breakfast.

Breakfasts in Jack's office started on a rainy Friday when he offered us donuts from a bakery box. They evolved into meals that provided warmth and camaraderie. Jack ran heavy duty extension cords from his wall outlets to a variety of electric skillets, toaster ovens and a microwave. Sometimes the appliances pulled so much current from the ancient wiring that the lights would dim momentarily or plunge us into darkness. In that case, Jack would cheerfully wipe his hands on a towel and trot to the metal box in the hall to throw the breakers. It was all forbidden, of course. It was against the rules to have small appliances in an office and the thought that we would "waste" thirty minutes in conversation and coffee would certainly have been scandalous to administrators. Perhaps they never noticed, since we were housed in a remote building at the edge of the woods. Or maybe Jack simply slipped a plate of eggs and biscuits to any supervisor who came by.

I had hardly finished hanging up my jacket when the desk phone rang and Jack summoned me. "Good morning Kate. Breakfast is almost ready." When I pushed open the door to his office, Dr. Levy and Liz were already be in attendance, each nursing a cup of coffee while they watched Jack scrape eggs from the skillet.

This Friday we had venison tenderloin with our eggs because Jack had raided his freezer at home to clear it out for the next hunting season. I helped myself to a cup of coffee and took my seat, glancing at biscuits browning in the small toaster oven. It had been a grueling week. There were more court-ordered juveniles than there were beds. While cursing and hollering threats at each other, the Property Department had rolled beds and mattresses from other buildings to the "frontier" of Hardy Hall.

Dr. Levy began our conversation by recounting the bizarre events that had been described during yesterday's Morning Report in the superintendent's office: George Beam, a patient who was best known for his stunning pencil sketches of beautiful women, had absconded with the corpse of a patient who died in the bed next to his. No one knew how George had managed to sneak an adult-sized corpse from the ward, but it was obvious that he had the help of Randall Finch, another patient who followed George like a puppy. The two of them had successfully hidden the corpse for two days, moving it from one thicket to another. Each time the security guards believed they had followed George to the hiding place, they would be detained in a nonsensical discussion while Randall moved the body. They had not locked George on a unit for fear that they would only then find the body by a sickly scent of decay. Rashan, the head of security announced that he felt sure the officers would be able to locate the body by tomorrow due to the presence of vultures that were roosting in the woods closest to Edmonds Hall.

Liz had had encountered another language calamity. She was driving through the parking lot yesterday where she was flagged down by Gracie, a statuesque R.N. whose gap-toothed smile was good natured and sincere. "Dr. Liz!" Gracie called, waving her great arms to get Liz's attention. As she slowed the Jaguar to a stop and rolled down her window, Gracie leaned her head in the opening. Her gray hair fell straight and limp around her broad face. "Dr. Liz, you want some kitneys?"

Liz said she thought about the calf liver, pork brains and beef kidneys that were wrapped in cellophane at the Madrid Piggly Wiggly. "I don't think so, Gracie," she demurred, but then seeing the crestfallen expression on Gracie's face, she added, "What in the world would I do with them?'"

"Oh my, Dr. Liz," Gracie insisted, "you just _play_ with them!" Liz immediately conjured a vision of herself, juggling the organ meats into the air. She hesitated, wondering how she could refuse Gracie's offer without causing hurt feelings.

While she mulled over the possibilities, Gracie continued. "I got four kitneys and a mama cat and that's just too much for me. Are you sure you cain't take at least one?"

Relieved that she was being offered a mewing pet, Liz said she would think about it and let Gracie know. "I'm seriously considering it," she told us as she spread a thin smear of butter across the steaming biscuit. "It would be nice to have something to come home to. As it is right now, the only thing I see when I'm in the house is the tower of the Administration Building, and if that wouldn't cause depression, nothing could."

I smiled at Jack over my last forkful of scrambled eggs. "Delicious! Thanks for the breakfast." He nodded, "Glad to do it." I dropped my paper plate into the trash can. I had long since stopped offering to help him clean up. Each morning after we had left his office, he stood patiently over a sink of sudsy water in the abandoned kitchen across the hallway, methodically washing and drying each pan. I tore a piece of paper towel from the roll that stood like a centerpiece on his desk. Wiping my mouth, I left his office for the conference room.

Most of the staff was already seated at the conference table. I took a seat on the right of the doctor, placing manila folders on the table in front of me. Dr. Levy ran the meeting like Grand Rounds at the Mayo Clinic. He asked for test data from the psychologists, explained psychodynamic theory, and taught us to defuse explosive situations by joining psychologically with the furious parents. He encouraged us to look at the "purpose" of each boy's negative behavior. What did the disruptive behavior accomplish for this child? What unconscious forces were at work? As Liz and I debated different theoretical approaches with Dr. Levy, Jack slipped into the room unnoticed. I looked up to see him watching me closely, his eyes shining with pleasure at my passionate debate.

While Dr. Levy was our doctor, each teenaged boy was interviewed at length and some were invited to come to the head of the table and sit next to him while he explained to them such Yiddish wisdoms as "God counts every tear that a mother cries." Or homilies such as "If you're smart, you learn from your mistakes; but if you are brilliant you learn from the mistakes of others." He characterized parents who arrived for treatment team with multiple piercings on their face as giving the world the non-verbal message of "F___ you." He explained, "Everybody else has to look at that disfigurement in order to interact with them."

When Dr. Levy was transferred to the acute men's unit, we felt like we had lost our papa. Liz and I moped around Jack's office, pushing our breakfast food to the edges of the paper plates and whining about the unfairness of the situation while Jack listened patiently. He had seen too many good alliances at the hospital disturbed by transfers. He couldn't see this one as anything but a random act of thoughtlessness. "It's the Western Way," he summarized, shrugging his shoulders. Shortly after Dr. Levy was transferred, Dr. Liz developed health problems and retired from the hospital to move closer to her daughter, leaving Jack and me as the last sentinels of what had become an extended family for me.

Being confined in a warm house while the wind blew ice pellets against the windows gave us an immediate sense of familiarity, and we began to see each other after work and on weekends. We had dinner in town several times each week and, by unspoken agreement, divided the check before we got to the cashier. Saturday afternoons were spent with either a group of Jack's friends or in outdoor activities. I felt a persistent attraction for this unassuming man, but I was reluctant to let myself slide into another serious relationship so soon after my divorce. We spent several weeks telling each other our histories: how we were raised; how we came to be at Western; how we married and ended our marriages. Trading stories of our ex-spouses, I saw us as two disillusioned travelers in a world of couples.

Jack, who got a job at Western State immediately after high school, worked as a tech while he was waiting for his girlfriend to finish the twelfth grade. Marrying young was widely accepted at that time in Madrid, and both of their families approved the match. But three years into the marriage, Jack had been faced with unavoidable evidence that Pam was unfaithful and when he confronted her, she had tearfully confessed that she was having an affair with one of Jack's co-workers. In answer to his question *why*, she responded with an indictment of Jack's emotional failures and then declared that she had never really loved him. The stinging accusations propelled him to sign the divorce agreement without reading it. He moved his clothes into his parents' house on the Western grounds and enlisted in the Air Force. Jack had never been out of Mississippi until Uncle Sam gave him a tour of duty in Germany, then back to the states for assignment first at Minot, North Dakota, and finally at Eglan in the Florida panhandle. Jack didn't mind the structure of the military: with its erratic jumps and stalls ("hurry up and wait"), the Air Force reminded him of Western State Hospital.

His mother died in an automobile accident a year before his discharge from the military. His father, helpless without his wife of 45 years, began drinking heavily and made long, rambling phone calls to his only child. When his father developed pancreatitis, Jack's enlistment was coming to an end. He dutifully returned to Madrid, resumed his job at the hospital and moved into his parents' house to care for his dying father. He told me he had felt like he was shackled to someone else's life.

"I know I don't want to work at Western from here on out," he said, looking across the café table. "But for right now, it's as good a place as any. For one thing, I need to get my dad's estate settled…and finish going through my mom's things. After she died, my dad never touched anything that belonged to her. Her pill bottles are still in the medicine cabinet, and her purse is still on the table where he dropped it when he came back from the emergency room. Every piece of her clothing is hanging in the closet. It's like he expected her to come home before too long." He splayed his fingers on the table in exasperation.

People with bright blue eyes shouldn't be allowed to sit in direct sunlight, I thought ruefully, as the sun streamed through the café's plate glass windows and illuminated his face. I looked away to keep from being mesmerized. I told Jack how my father had thrown away my mother's belongings a week after her death, leaving me with only a few trinkets. He took the small photograph of my mother that I handed across the table. My mother's head was tossed back in laughter, the dark locks fanned over her shoulders. "You look like her," he commented, glancing from the picture to my face.

On a day in February, while we were having a late lunch hour at the café, I told Jack the story I had carefully avoided. He had come to a pause in his comments about Pam and without warning, I had a strong impulse to talk about Russ, to say his name as more than a passing reference, to tell the whole truth about my divorce instead of commenting that we discovered we were incompatible. The truth as I saw it from the current vantage point was that I would still be married to Russ, if not for my pregnancy. I thought I was ready to divulge this central fact of our marriage, ready to let Jack see the bruised part of my life but I was mistaken: A few words into the narrative, and I knew even the curious stares of waitresses would not be enough to restrain the flood that was gathering behind my eyes. I interrupted myself and gave Jack a sudden summation, concluding with, "I had a miscarriage and that pretty much ended the marriage as we knew it."

Searching fruitlessly for a tissue in my purse, I avoided his sympathetic gaze until he pushed a napkin across the table to me. "I hate it happened to you, Kate," he said quietly, the pity in his voice worse than indifference could have been. "You didn't deserve that." I choked on a backwash of salty tears, feeling that any second I would have to lay my head on the formica table and weep. Swiping at the tears running down my cheeks, I asked, "Can we go now?"

Wordlessly he stood, leaving money on the table for the undelivered food, and walked me to the door, one arm draped over my shoulders. I felt like I should just give up my unsteady attempt at control and bury my face against his shoulder. I don't believe either of us said anything as he drove from the restaurant. He nosed his truck in Adele's driveway, asking if I'd rather just go home for the day, offering to sign me out on the attendance sheet. He told me he'd get the VW to me later in the day. Relieved, I gave him the key to my car, walked the few steps to my room and collapsed on the bed. The next morning the VW was parked in the driveway and in the front seat was a scrawled note that said, "Call me when you get a chance—Jack"

KATE

Chapter 37
Approach-Avoidance

A few weeks later, on a sunny day in March, we were riding on Jack's four-wheeler, enjoying the promise of warm weather. I was too aware of the intimacy that the 4-wheeler demanded to relax. If I leaned forward and encircled his waist with my arms, we would be in a quasi-embrace. Instead, I tensed my back to a ramrod straightness and locked my thumbs into a strap behind me. Jack drove through the trails and past the ghost village of long-abandoned farm buildings, scouting for the deer and turkey that owned the woods. When I asked him if he knew about the cemetery, he throttled the engine back to a low gurgle and answered over one shoulder. "Sure. It's close to the Neshobee. How'd you know about it?"

"I was out walking and just came up on it…Who's buried there?"

"Patients…mostly."

"How come some of them have nice markers and some have numbered bricks?"

"Depends on who's buying. If the state buys, it's the cheapest way to go."

Jack cut the engine and abruptly dismounted from the 4-wheeler, walking into the barn as if he had forgotten I was with him, decisively ending the conversation about the cemetery. From the cool darkness, he turned in my direction and flashed me a quick grin. "It's been a long time since I've been in here. This place used to be filled with forty head of dairy cattle." The fragrance of hay and grain still lingered. "It's a shame they had to stop all the farming operation. For a lot of the old men, this was their life. They couldn't wait to get up in the morning and come down here to see about the cows." He craned his neck to peer in the closest stall. "I think the patients were happier here than sitting in front of a TV all day long."

We stepped back into the blazing sunshine, strolling along the wooded edge before we drove back to his house and shared a simple supper. While he washed up the dishes, I stood at the living room window, a half-finished glass of tea in one hand, staring at the unruly column of daffodils that bloomed in the front yard of this humble cabin. Jack walked up behind me, took my crossed arms in his hands and quietly held me against his chest. It had been months since anyone had touched me in that way. I wanted to lean against Jack and luxuriate in the warmth of his embrace. But my heart began racing and all I could think of was flinging open the door and escaping. He's not Russ, I told myself, exhaling slowly, as fear, attraction and regret battled for supremacy.

"Kate," he said slowly, his southern accent drawing out even my one-syllable name. He gathered my hair with one hand and kissed the hollow of my neck. Immediately I felt Russ's impetuous hug, felt his unruly curls against my cheek. I wheeled around to face the man who had dared to hold me, who had dared to see me as a woman worth knowing. "It's too soon. I can't…" I stammered.

He hesitated only momentarily before he quietly said, "It's okay."

"I need to get home," I announced abruptly. I put the glass on the end table where his mother's purse was settled like a dozing black cat and dashed to the door.

The next week, Jack announced that he was going to be off from work to begin sorting through his parents' belongings. And as a reward for his labors, he would take a few days toward the end of the week to go camping at Chickasaw. As we walked to our cars one afternoon, he asked if I knew where Chickasaw was.

"Sure. I took a picnic there one time when…" I swallowed and broke off my sentence before referring to Russ.

"Well, I plan to be up there Friday and Saturday. So if you get bored, you should come on up."

I hesitated, then smiled. So like Jack to issue a casual invitation. "I might do it," I told him noncommitally.

With Jack gone for the week, I was plunged back to a routine of isolation at work and boredom at home. I spent time in my room at night, writing in a journal or making lists of what I knew and didn't know about Jack. Each morning I grabbed a snack from Josephine's kitchen, and at noon I ate a silent lunch at my desk. On Wednesday, I decided to take my sandwich to a picnic table that stood in a grove of oak trees in front of the Claiborne Building. I ate three bites in peace before an unknown male patient shuffled to the table and sat across from me uninvited.

"You the new social worker?" he asked with an intent expression.

"No. I work in psychology," I informed him, holding up the badge with my name.

He glanced from the badge to the branches above and began to repeat in a singsong, "I've been here thirty-two years. Thirty-two. Thirty-two years. I've been here thirty-two years. Thirty-two…"

With my sandwich raised halfway to my lips, I sat like a statue, hoping for a pause to insert my farewell. After five minutes, I put the uneaten sandwich back in the brown paper sack and tiptoed away from the table. I don't know how much longer he continued but when I looked back from the front door, he was still sitting at the table, his Adam's apple bobbing as he conversed with the trees.

I so wanted to tell Jack about my uninvited lunch companion and wondered how he would have responded to the man: Jack had a way with the patients—adults and adolescents alike—an easy familiarity with them. They responded to his suggestions and requests as if they wanted to please him. I imagined Jack with his arm thrown over the patient's shoulder, guiding him back to the courtyard.

Before the week was over, I was thinking of Jack a hundred times a day. I imagined him on his knees, sorting through his mother's collectibles, and I imagined him squatting in front of a campfire at Chickasaw Park. From those innocent images, I progressed to wondering how he had filled up the years after his divorce, wondering where the women were who had once loved him. Finally I began to wonder how he would love me if I could ever see a way to give him the chance.

LANA

Chapter 38
The Search

Billy Wayne arranged the second trip from the hospital as he had the first, presenting the paperwork at the door to Lana's unit. This time, Rita scanned the approval form before she stared at him. "I want you to be careful, Billy Wayne."

He smiled back, playfully bantering, "I'm always careful, Rita. You know I've never even had a wreck."

She slipped the form in her clipboard and told him, "You know what I mean…"

"Yeah," he answered, catching sight of Lana as she trotted down the hall. He waved her on and she caught up with him breathlessly, calling out her goodbyes to Rita as they went through the door. As soon as they had left the building, she grabbed the crook of his arm, skipping beside him on their way to the truck.

"You look pretty today," he told her, taking in her glossy curls, clean blouse and slim blue jeans.

She beamed at his compliments as he put the truck in gear, and they began the journey that was to be repeated for the next month. He would guide the truck through Madrid, north to Highway 200. Then he would turn on the rutted road that ran past the house where she had lived with her family. Staring out the window, Lana would choke back tears as she convinced herself, again, that her family was absent. They would continue to the shanties and shotgun shacks, leaving the truck together, but never hand in hand. Billy Wayne would climb the stairs to the front door while Lana stood behind him in the yard. If someone came to the door, they quickly said they knew nothing of the Gray family. They disappeared from their screened doors without saying goodbye. Once, however, an elderly woman appeared at the door with several grandchildren clinging to her skirt. She looked familiar to Lana, but the woman made no comment about knowing the slender young woman who stood in her dirt yard. She said she had heard that the Grays had moved closer to Clemmons, but she wasn't sure where.

Every Saturday ended in the same way: Exhausted from having her hopes raised and dashed, Lana would instruct Billy Wayne: "Stop at Daddy's house." She would lead him from the truck, stopping to reminisce aloud about her brothers' rusted toys or her father's favorite place to sit on a summer's eve. Her despair, breaking through attempts to remember happiness, propelled her into the darkness of the abandoned house and into desperate lovemaking on the torn mattress. Billy Wayne finally told her they didn't have to go to her daddy's house to be together—they could have the same privacy at his home.

And so the Saturdays of driving and searching gradually became a day to spend together at Billy Wayne's house. She took full advantage of the isolated location, wandering with him to the water's edge, fishing from the bank, picking wild flowers in the clearings. She made unhurried love to him in a bed that had sheets and pillows. Although she was despondent at having to leave his house at twilight, she assured Billy Wayne that these were the happiest days she had known. He struggled with the duty of escorting her to the ward and hearing the key turn in its ancient lock.

When school began in September, Billy Wayne enthusiastically told Lana that he had another idea of how to find the Gray family: They could talk to the superintendent of schools. "The boys got to be in school somewhere in the county," he assured her. He carefully wrote out the request for Lana to have a pass on a weekday, and they arrived at the superintendent's office on a Wednesday morning, both of them wearing clean and pressed clothes. The secretary sniffed her disapproval at them and asked pointedly what they wanted. Using a politeness that he found humiliating, Billy Wayne carefully explained their request and cajoled her until she grudgingly slid a piece of paper and pencil toward him. She instructed him to write down the boys' names, muttering, "I'll check the enrollment records and let you know next week." Billy Wayne thanked her profusely and then despised himself for being grateful.

The next week, the secretary informed them that no names had matched the brothers' in any county school. "Sorry," she said curtly and swiveled in her chair to turn her back to the ordinary young couple.

When they were back in the truck, Lana rested her temple against the seat. "They're gone out of this county," she whispered. And then with a resignation that was painful for Billy Wayne to hear, she added, "I don't want to look for `em any more."

LANA

Chapter 39
Playing with Fire

Saturday morning after a leisurely breakfast, they were in the porch swing, Billy Wayne sitting at one end and Lana stretched out across the full length. Her platinum hair spilled from his lap, and he absently stroked it with one hand. "Billy Wayne," she whispered. "I got something I need to talk to you about."

"Okay, Darlin', what is it?" he asked, gazing at her rapt expression, his hand coming to a stop.

She bit her lower lip, hesitating. "I..I missed my monthly."

His hand dropped to the arm of the swing. The enormity of her news began to sink in. "You sure? You sure you didn't misfigure?"

She shook her head. "No. It should've come `round the end of last month."

His mind raced backward with calculations. This was September 12th, so she was two weeks late. "You ever been late before?"

"Only once." She told him, pausing for what seemed an eternity before she continued, "And that time, I had a baby on the way."

He swallowed hard to keep the bile from seeping into his mouth. Stories of Jerry's abuse often haunted him, and now the thought of Lana, pregnant with that man's child, made him nauseous.

When he asked Lana what had happened, she responded, "I lost it," her voice as flat as if she were telling him she lost a key.

He pressed her to tell him how. "I fell out of the bed," she said simply, but he knew instantly what had happened, correcting her account: "You mean he knocked you out of the bed." Billy Wayne felt his eyes sting with rage. He balled his hand into a tight fist, boring it against the rusty chain of the swing. "I'd like to kill that son-of-a-bitch!" he said through clenched teeth.

She was silent, at a loss for how to console him when her own pain had long ago been buried.

"Lana, I promise you he'll never lay a hand on you again. I swear it! I'll kill him if he tries!" he rambled on. With her head lying against his leg, her mind roamed from the night on Jerry's bloody floor to the Christmas Day when Jerry's slap sent her into the road, wearing only her nightgown. What if Billy Wayne had killed Jerry before any of this had happened? Would she still be at the hospital? Would she have met Billy Wayne? Could they have been married by now?

In his silence, Billy Wayne let each possible catastrophe present itself. Then he let out a deep sigh and patted her awkwardly on the arm. "It's gonna be all right," he told her, reassuring himself. "If you're expecting, we'll just get married a little sooner than we planned." Lana glanced at him through half-closed eyes and then sat up in the swing, a surge of heat rising from her pelvis and spreading pleasurably through every nerve ending. She took his face in her hands, kissing him urgently and forcefully.

In the weeks that followed, Billy Wayne was unfailingly solicitous. Each time he saw Lana in a hallway or at a table, he asked how she was feeling and was reassured by her small smile. Although he tried to present himself as only a concerned staff member, his devotion did not go unnoticed. His brother Clyde asked Billy Wayne for some help one night in the kitchen.

"Gimme a hand so I can get these scraps out to the hog barn," Clyde directed, turning a warming tray on its side so that the leftovers ran into a large bucket.

"Sure," Billy Wayne said, absentmindedly. He glanced around the kitchen where patients were scrubbing the pots. "I thought Big John helped you with this."

"He does," Clyde answered tersely, "but tonight he's busy."

Billy Wayne shrugged and then pulled an empty pail across the floor to replace the one that was full. After they put four of the buckets in the bed of the truck, Billy Wayne settled into the passenger seat. A few yards down the road, Clyde turned off the ignition and let the truck roll to the shoulder. He twisted in his seat, draping one arm over the steering wheel. When Billy Wayne turned toward him with a startled expression, Clyde felt a small stirring of pleasure at this element of surprise.

"I promised Mama `fore she died that I'd look after you," he began with tone of resignation. "But you sure have made it hard for me to keep my word! You must be one of the dumbest bastards to ever get a job out here."

His temper rising, Billy Wayne demanded, "What're you talking about, Clyde?"

"You know what I'm talking `bout! Getting passes for that girl, takin' her for rides in your pickup, bringin' her back with her hair all messed up. You think I was born yesterday? Hell, I ain't the only one who's noticed. Even the help in the kitchen's talkin' `bout it!"

Billy Wayne glared at him. "What if it *is* true? What difference does it make to you?"

"You are playin' with fire, lil brother," Clyde sneered, waving his index finger in Billy Wayne's face. "That girl's a married woman. And her husband lives right here in Monroe County. Jerry Wright's a knife-totin' son-of-a-bitch, and he's been known to get the best of men twice your size."

"I can take care of myself."

"Yeah, I can see that," Clyde responded cynically. He turned the key in the ignition and rammed the truck into gear. "Just consider yourself warned, lil brother. If you wind up with your liver carved out, just remember this: I told you." The truck lurched forward and Billy Wayne, his face red with fury, silently plotted his next step.

LANA

Chapter 40
A Vortex of Panic

Jerry first heard about Lana from a drinking buddy, who said he had seen her riding through town with a young man. He spent several Sundays sitting in his truck, parked close to the hospital rose garden, but his boredom pushed him to assume he had heard the truth. When he appeared at the Administration Building one Tuesday morning, he was brusque with the operator and demanded to speak with Dr. Lundsford. Sitting on the other side of the walnut desk, Jerry began by reminding the doctor that he had brought his wife to the hospital more than a year ago for treatment. "I hear that Lana's pretty much back to her old self now, and I wanna take her on home."

Placing his palms together in a prayer pose, Dr. Lundsford tapped the ends of his fingers against his lips. "I don't see a problem with that, Mr. Wright," he began after a short pause. "If she's recovered, she could go back to her normal activities….We can discharge her tomorrow morning."

Jerry bolted from his chair, shook hands and said from the doorway that he appreciated all the doctor had done for Lana. Dr. Lundsford returned to the newspaper article he had been reading and didn't venture into the ward until later that afternoon. As he visited with Helen, he mentioned that Mrs. Wright needed to be readied for discharge.

"Tomorrow? I didn't expect it," Helen mused without asserting her previous opinion about Lana's ability to cope with her abusive husband. She casually remarked that she would let Rita get Lana's belongings together.

However, when Rita heard the plans for sending Lana home, she was aghast. She asked Helen to talk to the doctor and stop the discharge.

"For what reason?" Helen demanded, as she leaned against the edge of her desk, her clipboard held like a piece of armor across her chest.

"Because her husband's abusive and she's afraid of him!" Rita insisted.

Helen had fully acquired Dr. Lundsford's views in the months they had been sleeping together and now spoke as his representative. "We've been through this a hundred times with women just like her! Mrs. Wright is married; her husband committed her to this hospital and he has the legal right to take her home."

"We've got to stop him!" Rita insisted, her panic rising. "I'm scared to death of what'll happen if she goes home."

"I think you've gotten too attached to her," Helen coolly observed. "You need to learn to be more objective, Rita: Mrs. Wright is ready to go home."

Rita collapsed in the corner chair, covered her eyes with her palms and began to cry. "I can't believe this! I can't believe we're going to send Lana home with that man."

Her patience spent, Helen pushed away from the desk and walked to the door. As she opened it, she ordered, "Get yourself under control before you leave the office."

Rita refused to talk to Lana before her shift ended, frantic to avoid telling Lana such frightening news. She vainly hoped that someone else would inform Lana of her discharge. However, at her arrival early the next morning, it was obvious that Lana knew nothing. With a sinking dread, Rita pulled her away from the group and back to her bedroom. As Rita explained the discharge, Lana began to scream, and she darted from the room like an animal trying to escape its hunter. Lana streaked from one end of the ward to the other, her panic creating a vortex on the unit. Patients who had hardly acknowledged Lana's presence during the year she had lived among them suddenly became agitated. Some women paced in ever-faster circles; some cried out "No! No!" mimicking Lana's shrieks. A few scuffled with their peers. Lucy, hopping on one foot, looked like a sparrow with a broken leg. A frail woman sitting in the Day Room rocked violently in her chair and screeched.

Threatening the women she passed, Helen marched into Lana's room and ordered her to sit down and be quiet. With her heart pounding wildly, Lana knelt and placed her flushed cheek against the tile floor. A vague, powdery dust rose to her nostrils. Like a naïve child, she believed the nurse held the reins of power in this place, and she was desperate to stir compassion in Helen. "Don't make me go, Miss Helen! Please, let me stay here!" she begged. "My husband…my husband, Jerry…"

"Let go of my ankles!" Helen barked. Lana tucked her hands under her chest, still crouched on the floor with her forehead pressed against the tile.

"Jerry, he's hurt me. Please…"

Rita turned her face from the scene, feeling that she would vomit if she had to see any more degradation, but Helen seemed to be made of the same stone as the hospital's foundation. "Lana! You are making a big fuss for nothing! You have improved. Your husband wants you to come home." As Lana raised her head to look up at Helen's firm jaw, Rita saw tear tracks on her flushed cheek. "You'll be discharged later this morning," Helen informed her, turning on one heel and marching from the room. "Deal with her," she instructed Rita as she passed through the door.

Rita knelt beside Lana, patting her back, feeling her spine through the thin dress. "Come on, Lana, let's get up. Come on."

Sobbing against Rita's shoulder, Lana begged for help. Her pleas felt like a knife twisting into Rita's stomach, as she listened helplessly to the fears. Rita wiped her own eyes and pulled Lana against her side. "Sweetie, I don't want you to go, either," she whispered.

The early morning hours went by in a blur for Rita, who packed Lana's clothing and the small trinkets that Billy Wayne had given her at Christmas, while Lana sat on the side of her bed, staring into space and clasping the pink teddy bear. At 9:00 a.m. Helen appeared in the bedroom door and announced that Mr. Wright was waiting in the foyer. Rita took Lana's right hand and tucked it in the crook of her elbow. The slow procession gathered patients as it neared the door, the women leaving their chairs to trail behind Lana and Rita in a tragic parody of a wedding march. Keeping up a steady stream of soft assurances, Rita's gaze was fixed on the metal door, where Helen waited impatiently with a large ring of keys.

Jerry stood in the foyer with his legs wide apart and his arms crossed over his chest. He looked Lana up and down and then took the battered suitcase from Daisy. "Much obliged," he said, marching Lana away from the unit.

At the last moment, Lana thrust the teddy bear against Daisy's chest. "Take him!" she insisted.

Jerry jerked Lana away from the group huddled by the door. She stumbled beside him, her face turned to the little farewell party. He pitched the suitcase to the bed of the truck while his other hand clamped her wrist like a vise. Lana felt as if she were watching this scene from the window of the unit. She could see Jerry's brow creased in fury and could see her own numb helplessness, could imagine herself as his prisoner, being escorted to a sheriff's car. Glancing back to the fortress that had been her home for so many months, she longed to be locked on the unit, sitting in blissful anonymity against the cracked plaster walls with the collection of mute and dozing patients. With an edge of panic, she wondered how long it would take Billy Wayne to discover her empty seat at the cafeteria table.

Opening the driver's door, Jerry shoved her across the seat, then looped a belt around both of her wrists. She winced when he jerked it tight, but bit her lip to silence any whimpers, knowing that an expression of pain would only thrill him. Except for the grinding of the truck's gears, the drive home was soundless.

At their house, Jerry pulled her from the truck with her hands still bound, slung open the kitchen door and shoved her inside. Lana tripped, catching herself against the edge of the kitchen table.

"Sit down!" he commanded, pushing her into a kitchen chair. She leaned her spine against the wooden back, lifted her chin and willed her eyes to become unfocused. "I hear you been a busy girl a'that hospital," he sneered. "Feeling right frisky!" He paced back and forth in front of her. "You didn't think I'd hear 'bout any of that, didja, Lana?"

He stopped at the corner of the table and spun around to face her. "I ain't gonna have you whorin' 'round all over this county!" he thundered, pounding the table with one beefy fist. You're a married woman, Lana Wright, and you gonna act like one! You hear me?!"

He leaned his nose an inch from hers and she could smell the whiskey and soured saliva on his breath. "I'm your husband an' you're gonna do what *I* say!" She let her eyes flicker to his for an instant, taking in the bloodshot rims, feeling terror gnawing at her. "You understand me?" Silence. "You... understand... me... Lana?" He was even closer and as he punched out his words, a shower of spittle sprayed across her face. "Answer me, Bitch!" He backhanded her, the blow so forceful that she leaned precariously toward the floor. The iron taste of blood seeped into her mouth, and her mind slowly reeled into a well of numbness.

"I hear you," she said quietly.

"Don't you get smart with me, Slut!" He slapped her again, and she caught herself with her belted hands on the edge of the table. The blood ran from the corner of her mouth, trickled down her chin and dropped in blossoming stains on her dress. Suddenly she knew he was going to keep hitting her until she fell; until she was too weak to raise an arm to protect herself; until her life blood ebbed out and she lay dead on the stained kitchen floor. She whimpered her surrender.

"I give up," she mumbled, but her lips were too swollen to move over her teeth, and the sounds came out as an insensible gurgling.

He stepped to the edge of the chair and grabbed the forelock of her hair, pulling her from her seat. Pain from the torn roots drew a sharp, ragged gasp and a cry. "I'm gonna have your respect," he bellowed, slamming her forehead onto the edge of the table. The searing stab started at her eyebrow, flashed stars across her vision and brought the bitter taste of vomit to her throat. Groaning, she slid to the floor, toppling the chair, falling gratefully into the black well of unconsciousness. Jerry stood over her with his hands on his hips. He coughed up a piece of phlegm and spat it on her face, then strode out of the house and roared away in his truck.

LANA

Chapter 41
The Journey Back

Jerry believed that Lana was too bruised and weakened to leave the house, so he made himself comfortable in a bar on the outskirts of Clemmons and ruminated about his next strategy for dealing with his errant wife.

But when she regained consciousness, Lana slid the belt off her wrists, using the edge of the table to leverage it. She crawled to the sink, splashed water on her battered face and steeled herself to walk away from the house. Perfunctorily checking her underclothes for blood, she was reassured that the baby she carried had not been harmed. She stumbled to her feet and began to walk toward Madrid. In the heat of a dry, autumn day she followed paths through the forest where she could. When she was forced to hike by the roads, she trudged through the brush that lined the asphalt.

As she traveled away from the house that had been the source of so much of her suffering, anger overtook the throbbing headache and the leaden exhaustion in her limbs. With each step, her determination grew. She swore she would never again endure Jerry's touch. He had used his hands to draw her blood for the last time.

Lana believed she could count on Billy Wayne's support, but she began to let her doubts overtake her. She worried that he had grown tired of having to solve the endless problems that trailed in her wake, and she fretted that he would quietly disappear from her life. If that were so, she reasoned, she would have to find a way to live so that Jerry could not find her. She considered throwing herself on the mercy of Adele Cearley, even though she would be unable to earn her keep for the next few months. She thought about the Memphis homes for unwed mothers but quickly dismissed that idea with a shudder, knowing that she would be forced to give up the baby for adoption. She even fiercely considered returning to Western and begging for help, but the dangers of relying on Helen's sympathy seemed overwhelming. Finally her thoughts returned to Billy Wayne, and she reassured herself that he would take care of her, if she could only travel unrecognized to his door.

By sunset she had walked to the northern edge of Madrid. With sinking desperation, Lana realized that nightfall had made further travel untenable. Her feet dragged through the gravel at the side of the road; her arms hung listlessly at her sides and her mouth seemed to be coated with a layer of dust: thirst consumed her every thought. As she moved toward lights glimmering in a row of trees, she thought of every dipper half-full of water that she had tossed aside after drinking. She remembered Western's faucets that had gushed water through her fingers. With a pang of remorse, she realized how wasteful she had been. If she only had one sip of the water she had squandered!

The house she saw through the trees was a columned, two-story house with unpainted sheds on the edge of the lawn. Praying there would be no dogs in the yard, Lana slowly shuffled toward a carriage house and stumbled in the dusk against an outdoor faucet. Gratefully she sank to her knees, cupping her hands to drink while the water splattered against a flat rock at the base of the pipe. She drank greedily from her palms, thanking her lucky stars for the cold water she splashed against her face. Once her thirst was slaked, she moved to the carriage house where a grimy Oldsmobile was parked in the shadows. In the musty backseat, she lay on her side, her bruised face resting against one arm, and immediately fell asleep.

The insistent crowing of a rooster roused her before sunrise. Awaking in a car was confusing, but she groggily remembered the events of the previous day when she saw the tall columns of the house. She avoided the sight of her damaged face in the car's mirror, ducking her head as she slid across the seat to the door. The smudge of purple in the east prodded her to hurry.

Billy Wayne's house was empty when she arrived at his door in mid-morning. When Lana had been missing from the cafeteria the day before, he had jogged back to the unit and found Rita, whose tearful description of the discharge tumbled out nonsensically. He had run to his truck, pulling the pistol from the glove compartment as he raced down the hilly roads to Jerry's house.

Expecting to find Lana hidden inside, he pounded on the door with his left hand, his right hand loosely holding the revolver in his pocket. He had kicked open the door and marched into the house without a plan and as he threw open the bedroom door, he had a fleeting realization that his recklessness had overtaken all reason. He stood panting in the doorway for a moment, knowing he had forced his way into the lair of a dangerous man. Surveying the disheveled quilts, he roughly pushed away an image of Lana and Jerry tangled together on the sheets. He turned back to the kitchen where he found the overturned chair and the blood on the edge of the kitchen table. Then he knew that Lana had been beaten, maybe to death.

Desperation mounting as if a time bomb were ticking against his throat, he had run into the yard, screaming her name before he left the property to drive the back roads. He spent most of the day looking out his side windows for a flash of white-blonde hair. At one point, he decided Lana might have taken shelter in her father's old house so he had marched through the rooms, calling for her, his voice echoing through the emptiness as hers once had. He had returned repeatedly to his own house, fighting hopelessness by imagining he would see her sitting placidly in the front porch swing.

By nightfall, his fear was palatable and the sour lump at the back of his throat was constant. Since he could no longer see the sides of the road in the darkness, he had gone to Clyde's house and had found Betty alone in the kitchen. Collapsing in a chair, he had confessed everything to her, including his imminent parenthood.

Betty had patted him on the shoulder and told him there was nothing else to be done in the dark but that she would help him look the next day. She had also told him that she would do whatever she could to help Lana through her pregnancy. He swept her in a grateful hug before begging her not to tell Clyde.

An hour after she had turned the knob on Billy Wayne's door, they found Lana lying in her soiled clothes on the knotted sheets.

Billy Wayne crawled into bed and leaned over her face, his palms lightly touching her arms, rage filling his eyes with tears at the purple, swollen eye, the crescent bruises marching across her cheeks, the jagged cut on her forehead. Betty stood by the side of the bed, wringing her hands.

"It's okay, Billy Wayne," Lana whispered to him between swollen lips. "The baby's all right."

Abruptly leaving the bed, he stalked to the living room, jerked open the closet door and reached for his shotgun. Betty pulled at his elbow. "For Heaven's Sake, Billy Wayne, what do you think you're doing?"

"I'm gonna kill that son-of-a-bitch," he told her matter-of-factly, his fingers swiping the top shelf for the box of shells.

"Billy Wayne, you can't hunt somebody down like they was some kind of animal!"

"That's pretty much what he is," he commented, jerking away from her.

"But that young lady in there needs.."

"Billy Wayne!" It was Lana's insistent voice that wheeled him around to see her leaning weakly against the jamb, her disfigured face turned toward him, her left eye so swollen than he momentarily wondered if she had located him by sight or by sound. "Don't do it," she pleaded in a child's voice. "I need you to be there when…" She broke into a sob, taking a hesitant step toward him.

A shaft of pain drove through Billy Wayne's chest. He couldn't refuse her: He put the shotgun down on a chair and took her carefully by the arm, guiding her slowly back to the bed. She murmured her pleas as they crossed the floor, and his baritone answered in reassurance.

At the point that Lana was again in the bed, Betty decided to take charge of the chaos. She told Billy Wayne to get ice for Lana's injuries and when he disappeared, Betty gathered up the shotgun and stashed it in the abandoned smokehouse at the edge of his property.

Returning to Lana, she sat on the side of the bed, saying, "I'm

Betty, Billy Wayne's sister-in-law. Do you feel like you could drink something, if you had a straw?" Lana nodded. "I think you need some nourishment." She added shyly, "Since you're eating for two." Lana, too weary to speak, simply nodded again. "Let's see if we can get you some milk to drink and an ice pack for your eye. Then we'll decide what to do next."

The rest of the noonday was spent with Betty and Billy Wayne hovering over her pillow. Around 2:00, while Lana was dozing, Betty suggested that one of them go to the hospital and approach a nurse about readmitting her. "She can't stay here," Betty pointed out. "It's not safe."

"I don't want her back at the hospital. Those are the very people that handed her over to Jerry Wright yesterday!"

"I know, Billy Wayne, but I think once they see the shape she's in, they'll take her back... and keep Jerry away from her."

Billy Wayne sat in a chair with his elbows resting on his knees and his big hands dangling between his legs. He could hear the blood pulsing through his ears. "I almost lost her this time," he said, shaking his head. "I'm not gonna take another chance like that."

Betty took a deep breath and asked, "Well, what ideas do you have? You know she can't stay here."

"I don't know why not," he argued, glaring at her.

"Well, for one thing, this house doesn't have a lock big enough to keep out an angry husband! For another, you have to work, which means she'd be here eight hours a day, like a sitting duck! The last thing is, the sheriff won't be helping you keep some other man's wife, so you'd have Jerry after you and maybe the law, too."

He met her argument with a request that Lana stay at their little hospital house, but Betty counseled the virtue of patience, saying she would have to work everything out with Clyde before Lana could move in. Finally Billy Wayne said he thought Rita Grantham might help, and Betty volunteered to find her when the shift ended.

As a friend and an ally, Rita immediately came to assess Lana's injuries. She overcame her initial horror at the swollen, purple smudges and angry cuts to lean over Lana and stroke her hair. She focused on the unblemished eye that searched Rita's face for reassurance. "You'll be safe with me at Western," she whispered. "I'm going to see if we can get you readmitted today." She looked up at Billy Wayne and Betty, standing in the doorway. "I think Dr. Lundsford will say yes." she told them.

Lana wearily closed her eyes. She was too exhausted to campaign for other possibilities, and she reminded herself that in spite of the locked doors and the sameness of each day, she had only been beaten as a free woman.

LANA

Chapter 42
Resettling

Within an hour, Lana had been driven to the hospital and guided through the locked doors. Even though her friends were horrified by her injuries, they were nonetheless thrilled to see her return. "Your pretty face! Your pretty face!" Daisy moaned, peering unabashedly at the bruises. Lucy trailed down the hall behind them, whistling like a mourning dove and dabbing at her eyes. Shuffling to the bed where clean sheets had been tucked tightly under the mattress, Lana fell on the covers still dressed in her blood-splattered, muddy clothes. When she awoke the next morning, sunlight was making a square patch on the blanket, and the pink teddy bear was gazing at her from her pillow.

For several weeks, Lana lived in the hospital without leaving the ward. She had no desire to walk across the lawn for fear she might be seen by Jerry. Billy Wayne brought his coffee to her room in the mornings and sat on her bed while she, nauseous from morning sickness, picked at her food. Before he went home for the day, he brought her the news of Western. The other women were usually in the dayroom watching TV, allowing Billy Wayne and Lana a few minutes of privacy each evening. Sitting on her bed, he would hold her hand and talk about his day while Lana sat silently beside him, preoccupied and anxious. Before he left for the night, he would kiss her on the forehead and whisper, "I'll be here tomorrow morning. Try to get some rest."

By the time the fall weather finally broke the shackles of the late summer heat, Lana's bruises had healed and her nausea had subsided. Billy Wayne began to see a curve to her abdomen and a softening to the angles of her face. She told him one evening, as they were sitting in her room, that she wanted to go to his house.

He was taken aback. "Baby, you know I'd love to bring you to my house, but I don't think it's safe."

"Why not?"

"I don't know if Jerry could follow you there and try to hurt you."

"You'd stop him, wouldn't you?" she asked pointedly, her gaze boring into him.

"I'd do everything in my power to stop him!" he assured her. "But we don't need to be takin' chances. Not with you and not with the baby." She noticed him glancing at her abdomen, and she took his hand, placing it tenderly against her thickening waistline.

"Pretty soon you'll be able to feel the baby when he kicks," she mused quietly.

"Hm," he said, letting himself luxuriate in the thought of his child, moving unseen against his warm palm.

She shifted her hip against the bed. "Billy Wayne, what happens to ladies when the nurses find out they're expecting?"

He withdrew his hand. "I think it's different, depending. Sometimes the ladies go home and have their babies there. Sometimes the babies are born here."

Raising her eyebrows, she questioned further, "Then what happens? They're not raised here."

"No. They're not." He hesitated and she pressed him. He swallowed hard before mumbling, "Sometimes they're adopted."

"I don't want this baby adopted, Billy Wayne!" she loudly insisted.

"Sh-h! I've already thought of that. I've been talking to Betty and I think you'll be able to stay with her when it's time to have the baby. That's still on the grounds, but it's not on the ward."

He could still see alarm in her face. "Did Betty say 'yes'?"

"She said she'd help us any way she could, and she said you could stay there while you're expectin'."

"But, Billy Wayne, what'll happen after the baby's born?"

"I'm working on that!" he said impatiently. "I'm going to talk to a lawyer about getting you a divorce."

"A divorce?" She squeezed her eyes shut in disbelief. "Do you think Jerry Wright will ever let me have a divorce?"

He swallowed hard and then said, "I don't know, Lana! But I do know Mr. Jamison's a smart lawyer and he's gotten divorces for plenty of other people."

She raised her chin defiantly. "I'm ready to go to Betty's house right now!" she demanded, her eyes flashing with a brittle anger he had never seen.

"No. Not today."

"Tomorrow, then."

"Lana, you're just going to have to be patient! I'm tryin' to work it all out, but I have to get Dr. Lundsford to say 'yes.' And Clyde has to be told about it. You're safe here for now. Don't you feel safe here?"

"No! I don't." She spat out the words with contempt.

He miserably turned his gaze to the square of darkness framed by the window. He couldn't stand to meet the disdain in her eyes. She continued angrily, "Billy Wayne. If somebody figures out I'm expectin', they'll take this baby away from me! You're the father and you need to do somethin' about this! Now!"

"Nobody's going to take our baby anywhere," he said with finality. "I promise you that's not gonna happen."

Her heart was racing with the scenes she had spoken into reality. She looked down and folded her hands protectively over the curve of her stomach.

"I haven't got all the details worked out yet," he pleaded. "I think we've got a few more weeks before people can tell. I'm gonna get you outta here before then," he assured her.

She looked back at him and scornfully said, "You need to make it happen soon."

The brisk air was a tonic to Billy Wayne, as he left the stuffy building and walked to his truck. Glancing back, he saw Lana standing at the window, her hands framing her face. He felt her eyes following his unfettered steps to the truck that would take him away from the campus, and he felt a pang of failure and shame.

LANA

Chapter 43
In a Dark Hall

A week later, Lana was the straggler, the last one to leave the Administration Building's darkened kitchen after a light supper. As the line of patients filed out of the cafeteria, she returned to the serving line to add leftover bread to Mavis' tray. Mavis was confined again to the unit and Lana was assigned to bring her evening meal to her. The bread was for Lucy's birds, a small present for someone who could only beg with her eyes. She pushed through the double metal doors with her hip, then allowed them to swing shut behind her. Lana was faced with darkness so intense that she stopped walking to allow her eyes to adjust to the gloom. She considered returning to the kitchen and calling for someone to turn on the light, but then she convinced herself that she knew the hallway well enough to walk to the ward. The sound of a metal door, creaking open at the unit reached her. She took a few steps toward it before she heard the heavy foot, being carefully, almost daintily, placed on the tile floor behind her.

"Who's there?" she called, wheeling to face the noise. She stilled her breathing so that she could hear any movement. "Who is it?" she demanded. There was no sound but the echo of her own words, slithering along the bare, plaster walls. Someone waiting in the darkness had halted when she stopped. Terrified, she turned to run to the kitchen but in an instant, the tray was flung from her hands and clattered to the hard floor, the dishes shattering on the tile. She drew in a breath to scream and felt a huge hand, cupped over her nose and mouth. She rushed backward in tandem with her attacker's steps, as if they were dancing some bizarre tango. Her back slapped against the wall and she felt the air leave her lungs in a violent gush. The powerful man started to jerk at her blouse. Buttons popped loose, spilling to the floor and rolling like a broken strand of pearls. She grabbed his wrist with both hands and tried to move the palm away from her mouth. When she screamed, her horror was muffled, even to her own ears. The veins in her neck stood out in blue, throbbing coils.

He was breathing heavily now, with the effort of holding her against the wall. She could feel his hot breath on the side of her face and could smell the acidity of his sweat and a just-finished meal. As he tore at her blouse, his erection pressed insistently against her thigh. He thrust a large, calloused hand against her breast and then grunted as he moved his hips away from her and unzipped his pants, taking himself out with one hand.

Her mind paralyzed, Lana could only think of jerking her shoulders away from his chest and pulling repeatedly at his wrists. Thoughts ran in helpless circles: *I can't breathe! I can't breathe!* Her efforts were accomplishing nothing. She could feel his free hand urgently seeking the space between her legs, and she tensed her thighs together, imagining a band of steel to hold them tight. He was so strong that her body felt like it was made of clay, as if it were being molded by his huge hands. He pushed one knee between her legs and pried them apart.

Astonishingly, a clang of metal ricocheted off the wall and echoed four or five times before it died. The powerful man hesitated and turned his face to the side before he dropped to his knees. Lana slid her spine down the corner until she could feel the hard floor against her buttocks. She clutched the torn pieces of her clothing with both of her hands, pulling her skirt over her knees and covering her breasts with the ripped blouse. Cold, precious air rushed into her lungs as she gasped for breath.

"Son of a bitch!" Clyde exclaimed as Big John fell in a mountainous heap at his feet. When John pulled himself up on one elbow, Clyde let the iron skillet fall on John's head as if he were pounding a spike with a sledge hammer. Big John moaned once and lay without moving.

Stepping over the unconscious man, Clyde grabbed Lana by one arm and jerked her from the floor, only momentarily glancing down at her clothes. "Son of a bitch," he repeated in wonder. "I can't believe he did this." He caught John's arm with the toe of his boot to test his unconsciousness before propelling Lana to the dim kitchen.

"I was just about to head home when I thought to check the freezer door," he said, more to himself than to Lana. Her hair swung from side to side as she stumbled next to Clyde. "Son of a bitch! I just can't believe he'd go off like that." He opened the door to his office with one hand and slung her to the vinyl chair opposite the desk. She crumpled into the seat, pulling her legs up and circling her knees with her arms. Hot tears ran down her cheeks and spilled onto the ruined blouse. Fiercely she rubbed them away with the collar of the blouse, rocking back and forth as if she had a colicky baby at her breast.

"Hush now, so I can think, Girl!" he commanded, running the fingers of one hand through his thin forelock. Clyde's thoughts quickly jumped to the various scenarios: If he were to approach the superintendent about this incident, Dr. Lundsford might want to nose around the dietary department and make "improvements" in the security. He might be angry about the lack of supervision in the kitchen and demote Clyde. Whatever the outcome, Clyde was sure it would be negative. He hoped he could avoid all of the impending trouble by taking care of the problem on his own.

Like an inconsolable toddler, Lana was oblivious to his commands. She rocked in the chair and wept while he paced to the window and back. "C'mon," he told her as the plan became clear to him. He marched her to the truck, opened the door and deposited her in the seat with no more ceremony than if she had been a large sack of flour.

"I'm takin' you home to Betty," he informed her as he slid behind the wheel. "Then I'm goin' back to the men's unit and get some help with Big John." He turned the key and the truck chugged toward the road. "I'll let somebody on your ward know that you'll be with Betty tonight," he added as an afterthought.

The truck bumped over the pitted road and then jerked to a stop in front of the cottage. As he opened the door, Clyde began to yell, "Betty! Betty! I need some help here!"

Betty wiped her hands on a dish towel and surveyed the shadows shuffling down the path. She scurried down the wooden steps. "Sakes alive!" she exclaimed. "Child, what has happened to you now?"

"Big John attacked her," Clyde explained curtly as he escorted Lana through the door. Released from his grasp, Lana fell headlong onto the cushions of the couch. Her keening rang through the little room, scratching the clean windows and grating against the pictures that hung neatly on the walls. "For God's Sake, Girl, Be Quiet!" he yelled, glaring at Lana. "I can't hardly think with you goin' on like that!"

Casting an angry look in Clyde's direction, Betty stepped to the couch and bent over Lana. "Be still now, Honey. You're safe. You're all right." She patted Lana on the back as if she were a small child, then straightened up and walked to the porch, motioning for Clyde to follow her. "What do you mean, 'Big John attacked her'?" she whispered loudly.

"He was all over her. Had her pinned up against the wall. I guess he was trying to rape her."

"Did he?"

"Not that I know of. He tore her clothes pretty good, though."

"Poor thing!" Betty said. "That child has had more trouble!"

"Yeah, well, I'm gonna have some trouble if I don't get back there and get the mess cleaned up. I knocked John out and left him on the floor. He was bleedin' pretty good."

Her eyes darted back to Clyde's face. "You just brought her here, first thing?"

"Yeah...I..."

"You sweet thing!" she said, impulsively kissing him on the cheek. "I'm so glad you did."

He was mildly confused by her gratitude but decided not to explain further. He murmured his promise to be back soon and retreated to the truck.

"Clyde?" She interrupted his steps. "Go by and get Billy Wayne before you come home. You know she'll be askin' for him."

He could think of a thousand reasons not to get Billy Wayne. The primary one being that a state of confusion would reign at his house, and he would have no hope of getting any sleep. But part of him did not want to disappoint his wife, after he had just risen in her estimation. He nodded his consent and disappeared into the cab of the truck.

John was still unconscious when Clyde opened the double doors of the kitchen, followed by two aides from the men's unit. If anyone noticed the little pearl buttons that had rolled into the corners, there was nothing said. Big John was unceremoniously dragged down the hall to the unit, his head sliding along the tile floor and leaving a smear of blood.

The conversation at the door of Lana's locked ward was swift and to the point. Lana had gone to spend the night with Betty, who needed some help with housecleaning in the morning. The sleepy aide who had answered his knock nodded twice and said she'd mark it on the bed count.

Clyde steeled himself for the next stop on his journey: the homeplace. He decided to give his younger brother the simplest explanation possible and send him on to see about Lana, while he, Clyde, made himself comfortable in his childhood home. The plan, hatched as he drove the short distance from the hospital, seemed as if it would benefit everyone.

Taking no chances that Billy Wayne would mistake him for an intruder, Clyde gave two short blasts on the horn as he pulled into the yard and repeatedly called Billy Wayne's name when he stepped on the porch. He marched three confident steps toward the door, reaching for the handle in the darkness. His younger brother appeared at the door, his thatch of hair wildly unkempt.

"What the hell's the matter with you, Clyde?" he demanded.

"It ain't me," Clyde sneered. "It's that little girlfriend of yours."

Billy Wayne was instantly awake, as if the moisture in the night air had become a deluge of icy droplets, thrown from the front door. "What? What's wrong with Lana?"

"She got in a scuffle with Big John, outside of the kitchen She…"

"Is she all right?" Billy Wayne persisted, holding Clyde by the shoulders.

"She's okay," Clyde said, breaking the grasp by flinging his arms in a wide backstroke. "Betty figured you'd wanna come check on her."

Billy Wayne was already in the house, pulling on jeans and rummaging in a pile of clothes for a shirt.

"Listen, Billy Wayne," Clyde continued, as his brother frantically threw clothes on the floor. "I think I'll just spend the night here, and you can stay up at the house with Betty and her," he ventured. "That way there'll be more room for everyone…"

Billy Wayne was ramming one arm into a sleeve of his shirt. "Yeah, that's fine.." He ran out the door, clattered down the steps and started his truck.

Clyde listened to the roar of the engine as it faded away through the woods. He went to the kitchen, stood in the light of the refrigerator for a few minutes, found a beer and opened it. With a kitchen chair in the other hand, he retreated to the front porch. There were still a few crickets calling, but otherwise the night was silent, he thought, recognizing that colder weather was imminent. He sipped the beer and tried not to think of all the trouble that girl of Billy Wayne's could bring to him and Betty.

LANA

Chapter 44
The Plan

She stood in the doorway of her cozy living room, watching the lovers in their dreamless sleep. They lay on the sofa together, Billy Wayne's left hand curved protectively against Lana's abdomen. Lana rested on her side, her cheek against his chest, her blonde hair obscuring most of her face. They were the very picture of lovers long separated, and now finally united, she thought.

Betty was middle-aged and heavier than she had ever been. Tight socks swaddled her fat ankles, and the floral house dress hung shapelessly from her broad shoulders. One of Lana's long calves was flung carelessly over Billy Wayne's leg, its delicate curve a reproach to Betty's dimming femininity. A quick succession of thoughts tormented her as she knew she had never been that beautiful, that slender, that sexual, that adored by any man. Betty felt her sadness spread through her limbs as if she were carrying an armful of stove wood. Clyde had never loved her as profoundly as the love she saw in Billy Wayne's face. The loss of what she had dreamed of, but never captured, brought moisture to the corner of her eyes. With a rising sense of embarrassment at her intrusion on their privacy, she averted her eyes.

Betty scooped the coffee into the percolator and plugged the cord into the wall, turning when she heard the creak of springs from the couch. As she watched from the kitchen, Billy Wayne took an afghan from the arm of a nearby chair and unfolded it over Lana's legs. He whispered as he came in the kitchen doorway, "I'm glad you're awake, Betty. I need to talk to you."

She leaned against the edge of the counter, her hands folded in front of her. "I've got to get Lana outta the hospital." He glanced at her solemn expression. "Now… Today. Once the baby gets here safe, I might could have things worked out with a lawyer so she'd never have to go back to Jerry or to Western. But something's got to be done now to get her out of harm's way."

Betty nodded slowly. "I was up half the night, thinkin' the same thing," she confessed.

He paced toward the kitchen window, ran his fingers through his sandy hair and continued, "I've thought of a couple of ways to do this. I could ask for a meeting with Dr. Lundsford and tell him that Lana's expecting and needs some place to go 'til the baby's born."

Betty was already shaking her head. "That won't work. He'll just say she can have the baby in the hospital and..."

"Give it away..." Billy Wayne ended her sentence bitterly. He continued, "If I told him Big John tried to rape her, he'd see that Lana's not safe as long as..."

"He wouldn't be worried 'bout that 'cause they're both patients," she pointed out.

Billy Wayne went back to pacing between the table and the window. "There's got to be a way!" he insisted. "Think! Think of some way it would help Dr. Lundsford to have Lana out of Western!" He smacked his forehead in frustration, as if the blow would free a trapped idea.

The sound of the gurgling percolator dominated the kitchen as both Billy Wayne and Betty silently considered the options. Finally, Betty said, "You know, Billy Wayne, the best way to handle this might be the simplest. What if Clyde and me just asked Dr. Lundsford to let Lana live here for a while so she could help me with some cleaning? Other people have patients who do their housework. We've never asked for any help, so I'd say it's high time that we had some." She smiled at him, one eyebrow cocked up to ask his opinion.

"I don't know... I mean, nobody else has patients stayin' over night. They work during the day and then go back to the ward."

"As far as we know," she pointed out. "But really, the grounds are so spread out and there's so many wards that there could be patients spending the night anywhere and we'd never know it."

He considered it but found it all very unlikely. "I keep thinking we'd be better off to get some kind of medical leave for her. I just don't know how to do it."

Betty fell silent and then started again, "How about this? We talk to Dr. Lundsford and tell him Lana is expectin', and it happened when her husband took her back home in September. She needs to be kept safe. Why, if Jerry caught her out on the campus, he could kill her or hurt some of the staff. Then there'd be a big, messy investigation from the governor's office. So it'd be best to keep any of that from happenin'." Her eyes were shining as she built the story and found the hook to snag Dr. Lundsford's cooperation.

Billy Wayne looked disgusted. "It makes me sick to my stomach to even say she's expecting Jerry Wright's baby."

"Believe me, Billy Wayne, I understand how you feel, but this will work! I just know it will!" she insisted.

In the end, he added the incident with Big John and agreed to the fabricated paternity because he was at a loss to suggest anything better. They sat down at the table, drank their cups of steaming coffee, tilted their heads together and conspired about how they would convince Clyde that Lana should spend the next 6 months in his home. Lana dozed on the couch, rousing momentarily when a cabinet door was closed or the smell of frying eggs drifted into the living room.

Clyde, who had gone directly from the homeplace to work, watched warily for any signs of investigation while he commanded the patients who moved between the stoves and the sinks. By 11:30 a.m. the midday meal was finished, and he was free to go home until evening preparations were started. He had half-forgotten that Lana was deposited at his house the night before and was surprised to see her sitting at the kitchen table with his wife and Billy Wayne.

As Clyde's heavy footsteps fell on the porch, Billy Wayne gave Betty a knowing glance and pushed his chair away from the table so that he would be standing when Clyde entered the kitchen.

"Good mornin', Brother," he greeted him.

"Mornin'," Clyde responded gruffly, avoiding any notice of Lana as he made his way to the percolator.

"Thanks for the breakfast, Betty. Think we'll get out and take a walk," Billy Wayne announced. Lana looked up from her plate with a questioning stare before she wiped her mouth and stood by his side.

When Clyde heard the sound of Billy Wayne's truck starting, he fell heavily into the chair next to his wife. "If this ain't the biggest mess…"

She placed both of her hands on the table and folded them around her crumpled napkin in a loose fist. "Clyde, I been up half the night and I got a plan." Initially, he looked surprised but then brightened to hear that Betty could have resolved all of his problems. "First off, is there anything bein' said 'bout Big John this mornin'?"

He shook his head. "One of the patients told me John was in bed on the ward and that he had two black eyes. He thought John'd been in a big fight."

"But none of the aides asked you anything about it? Not even the ones who helped you move him?"

"No. I told them I found him on the floor and that he must-a been fightin'."

"Good!" she responded, clapping her hands together in glee. "That's good! Everybody pretty much believes the story, then. And John's not about to tell 'em any different." Clyde nodded. "Now, here's my plan," she said, returning his attention to her words. "I think you and me need to go see Dr. Lundsford and let him know that Lana's in trouble." Clyde was already shaking his head at the mere mention of the superintendent's name. "Hold on, Clyde! Let me finish!" He took a deep breath and set his mouth in a grim line. "You didn't know this, but Lana's big problem is that she got pregnant while she was at home with her husband." She paused to see how this fabrication would play to a fresh audience.

"What? She was beat all to hell before she ran away from him! Are you tellin' me he had relations with her and then…" Betty sat quietly, letting him digest his own words. He looked at the floor, shifted in his chair and forced his disgust through his teeth in a rush of breath. "How you know it ain't Billy Wayne's?"

"Because he says it's not," she answered with finality before continuing her initial line of reasoning, "So now, Lana's expecting a baby and Jerry Wright's so dangerous that he could come to Western and try to kill her. `Specially if he sees she's expecting."

"Especially if he sees she's expectin' another man's baby," he countered sarcastically.

Betty glared at him. "It don't matter whose baby it is, Clyde! Jerry could hurt some of the staff while he was trying to get at Lana. Wouldn't there be a big investigation then? The governor'd probably send somebody down here to see why the heck she wasn't kept safe! We've already had Big John attack her! He could have killed her!"

Clyde had leaned back in his chair with his beefy arms folded across his chest. "Don't nobody have to know about what happened with Big John; you said so yourself."

"Nobody has to know how it happened or where. The patients roam around the grounds `til bedtime, and you know as well as I do there've been patients having sex in stairwells and closets as long as Western's been here!"

He winced at his wife's assessment. "So let me get this straight…You're sayin' that you and me should go see Dr. Lundsford and tell him that Lana's expectin' and that she could be hurt here in the hospital…" Betty nodded, her eyes locked into his. "And then what?"

"And then we ask Dr. Lundsford if she can stay with us 'til she has the baby."

He didn't see the conclusion coming. His mouth dropped open and he twisted in the chair, turning his contorted face away from her. "Aw-w-w Betty! What're you thinkin'? I don't want her here in my house!"

"Well, I do," she said in a voice so quiet and firm that it arrested him in mid-argument. "I want her here so as I can look after her."

He turned back in the chair to face his wife, disbelief still written across his face. "Why? Why you wanna do that?"

She leaned across the table and took one of his hands in both of hers. "I don't know if we're ever gonna have a baby of our own, Clyde. I would love to see this baby brought safely into the world. To get to hold him and take care of him, even if it's just for a little while. And I'd be helpin' somebody who's had more sorrow in her life than anybody I know." She implored him with her eyes. "I've never asked you for somethin' this big," she admitted. "But this is important to me. And I'm beggin' you to understand."

He noticed that she was not asking permission so much as asking for his acceptance. She looked at him with an unblinking stare. Clyde felt overwhelmed by the request, and instinct told him to refuse her, but he could not find the words to tell her no. When he bent his head and mumbled "okay" under his breath, she leaped from her chair and threw her arms around him.

LANA

Chapter 45
The Doctor's Support

Clyde paced to the window and back while Betty sat placidly in the waiting room. His anxiety had built to the point that he was having difficulty remembering the story he and Betty had rehearsed. When the door opened, Helen exited, looking back over one shoulder to smile at the doctor. "He can talk to you now," she said, gliding past them.

They stepped into the walnut-paneled office, their footsteps muffled by a thick Oriental rug. The wide desk and Dr. Lundsford's disinterest created a palpable gulf between them. They waited quietly while he flipped through a medical journal and then tossed it on the desk.

"Hello, Clyde," he said, briefly glancing from him to Betty. "What can I do for you?"

"Sorry to take up your time, Dr. Lundsford, but me and Betty wanted to talk to you 'bout a problem."

"Betty, too?"

"Yes, Sir. She's in on this, too."

After Dr. Lundsford gave them permission to take a seat, Clyde blurted out, "We found out that one of the women patients is in trouble and we want to help out."

The doctor was moderately interested. "Trouble? How so?"

Clyde's anxiety had risen again and he stammered, "It's Lana...Lana Wright and she's...she's..."

Betty took the lead. "She's expectin' a baby."

Dr. Lundsford stopped tapping his fingers against his lips and held them in midair. "Pregnant? By whom?"

"Her husband," Betty quickly replied, afraid that Clyde would give the wrong name. "It must've happened when she went home back in September."

"Hmm," he mused, thoughtfully. "Didn't she come back to the hospital bruised and battered?"

"Yes, Sir," Betty responded. "Lana says her husband beat her."

"Yes, well the pattern of injuries would be consistent with that," he commented with a clinician's interest.

"Her husband is a violent man, Sir," Betty continued. "Lana's afraid he'll try to kill her if he sees she's pregnant. And Clyde and me, we're afraid that an aide or a nurse could be hurt while tryin' to protect her."

The doctor let the scenario play in his mind and then commented, "So we need to keep close tabs on her, maybe keep her confined to the building."

"I'm not sure that's the answer either, Dr. Lundsford," she tactfully disagreed. "The reason bein', she got attacked yesterday, inside one of the buildings."

His eyes grew wide and he dropped his hands to the edge of the desk. "What?!" He looked at Clyde.

Betty nudged her husband with her elbow, startling him. "Yes, Sir. Yes, Sir… Big John tried to rape her."

Looking from the Gordons to the ceiling, Dr. Lundsford exclaimed, "Holy Mother of God! How did *that* happen?"

Clyde's discomfort was choking him. He ran one finger between his shirt collar and his Adam's apple while Betty answered the question. "We're not sure how it happened, Sir, but Lana's clothes was all torn. She says she fought him off and John's got the black eyes to prove it."

Dr. Lundsford drew in a deep breath between clenched teeth. "Good Lord! Big John? Isn't he the one that smashed the guitar over the bandleader's head?"

Clyde nodded. "Yes, Sir, that's him."

Dr. Lundsford considered the options as the stately grandfather clock ticked loudly against the silence. Betty interrupted his thoughts. "Dr. Lundsford, we're worried 'bout the governor sendin' somebody down here to check on all this. It's happened before, when somebody got hurt or killed and there was family wantin' to make trouble."

He leaned forward in his chair. "The governor?" That was all he needed: some idiot from Jackson investigating things at Western. Someone who would interview the mental patients, of all things, and take their word for the truth. "Damn it to Hell!" he hissed.

Betty felt a small stirring of satisfaction as she watched Dr. Lundsford's reaction to her story. Even though he was a doctor, he wasn't so different from Clyde, she thought: They were both primarily interested in protecting themselves. She waited silently, allowing the doctor to stew over the possible disasters that could befall the hospital and by association, the superintendent. Then she said softly, "Dr. Lundsford, Sir, Clyde may have a way to steer clear of this." She gave her husband a purposeful nod.

He removed his finger from his collar and hurriedly said, "Lana could stay with us at our house."

Dr. Lundsford raised his eyebrows and looked back at Betty. "And you'd approve of that arrangement?"

She nodded. "I think it'd be best for Western to get her outta harm's way. We live right on the grounds but far enough from the main building to keep her out of sight. And 'til Lana gets too big to work, I could use some help around the house." She paused to let him digest the details before adding, "We've never asked for help with our chores, Sir, so I'd appreciate it if we could have Lana come." She folded her hands in her lap and smiled pleasantly at him.

To Dr. Lundsford, the information Clyde and Betty brought was like being informed that he had a serious and potentially fatal disease. He had never had to deal with this many problems related to one very pretty but very disturbed patient. His mind moved logically and with the speed that had put him at the top of his chemistry classes. He supposed that his head nurses had always handled these predicaments without bothering him for a decision. But this time, the problem was beyond the unit, in fact, beyond the hospital. He quickly assessed that he had no control over Lana's violent husband and little, if any, way to predict which male patient might come in contact with her. Worse yet, Betty was correct in her assessment of the governor's penchant for becoming involved in sensational scandals among the department heads. The new governor would relish the opportunity to send an envoy to the hospital, investigate the death of a patient or staff member, and then announce sweeping "reforms" to the press! Unfortunately, a superintendent could be labeled as "the problem" and could be quickly removed to make way for the governor's own nephew or grandson.

Part of him wanted to jump at the chance to get Lana out of sight. As her pregnancy advanced, she would be a constant reminder of the peril that lurked behind every quiet moment, every well-organized nurses' station, every docile "trustee" cleaning his house. Despite his review of possible catastrophes, however, the Gordons' solution made him vaguely uncomfortable. He could not recall another patient who had been allowed to spend weeks or months away from the ward. He hesitated, reviewing the possible decisions and their consequences, as if he were meditating over a chess game. Abruptly he stood and told Clyde and Betty they could take Lana to their home.

"She is to remain on this campus," he warned, punctuating the air below his hand with his index finger. "No trips off the hospital grounds." Betty nodded solemnly as he continued. "And I want a weekly report on her condition. I want to be informed about any attempted contact from her husband." He took several steps toward the door with Clyde and Betty following him. "Come to think of it," he said, wheeling around to look at them. "I want one of the aides from her unit to come to your house and check on her from time to time. Those visits will, of course, be unannounced." He was pleased with this addition to the plan, feeling that his authority had been reinstated.

"Sure," Betty agreed pleasantly. "I'd be glad to have company."

He nodded at her absently and continued. "And when Lana has her baby, we'll review the options at that time...adoption and such."

Betty's throat constricted, but she nodded again and said, "Yes,

Sir."

They had reached the door to the waiting room. Dr. Lundsford opened it as he told Clyde, "Thank you for making me aware of this problem. I appreciate your vigilance and your desire to protect the hospital."

Yes, Sir," Clyde responded quickly. "Sure bet."

The door closed behind them and the couple walked briskly out of the Administration Building and into the road. When they were a distance from the building's shadow, Clyde broke the silence by saying, "I'm glad that's over with. I thought he'd be mad at us."

"Me, too," she confessed under her breath. "But I think it went pretty well."

They walked again in silence. As they rounded the last curve toward their house, Clyde said, "I hate to have to go in there and see her."

Betty took him by one arm and said firmly, "Now, Clyde! We talked 'bout all this before we went to see Dr. Lundsford, and you *agreed* that Lana could stay with us. You need to hold up your end of this bargain 'cause I don't wanna hear you complain every single day she's with us!" He was momentarily surprised by the sharp tone but ruefully recalled that she had lately been more strident. "Do I have your word on this, Clyde? That you're gonna give it your best?"

He stepped back from her, taking in the grim set of her mouth before he observed, "I don't guess I got a say in it, do I?"

She shook her head. "You already *had* your say. We are gonna give Lana the back bedroom, and she's gonna live with us 'til she has her baby. And Clyde, if that's too much for you, you can stay with Billy Wayne. I'm sure he'd be glad to have the company."

Clyde rolled his eyes heavenward. He jammed his hands into the pockets of his pants and strode toward the house.

LANA

Chapter 46
Christmas 1956

For the rural South in the fifties, Lana's confinement was replete with daily luxuries: a bounty of food, plenty of rest in a comfortable bed, only light chores, and free time for gardening and sewing. Each afternoon, when Billy Wayne parked in Clyde's yard, his heart quickened at the sight of Lana. On warm days she sat in a rocking chair on the front porch, sewing baby clothes, the pastel fabric falling over her knees. Or she knelt in the yard planting the bulbs she had asked him to buy.

When he got off from work, Betty was usually cooking supper, and she would turn from the stove, a fork in one hand, to smile at the young couple. Billy Wayne would stand behind Lana and wrap his arms around her expanding waist, kissing her on the neck as she giggled.

"I declare! That baby's goin' to be born a-laughin'!" Betty would tease before turning back to the skillet.

Clyde ate supper with them some nights. At other times, he came home after dark, when the women were sleeping. He frequently rose before dawn, fixing his own coffee and enjoying the silence of the little house as he sat alone in the kitchen. Some nights, when Lana and Betty were listening to the radio, or talking excitedly about the baby, or baking cakes that Lana decorated in a wild medley of fruits and candies, Clyde would wordlessly resettle his cap on his head and drive to the homeplace to spend the night.

On Saturdays, Clyde and Betty drove into Madrid to buy staples for the household, leaving Billy Wayne and Lana alone. During those leisurely afternoons, the lovers had privacy and freedom they only rarely found. When Betty and Clyde returned, they usually found Billy Wayne sitting in the living room, thumbing through a newspaper while Lana slept dreamlessly in the bed.

≈୬ঙ৯

As soon as Thanksgiving passed, Lana began to look forward to Christmas as if she were a child. She worked with scraps of material, making gifts for them all. On Christmas Eve Billy Wayne cut a cedar tree and brought it to the house in his truck. With Bing Crosby singing "White Christmas" on the radio, Betty and Lana decorated the tree with strings of popcorn and ornaments, cut from glittered construction paper. While the women circled the cedar, chattering and laughing, Billy Wayne patiently strung popcorn on sewing thread, and Clyde glumly lounged in his chair.

After the tree trimming, they opened the humble gifts they had assembled. Billy Wayne remembered the previous Christmas on the women's ward when Lana, seated in a circle of patients, had waited obediently for the state's presents. Now she danced from the tree and back, distributing the packages to each of them and watching excitedly as they unwrapped her homemade gifts. This year, Lana tore into the packages meant for her, leaving the crumpled paper and ribbons on the floor.

Billy Wayne had spent a lunch hour at the drugstore in Madrid, buying fanciful gifts for Lana: a box of chocolate covered cherries, a bottle of perfume and a pair of white gloves with lace along the hem. But his most meaningful present was the baby cradle, which he had retrieved from the tool shed and painted a dazzling white. Even Clyde seemed to momentarily forget his irritation long enough to thank Lana for her gift: a fine cotton handkerchief that she had embroidered with his initials.

The festivities done, Billy Wayne and Lana stood on the front porch to say goodnight. He broke their embrace to open with trembling fingers a small box. The ring had a diamond chip set in the band, and as he slid it onto her left hand, he explained, "This is my engagement ring…so every time you look at it, you'll remember that I intend to marry you." She had stopped questioning how he would manage to release her from Jerry's custody. She simply kissed him and told him she would never take it off. "And come next Christmas," he promised, "I won't be havin' to get up and go home. We'll be opening presents together under the tree in our own house with our baby watching."

She leaned in to hug him tightly and they both felt the hard mound that was the baby as it pushed them apart. Lana nuzzled his neck. "I love you, Billy Wayne," she whispered, aloud and then followed her declaration with the wish that their next Christmas would be just as he had predicted.

LANA

Chapter 47
The Attorny's Office

It was early January and the downtown streets were dusted with snow. Billy Wayne paused at the door lettered with gold and then ducked into the attorney's office. He knocked tentatively at the interior door.

"Come in!" a voice bellowed.

Billy Wayne opened the door to a smoky paneled room lined with bookshelves. The desk had so many papers piled on it that he could only see Mr. Jamison's forehead and bald dome when he settled into a chair. Mr. Jamison craned his neck to see around one stack, removed the cigar from his mouth and gruffly demanded, "What can I do for you, young fella?"

"Sir, I'd like to make an appointment to get some legal advice."

"Humph. What kind of legal advice?"

"About a divorce, Sir."

"A divorce? Why you don't look old enough to even be married! What you want a divorce for?"

"No Sir. It's not about me. It's about .." He hesitated. Should he say "a patient"? Or maybe "my girlfriend"? That sounded too trivial. What about "the girl who's having my baby"? He swallowed hard.

"Speak up, Son. Who wants the divorce?"

"Sir, I need to talk to you plainly, but I need to know if this is private. I've got the money to pay you for your time."

"Of course, it's private!" Mr. Jamison barked. "Haven't you ever heard of attorney-client privilege?" Billy Wayne shook his head. "Well, that means I can't discuss anything you tell me with anyone else." Snapping his teeth down on the cigar, Mr. Jamison glared at Billy Wayne and waited impatiently for him to continue.

Billy Wayne swallowed again before he began. "Sir, I'm afraid I got myself in a real jam. I…I met this girl who was married. Her husband had been beatin' her pretty bad, so she wasn't livin' with him when I met her."

"And so you started going with her," he deduced while Billy Wayne nodded, "and now, lo and behold, she's pregnant!"

Startled by this quick summation, Billy Wayne wondered if Mr. Jamison was some kind of seer. He couldn't imagine how the old lawyer would know these details.

"So she needs a divorce to marry you and that's why you've come to see me," the attorney continued with the cigar bobbing up and down in the corner of his mouth. "Well, that's likely to be a rather expensive proposition."

"I've been saving up," Billy Wayne insisted.

"Humph!" Mr. Jamison grumbled, signing a typed page with a flourish before firing questions at Billy Wayne. "Where is the husband?"

"Outside of Braggadocio."

"What's he do for a living?"

"Sharecrops."

"Where does your girlfriend live?" Billy hesitated, raising the ire of the impatient Mr. Jamison. "Hell, Son, how am I supposed to help you if you can't answer my questions?"

"Well, Sir, there's a part of this I haven't told you..."

"Go on then!"

"Sir, my girlfriend has been a patient at Western State."

Mr. Jamison's mouth dropped open slightly before he realized he was about to lose his cigar. He quickly snapped it shut. "A patient! Is she crazy or just dumb?"

The hairs were standing up on the back of Billy Wayne's neck. He fought his anger down and answered between clenched teeth. "Neither one, Sir. Her husband put her at Western after he'd beaten her senseless. It just took a little while for her to get over it, that's all."

"Have you been a patient, too?" Responding to Billy Wayne's shake of the head, Mr. Jamison persisted. "Then you work out there?"

"Yes, Sir."

"Well, I'll be damned!" He leaned back in his leather chair and laced his fingers behind his head. "You work out there and you've been shacking up with one of the crazies! And now she's pregnant and you want to know what to do next!" He abruptly leaned forward and measured Billy Wayne with his eyes. "You must be the dumbest white man I ever met!"

Billy Wayne bolted from his seat and slammed a fist into a stack of papers. "You need to shut the hell up!" he shouted. "If you can't help me, just say so! There's other lawyers I can hire!"

Taking the cigar from his mouth, Mr. Jamison smiled malevolently. "Sit down, Son! No need for high drama! I didn't say I wouldn't help you."

Billy Wayne looked around the office in confusion and then dropped into the chair.

"Now then." He took out his fountain pen and began to scratch the date along the top of a legal pad. "I'm ready to take your name and the other information I need," he explained.

An hour later, Billy Wayne stumbled from the smoky office into a bracing January afternoon. He felt completely drained and more confused than when he had first walked through the tall, oak doors. Mr. Jamison had thought their situation was currently impossible. There would be no divorce unless someone could gather proof that Jerry was being unfaithful to Lana. And how would a judge react to that accusation from a wife who was pregnant with another man's child? "It would be like the pot calling the kettle black!" Mr. Jamison had admonished him. It might be better to wait until the baby had been born and then bring proof of Jerry's unfaithfulness, Mr. Jamison had counseled.

"And what about the baby?" Billy had asked.

"He.. or she," Mr. Jamison had added as an afterthought, "would be considered Jerry's child, since Jerry was still the husband."

"And what if Lana swore the baby was mine?"

Mr. Jamison had stared àt him before he shook his head and answered, "You really wouldn't want to make a point of that, now, would you, Son? Since that would cast your girlfriend in a negative light."

After he had passed the towers of the Administration Building, Billy Wayne could see the yellow lights from Clyde's small house. Wearily he pulled up the emergency brake and shuffled to the door. The three of them were eating silently; Clyde was at the table and preferred a lack of conversation at mealtimes. Billy Wayne returned Lana's quizzical smile with a small nod, pulled a chair next to hers and began to serve his plate. When supper was finished, Betty sensed that they needed time alone and hurried Clyde from the kitchen.

Pulling Lana close to his side, Billy Wayne began, "I went to see a lawyer today."

"About getting married?"

"Yeah. But first we've got to get you divorced from Jerry." She was silent, waiting with dread for the lawyer's assessment. "You know it's not going to be easy, don't you, Lana?" She nodded. "From what the lawyer said, we can't do anything 'til after the baby comes."

Lana craned her neck to look at his face which was stricken with regret. She momentarily forgot her own feelings of defeat. "It's okay, Billy Wayne," she reassured him. "The baby'll be here by May. That's not so far away!" She measured his glum expression. "You're not afraid they'll take the baby away from me, are you?"

He violently shook his head. "No. That's not gonna happen."

She pressed him to tell her the details and he continued: "It's just that I want the baby to have my name. I'm the father." He almost added, "not Jerry," but thought better of bringing that worry to her. "I'm the father," he repeated.

"Well, we'll give the baby your first name," she answered with a gaiety she did not feel. "It could be Billy Wayne for a boy or Billie Jane for a girl."

"You don't understand, Lana," he said, pushing away from her to stand with his back to her questioning expression. Billy Wayne did not want his child to be saddled with the burden of illegitimacy. He had been in school with those children: angry, fatherless waifs

301

who were forced to fight for their mother's honor on every playground and parking lot. Even though his family lived in poverty, Billy Wayne had a mother and a father. He knew that the children of married parents walked with the confidence of their father's surname and the fellowship of his kin. He took a deep breath and tried to explain. "All my life, I've known kids who didn't know their daddies. They were called every ugly name you can imagine and their mothers were, too. My family never had much, but I knew my daddy'd be home every night. It was him that taught me how to hunt and fish and how to make a livin'. I just want the same thing for my kid…"

Impulsively, she stood behind him and wrapped her thin arms across his chest, bowing her back to make room for the baby. "I love you for wanting that, Billy Wayne," she whispered against his shirt, "and this baby will, too."

LANA

Chapter 48
Wading in the River

Warm, windy weather heralded an early spring that year. Recently Billy Wayne had found Lana on the back porch, planting flowers in the huge tin cans that had been emptied in Western's kitchen. Lana's garden of crocuses and hyacinths bloomed above the weathered labels depicting scarlet tomatoes and Kentucky wonder beans. Billy Wayne was touched by Clyde's kindness in supplying the commercial-sized cans, but he never thanked him, believing his gratitude would be met with a gruff embarrassment.

The March wind whipped Lana's hair into a swirl of platinum and smoothed the cotton dress around the curves of her abdomen and breasts. Although she seemed oblivious to having her pregnancy revealed, Billy Wayne and Betty were terrified that another employee would notice her and begin a chain of gossip. They begged her to stay inside; but when that tactic failed, Betty insisted that Lana work in the backyard, shielded from the road.

Sometimes Billy Wayne wondered how this extended home pass could have worked so well. Rita was sent to check on Lana during the first month she lived with Clyde and Betty. After that, Dr. Lundsford seemed to forget that Lana was not on the ward for bedcheck and dear Rita, who believed Lana would benefit from a lack of official attention, had decided not to continue the visits unless she were reminded to do so. If Jerry was still interested in Lana's whereabouts, it was not apparent to any of the aides or other employees.

Lana's health had been excellent and no one had suggested she needed to see a doctor. She seemed to be, at times, a little headstrong and too carried away by the spring weather. Sometimes she wanted to pace around the kitchen talking and giggling. But these periods of excitement, which Billy Wayne believed were due to the pregnancy, were brief. He was usually able to channel her restless energy into brisk hikes down the wooded trails that ran to the river. Once at the shore, she would gaze at the water with reverence and talk about its spirit. The fresh air and the fast walks seemed to tire her, and she was usually ready to sleep when they returned home.

In early April, Betty woke to a stillness that was unsettling. She threw the bedspread to one side and pulled on her robe as she walked. The door to Lana's bedroom was open and the sheets were flung to the floor. She walked to the kitchen and was confronted by more silence. Opening the back door, she looked across the grass to the dark tree line. "Lana?" she called, scanning the yard. Surely, Lana wasn't out in the front yard, in view of anyone who happened along the road, she told herself as she scanned the lawn.

Hurriedly Betty pulled on a pair of Clyde's overalls and cinched them with her belt. She jogged through the backdoor, holding a flashlight in one hand. Her shoes grew soggy with the dew as she followed a dark trail in the grass where someone had already walked. The hunt became more difficult when the grass ended at the woods. Betty called Lana repeatedly as she searched for a way through the undergrowth. After a few steps she found the well-worn path that led to the river and hurried toward the water in the gathering light.

Holding to saplings as she slid down the last hill, she could see Lana standing in the water of the Neshobee, her arms raised over her head, her mouth moving in a silent hymn, her ungainly body swaying to the music of the wind.

"Lana!" Betty called sharply. "Lana, what do you think you're doing?"

Lana turned slowly to face Betty, her hands still held above her head, the muddy water streaming around the calves of her legs. Her expression was beatific and so haunting that Betty abruptly stopped her descent, gasping for breath. Then she plunged into the water and grabbed Lana by the wrist. "Get out of the water this instant, Lana!" Her voice was raised in shrill terror. "Get out now! Before a cottonmouth bites you!"

Lana smiled at her quixotically. "This river…this is my spirit river… spirit," she murmured.

"Stop talkin' nonsense and get out!" Betty commanded, pulling her toward the shore. The mud sucked one of Betty's shoes into the abyss and left her temporarily unbalanced. She stumbled, releasing Lana's wrist and putting one hand against the bank to steady herself before she turned to Lana again.

Lana extended her hands toward the sky. Gazing upward, she said in a singsong voice. "Thank you, Jesus. Thank you for my spirit…river… spirit!"

Betty took two tentative steps toward Lana and looped her arm around her waist. "Come on, Lana. Let's go home. Billy Wayne'll be worried sick," she pleaded.

Lana let her arms drop to her side and she looked blankly into Betty's distraught eyes. She allowed herself to be guided toward the bank. Betty scrambled up first, wearing only one shoe, and then reached down to pull Lana from the current. The thin cotton nightgown was wet to Lana's hips and clung to her huge abdomen. As Lana began to shiver in the cool breeze, Betty pulled her to her side and tried to cover her with her arms. They hobbled toward the house as if they were practicing a "three-legged race."

The little house seemed to be floating on an early morning fog. Betty guided Lana up the backstairs and settled her on the side of the tub while she ran a stream of warm water. She had heard stories of the Neshobee's legacy of death and disease all her life, and she was unwilling to take a chance that Lana had contracted some dread illness. Betty directed her to strip away the muddy gown, averting her eyes as Lana let the wet clothes puddle around her ankles. Lana settled into the tub and began to play with the water, moving her palms to make ripples around her knees.

Using a soapy cloth, Betty washed her own feet and ankles while she frantically tried to decide what to do next. Should she put Lana to bed? Bring her to the kitchen and insist she eat breakfast? Guard her until Clyde came home at lunch, then dispatch him for help? She was angry at Lana's foolishness and worried about what this behavior portended. In the end, she was saved from making a decision by the sound of Billy Wayne's truck.

She met him at the front door, wiping her hands on a towel. Her dark hair was damp with the steam from the bathroom and the effort of cajoling Lana.

He waited in the living room, while Betty pulled the plug and allowed the water to drain, leaving behind a smear of silt on the bottom of the tub. He could hear Betty's voice but although he strained to make out the words, he could hear nothing more than a low murmur from Lana. When she appeared at the door, wrapped in Betty's robe, her hair was dark with water that dripped onto the collar. She smiled broadly, stepping toward him and taking his face in both hands to kiss him deeply. She allowed the edges of the robe to swing open. "Oh! Billy Wayne! Am I glad to see *you*!" He backed away, pulling the robe closed across her stomach. As he fumbled with the tie, she stepped forward and tried to kiss him again.

"Lana!" he said sharply. "Stop! This ain't the time for that!"

She looked bewildered for a moment, and then a dark cloud of fury passed over her eyes. "You were happy to make the time for me when I was up at your house!" she accused. "You used to love to see me like this!" She pulled the robe apart again, exposing herself to both of them. Betty turned her head away and primly closed her eyes. She could hardly stand to see Lana so swollen, looking like some obscene fertility goddess. Billy Wayne took Lana by the shoulders and wheeled her around, marching her toward the bedroom, the thin robe fluttering at her sides.

At the sound of the door closing, Betty looked up to see that they had both disappeared. She could hear the low, pleading of Billy Wayne's voice and the sharper, insistent sound of Lana's. Then begging and sobbing from Lana. When she heard the sound of the bed springs, gently creaking under their weight, she went to the kitchen and busied herself, making as much noise as possible to drown out Lana's moaning.

An hour later, Billy Wayne stumbled to the kitchen and glanced at Betty with a rueful expression. "Sorry about that," he said.

She sharply confronted him. "Sorry? You don't look sorry to me," she said as she turned her back. "You know, Billy Wayne, I can hear every little thing from that bedroom, whether I want to or not! It's hard enough to deal with all Lana's shenanigans without havin' to feel like I'm runnin' a motel here!" She turned to glare at him.

Billy Wayne leaned his weight into the counter, and whispered urgently, "I didn't have a choice! I tried everything I could think of to get her mind on something else! I talked 'til I was blue in the face, tryin' to reason with her." He turned his palms up in supplication. "When she gets like that, she won't take 'no' for an answer." He let his voice trail away. Pushing away from the counter he added ironically, "At least she'll sleep for a while now." He started for the living room.

"It's a good thing Clyde isn't here," Betty warned, trailing behind Billy Wayne. "He'd be hauling her back to the hospital about now!"

The threat pulled Billy Wayne back to face her. "Is that what you want, Betty? 'Cause if you don't want Lana here no more, you need to just come out and say it."

She shook her head slowly. "No, that's not what I want… What I want is for her to stop this foolishness and act like a lady. A lady who's about to have a baby! Lana scared me to death this morning!" she said, her voice breaking with emotion. "I couldn't imagine where she'd gone to. Then, when I saw her standin' in that river, I just knew she was gonna drown 'fore I could get to her! It scared me to death," she repeated.

She took off her apron, flinging it on the kitchen table, and went to sit in the glider on the front porch. Within minutes, her eyes were closed and her head had lolled to one side.

KATE

Chapter 49
The Camping Trip

The VW's engine whined in protest as I crested the last hill to Chickasaw's campground. I had second-guessed my decision to join Jack from the moment I threw the duffle bag in the back seat. I kept wondering how I could be meeting a man who had issued the most casual of invitations. If I were lucky enough to find the campsite, would he be there? What should I say as I got out of the car? Would it be possible that some other woman would already be sharing an evening meal with him? I was so concerned about appearing foolish that I stopped the car three times to gather my courage.

The sun was low on the horizon, visible only in a lacy pattern behind the trees when I saw his truck parked in front of a small tent. The campfire blazed cheerfully against the gathering darkness, throwing Jack into silhouette like some character from a Western movie. He crouched in front of a grill that spanned the flames, a fork in one hand. He was alone. The crunch of gravel stirred him to look in my direction. It was too late to change my mind, I noted wryly, willing my pounding heart to slow to a sensible pace.

Jack smiled broadly in greeting, sauntering toward my car. I leaned against the door frame, hoping my trembling knees would steady before I took a step away from the car.

"I'm so glad you came!" he told me, with an earnest expression. "Have you had supper yet? I just cooked some eggs and bacon!"

It was easy to relax into the familiar routine of Jack's invitations for dinner. We ate at the picnic table, the shadows stealing across our faces, the small lantern casting a weak glimmer at the end of the table. As we shared the simple meal, he assured me that if he had only known I would be coming, he would have brought steaks to grill. His comments maintained the illusion that my drive to the park was for nothing more intimate than roasting marshmallows.

"Finish your eggs and I'll get these things rinsed off," he suggested, as he gathered utensils from the table. I watched him moving into the darkness with a confidence I could hardly imagine.

When he returned, he put the skillet close to the campfire to dry, then leaned over the ice chest. "Want a beer? I know it doesn't really go with eggs and bacon, but it's all I've got," he observed. He moved to the ring of campfire stones and settled against a log, beckoning me with one hand. "The seats aren't soft but the entertainment's good." A swirl of sparks floated to the black outline of branches.

I left the table and sat next to him, watching the fire as it collapsed a log into the red coals. Even though my face was hot from the flames, my back was soon cold from the chill of night, and Jack must have been cold, too. He went to the truck and returned with the tattered plaid blanket. I laughed when I saw it, remembering the day he had towed Karla's car from the ditch. He must have thought of the same vignette as he spread it across my back, because he said, "This old blanket's been through some real adventures!"

We sat silently for a long time, cocooned in the blanket, mesmerized by the dance of the flames until drowsiness crept over me and I leaned my head against his shoulder. He encircled my waist with his arm, then pushed my bangs back from my forehead, kissing me on the brow. "It's time to turn in," he observed. "You want to stay? Or are you going back to Madrid?"

It was the moment of absolute truth, the moment when I made the unalterable decision at the fork in the road. I hesitated for only an instant, then told him softly, "I came to stay."

"I'm glad," he whispered, pulling me up to stand in front of him. He kissed me first softly and then persistently before he took my hand and led me to the door of the tent. I crawled into the little tent behind him, and he pulled down the flaps, securing each one with a knot. The moonlight filtered through the trees in shafts of silver, leaving a weak glow inside the canvas. Since the ceiling was too low to stand, we knelt in front of each other, tenderly unbuttoning the other's jackets and shirts. I pulled open the snap on my jeans, and he hooked his thumbs into the waistband, sliding his hands along my hips, forcing the soft denim around my knees. The cold night air and the anticipation of what was to come made me shiver. Holding me at arm's length for a moment, Jack lingered over the sight of my bare skin in the half-light. A soft moan escaped his parted lips before he pulled me to him. "I've been waitin' for you a long time, Kate," he said, choking on his words. "I …"

I didn't let him finish. I put my arms around him, and we were locked into a kiss so deep that I was left panting for breath. We fell on the soft pile of sleeping bags and the long, slow lovemaking began. All of the things I believed about Jack were knowable that night: his patience in waiting for me to ask for more, his delight in my pleasure, his steady and sure hands moving along my flank, inside my legs. When I let him know I was ready for him, he poised above me, his weight resting on his forearms, tenderly searching my face before he slowly entered me. I closed my eyes and let myself be moved with the waves, let him wash over me and inside of me, let him bring me to the edge until I fell backwards into the abyss where time and space are heedlessly one.

Afterward, when he gathered me against his side in a loose embrace, I knew that I had survived the tempest and come to a safe harbor. Contentment settled over me. I nuzzled against his neck, reveling in the smell of wood smoke and damp masculinity.

He shifted his arm, turning his face to me so that our noses almost touched. "Kate, d'you think you could ever fall in love again?"

"I do," I answered too ardently, immediately embarrassed at giving the bride's response. I was sent into an attack of hilarity, flustered and giggling. He pulled me close again, chuckling, "I may have to hold you to that one, Darlin'." He kissed me on the temple and then fell asleep with one arm under my head and the other hand resting lightly against my waist. I drifted off to the rhythmic sound of his breathing.

The rest of our time at Chickasaw was spent discovering each other. After lovemaking, unguarded and vulnerable, Jack reminisced about his childhood, his parents' failures and heroics, his own fears and his shortcomings. I finished the story about Russ and my mother, the two biggest losses of my short life.

By the time we folded the tent on Sunday, I thought I knew everything important that there was to know about Jack, and I believed he knew me in ways that no one else had ever questioned. And the fury I had felt toward Russ was simply gone: Russ had loved me in the only way he knew, and his failings had allowed me to open a door for Jack.

∽୧∽୨∼

When we returned to Madrid, everything had changed for me, and evidently other people read the sexual energy and optimism. The uncomfortable young social worker ventured to ask me out for lunch "sometime." Patrice caught a few words between Jack and me one afternoon as we were leaving the building and then teased me mercilessly about my "main squeeze." Adele asked me who had called for me the night before without bothering to come to the front door. She then expressed her opinion about the character of such men.

"Jack Gordon? He's Clyde's boy, isn't he?" She put down her fork and wiped her mouth, leaving a burgundy smear on the damask napkin. "Kate, you don't have family here to advise you, and I think too much of you to stand by and watch you make a bad decision…"

"What bad decision?" I demanded, my face flushing.

"The decision to get involved with Jack Gordon! His father was a drunk. His people made their living sharecropping until they got low-level jobs at Western State. No one in that family had any higher education. They are simply not your class of people."

"Jack can't help it if his father had a drinking problem!" I countered, my voice raised in anger. "And what if his grandfather was a farmer? What does that prove?"

I stood against the tablecloth, threw my napkin to my plate and stormed to my room, suddenly feeling like a spiteful adolescent. Before the door to my room slammed, I saw Josephine in the hallway, her troubled face turned toward me as she slowly wagged her head in disapproval.

Josephine was waiting for me the next morning as I stepped outside. Standing on the brick patio, she held a greasy paper sack in her gnarled hands. "Got some ham and biscuits fo' you," she whispered conspiratorially. I reached for the sack, giving my thanks, but she held the rolled edge tightly, waiting for me to meet her eyes. She continued, "I been knowin' Mr. Jack since the day he was borned and he a good man! His daddy and his mama fine people, too." She nodded decisively, releasing the sack. "Don't you pay Miss A-dele no never mind. She don't know Mr. Jack like I do!" With that, Josephine flashed her brilliant smile and shooed me off to work.

LANA

Chapter 50
The Birthday

The baby, a healthy boy, was born on April 28th as a vigorous storm roared across Monroe County, sending the fortunate to their basements and root cellars for shelter. Lana had been pacing through the house all night, constantly stopping at a window to marvel at another fork of lightning and repeatedly being admonished to stay away from the glass. She excitedly pointed to the trees that bent at alarming angles and called Betty and Clyde to the rattling windows to look at the hail that bounced in the yard and shredded the daffodil leaves.

At 7:30 Lana was stopped in midstep by the sensation that something had knocked insistently against her pelvic bone. The second rap sent shock waves up her spine. Suddenly, her water broke and amniotic fluid began to run down her legs. As the first contraction began, she grabbed Betty's arm and looked at her with a frightened, wide-eyed stare.

"Lord, have mercy! I believe that baby is comin' tonight!" Betty exclaimed. She hobbled with Lana to the bed, sending Clyde to fetch Billy Wayne and the midwife. Thirty minutes later, the three of them arrived in drenched clothes. The wizened midwife, who held an antique leather satchel with both hands, glanced into the bedroom where the enormously pregnant woman was writhing in tangled sheets, Billy Wayne was bent over her. Miss Josephine set the bag on a bedroom chair and marched toward the bathroom where she unhurriedly washed her hands, ignoring Lana's piteous cries. She gave commands to Clyde and Betty for towels and basins of water, conscripting them as assistants. Then she stepped to the bed and ordered Billy Wayne from the room. Through the narrowing crack in the door, she told them, "I'll call y'all if I need you."

Lana's cries rose in terror until they seemed to grind against the rusty hinges, and Billy Wayne wondered if the door would be blasted from its moorings. He argued with himself about rushing in to save her but then reminded himself that he was powerless to do so. After a few minutes of screaming, the bedroom grew so ominously quiet that he could hear the howling of the wind. Billy Wayne tiptoed forward to listen through the crack just as Lana's screams began again. He and Betty consulted constantly with each other, trying to recall any stories they had heard about family births and how many hours the women had been in labor, while Clyde retreated to the kitchen.

At 12:10 a.m., Billy Wayne glanced at his watch as a loud, guttural shout began. He was sitting on the couch with his head in his hands, wanting to cover his ears but feeling that somehow it would be less than gallant to do so. Instead he ran his fingers through his hair so vigorously that Betty wondered if he would pull it all out. At 12:15 the shouts stopped. First silence seeped from the cracks around the door and then the wavering cry of a newborn. Billy Wayne jerked his head up, grinned at Betty and bounded to the door.

"Lana!" His call was met with the sound of bustling and footsteps shuffling across the plank floor. "Miss Josephine!" he shouted. He stood frozen to the spot, waiting to be acknowledged. Several moments later, Josephine opened the door, holding a swaddled infant in the crook of her dark arm. She was grinning broadly, her perfect white teeth dazzling against her ebony skin. "You've got yourself a boy-child!" she told Billy Wayne, proudly thrusting the bundle toward him. He hesitated. "Go on and take him," she chuckled. "You ain't gonna break him!"

Billy Wayne craned his neck to see past the midwife where Lana lay sprawled on the bed. Josephine had taken the time to cover her with a sheet and although the sheen of perspiration glazed her face and shoulders, she made no effort to fling it to the floor. "Take him on over there and let his mama have another look at him," she instructed Billy Wayne. Betty was at his elbow, marveling at the child's miniature features as Billy Wayne walked slowly toward the bed, unable to look away from the tiny, red face. After so many months of feeling his son kick against his palm or watching him move under Lana's skin, he could hardly believe he was now gazing at him. He settled one hip on the bed and awkwardly turned his elbow for Lana to see the baby's face.

"Look at how beautiful he is," he whispered, more to himself than to the still figure lying in the damp sheets.

Lana fluttered her eyes. "He looks just like you," she observed, her voice hoarse and ragged. "We'll name him 'Billy Wayne'." Her breast heaved with a deep sigh. The midwife bent over her and wiped her damp hair away from her face.

"You did just fine, lil mama," she chuckled. "Now it's time to get you all cleaned up. She shooed Billy Wayne and Betty from the room and began kneading Lana's abdomen to deliver the placenta. The baby slept in his father's arms while he and Betty admired his uncommon beauty and reverently talked of his bright future. Clyde roused himself from the kitchen chair long enough to congratulate Billy Wayne on his son's birth, letting them know that he had long ago dismissed the fictional account of Lana's pregnancy.

For the first week, Billy Wayne constantly hovered over Lana and the baby. He rushed to work with enthusiasm for finishing his duties by noon. Within days he had bounded into Mr. Jamison's office to announce that he was a father. As he proudly slapped a twenty dollar bill on the desk, he told the old lawyer to begin work on a divorce.

Lana was weepy and lethargic. The baby lay against her breast, nursing while her salty tears splattered on his cheek. His birth had brought her worries about adoption to a boil. She imagined that any sound of tires on gravel would be Helen, coming to take the baby to an orphanage. When a vehicle turned around in the yard,

Lana grabbed the baby from a peaceful nap and ran to Betty's ancient chifforobe to hide among the wool clothes. She crouched in the musty darkness, inhaling the sharp odor of mothballs and vainly shushing the baby's cries.

Betty was relieved that the baby was healthy despite his mother's unorthodox activities, but she could hardly enjoy him for the dread she felt about his family's future. She scrubbed and mended and cooked as if her work would keep Dr. Lundsford from their door. Clyde glumly asked when he would have his house back and reminded Betty that he had not agreed to live in a nursery forever.

LANA

Chapter 51
The River Owns Them

Betty awoke to the sound of the baby crying and then a footstep toward the cradle that was too firm to be Lana's. She heard Billy Wayne talking to the baby, trying to soothe him as he walked to the kitchen. Then she heard the back door creaking open and the footsteps quickening. "Betty!" He flung open the door to her bedroom without waiting for an answer. "She's gone, Betty! Lana's gone!" His eyes, rimmed with fear, searched her face, while the baby waved an angry fist and cried more insistently.

"What do you mean 'she's gone'?" Betty demanded, pulling on her robe as she walked toward them. "It's 5:30 in the morning." Instinctively she put her palms out and took the baby, then looked down at him, making comforting noises.

"I'm goin' out to find her," Billy Wayne declared as he pulled work pants and a jacket over his pajamas. The screen door slammed and he clattered across the porch. Betty was framed in the door, bouncing the squalling baby in her arms, her forehead creased in worry.

"Billy Wayne!" she called. "Last time Lana left early in the morning, she was down at the river."

He turned immediately and began running through the woods toward the Neshobee. His shoes were sodden after only a few steps across the grass. The leaves of the forest, wet with a heavy dew, scraped against him, leaving dark smears on his pants. With a staccato beat, his heart drummed faster than his racing thoughts, which had already reached the edge of the rain-swollen river. "Let her be standing on the shore," he whispered to an unacknowledged deity. "Let her be okay."

His breathing grew faster and more shallow as he zigzagged through the brush and saplings. He remembered how quiet and withdrawn Lana had been the night before, how he had found her crying when he laid the sleeping baby in his cradle. She only shook her head to his questions and although he tried to comfort her, she was limp in his arms, so quiet that he momentarily wondered if she had stopped breathing.

As he rounded the last hairpin curve, he caught his first glimpse of Lana, wading toward the middle of the river. The hem of her gown billowed out like a bridal train, carried by the cold fingers of the current. In the early morning breeze, her blonde hair grazed her shoulders, flying in small tendrils. She stood momentarily with her arms at her side and then resumed her journey, the muddy bottom pulling at her feet, crippling her.

"Lana-a-a! Stop!"

She turned toward his voice and their eyes met for an instant as she tilted her head to find him on the bluff. She raised one opened hand to beckon him and then, without a word, she bent her knees and let the water carry her with the leaves and branches that the storm had sent down river.

"No-o-! Lana!" He scrambled down the bluff and ran into the water, his legs pumping a spray of brown droplets. Splashing into the current, he began to swim toward her, stopping after a few strokes to catch sight of the blonde head that bobbed in the water. He swam furiously, but each time he stopped to find her, she seemed farther away. With the river roaring in his ears, he scanned the next tight curve and saw Lana being flung onto the branches of a downed tree. He was exhausted from the race to the water, but he pushed himself to kick harder.

Suspended against the tree limb, Lana's face settled into a baffling, serene expression before the brutal current somersaulted her below the surface. He gulped a breath of air and dived below. The muddy water made it impossible to see anything. He swept his hands in wide arcs, trying to touch her, his fingers raking against rough bark and coming up empty with every reach. At one point, he thought he saw a wisp of white-blonde hair, and he raked frantically but was unable to touch it. He needed to breathe, he thought with a pang of shame: He had to get to the surface to save himself. He stopped groping for Lana and started swimming upward. His ascent was stopped with a jerk. The laces of his boots were tangled in the branches. He was trapped.

At first Billy Wayne struggled, and his lungs felt as if they would burst into a thousand flames. He pulled his foot away from the branch to find that the force of the water held him fast. He had no breath to cry, but there was a pain in his diaphragm like a trapped sob. She had been so close to his fingers! His beautiful Lana—her hair an impossible beacon. His Lana, taken away by the very river he had been so eager to show her.

The ache of regret washed over him and for a moment he forgot that he, too, was held prisoner. And so when the muddy water ran in his mouth and rushed through his lungs, he was only thinking of Lana and the life he had planned to share with her and his son. In rapid fire succession, he could see her as she sat that first day on the porch at the 'Y'; he could see her standing in the moonlight, pointing at Orion; he could feel the brush of her lips when she first leaned against him and kissed him on the shore of this river; he could hear the excitement in her voice as she talked about the Neshobee, running its course to the sea; his body ached again with the marvel of how she moved against him the first time they made love in her father's abandoned house. He could see her face as if she were standing before him, the ironic smile suggesting a question to follow. He could see their baby, Billy, cradled against her breast and suddenly he could imagine Billy as a toddler, calling "Daddy! Daddy!" in a high pitched voice and running to greet him.

As the water pooled against the deep recesses of his lungs, a peace that was stronger than the river, flowed over Billy Wayne, weighting his legs and arms and yet freeing them to float. The last vision was Lana standing before him, bathed in a shaft of sunlight, the blue eyes locked into his. She held out her arms for his embrace, and he pulled her against his chest, inhaling the scent of her clean hair.

LANA

Chapter 52
Finding the Beloved

For the rest of her life, Betty would remember the cloudless May morning as if it were a crazy quilt of beauty and dread. The exuberant green saplings that framed the house; the outraged cry of the newborn who rooted against her calico dress, pressing his mouth against her empty breasts; the brilliant spring sunshine that left a carpet of diamonds in the grass; the fear that lodged in her throat as she thought of the day she had found Lana standing in the muddy river; the baby's downy blonde hair, pressed against her feverish cheek; the anxious impatience to see Clyde's truck rolling to a stop in front of the house; the unruly clumps of buttercups, defiantly asserting their right to survive the last storm's browbeating; the heavy, cloying fragrance of honeysuckle; the dashed hopes each time the underbrush stirred without yielding up Billy Wayne and Lana. She ached to see them bursting through the edge of the woods, Billy Wayne with his arm around Lana's waist, laughing as he escorted her home.

Within an hour of Billy Wayne's sprint from the house, Betty knew that they would not be coming back. As the tears streamed down her cheeks, she rocked and jiggled the screaming infant until she remembered the Pet milk in her cabinet and mixed it with boiled water. She had no bottle. She repeatedly wet a twisted, clean dishcloth in milk and let the baby suck on it until he was too exhausted from the effort to stay awake.

Clyde came home at 10:00. With her face turned resolutely away from him, she sternly ordered him to go to the store for bottles and nipples, sending him away with no more than a brief description of the early morning events. "Lana went for a walk and Billy Wayne's gone to find her." The baby came first, she thought. Once Clyde returned, she would tell him the story and let him decide how to look for them.

Fiercely, she gazed at the fitfully sleeping infant, vowing to herself that this baby, this last remnant of Billy Wayne and Lana, would safely live with his blood kin, would never be handed over to a stranger.

As he put the rattling sack of bottles on the kitchen table, Betty began to tell Clyde about Lana's absence and Billy Wayne's search. Clyde left immediately for the river as if he would be able to discern from the shore the fate of the two young parents. Cursing under his breath, he stood where the footprints ended at the raging water's edge, then trudged back to his house.

He decided to alert both Dr. Lundsford and the sheriff's department. He told the sheriff that he didn't believe he would ever see his brother alive but hoped the deputies could find his body, so that Billy Wayne could be buried with his family. As he drove back to the hospital, he found himself roughly wiping away tears and wishing he had told Billy Wayne that in spite of their differences, he did love him.

The sheriff's deputies put their johnboats in the river at Russell's Landing and slowly motored northward, halfheartedly peering into the bushes that lined the shore. They found Billy Wayne's body, still held by the tree where he struggled and died. A day later, a fisherman found Lana's body, washed on the shore like a rag doll, stolen from its passage to the sea by the river's eddy. The tiny chip of diamond in her ring glinted in the sunlight.

Despite Clyde's arguments, Betty insisted that Billy Wayne and Lana be buried together, just as if they were man and wife. "You know, Clyde, that they were married in all the important ways— just not in a church." His distraction at informing the out-of-town brothers allowed her to finalize the arrangements. She talked to Dr. Lundsford, who seemed to be pleased to assign Lana a permanent bed in death, since he had been unable to do so in life. The doctor agreed to bury Lana in the hospital's cemetery, and he gave the dispensation to allow his employee, Billy Wayne, to be buried next to her. At their meeting, Betty was prepared to resort to any tactic to keep the baby, but Dr. Lundsford was exquisitely disinterested in the results of Lana's pregnancy and simply did not ask.

Betty stayed cloistered in the little house for several more weeks and then appeared in town with her new baby, who had a broad face, round blue eyes and sandy hair, the color of Clyde and Billy Wayne's. She took him to the Health Department and explained the circumstances of her at-home delivery, carefully printing "William Jack Gordon" on the birth certificate form and writing Clyde Thomas Gordon and Betty Lindsey Gordon on the line for parentage. Despite his initial resistance, Clyde grew to love the toddler who ran to him each evening when he arrived from work.

During early spring days, the little boy would pick a fistfull of buttercups and bring them to the door for Betty to display in mason jars. The picture of William Jack, his blue eyes shining over a display of Lana's flowers, always brought tears to Betty's eyes. In a cedar chest, Betty carefully packed the few mementos of Jack's heritage: photos of his young parents and the pink teddy bear Lana had carried, just as a child would carry a talisman. Betty told Clyde that she would relate the story of Jack's parentage someday, perhaps when he had children of his own, and she swore Clyde to secrecy until that time should come.

William Jack grew up with the confidence of his father's surname and the fellowship of his kin. As a child of the hospital, he was unafraid of the patients or the staff and was treated as a persona grata. He rode his bike throughout the campus, stopped at the dairy when he was thirsty, bought fishing worms from Luther and played pool in the patients' activity rooms. He attended the hospital festivals and dances as if he were the child of royalty, and he grew tall and moved with an athlete's natural grace. He was kind to all and treated each patient with the same respect he was taught to give his parents, Clyde and Betty. William Jack became a man about whom it was said, "I never heard anyone say a bad word about him."

KATE

Chapter 53
Inravelled by Degrees

I ignored Miss Adele's ominous warnings and continued to see Jack. We soon began the arduous process of sifting through the flotsam of his parents' long years of marriage. Three piles grew in the guest bedroom, where we methodically stacked the items to be thrown away, given to charity and kept. His mother's cedar chest was the last piece of furniture to be searched, and it yielded a confusing array of photos, knick knacks and baby toys.

When he found the manila envelope labeled in block letters "FOR JACK" he glanced up at me with a look of dread, before running his fingers under the seal. The first photo he extracted showed three adults and a baby. On the back of the image was printed "Clyde, Billy Wayne, Lana and Baby, May 1957." I suppressed a gasp as I realized I was finally being introduced to the lovers buried in the hospital cemetery. Their faces looked out at us through more than thirty years: A beautiful, young woman with long, flaxen hair, awkwardly holding a swaddled infant; a young man with a broad face seated next to her, one arm protectively thrown over her shoulder.

When Jack identified his father Clyde as the tall, frowning man who stood behind the young couple, I felt a spasm of disbelief for it was the young man's face, not Clyde's, that was hauntingly familiar.

I took the photo from his hand. "Jack, this man looks just like you!" I whispered, pointing.

He peered at the photo. "That's my Uncle Billy Wayne."

"And this woman must be the Lana who's buried next to him."

Silently Jack turned the photo from front to back, peering into the eyes of the young couple and re-reading the names. He carefully laid the picture on the bed and reached into the envelope again. He pulled out a high school photo of Billy Wayne in a football uniform, kneeling next to his helmet. The last picture was of Lana, enormously pregnant and attempting to disguise her protruding belly with an armful of daffodils. She smiled coyly over the blooms, her pale eyes seducing the camera with a frankly sexual gaze.

Sitting on the floor, his back against the plaster wall, Jack mulled over his findings and sipped slowly at the beer he had retrieved from the kitchen. I felt a stirring of pity for him, for a man who was having to rethink everything he thought he knew about himself.

When he finally spoke, his voice sounded almost rusty. "The baby in that picture…it's either me or I've got a cousin somewhere I never heard about." I leaned my head against his shoulder, wishing my heart would stop its race. I was so close to knowing the answers to the enigma at the cemetery, but this was Jack's very life and this discovery should unfold in his time.

"What's the chance of that?" I asked cautiously.

"A cousin? Not much." More stillness. I heard a mockingbird outside the window, running through his repertoire at lightning speed, breaking open the stillness of the day just as we had broken open the envelope to the past.

"It has to be me, Kate," he finally surmised, sighing and looking at me with a pained expression. "And, if that's true, then Lana must be my mother… my biological mother," he corrected himself, using the clinical jargon we bandied back and forth in treatment team. "I mean, she's pregnant in this picture…"

"So that would mean Clyde and Betty adopted you?" I ventured.

"I guess so…anyway, they were the only parents I ever knew."

As I sat in sympathetic silence, Jack began to unravel the years of his childhood and adolescence and like a cuckold husband, he realized by degrees the deception that had been perpetrated. All of those older women who had demurely commented that Jack didn't look a *thing* like either parent; the time he had heard Clyde tell Betty in an argument "Jack's just like his father." He had wondered then why Clyde would make a negative comparison to himself but had dismissed his eavesdropping as too unreliable for worry. As a young teenager, he had felt a passing concern about how his parents, with their brown eyes, could have produced a child whose eyes were crystalline blue.

Then there was the patient cemetery: his mother had tended Billy Wayne and Lana's granite headstone in virtual secrecy; clamping poinsettias to the top at Christmas; planting daffodils along the border of the plot in late winter. Jack remembered riding his bike through the aisle of trees on a summer morning when he was nine and finding Betty kneeling beside the grave, so deeply in thought or prayer that he had secretly watched her for what seemed like an hour, before he rode away.

He thought of the few times he had asked about his uncle and the woman, Lana, and how Betty had deflected his questions with promises that they would discuss it further "some other day." He had grown up believing there was something vaguely disgraceful in Billy Wayne's death and his final resting place among the patients, something scandalous about a headstone so incomplete and yet so tantalizing.

I remembered Josephine's comments the morning I left the house, still smarting from Adele's scolding, but when I repeated them to Jack, he was pessimistic about Josephine's ability to give any answers. However, with considerable persuasion, he agreed to visit her.

Chapter 54
Epilogue

The brick path through Adele's garden led to an unpainted cabin. Before we could announce our presence, Albert opened the door to a soft glow of kerosene light, revealing Josephine at a table covered with a tattered oil cloth. She pushed away from the table and stepped close to Jack, searching his face before I could introduce him. "You got your mama's blue eyes," she pronounced and then added proudly, "I knowed who you was, when you come in the do'."

He laid the pictures on the tablecloth and asked about the images, his hands resting on the edge of the kitchen table. Josephine said she was not privy to the reason for Lana's admission to Western but told Jack that Lana had come to live there at a time when the hospital housed the poor, the elderly and the unwanted. She told him about Lana's creativity that extended from gardening to sewing and recounted the stories she had heard of Billy Wayne's steady generosity and compassionate heart. Josephine said that Lana was married to Jerry Wright when Jack was born, but she was sure his father was Billy Wayne Gordon. Recounting the night of his birth, she told the story of Billy Wayne hovering over Lana and holding his newborn son.

Jack finally asked about his parents' deaths, but Josephine slowly shook her head, saying she did not know for sure. She had heard people say that Billy Wayne was trying to save Lana from drowning, when the Neshobee took them both. She believed that Billy Wayne was so in love with Lana that he would have heedlessly plunged in the river without a thought for his own survival.

At the end of her account, she leaned across the table and patted Jack's hands. "I waited a long time fo' this, Mr. Jack," she said, nodding confidently. "Miss Betty, she be meanin' t'talk t'you 'bout your kin, but I 'magine the Lord took her 'fore she got 'round to it.

I'm glad you come t' me. Your mama and daddy, they was as in love as any two people I ever seen. They was fine folks, too, and don't you ever let nobody tell you any diff'rent."

Sitting next to Jack, I leaned against his shoulder, wishing my touch could heal the wound that must be as painful as any I had suffered. He swiped the back of his hand across his eyes one time before he stood and thanked Josephine for the memories she had shared. As she took his hand in both of hers, the ebony fingers that had safely guided him into the world warmly encircled his fingers.

∽৸৹∾

I am standing, again, at the grave that began my odyssey. I have walked through the allee of interlocking trees many times but never before with Jack at my side. He lays the silk flowers atop his parents' headstone, and my eyes linger on the inscription again: "Death could not part us."

Jack and I have talked to those who knew Lana and Billy Wayne, even approaching Adele for her memories, and so the pieces of the puzzle are finally together. Now, I see a devotion so immeasurable that Billy Wayne lost his life in a vain attempt to save Lana from herself. I see a love, young and naïve, and a mental illness that was only partially acknowledged. Their love transcended the family who opposed them, the staff members who were cruel or simply indifferent, the laws that prevented their marriage, a spurned husband who raged against them, and a prejudiced era that sought to separate them. Neither of them left any written account of their lives, yet their shared legacy is standing next to me— generous, steady and strong.

I pull one of the silk daffodils from the spray, walk to the edge of the bluff and let it fall into the swift waters of the Neshobee River.

Main Street Publishing, Inc.

206 E. Main Street, Suite 207
P O Box 696
Jackson, TN 38301

Toll Free #: 866-457-7379
or
Local #: 731-427-7379

Visit us on the web:
www.mainstreetpublishing.com
www.mspbooks.com

E-Mail: *editor@mainstreetpublishing.com*